THE WATERFALL

By

Nancy Rogers Yaeger

Nancy Rogers Yaeger

ISBN: 1-4033-6247-5 (e-book)
ISBN: 1-4033-6248-3 (Paperback)

Library of Congress Control Number: 2002093770

This book is printed on acid free paper.

Printed in the United States of America
Bloomington, IN

1stBooks – rev. 12/16/02

DEDICATION

To my children, Robin, Jonathan and Suzanne.

loving ... thoughtful ... extraordinary

In memory of my beloved David & our beautiful Lisa.

"I am not resigned to the shutting away of loving hearts in the hard ground." Millay

THE WATERFALL

by Nancy Rogers Yaeger

PROLOGUE 1995

The woman slid off the bicycle, guiding it to rest against the base of a nearby Mahoe tree. Absently she brushed beads of sweat from her forehead and cheeks with the back of her hand; ahead, the tangle of flowering plants and shrubs struggling to survive in a thicket of choking grasses and weeds filled her with dismay.

This is de place. I know it.

Shielding her eyes from the sun's oppressive glare, she moved slowly toward the natural barrier. Two sparrows chased each other amidst the branches of a dead cottonwood tree. Distracted by their antics, she looked up and caught a glimmer of coralstone, barely visible under a rich profusion of vines and lichen. Forbidding arms of bougainvillea with spikes so thick they would tear her skin to shreds brought her to a standstill. She was sorry now she hadn't borrowed her husband's machete, but he would have asked where she was going, why she had need of it.

In her impatience and longing to see once more the place which had indelibly marked her life, she had forgotten the vengeance extracted for desertion and neglect in the tropics. Tears came, unbidden. She lowered herself to the ground, crossing her arms in a consoling hug. Rocking gently back and forth, she struggled to accept the futility of her quest.

CHAPTER I

1979

Spring was a bonus, but summers were just plain hell. So was the traffic. After three years, Tyler decided he'd had his fill of Atlanta. *Time to move on, buddy-boy.* He liked the idea of being free to do '*whatever I damn well please.*' He'd never forgotten his days as a salesman for a glass company in upstate New York: *all the married guys spent every month sweating loan payments and medical bills, running their balls off to meet the department's quotas while trying to scrape up the extra cash for some damn appliance 'the little woman' had her eye on.* 'Not for me' he'd decided, wanting no part of encumbrances like kids and a mortgage.

Once he made up his mind to move on, Tyler began checking the classified ads appearing at the back of HOTEL MANAGEMENT, religiously answering those with the most appeal. Weeks went by without a response and his buoyancy wilted. In May, a new listing caught his eye:

WANTED: EXPERIENCED BARTENDER. *Single, reliable, willing to relocate. Management position available in exotic tropical locale. All queries confidential.*

A million guys will be after this one, but what the hell. He dropped his resumé in the mailbox on his way to the laundromat and promptly forgot about it.

Tyler's shift at the Lounge Bar of the Airport *Sheraton* coincided with the daily 'happy hour.' Young executives in button-down shirts and polyester suits swarmed in from nearby offices looking for a pickup as alternative to dinner alone. At their heels came a stream of freshly perfumed and mascared secretaries, all eager to oblige. The midweek scrimmage had a rhythm all its own: at 5:30, relaxed bursts of laughter could be heard above the mellow drone of conversation; an hour later, the laughter was more strident. By 7:30 the Lounge would begin emptying out, leaving the unbidden to finish their drinks in resigned solitude.

"Another round of *Miller's* for the table of five and one glass of milk with a dash of nutmeg," the waitress called from the end of the bar.

"This isn't the *Dairy Queen*, Carrie."

"I know that, Tyler darlin', but the customer, she ain't figured it out yet." Carrie rolled her eyes in the direction of a table near the entrance where a woman of leviathan proportions sat alone facing the bar. She reminded Tyler of a Buddha he'd seen once in *National Geographic*. Her features, buried in the fleshy folds of her face, were like a sprinkling of raisins in uncooked dough. Heavy gold chains were splayed across her bosom and a green metallic turban encircled her head.

He winked at Carrie, "Now that's some broad."

"Spare me your tired jokes, darlin'. Just gimme the milk."

A lull between the cocktail hour and the arrival of the after-dinner crowd gave Tyler a chance to relax and have a smoke. Leaning his back against the bar, he fished in his pocket for a *Kools*. Carrie leaned over the counter. "The lady wants to talk to you," she hissed.

"Which lady?"

"You know, the 'broad' one over by the door."

He checked the room with his eyes: the only customers left were a solitary drinker at the end of the bar and a couple holding hands in the corner. Reluctantly, he put away the cigarette and strolled over to the table.

"Tyler Scranton?" The accent was pure Henry Higgens.

"You know my name?"

She ignored the question. "Can we talk?"

"No ma'am. I'm still on duty. My shift doesn't end 'til eleven."

"Fine. I'll have dinner and meet you back here at eleven."

He spent the rest of his shift trying to figure out who the woman was, how she knew his name and where he worked. When the time came to join her, he was clearly in a truculent mood. She waved him to a chair.

"The name is Caswell, Leona Caswell. I can tell by the look on your face, Mr. Scranton, you did not like my silly game. I apologize. But it's such jolly fun playing 'the mysterious fat lady.'" She giggled softly, enjoying some private joke of her own. "May I buy you a drink? This may take some time."

He shook his head. "Mind if I smoke?"

"Please do. I could use a light myself." He watched in fascination as she took from her handbag an ivory cigarette holder into which her thick, ringless fingers delicately inserted a cigarillo. She took several languid puffs before speaking. "Some weeks ago, Mr. Scranton, you answered an ad for an overseas position. I am here in Atlanta to interview you for that job."

Selecting her words with care, Caswell described in a trenchant voice an island in the eastern Caribbean Tyler'd never heard of named Lutigua and the hotel, Belle Jours. "It's not a large hotel," Caswell explained, "but it has a distinguished past. Plans for a complete facelift are already underway. Since we are seeking to attract an upscale clientele, Mrs. Foster-Jones, the owner, places great emphasis on acquiring dependable and experienced staff."

She outlined the responsibilities that went with the task of managing the bar, stressing the long hours, the difficulties inherent in training the locals, the frustrations of importing supplies, adding cooly, "Forget whatever illusions you may have, Mr. Scranton, about chatting up bikini-clad young ladies under the palm trees. My employer has strict rules about co-mingling with the guests."

She's really laying it on with a trowel.

The Englishwoman honed in on his private life: Divorced? Any children? A police record? Would he sign a two-year contract?

Before Tyler had a chance to ask one of a dozen questions racing across his mind, Caswell made an elaborate show of checking her watch with the clock over the bar.

"It's long past my bedtime, Mr. Scranton. I have a plane to catch tomorrow. Please ring my room before nine if you wish to be considered for the position we have just discussed. I will get back to you in a week or so. I have another candidate to interview." The obese woman struggled from her chair. "Now, if you would be so kind as to help me to the Reception Desk ... my legs ...all this sitting."

* * * * * * * * * *

An ebullient sun spread its arms over the horizon as Danielle watched her brother's old Morris, spewing the perennial dust of the dry season, disappear down the road. In the sweetness of the early morning, every leaf and blade of grass glistened; a chorus of chattering sparrows and yellowbirds accompanied her as she hurried on her way.

Thank you, Lord. I truly thank you, she whispered, still unable to believe her good fortune. The bank manager's recommendation had freed her from the dank, fetid confines of the of the shipping firm's offices down on the wharf, where each morning she had to cross the threshold of the dark-timbered warehouse, skirting rotting planks and rat droppings to get to her small cubicle. The job of bookkeeping at *Benbow & Otis* had been offered to her after completion of a secretarial course in Jamaica. Steady work was much prized on the island, and knowing how pleased and proud her father was, she spoke of her unhappiness to no one.

Months later, the letter to her father arrived from Mr. Braithwaite at the bank:

...Mrs. Foster-Jones, daughter of the original owner of Belle Jours, is returning to Lutigua to reopen the hotel for the winter season....seeks a reliable and honest young woman to perform light secretarial duties and act as general factotum in her absence ...highest regard for your daughter ... with your kind permission ...

Danielle slowed at the sight of the twin coral pillars guarding the entrance to the hotel grounds. Beyond them, towering royal palms marched like sentinals down each side of a wide strip of freshly tamped earth to the sea. At irregular intervals, mounds of rotting vegetation waiting to be burned, gave mute testimony to the struggle to clear the land.

Several hundred yards before the sea came into view, a paved road branched off to the left. Following it as instructed, Danielle found herself on the curved driveway fronting the entrance to Belle Jours. Several vehicles were parked along the curb, among them a red Chevy truck which she recognized immediately. It belonged to Farrell Cafferty, a white plantation owner and the island's leading contractor. Demanding to be addressed by the unearned rank of 'Captain,' he represented the third generation of Caffertys on the island. Rumor had it that his grandfather Sean had escaped from Ireland with the law at his heels, bringing with him a serving girl from the local tavern who was no stranger to his bed. Did the couple disembark in Brazil? Or was it Guyana? No one knew for sure, nor why they decided to settle in Lutigua. They arrived with their infant son aboard one of the small schooners plying its trade between the islands. Within a year the fugitive had purchased a modest piece of property on the northern side of the island and set about establishing a dynasty.

Sean Cafferty's progeny were known for their industry and stubbornness, their partiality to malt whiskey and all things Irish ... and their abiding contempt for anyone with dark skin.

Danielle caught her breath at the sight of Cafferty's grizzled white head and unshaven jowls as he emerged from the arched entranceway of the hotel. He barked a final order over his shoulder and stomped down the steps. Glancing around he saw her standing motionless in the forecourt.

"Hey, girl. You! You Danielle Mapp?"

"Yes, sir."

"'Bout time you showed up. Come over here," jerking his thumb towards the truck. "I've got some letters for you."

He wrenched open the door of the cab, leaning his thickset body against the steering wheel in his search; retrieving the cache of mail, he held it aloft in his fist like a jubilant prize fighter.

"Come on. I haven't got all day." He shoved a thick pile of envelopes at her. "There's other stuff in there too, addressed to the hotel. Some boxes came yesterday. I had the boys clean out the dining room and we stored 'em in there."

Danielle smelled the rank odor of his body, his sour breath as he stepped closer, pinning her gaze with his bulging eyes. "Look, girl. You do your thing here and you won't get no trouble from me. But mind you, stay clear of my boys. No monkey business . Understan' me? Got any problems, you see Forbes, my foreman."

"Yessir."

Beneath the generous arms of an ancient mahogany tree on the hotel grounds, she pored over the several pages of typed instructions, each one signed, '*Leona Caswell, on behalf of Mrs. Foster-Jones.*' Overwhelmed by her duties and responsibilities, she fought back an urge to flee, steadying herself with the litany, <u>Help me, Lord, to please this lady.</u>

* * * * * * * * * * *

The taxi coughed and sputtered to a halt alongside three steps ascending to a murky interior. Flying ants and moths danced an arabesque around a lighted fixture on the outside wall.

"You sure this is the right place?"

"Yes, please. It's de Belle Jours hotel. Dey been workin' here for some time now."

Gripping a suitcase in each hand, Tyler moved cautiously along the shadowy stone corridor towards a glimmer of light. He paused at the threshold of a large rectangular room where a solitary woman, head bent in concentration, stood behind a makeshift counter, her finger moving slowly down the page of a ledger. He cleared his throat. "Hello. Tyler Scranton here."

She looked up. Tiny ringlets of moisture at the hairline and on the upper lip glistened in the refracted glow of the small lamp at her elbow. The sculpted lines and angles of her face, almond-shaped eyes pulled back slightly at the corner and the full, soft lips of her African ancestry: Neferititi incarnate, fifteen centuries later. Perplexed, she stared at the tall, attractive stranger in the rumpled white shirt, whose face with its classical nose and deep-set eyes reminded her of the Prince in a book of illustrated fairy tales her mother read to her when she was a child. "Mr. Scranton? But you are not to come until de day after tomorrow," the words uttered in a sweet, lilting cadence endemic to the islands.

"Sorry. Guess I should have sent a cable." He dropped the luggage to the floor.

"The wireless is down for many days now. Government sayin' it will be fixed 'in good time,'" her sigh brushed the air like a feather, "but then de government makes many promises it cannot keep."

"Too bad I can't evaporate into thin air. Looks like you're stuck with me."

"Not to worry. Welcome to Lutigua, Mr. Scranton," she said, closing the ledger and moving from behind the counter. "Welcome to Belle Jours. I am Danielle."

"Pleased to meet you, Danielle." His voice lingered over the last syllable, lightly mimicking her own pronunciation while his eyes teased her to return his smile. She did not.

"I assume there's a bed for me somewhere."

"I will see to it. Please to wait here."

He shrugged and pulled a handkerchief from his pocket to wipe the back of his neck and face; heat and humidity swaddled his body like a thick gauze bandage. The newcomer gazed around the room: it was freshly painted and barren, except for a broken rattan chair and several cans of paint at the foot of a handmade wooden stepladder. Curved arches like giant thumb prints stood at either end. In the distance could be heard the faint rush of the incoming tide.

From the shadows, Danielle reappeared hugging to her chest bed linens and towels, leaving the other hand free to wield a small electric torch. "You will find some candles under de counter. Please to bring them and follow me, Mr. Scranton."

Above, the sky was starless, the night black and sullen with the promise of more rain. The din of crickets filled the air as he trailed behind her, stumbling along the uneven stone pathway that curved behind the main building. Suddenly, something wet and slimy crossed his open sandal.

"What the hell!" Tyler roared.

The woman whirled around, the glare from her torch momentarily blinding him.

"A snake. A goddamn snake ... it touched my foot."

"Not to worry," she said calmly, hearing the fear in his voice. "No snakes live on de island, only lizards and toads and when it rains, de toads are everywhere." She watched as he struggled to regain his composure.

"May we go on now, please?"

"Yeah, yeah. Keep going."

Abruptly the stone path ended and Tyler's leather sandals sank in mud. "Great, just great," he muttered under his breath. Rivulets of sweat poured down his back and legs; his shoulders ached with the weight of the suitcases. They continued in silence.

"Please to take care," Danielle cautioned at the start of a shallow incline, "it is slippery here."

A few seconds later the torch's beam traced the outline of a wooden house perched on stilts of concrete block and surrounded on three sides by hovering palms. The Lutigan mounted the steps and moved across the planked porch to a screen door, nudging it open with her shoulder. Tyler, at her heels, heard the click of a switch. She held the door open for him.

"Mr. Scranton ..."

"Drop the 'mister' bit, Danielle. The name's Tyler, o.k.?" She pointed the way to his bedroom and waited until he had shed his luggage before continuing:

"Ty-ler. This cottage is for you to share with Mr. Preston, our bookkeeper. I'm sorry your room is not ready, but you were not expected." She might have been addressing a class of slow learners. "There are no shelves in the kitchen; Mr. Yarde, the carpenter, has been busy in de new guest wing but when he is done, he will come to put them up. A refrigerator is on order. God willing, it will arrive in de next container."

"Is there running water, or must I wait for that, too?" Scranton's voice was sharp with the cumulated reservoir of disappointment. He'd risen before dawn, eager for this new adventure to begin, blunting his impatience with double Scotches on the long flight to the Caribbean. His spirits sagged as he waited in a stifling shed to be cleared by Immigration; later he watched in impotent fury as an overbearing Customs' officer pawed through his belongings. His sense of grievance was further aggravated by the starkness of his living arrangements, his cool reception. *Stuckup bitch.*

"Water is no problem," she said with asperity. "God has been generous with de rain this season."

"I could use a drink. Something a little stronger than water."

"I will see to it. If there is nothing more, Mister Scran-, Ty-ler, I will say 'good evening'."

With a litany of curses, he unbuttoned his shirt, tossed it on the floor and made the bed. As he rummaged through the larger suitcase searching for his toilet kit, Tyler heard a soft rap on the screen door. *Now what?* He crossed to the front of the cabin and yanked it open. A diminutive, wizened black man in a white dinner jacket blinked up at him. The tray he carried was thrust forward for Tyler's inspection like a child exhibiting a scratched knee.

"Welcome to Lutigua, Mister Scranton. Mis Danielle send me to bring you some refreshment." The voice was dry and sweet.

"Come in. What's your name?"

"I was baptized Jeremiah Washington Wilson," he replied with quiet dignity, "but folks here, dey calls me Wash."

"Glad to meet you, Wash," Tyler said, his good humor instantly restored by the incongruous sight of formal attire in the middle of a tropical thicket. "Here, I'll take that tray."

"Please to let me set it down for you, Mister Scranton."

"What's this?" the American asked, pointing to an unmarked green bottle next to a thermos of ice.

"Dat's rum. We makes it here."

"No Scotch?"

"No, sir. Rum's all we got."

Eschewing the energy needed to unpack, Tyler shed the rest of his clothes and stretched out naked on the cot, head propped on a pillow, one hand balancing a fresh drink on the flat of his stomach. Overhead the fan sent washes of tepid air across the room, making him grateful for the cold oasis the ice-filled glass made on his warm skin. He listened to the rain beat a light tattoo against the corrugated roof and watched in fascination as two lizards chased each other along the window frame.

Scranton, ole boy, coming down here will turn out to be the smartest move you ever made or the dumbest.

* * * * * * * * * * *

The weight of her responsibilities at the hotel meant Danielle was often late returning home, but her father never failed to keep a plate of food warming in the oven for her. One evening after she finished the washing up, she joined him on the porch. Ensconced in his favorite rocking chair, Mapp's gaze was focused on the clear night sky.

"Looka! Looka there!" he pointed. "You can see Orion, clear en sweet as well water." Josiah Mapp was a life-long student of the constellations.

Lowering herself to the the bare planked floor, Danielle leaned back against the railing and closed her eyes. Thrusting aside the cares of the day, she listened to the familiar night sounds surrounding them and filled her lungs with the fragrant air. Moments later she stirred and softly broached the subject uppermost on her mind.

"Tell me, Daddy, Mrs. Foster-Jones... what manner of lady is she?"

"Been a long time since *that name* spoken round here," he replied, inhaling deeply on his cigarette. "But folks of a certain age on this island ent forgotten Laura Gallon... *Gallon* was her name, you see, 'fore she married. ...Her Daddy was George Gallon. His people tried their hand at growin' de cane, but they didn't have no talent for it; their eldest son (that bein' Mister George) he had his head set on ownin' a hotel, en he settled on a place in St. Mary's Parish... Everbody makin sport of him 'cause the house he bought was in such a sorry way, but they stopped laughin' after Gallon cleared de land en fixed de place up to be lookin' most fair. Nowadays, to own a piece of land by de sea, you needs be a millionaire; but back then, land could be had for a handful of shillings. Gallon, he named de place 'Welcome Inn' 'til his wife come along en fussed at him to change it to Belle Jours...guess she had her reasons.

"Gallon, now, he was truly blessed with a good woman. Mistress Alice, she come over from England to visit her cousins, the Shelbys up by Dugan Hill. Soons he meets her, Gallon have it in mind to make her his wife. He courtin' her like a one-way mule 'til she say, 'Yes.' It was a good match.

"Early on, de hotel was empty more'n it was full en Mistress Alice, she don't know a lazy day ... what with the cookin' en lookin' after de guests. But in time, de rooms at Belle Jours' filled up year round en they takes on regular staff.

"When de baby come, Gallon, he's so proud he's treatin' half de parish of St. Mary's to rum drinks to celebrate Mis Laura's birth. But poor Mistress Alice, her health ent never the same after de birthin'. She took to her bed most days and Jessie, your great auntie, she came to stay, to look after her and de baby.

"Early on, Mis Laura was sweet to look at. Your own Granny used to say, 'Dat chile's so beautiful, she puts de moon to shame.' Soon's she could walk, her Daddy's takin' her everywhere, showin' her off in fancy dresses en de like he ordered from overseas. She even had a pony for her very own when she was only six years old! Not a thing that chile was wantin' for. No wonder she grew up headstrong en spoiled."

Traditionally, Lutigua's white plantation owners and wealthy trades-people sent their sons and daughters abroad to England for their schooling, Mapp explained, but when it came time for Laura to go, her parents quarreled: Gallon couldn't bear the thought of his beloved child being so far from home; his wife, however, insisted their daughter needed to acquire the social graces and discipline that went hand-in-hand with a proper education. In the end she prevailed and Laura was sent off to a convent school near Reading. All during the months she was away until her return for the summer holidays, Gallon looked as if he were in mourning. He never did grow accustomed to his daughter's long absences.

"The summer Mis Laura was seventeen, de boys come swarmin' round by de bushel basket, she was such a beauty. En lively, too! Her wild ways caused talk... some sayin' she was a terrible tease en cruel to more than one young lad. But I'm guessin' it was the womenfolk who were passin' those tales out of jealousy en spite. Your auntie Jessie said there was nothin' that chile wouldn't do for her Mummy."

At the end of August Laura was to sail back to England to begin her studies at University. But the news from Europe was disquieting: Germany, under Hitler's sanguine and ruthless leadership, was once again on the march. George Gallon didn't want his daughter stranded in a country that might be drawn into war. But Laura belittled his fears, reminding her father that Chamberlain's signature on the Munich Pact - as the Prime Minister had assured his countrymen - guaranteed England 'peace in our time.'

"Daddy, the Prime Minister gave his *word.*" Reluctantly he agreed to let her go. Three days after the ship left Lutigua with Laura on board, the *BBC* broadcast news of the German invasion of Poland.

Mapp sighed. "So many fine young menfolk went off to fight that war en never come back." He lit another cigarette and fell silent.

The stillness of the night was broken by a choir of raucous crickets and the dull, rhythmic thud of the rocker on the hard, wooden floor. Danielle waited patiently for her father to speak, but he seemed lost in a tangle of memories.

"Daddy," she said softly, "please tell me more. There must be more."

"Yes, chile. There's more. But my old head has taken to wanderin' in de past, en my throat's gone dry."

She jumped up, "Coconut water will ease de dryness." Returning swiftly from the back of the house, she handed him a glass of the cool liquid and returned to her place on the floor.

"Now what was I speakin' of? ...Oh yes, de war. De Devil's invention, that's what war is. But here in Lutigua we could count our blessings. De Lord blessed us with plenty of sunshine en rain to make de crops grow, while those poor folks in London, they all de time dodgin' bombs en can't get fresh greens en fruit."

"Laura Gallon. What became of her, Daddy?"

"Well, soons he hear de news, Mister George sendin' one cable after de other beggin' Mis Laura to take de first passage she can find en come home. She's cablin' back not to worry, that de University was in de countryside, away from de bombs en besides, she wasn't havin' a wicked man like Hitler keep her from her studies... I tole you she was headstrong."

To her father's chagrin and sorrow, Laura was to remain abroad for several years. ("Three, I'm guessin', maybe four.") In the early days of the conflict, Gallon talked of enlisting, but it turned out to be just that—talk. He couldn't bear to leave his ailing wife and in any case, in mid-1940, the British government requisitioned Belle Jours for 'special cases' -pilots who'd flown too many missions and needed a place to rest. Each week a new batch was flown in from England to replace the ones who returned to duty. One day Gallon received a letter from his daughter with a London postmark, telling her parents she'd left University and signed on to be a driver for the military. Mail from overseas was slow and sporatic in those days, but every evening the *BBC* broadcast fresh reports of another bombing raid on London. Overnight, George Gallon's hair turned white; a few weeks later, his wife suffered a stroke.

"One whole side of her stiff as a board. Trouble pile on trouble for that poor man...got so folks here could hardly bear to look at him, he was in such a pitiable state."

When his wife suffered a second stroke, Gallon again cabled his daughter, but Laura was unable to book passage: all available space on British ships was allotted for desperately needed supplies. Her mother's illness weighed heavily on Laura's mind; from time to time she sent money orders to Jessie asking her to buy a few yards of material so the local seamstress could make a robe or nightgown for Mrs. Gallon.

Weeks slipped by and then a cablegram arrived at Belle Jours: *My darling Edward is dead. His plane shot down over the North Sea. I am desolate. Thank God they still need me at the Ministry. Work is all that keeps me from falling to pieces. Love to you and Mummy. Laura.*

Her father was puzzled by its distraught tone: who was this Edward? A special beau of Laura's? Three months later a letter reached Lutigua with the answers.

While at University, their daughter had met and fallen in love with a young Englishman. When his country declared war, Foster-Jones joined the RAF; Laura quit school to be near him and quickly found work in London. As soon as he completed his training, they were married. The young couple had one long weekend together in the Scottish Highlands before he reported for active duty. Happiness flowed from every line as she described her new husband, his background and family, their courtship and the simple wedding ceremony ... her exuberant rhetoric expressive of a young woman very much in love. With the careless optimism of youth, she outlined their plans for the future, where they would live and the children they would have. '*I can't wait for you to meet Edward. I know you'll love him as much as I do!*.' She signed the letter 'Mrs. Edward Foster-Jones.'

"Oh Daddy, what a sad story."

"Plenty of sad stories come out of that war." Mapp slowly rose from his chair . "These old bones is weary. I'm off to bed now. You best be gettin' to bed, too, Dani."

"What happened to de lady after she lost her husband?"

"Patience, daughter. Patience. I'll finish de story, or what I knows of it from Jessie, soons my throat's had a good rest. Good night. Leave de porch light on for your brother."

* * * * * * * * * *

Tyler stared groggily at his watch: 5:30. The golden rays of an early sunrise shimmied and pranced across the room like a gleeful child at the end of a school term.

Shit. Look at the time.

He rolled over and shut his eyes, but it was no use. He was wide awake. Muttering a stream of expletives, he left the bed in search of his swim trunks. Stepping from the cabin into air washed clean of the oppressive mugginess of the night before, he retraced his steps until he was within sight of the hotel and the sea. He stopped in his tracks and gave a low whistle of appreciation. The owner had taken full advantage of the chromatic drama provided by the island's flora and fauna: masses of pink and red hibiscus were banked against the main building's pearly coral walls; clumps of Jacob's coat, Beaumontia and variegated leaves of Croton were scattered along pathways to the two els extending from it . Coconut palms in groups of two or three, some towering 60 feet or more, were placed at intervals around the entire perimeter, their swaying, rustling fronds and scarred grey trunks providing a theatrical touch as well as essential shade.

A low, wrought-iron fence, it's chipped black paint barely visible beneath scrambling arms of magenta, white and terra-cotta bougainvillea, separated the main grounds from the beach. Just beyond, the tantalizing pull of a gently rolling surf moved towards the shore.

The American had never seen sand so fine and white, water so clear and enticing, its color changing from pale green to deeper shades of brilliant turquoise. He waded out from the shoreline and dove into an oncoming wave, swimming with sure, crisp strokes away from land. Later, as he lay floating on his back eyeing the compound from a distance, he was overcome with a surge of optimism: *It's about time your luck changed, buddy-boy. This place is a beauty.*

The dining room, open on three sides, faced towards the sea. It was barren save for a few metal folding chairs around a long trestle table similar to the ones used by the *Sheraton* for banquets. At its center were a handful of mugs, a covered sugar bowl and tin of evaporated milk. But no sign of a coffeepot. Tyler firmly believed that what stood between man and his inhumanity to his fellow beings was a cup of steaming, caffeine-laden coffee.

"Hey! Anybody home?" A few seconds later the door to the kitchen swung open and an ebony giant emerged carrying a large aluminum coffee maker.

My God, every team in the NFL would kill for a build like that.

"Good morning, sir." He gave the newcomer an inquiring glance as he set the pot down.

"I'm Scranton, the new bar manager," Tyler offered, extending a hand.

"Corbin's de name, Belle Jour's master chef," said the giant, grabbing it in his large paw. "Pleased to meet you, Mr. Scranton," he grinned widely, exposing the absence of several teeth. The chef's bald skull was offset by a resplendent growth of salt-n-pepper sideburns and a thick, walrus mustache. An immaculate white tee shirt and pants embraced broad shoulders and muscular arms, a trim waist and solid thighs. "I'm guessin' you're from de States, New York?"

"No. Pennsylvania. Close enough to be its kissin' cousin. Say, you have a beautiful island here, Corbin."

"Dis aint *my island*," was the distainful reply. "No sir, I'm from Barbados. Mon, dis here Lutigua's a marl-hole compared to where I comes from."

Tyler ate alone, entertained by a pair of yellow birds making greedy passes at the crumbs scattered on his plate. His solitude was interrupted by the appearance of Danielle who had forsaken the westernized look of the night before: her hair was braided in corn rows, her feet bare and the simple cotton shift she wore with its bold splashes of color accented the beguiling curves of her body. She hugged to her breast a thick folder of papers.

"Good morning, Mr. Scranton."

"Morning, Danielle. It's *Tyler*, remember?

"It has slipped from my mind. Please to forgive me."

He was willing to bet a fiver it hadn't, but he was damned if he was going to let her studied aloofness get under his skin. "What's that, your homework?"

"Pardon? Oh these," she said, with a glance at the folder as she set it aside and helped herself to coffee. When she spoke again, it was in the same pedagogical tone of the night before.

"Miss Caswell sends instructions to me from Mrs. Foster-Jones. I am to see that all is done as she has written."

"So you're the acting field marshall."

"Yes please?" she asked, with a quizzical look.

"Nevermind. Tell me, what's she like, this Mrs. Foster-Jones?"

"I have not met de lady, nor Miss Caswell."

"I'm beginning to wonder if there really *is* a Mrs. Foster-Jones."

Danielle was not about to reveal to this stranger what she has learned from Josiah.

"Not to worry. She is real. Many months ago two ladies come to Lutigua from England. They rented a villa many miles from here, but every morning they come in Darius Owen's taxi to visit Belle Jours. Mr. Owen cannot keep a still tongue; he brags to folks that Mrs. Foster-Jones remembers his uncle who worked at Belle Jours many years ago . He sayin' de lady with her, Miss Caswell, smokes funny brown cigarettes and is ..." she pursed her lips in embarrassment.

"...very fat," Tyler added. "I've met her."

"I do not wish to be unkind," she said softly, abandoning her usual hauteur.

"Look, Danielle, I need to run some errands. One of the painters gave me directions to St. James. Are there wheels around I can borrow, or do I call a taxi?"

"If by 'wheels' you mean an 'automobile', there is a station wagon parked near de gardener's shed. It is for the senior staff to use, but Miss Caswell says de petrol tank must be full on its return."

"Thanks. I'm off then."

She rose and gathered up her notes. "Time is running fast, like a thief in de night, and much work is still to be done. Belle Jours must truly be made sweet for our guests. For if their time here is pleasing, they will tell others. With God's blessing, more tourists will come, more hotels will open and Lutigua will blossom like the angel trumpet when de sun goes down." She smiled and he watched as an expression of warmth and expectancy broke through her reserved demeanor.

CHAPTER II

The station wagon was a battered lime green Ford Fairlane with a V-8 engine, its paint and chrome so devotedly polished, it gleamed in the morning sunlight. Stuck to the dashboard was a hand-written warning: *Remember! Drive on the left-hand side of the road!*

Must be a legacy from our British cousins. He remembered Caswell mentioning that the island had once belonged to England, was independent now, but retained a plethora of ties to its former colonial masters including membership in the Commonwealth .

Driving with unusual care - old habits die hard, he discovered - Tyler inspected the alien landscape. A luxuriant riot of color assaulted the eye. He passed barefoot women in cotton dresses, some with heavy baskets balanced on their heads; two old men squatting knees-to-chin over a checkerboard in the shade of a shak-shak tree; spindly-legged boys, some lugging sacks of yams or cassavas, and young girls with gay ribbons in their hair. The children stopped and stared as the Ford came abreast and a few shyly waved. After a time, Tyler realized he hadn't seen a speed limit or stop sign posted anywhere. He slowed to a crawl at a crude intersection until he spotted a weather-battered wooden marker with the legend, barely visible, 'St. James, 5 kil', its arrow pointing in the direction of the island's capitol.

As the road rose and dipped, he saw on the horizon acres of green young cane, patchwork quilts against the hills and at the crest of one steep incline, caught sight of a thick forest hugging the side of a mountain. The houses along the way were mean wooden shacks perched on top of piled rock. Roosters, hens and what Tyler presumed were goats, occupied the front yards. (Later Wash would explain: "Our sheep, dey looks like a goat, but dey ent. You tells a sheep from a goat by de tail.") Tethered to the front lawn of a parish police station was an emaciated black cow with a cattle egret roosting on its neck. The disparity between this rural out-post and the State Patrol stations in Georgia made him shake his head in disbelief.

The surface of the road he travelled was hard-packed dirt. From time to time he was forced to maneuver around scattered chunks of coralstone and potholes 'the size of an elephant.' But he had the road to himself and did not see other cars until he reached the outskirts of St. James.

A merciless sun trailed him as he roamed the narrow by-ways of Lutigua's capitol, the pungent odors rising from open trenches on either side of the street stung his nostrils, making him want to gag. Vendors in from the countryside with their produce clustered along store fronts and at the corner of every intersection, filling the air with their mysterious argot.

"Buy a sweet mango, mistah. Two fo five dollah. Bes' mangoes you evah eatin.'"

On a modest slope at the center of the city was the structure that dominated it and was its namesake: the dignified and venerable Anglican Cathedral of St James, with walls of sandstone and windows covered by dark wooden slats in place of stained glass. The grounds skirting the west portico of the Cathedral were littered with crumbling headstones and vaults, some dating as far back as the late 1600's—the only touch of color on its parched and scraggly lawn being two gnarled frangipani trees, one bearing pink blossoms, the other white.

Flanking the Cathedral, like outstretched arms, were the main arteries of the city; they were filled with modest shops, government offices, several overseas bank branches and a postal center. The remaining thoroughfares were a crowded hodgepodge of dark storefronts and refreshment stands.

Tyler watched his optimistic shopping list shrivel under the weight of reality. Instead of bamboo shades for the bedroom window, the best compromise the single hardware store in St. James had to offer was a yellowing Venetian blind, four inches too narrow and covered with dust. Nor was a hideous glazed pottery table lamp the austere, modern fixture he envisioned. It took him the better part of two hours to scout for articles he could have picked up in less than half the time at a shopping mall in Atlanta. By the time he made his last purchases, three lurid paperbacks and a quart of *Haig & Haig,* his shirt was damp, his feet, swollen and sore.

Checking the time, he was further chagrined to discover he'd be late for his meeting with Wash.

As he pulled into the hotel driveway, he remembered Danielle's cautionary advice about filling the gas tank. "Shit."

"Tyler!" Danielle called from the office doorway as he hurried past, "Mr. Wilson, he looks for you an hour ago."

"I know. I'm sorry, but shopping in St. James was no picnic." *Why the hell am I making excuses to her?*

The elderly Lutiguan rose to his feet as Tyler approached.

"Sorry to be late, Wash."

"Not to worry, Mister Scranton. Dis list's still waitin' for you here in my pocket."

"How about dropping the 'Mister 'bit? Just call me 'Tyler'."

Wash was slow to respond, his serene black countenance registering discomfort as he shifted from one foot to the other. "I can't be doin' it, Mister Scranton. It's not my nature."

"Forget it. Call me whatever you like. Now then, let's talk about the lineup tomorrow morning. How many signed up to work the bar?"

"Thirty I knowin' of, but more will show up when word gets round."

"*Thirty!*" Tyler was stunned. "We only need *eight!*"

"Mis Danielle, she seen over fifty folk already. They come on de run when dey hears Belle Jours is openin' again. Steady work's hard come by on Lutigua, Mister Scranton."

"Look, Wash. Do you know any of these fellows?"

"Been here all my life, so I knows most of dem – de spoilt fruit and de sweet."

With phrases like, "He's kin to an apothecary's knife" (two-faced, not to be trusted), "De police has pressed his tail" (charged several times), and "You'll bite your finger when it's too late" (you'll regret hiring him), the old man eliminated a number of applicants.

"The last name on this list is 'James MacArthur Wilson.' He any relation to you, Wash?"

"True. James's my youngest," the Lutiguan said with pride. "His sixteenth year's near over en he's done wid schoolin'."

"In the States," Tyler said gently, "you must be 21 to work in places where liquor is sold. It's the law."

"Lutigua's got no laws like dat, Mister Scranton. James, he's a good boy, a hard worker."

"O.K. I'll see him tomorrow with the rest."

Men started arriving at the hotel at dawn; by seven, the line stretched from the steps of the dining hall to the pool area. They were uniformly neat, each wearing a freshly laundered shirt and pressed trousers. The American was impressed.

He spoke with them all, a task that occupied the entire morning. The few who showed undue servility were automatically ruled out: *I need guys who have the balls to handle mean drunks and dead beats.* When the last interview was over, he stretched wearily and reached for a cigarette.

"Mister Scranton, this here's my boy, James MacArthur."

A slim youth with with skin the color of dark honey and a face so perfectly proportioned it begged to be captured on canvas, stepped forward.

Christ, he's beautiful. There's no other word for it. Wash has sired a beautiful kid.

He was pleased with the boy's responses to the few questions he asked. *There's not an ounce of conceit in him and he bustin' to get this job. Not only to please his old man, but to prove something to himself.*

"Well now, James, since this is your first time out, suppose we take you on as bus-boy. You're to keep the tables cleared and make yourself useful to the crew at the bar. You'll draw a salary, but no tips. Do you understand?"

"Yes, sir, Mr. Scranton.

"Are you willing to put in long hours?"

"I'm not afraid of work, sir.

"Good. You're hired. Be here for the training sessions."

"*Yes, sir!* Thank you, sir!"

Any second now, he'll start turning cartwheels.

Wash reappeared as soon as his son was out of sight. "I thank you kindly, Mister Scranton." His voice was husky with emotion.

"Forget it," Tyler said brusquely. "I didn't hire James because he's your son, Wash. I hired him because I think he'll do a good job."

Later that afternoon he went looking for Danielle. He found her standing beside an open file drawer in a small room off Reception which served as a temporary office. Observing her in silence by the open doorway, he was unexpectedly stirred by the tantalizing arch of her neck, the curve of her thighs. *I'll have to work harder at thawing Miss Ice Queen.*

"Got a minute?"

"Yes, please. There is a problem?"

"Well, sort of." He flashed a rueful smile. "I need to clear something up. It's a matter of protocol."

"*Protocol?* I do not know this word."

"It's like this: Wash insists on calling me 'Mister Scranton', the younger men, 'Mister Tyler'. Makes me feel old as Methuselah. Just plain ole *Tyler* suits me fine. Then I notice you always say 'Mr. Wilson,' but I'm supposed to call the old guy, 'Wash.' It's damn confusing."

He was flattered to note a slight frown of concentration cross her brow, a sign she was taking his dilemna seriously.

"From de days when we belonged to England, all white men were called 'Mister,' de white ladies, 'Mistress.' Our old people, they cannot change their ways; but de young ones who were born after Independence, they do as they please. Since you're head boss at the bar, de men who work for you will show their respect by saying 'Mister'. I say 'Mister Wilson', because he is a fine gentleman with the weight of many years on his shoulders and he is deserving. But he would not be happy for you to call him anything but 'Wash'."

"Thanks. Put that way, it makes some kind'a sense. I don't want to get off on the wrong foot."

"All is not simple when one is a stranger in a strange land," she said kindly.

Well, well. Is that a civil tone I hear? Score one for me.

Deciding to close out the busy day with a swim before the sun disappeared, Tyler was at the cabin changing into his swim trunks when he was interrupted by a fist pounding on the porch door. Corbin's kitchen boy called out:

"Mistah Tyler! Mistah Tyler! De container come. Miz Danielle not lookin' for it today. We needs you to help unload it before de sun go down."

For the next two hours, Tyler and a small team of men hastily assembled by Wash, unloaded headboards and mattresses, kitchen equipment, chairs and bolts of material under the watchful eyes of two Customs officials, the shipping agent and Danielle. As he lugged yet another chair into the Reception hall, the American deliberately confronted her.

"What's the rush?" he asked accusingly. "Couldn't this have waited until morning? If the mosquitos don't get me, a hernia will."

"Tomorrow is Saturday, Mr. Scranton," she snapped, "and the day after, Sunday. The offices of de shipping agent are closed for de weekend. Please to know that for each day the container sits at Belle Jour unopened, the agent charges a high fee."

He could have kicked himself. *That poor broad has been at it since sun-up. Why can't you keep your big mouth shut, buddy-boy?*

Later the exhausted crew gathered around the trestle table in the dining hall and were served sandwiches and cold beer by Corbin, who'd exempted himself from their labors: "In my country, master chefs don't move' no furniture." With fatigue stamped all over her face, Danielle sat apart from the others, her food barely touched. Tyler slipped into an empty chair beside her.

"Foster-Jones was lucky to find you, lady," he said softly. "You're worth your weight in gold and then some."

She mustered a wan smile. "In Lutiguan or U.S. dollars?"

That night he dreamed he was being chased down a long, narrow tunnel strewn with gigantic pillows. Time and again he looked back over his shoulder, desperate to reach safety before his unknown pursuer caught up with him. The pillows, with the viscosity of jumbo marshmallows, caused him to stumble and fall to his knees. He rose, only to fall again. Lungs aching, he panted for breath, struggling to maintain his balance as the unseen menace moved closer. A scream of terror rose from his throat as the pillows suddenly transformed into faces and he recognized the doll-like features of Erly-Mae. Her voice filled the tunnel, echoing and re-echoing in a high-pitched vibrata that stung his ears. "Why Tylah ...Ah declare ...Ah declare ..." He covered his ears with his hands and the whining ceased, her face dissolved and was immediately replaced by another. In his confusion and fear, it was a second or two before he recognized Myra. His mother. It was *her* face he now trampled on, squashing it underfoot, *her* voice reverberating along the walls in a cold, mocking fury ..."Pretty face, that's all ...that's all ... that's all." Tyler wrenched himself from sleep and lay panting on top of the rumpled bed sheets, the panic and anxiety induced by his dream still vividly present. His fingers fumbled on the nighttable for a cigarette. *Now where the hell did I put that Scotch?*

* * * * * * * * * *

Myra Scranton, neeé White, was one of four daughters born to a coal miner and his wife in Wilkes-Barre. Her father was a drunken brute of a man who ruled his household with an abusive tongue and hard, pummeling fists. One night Mrs. White's screams were so piteous a worried neighbor called in the police; but the following week Mr. White broke the neighbor's collarbone, thus discouraging future interference with his homocidal rages.

Myra was nineteen when Hugh Scranton appeared at the Lakeside Presbyterian's annual ice cream social. When the dapper salesman politely asked if he could sit next to her and later, just as politely, asked if he could walk her home, it must have seemed to the unworldly girl like the answer to years of bitter prayer and petitions: Please, *please*, God, help me find a way to get out of this house and away from my father.

She was pregnant when they eloped 14 weeks later.

Despite the pall cast over the country by the Great Depression, Hugh Scranton with his bland good looks and the social adroitness of an Arthur Murray dance instructor, managed better than most as a jobber for *Alcoa* and its amazing new metal –aluminum. He brought his new bride to Thompson, drawn to the Pennsylvania town by its aura of Victorian stability and the fact that, by Hugh's reckoning, Thompson lay midway between his two biggest customers. The couple settled into a boarding house three blocks from the railroad station.

Hugh wrote to his mother in Dayton, Ohio about the marriage, promising to bring his wife for a visit after the baby came; but Mary Squires Scranton died two weeks before her grandson was born. She left Hugh a small legacy which he used as down payment on the frame house where Tyler grew up.

Herman Steinmenhausen, Hugh's paternal grandfather, was an adventuresome rake. At age 43, Herman sneaked out of the house and headed West, leaving a wife and three children to fend for themselves. En route, he passed several nights of frolicsome debauchery in a whorehouse in Scranton. In memory of this felicitous occasion–symbolic of his new freedom–and because "Scranton" is easier to spell than 'Steinmenhausen,' he adopted it as his surname without benefit of legal formalities. Herman made it as far west as Wichita where he took on a young, second 'wife' who bore him two sons, one of whom, Phineas, departed the Jayhawk state on his 25th birthday to seek his fortune. During a prolonged stopover in Dayton, he met and married Mary Squires, Hugh's mother. Phineas never left Ohio. He lost a leg in an accident at a lumber yard and drank himself into an early grave. His wife's family undertook the support of his widow and their two adolescent sons, Hugh and Tyler Lincoln.

Nowhere is it recorded that Herman Steinmenhausen's eyes were blue or brown, his hair sparse or thick, or any other hereditary feature that might have trickled down the genetic line. Except, of course, his peripatetic spirit.

How else to account for a son, Phineas, whose wanderlust was curtailed by an accident, or a grandson, Hugh, who casually stepped across the threshold one bright September afternoon, pulling shut the stained oak door, abandoning forever wife, beloved son, newborne infant?

Tyler was accustomed to his father's long absences from the house. At night, the small boy struggled against sleep, straining to catch that familiar, mocking bellow, "Anybody home?" accompanied by the thump of suitcases dropping to the floor in the narrow hallway at the front of the house. But the only sounds he heard were the reprise of branches scraping the side of the house, the groan and creak of old timber when the wind was up. Weeks slipped by and still there was no sign of him.

"When's my Daddy coming home?" he asked one morning at the breakfast table.

"Don't be pestering me with questions I got no answer to, Tyler," his mother snapped. "Finish your oatmeal."

With the approach of the Christmas season, his kindergarten class became absorbed in making presents for their parents. Tyler painstakingly cut a felt pin cushion in the shape of a tomato for his mother and fashioned a pipe rack out of popsickle sticks for his father.

"What you got there?" Myra asked when she came to clean his room, pointing to two garishly wrapped packages on the top shelf of his bookcase behind a model car.

"It's a surprise. For Christmas. For you and Daddy."

"Son, I hate to disappoint you, but your Daddy ain't comin' back. Not for Christmas. Not *ever*," emphasizing the finality of her declaration with a hard shove of the sweeper.

"He is too, he is!" rage and hurt lending him unexpected courage. "You don't know everything!"

Myra dropped the handle of the sweeper and approached him with quiet menace.

"Don't you ever sass your Mother again, Tyler Scranton," she warned, smacking his cheek with the flat of her hand.

In time, Tyler's memory of his father became a blur of scents and images: strong arms lifting him into the air, a twilight game of catch with a red rubber ball, the faint aroma of pipe tobacco on a tweed jacket, the scent of Brilliantine and licorish breath sweeteners. As the years passed by only an unexpected whiff of these was able to evoke a faint reminder that Hugh Scranton ever existed.

Myra made the best of a meagre education, a parochial mind and reduced expectations. America was at war on two continents and most of the able-bodied men were gone from Thompson. Justin Mooers, owner of the *Esso* station around the corner from their two-story frame house, hired her to be his cashier and general factotum. From a desk in the corner of a cramped and cluttered office–one grimy plate glass wall facing the pumps–she made change, kept track of ration stamps and sold scarce Hershey bars to favored customers. Sometimes Myra had to pump gas herself, a task she found undignified for a woman; but Mooers, a kindly man, allowed her to keep Tyler's younger brother Neddie with her, so she refrained from voicing her pique. After Neddie entered grammar school, she quit her job at the gas station to take up waitressing at Al's Diner, apologizing to Mooers: "With tips I can make more, Justin, and I need the money."

Whatever warmth and lightness of spirit the young Myra Scranton once possessed slowly shrivelled and died in the harsh reality of her husband's defection. No one, however, could accuse her of shirking her maternal duties. Neither cruel nor vindictive by nature, she was a conscientious mother, teaching the boys rudimentary good manners, seeing to it that their clothes were clean and mended, that a hot meal appeared at the table in the evening no matter how tired she was. When Tyler came down with a severe case of chicken pox, Myra sat by his bedside all night applying calamine lotion and cold compresses to relieve the itching and fever.

But after his father abandoned them, Tyler would catch her in an unguarded moment staring at him as if he were an uninvited guest who had overstayed his welcome. It was a look composed in equal measure of buried anger, pain and humiliation: she could hardly bear it that her older son looked exactly like his father, the scoundrel who had deserted her. None of this did Tyler understand as he struggled to both please and appease her. *What does she want?* He never found an answer. His mother's eyes never imparted the same affection and approval she gave unstintingly to Neddie. When Tyler reached puberty he stopped trying to win her over, accepting that Myra didn't love him. Neddie was the one his mother loved.

CHAPTER I I I

She reminded him of a kewpie doll he'd won pitching rings on the Boardwalk at Atlantic City: short, pudgy, skin the color of rice pudding, saucer blue eyes swimming in a sea of makeup and a cupid-bow mouth. Like a lowboy with its top drawer pulled out, her soft, thick body was dominated by casaba-melon breasts. He first laid eyes on her at 'Annie's Place,' a restaurant featuring generous portions of home-style Southern cooking located a few blocks east of the Atlanta stadium.

Situated on the ground floor of a three-story brick building, the restaurant had succeeded an Army Surplus store, and before that, it was rumored, an abbatoir. It's narrow interior contained a line of varnished plank tables against one wall and a small bar with six swivel stools against the other, its ambience reflected in the faded plastic flowers in old jelly glasses which adorned the tables. The majority of paying customers were men;

women rarely ventured into this battle-scarred part of the city.

Tyler sipped his beer, his eyes trailing the new waitress as she moved back and forth between the customers and the kitchen. He wasn't the only one. She had the undivided attention of every male in the room. A few of the bolder ones expressed their appreciation in half whispers, others by suggestive winks and nudges. She seemed oblivious to it all. Emboldened by her passivity, a long-haul driver in a checked shirt reached out and patted her fanny as she passed his table.

In a voice that ping-ponged around the room, she scolded, "Cut that out, mistah. Didn't your Mama teach you no manners?"

Tyler marvelled at her aplomb. *By God, she's shamed them all.*

Moments later when she emerged from the kitchen with his order, the heckling had ceased. With great care she set each item of Tyler's lunch before him.

"Can I get you anythin' else?"

"No thanks."

"Say mistah, you ever watch "Three's Company" on the television? Cross my heart, I swear you could be John Ritter's twin. You look just like him."

"What's your name?

"Everyone calls me Erly-Mae.

"Thank you, Erly-Mae, for that fine compliment, and from such a pretty young lady, too!"

He watched with amusement as a slow blush spread from her neck to the roots of her hair.

When he returned to 'Annie's a few days later, Erly-Mae spotted him and rushed over to take his order.

"Miz Annie says the trout's real fine today."

Annie Tompkins, proprietor, was born on a constipated, dust-and-weevil ridden farm in south Georgia and despite some twenty odd years spent in the wicked megopolis of Atlanta, retained all the prejudices and virtues of a small-town upbringing along with a deep and abiding faith in her Methodist God. Spirits were served at the restaurant, but her tolerance for the weakness of others did not extend to drunk and disorderly behavior: "If you cain't hold your likker like a gentleman, ya'll don't belong here," she'd say, pointing to the door.

Hers was a moon face, pale and perspiring, suspended over a shapeless lump of flesh whose considerable girth was hidden under a succession of faded gingham aprons and tentlike dresses ordered from the *Sears* catalogue. Under a flat forehead, grey-blue eyes, one slightly crossed, mirrored the soul of a warm and generous spirit. Miz Annie had taken Erly-Mae under her protective wing from the moment the girl showed up on the restaurant's doorstep in the pouring rain, her worldly goods crammed into a cardboard suitcase.

"'Please, ma'am. I gotta have work,'" Miz Annie relates, giving a fair imitation of the girl's singsong voice. "Course I took her on ...got her a room, too, up at Miz Brady's. The Lord was surely lookin' after me when He sent Erly-Mae, 'cause the very next day, my other girl, she ups and runs off with that shoe salesman from Macon."

Erly-Mae soon became the focus of a daily barrage of good-natured kidding from the regulars: "Hey darlin'! You get that hair style in Paris?" (hers being mouse-colored and stringy and fussed with constantly.) "Erly-Mae! How's 'bout you and me goin' out dancin' Saturday night?" The men were proprietary and fiercely protective of her, hissing a loud, **"Didn't your Mama teach you no manners?"** when a newcomer got out of line. She accepted their homage with modest grace, their teasing with good nature. A hardware salesman from Livonia voiced the prevailing opinion: "'Annie's' is more like family since Erly-Mae started workin' here, more fun, too."

The young waitress was playful and skittish with the others, but not Tyler. She found excuses to linger by his table, fussed over his food and blushed furiously whenever he turned lightly flirtatious. He was aware of her developing crush but thought nothing of it; for as long as he could remember, the opposite sex had been in hot pursuit. The first to voice her appreciation was a friend of his mother's, a grass widow named Melba

Talbot. The buxom divorcee seduced him in an alley behind the local RKO two weeks after his fourteenth birthday.

"You're some gorgeous hunk, Tyler Scranton," she whispered, unzipping his fly with shaking fingers, then pushing her hand inside, "the best looking thing I've seen around these parts in a dog's age."

"Damn it! I can't see a thing."

Tyler swung off *I-85* at the Stadium exit on his way to 'Annie's in the middle of a sudden, blinding downpour. Pulling the car up onto a low, grassless verge on the side of the highway he sat back to wait out the storm, his face settling into the flowering sulk of a small boy. He hadn't set foot in 'Annie's' in ten days having spent a rare weekend off sailing around Lake Hartwell with Herbie, the *Sheraton's* night manager. After sunset they guzzled beer and flirted with the local girls at a roadside tavern. Early that morning the two returned to Atlanta nursing hangovers. At his apartment Tyler gulped down two aspirin with black coffee and forced himself to take a cold shower. Before dressing, he examined his body in the mirror, noting with pleasure the mellow tan on his face and the upper half of his body. He couldn't wait to see Erly-Mae's face when he walked in.

Eventually, the storm levelled off and he was able to navigate partially flooded streets to the restaurant. He arrived to find the usual crowd had thinned down to a solitary quartet of Georgia State patrolmen dawdling over their cokes. Miz Annie emerged from the kitchen to clear off the tables.

"My goodness, I didn't expect to see you today, Tylah. It's way past your regulah eatin' time."

"Got caught in the storm and couldn't move, Miz Annie. Say, where's Erly-Mae? Hasn't quit on you, has she?"

"Poor chile took to her bed with the flu last Friday and ain't moved since. She begged to come in today, but I tole her she looked so sorry she'd scare my customers away. You hungry?" He nodded. "There ain't much left. Will you settle for meatloaf and hash browns?"

She returned shortly with his lunch. "I put some extra biscuits on the side, boy. I know how you favor them" Annie set his plate down before him and to Tyler's astonishment slid decorously onto the seat opposite.

Certain amenities were observed at the restaurant, an unspoken 'Roberts Rules of Order'. Topping the list was the dictum that one never invited Miz Annie to "sit down and join us." She wandered amongst the tables like a sovereign queen, pausing to exchange personal greetings, keeping a running score on the financial and emotional ups and downs of her regulars.

Folding her arms across her ample bosom, she silently watched him butter a biscuit.

"I've had it in mind to speak plain with you, Tylah," her voice, steady and low. "Now I don't hold with pokin' my nose into other folks' private business, but you bein' late and all, I took it for a sign: seems like the

Lord is sayin' to me, 'It's now or nevah, Annie Tompkins.'"

He was about to make a plea for enlightenment, but her next words took his breath away.

"It's Erly-Mae. I know *you know* she has a powerful feelin' for you. And no good can come of it, hear? No good a'tall."

"Hold it right there, Miz Annie. Are you trying to tell me you think some hokey-pokey's going on between me and that kid you have working here?" Self-righteousness fed his anger. "Gimme a break! I'm not so hard up I have to rob the cradle."

"I didn't say you was carryin' on ... not yet, anyways. But I know Erly-May and I know men."

"Well, you don't know me."

"That's the truth, Tylah. It's why I'm speakin' plain. 'Neath that soft puppy look of hers, there's a hide tough as pig's knuckle. Erly-Mae's had some hard times, been travellin' some rockbed roads. I could tell right off, though she don't evah say ... I've taken a real shine to her. Mind you, she puts in a good day's work, but more than that, she makes the folks who come heah happy ...". She paused, and for a moment the big woman seemed distracted... "Nevah had children of my own," she said softly. "Can get mighty lonesome sometimes ..." She sighed, suddenly aware of her audience, and hoisted her shoulders upright like a soldier coming to attention. "Nevah mind about me... I'm askin' you, Tylah, let her be. No good can come of chile her age gettin' mixed up with an older man like you."

"Damnit, Miz Annie. I've already told you. Nothing's going on between me and that 'chile' of yours."

"I prays not. I just hope the Good Lord is listening."

"If that's how you feel, I suppose I'm no longer welcome to eat here?"

"Now Tylah," she sparred, "did you ever know Miz Annie to be runnin' off a good customer?"

"But that's what you'd like, isn't it?"

She half rose from her seat and leaned across the narrow table, the upper weight of her body supported by two solid fists resting on its top.

"Boy, that's for you and your con-shence to decide."

* * * * * * * * * *

Tyler braked outside his apartment unit and waited for the closing bars of an old Dylan song before turning off the ignition. He was beat. The *Sheraton* had hosted a three-day convention of pharmaceutical salesmen and he'd put in a lot of overtime. *At least I have tomorrow off.* In the second or two before the headlights dimmed, he saw a familiar figure huddled on the steps leading to his building. Bounding from the car, he confronted Erly-Mae:

"What in God's name are you doing here?"

"Evenin' Tylah."

"Evenin' Tylah," he mimicked. "It's two o'clock in the goddamned morning and that's all you can say? What the hell are you doing here?"

"No need to be ugly, Tylah. If you'll just stop yellin', I'll explain. But first, lemme in your place. I've been sittin' here for three hours and I gotta pee real bad."

"You got a real cute place, Tylah," was her verdict after a silent tour of the livingroom. She stopped and stared at a picture on top of his bookcase. "That your steady girl?" It was a color photograph of Tyler with his arm around a tanned and beautiful strawberry blonde; they were both in swim suits against a background of white beach and blue sea. The adulation on her face as she gazed at him said it all. *Ah, sweet Betsy.* He'd picked her up at a singles' bar in Buckhead the year before; the affair had lasted six months. Betsy worked as a reservations clerk for *Delta*, and the roundtrip fare to Acapulco, where the photo was taken, was one of the perks open to its employees. After the trip, Betsy began dropping hints about a permanent liason. Despite the fact that she was fun to be with as well as an erotic and inventive bed partner, Tyler had no intention of settling down. With great reluctance, he'd broken off the relationship.

"No, just a friend. Besides, it's none of your business." He grasped her shoulders firmly, "Look Erly-Mae. I'm dead tired. I want to hit the sack. Come on. I'm taking you back to Mrs. Brady's."

"Don't you want to hear mah story?"

"You can tell me all about it in the car, damnit. Now come on!"

"'Fore we go, Tylah, can I have a coke? I'm about to die of thirst."

"I'll bring you a glass of water," he said through gritted teeth. On the drive back to her room, Tyler demanded to know who'd given Erly-Mae his home address.

"You been gone from Miz Annie's three weeks this coming Tuesday, Tylah, and I got worried you were sick or been in some kinda acc-ee-dent." She phoned the *Sheraton* and told the front desk she was a cousin of his who was passing through Atlanta unexpectedly and wanted to look him up.

Tyler grinned in spite of himself. "Ever think of entering the 'Guinness Book of Records' as a world-champion fibber? Now tell me, how the hell did you get to my place?"

"I told Ben I had this e-mergency, that mah poor ole aunty was sick and needed to see me real bad." Ben, a good-looking rogue, worked as a mechanic at a *Gulf* station near the restaurant. For weeks he'd been pleading with the young waitress to go out with him.

"You think Ben cared 'bout my ole aunty? No, suh. While we're drivin' over heah in his pickup, he tried to put his hand up mah leg, and when we come to a stop light, he takes a feel of mah boobs. I told him to quit his foolishness. Ah declare ...that boy's got no respect."

"Poor Ben. Imagine, no respect for your 'sick old aunty.'"

A week later she was back on his doorstep.

"Erly-Mae, this is getting out of hand. I have something better to do then run you across town after busting my tail half the night."

"No need to be takin' me back tonight, Tylah."

"Whadda ya mean? Of course I'm taking you back to Mrs. Brady's."

"Cain't!" she said triumphantly. "I left there for good this morning. See?" She reached behind the holly shrub at the side of the entrance-way and hauled out a shabby suitcase.

"Oh no you don't! You're not staying here, young lady."

"Got no where else to go, Tylah."

"St. Ignatius runs an all night shelter for strays and runaways. I'm taking you there. If they're full, I'm going to dump you in the middle of Peachtree Street and you can fend for yourself."

She lowered her head. "I didn't think you'd be so ugly, Tylah," she whispered.

In support of her entreaty, a splatter of raindrops fell from the darkened sky.

"Damn!" Tyler punched the air in defeat. He leaned down and grabbed her roughly by the arm. "Hurry up. Don't you know enough to come in out of the rain?"

She watched without comment as he hastily made up a bed for her on the couch, her innate buoyancy punctured by the sharpness of his anger. Tyler beat a fast retreat to his own room, where he drifted off to a restless sleep, the absurdity of the situation and its hypothetical consequences playing havoc with his nerves.

He woke with a start and glanced at the clock-radio by the bed. *Damnnit, it's after ten.* Pushing aside the tangle of covers, he rose to a sitting position, then remembered it was his day off and sank back on the pillows only to rise again like a shot. He'd forgotten. *That wacky kid's sleeping in the next room.*

The livingroom was empty, the bedding piled neatly on the floor by the sofa. From the kitchen came the aroma of fresh coffee and the strains of "Carolina in the Morning" in Erly-Mae's flat, sing-song voice.

"Mornin', Tylah," she beamed at him. "There's coffee on the stove, rolls in the oven, but I couldn't find any juice."

The barman poured himself a mug of coffee and sought refuge in the lounge chair at the far end of the livingroom where he leaned back and shut his eyes.

"You feelin' all right, Tylah?"

"Go away, Erly-Mae. I'm trying to think."

"Ah declare ...what you need, honey, is some cheerin' up."

Moments later he reluctantly opened his eyes and instantly wished he were on another planet. The purple t-shirt emblazoned 'Government Surplus' which Erly-Mae had been wearing lay in a heap at her feet while she engaged in a skirmish with the zipper on her jeans. Before she won the battle, his eyes had focused on the roseate darkness of nipples the size of silver dollars pressed flat against the confines of a peach lace brassiere. As the jeans joined her shirt on the floor, he was enthralled by the startling contrast between slim waist and butter-ball thighs.

"Cut that out! Put your clothes back on Erly-Mae!"

"Don't look so scairt, Tylah. You ain't the first."

Later, they lay in companionable silence on top of the unmade bed. Tyler felt numb, anesthetized by his romp on a playground of tremulous flesh, a quicksand of quivering breast and thigh.

"You got a funny look on your face, Tylah. Why?"

"I was just thinking, Erly-Mae, I don't even know your last name or where you're from."

"My Christian name is Erlene-May Adora Bigbee, but I prefers Erly-Mae. Sweet Water, Alabama is where my folks is, where I was baptized, but I aint laid eyes on Sweet Water for dawg's years."

"Sweet Jesus," he shook his head in bemusement, "that says it all. She snuggled closer and lightly teased his earlobe with the tip of her tongue. "Hey gal, enough already! . . What's Miz Annie gonna say about this?"

She moved away from him and sat up, unashamed of her nakedness, unaware of the erotic tumult her pendulous breasts with their shell-pink nipples might cause. "Miz Annie don't own me, Tylah. She's been real good to me ... treats me like I was kin and I'm grateful, but like I say, she don't own me."

"She won't like the idea of your being here," as if it were already settled. "What will you tell her?"

"I don't plan to be tellin' Miz Annie no fibs."

Declaring that 'her con-shence' wouldn't allow her to keep in her employ one who willfully ignored the Lord's commandments, Miz Annie said Erly-Mae had to go. Then she broke down and cried; Erly-Mae cried right along with her and they hugged each other goodbye. The girl from Sweet Water promptly got a job at *McDonald's* and was just as promptly fired a week later for 'hampering efficiency.' She hung on for three days at a fish & chips place, but couldn't stand the smell and quit. Next it was the lunch counter at *K-Mart*, but that didn't last long either. Eventually, she found work at an all-night diner on Moreland Avenue, an after-hours hangout for musicians and entertainers who played the nightclub circuit around Atlanta.

Her presence in Tyler's domain manifest itself a dozen different ways, "like a fire sale at *Macy's*" was how he came to think of it: undergarments and damp towels flung helter-skelter, tissues smeared with rouge and eye shadow in crumpled balls on every surface, a diaphram left casually to dry on the edge of the sink, tops for toothpaste, vitamins, deodorant -all mysteriously missing. And over the entire debacle hung the scent of gardenia bath salts. Erly-Mae's culinary abilities extended no farther than the first meal of the day and invariably, she burned the toast.

After adjusting to the idea that he'd been out-maneuvered and outsmarted by a kook from Alabama, Tyler relaxed. 'Schizoid time' was how he later referrred to the few months they lived together. At times he could have strangled her, but eventually he came to appreciate her sunny disposition, her indestructible optimism, and what he called her 'backwoods-country-road' directness and honesty. She never made his pulse race or his limbs ache with desire, but he enjoyed having her around.

He wasn't prepared for the stab of regret that followed her announcement that she was "movin' on," that Jocko, a trombone player she'd met at the diner, had captured her heart.

CHAPTER IV

Like butter in a heated frying pan, the days melted one into another as the date for Belle Jours' opening moved closer. Leona Caswell flew in from abroad to check the progress of the renovations and oversee arrangements for Laura's private suite. From a command post at the Reception Desk she issued marching orders in the form of individual assignments scribbled on a yellow legal pad and posted daily.

"Dat fat lady puttin' so much work on us, she don't care if Good Friday come 'pon Sunday," was how one Lutiguan expressed his pique.

Tyler was dispatched to a hamlet on the far side of the island: "Ask for Esme, the basket weaver. Bring back some samples. Tell her we may want to use them in the guest rooms."

Despite Wash's painstaking directions, the American lost his way several times in his quest for the remote enclave called 'Whimsy Gully' where the weaver lived. His search led him past an abandoned windmill, odd formations of sedimentary rock, crumbling sugar mills and a deserted plantation dense with tropical vegetation and dotted with palms of such extraordinary height, Tyler nearly swerved off the road admiring them. The sea was never far from sight and at times the road would crest above an inlet overlooking a small fleet of fishing boats. Unpainted wooden shacks dotted its hilly perimeter. It was after dusk when he returned to the hotel.

"I had the Devil's own finding that woman's house," he said, handing the baskets to Danielle. "God-awful roads and when I stopped to ask directions, half the time I couldn't understand the answer. That Esme's some character. Loves to talk, loves to bargain. She'd be right at home on the Chicago Exchange trading in pork futures."

"True. Esme has a way of burnin' up words."

"Speaking of 'burning up'. . . I need a shower and a drink, not necessarily in that order."

He was gone by the time Danielle remembered she was to tell him his cabinmate had arrived, but Tyler discovered that for himself when he flung open the cabin door and stumbled against a pyramid of luggage .

"Goddamn dumb place to leave suitcases," he muttered.

"Sorry, old man, I've been waiting for the boy to come and put them in my room." A reedy, cosmopolitan voice, with intimations of New England-prep-schooI-Ivy-League credentials and mahogany-panelled club rooms imbedded in its consonants, emanated from the far side of the darkened porch. Tyler edged around the bottleneck and switched on the light before turning to get a better look at the figure draped over the only extra chair in the cabin. He introduced himself, making a mental note of the expensive genealogy of the newcomer's rumpled linen suit.

"The staff here waits on itself, but I'd be glad to give you a hand."

"Preston's the name. Avery Preston, Keeper-of-the-Books. You'll excuse me if I don't rise, but I'm on my last legs. The entire day has been a series of minor catastrophes. At the moment I'm trying to work up the requisite energy to take a leak. Leona warned me this place was a little rough around the edges when in fact, it's positively primitive!"

Without further prompting, the newcomer launched into a litany of grievances beginning with a recalcitrant cabbie who wanted no part of six extra pieces of luggage -"I finally told the bugger I'd call the cops" - continuing with the airline: "They rush everyone on board so they can keep us waiting an hour while some damn fuel line is being rechecked; naturally, they shut off the engines and after ten minutes, the air is as foul as old sweat socks. When they finally get around to serving lunch, the steak's overdone, the champagne, lukewarm *and domestic* – this is *First Class*, mind you."

As the peevish phrases floated into the heavy night air, Tyler studied the New Yorker, his eyes registering the pencil-slim nose, skin like polished agate and sand-colored hair, meticulously brushed and parted to one side. Words tumbled from lips thick and piscine, reminding Tyler of the puckered mouth of a fish, and for a giddy moment he half expected to see a stream of bubbles emerge and go drifting over the porch railing. But it was the man's eyes, dark and heavily lidded like some prehistoric lizard, that were the most disturbing. *Only lizards don't have curly lashes.* The barman guessed he was in his mid-thirties.

An invading mosquito interrupted the bookkeeper's monologue giving the other man an opportunity to interject: "Look, dinner's at eight. I need to shower and change, so let me help you now."

"Right, old man." As Preston languidly rose from the chair, his figure evinced an encroaching flabbiness. It came as no surprise to Tyler that he ended up carrying most of the luggage while Avery busied himself supervising.

Absorbed in sorting out impressions of his new cabinmate, Tyler soaped himself under a limpid stream of water. *Damn pressure's low again.* Without being the least conscious of it, certainly without an iota of animus or self-pity, he automatically acknowledged the superiority of the Avery Prestons of this world.

Growing up in the small, rural community of Thompson near the northwestern border of Pennsylvania, he'd learned to accept at an early age the immutable demarcation between 'them' and 'us.' In Thompson, as in other towns settled before the turn of the century, the railroad acted as a social arbiter, separating those enfranchised by wealth, power and family name from the rest. In Tyler's hometown, 'them' referred to broad, maple-lined streets and the possessors of rambling Victorian houses embossed with gingerbread latticework, summertime lawns like carpets of emerald green, wicker porch furniture and ornate stone urns filled with clumps of brilliant red and pink geraniums.

Mooer's Park, a tired stretch of sand and crabgrass used as a playground cum baseball diamond, the Red Checker Depot and 'Al's Diner' - a garishly resurrected B&O passenger car - these were the signposts of Tyler's part of town.

As he towelled down, he decided, "That accent of Preston's is the kicker. 'Old man this ... old man that,' the guy's seen too many British films."

* * * * * * * * * * *

The staff at Belle Jours trickled into the dining hall for their evening meal savoring the freedom and leisure to do so, knowing it wouldn't last. Among the first to be seated were Danielle accompanied by Cleo, the young Lutiguan who worked under her direction in the office. They made a handsome pair: Danielle, with her classic features and Cleo, half woman, half child, slender and shy, oblivious to an innate, unstudied appeal which would ripen in time and mark her as a real beauty. At their heels came Leona Caswell and Ralph Martinelli, an engineer on loan from *Pittsburgh Light & Power* who'd arrived the previous day to supervise the installation of the hotel's generator and air conditioning . A blunt, outspoken man in his early forties, Martinelli made no bones about wishing to get his job done as quickly as possible so he could get back to Mrs. Martinelli and their five children.

Tyler sidled up to Danielle's chair and whispered in her ear, "That's some roomie I'm stuck with. More to the point, what's a guy like Avery doing in a place like this?"

"If you wish to know more about Mr. Preston III, please to ask Miss Caswell," she replied cooly.

"Well you can't shoot a guy for asking."

Moments later, with the consummate skill of one to whom all the world is indeed a stage, the bookkeeper made his entrance brandishing a bottle of wine.

"Ladies and gentlemen," he announced, "the last name is *Preston,* the first is *Avery* and anything else you may eventually decide to call me, I beg you, do so when I'm out of the room!" Laughter erupted as if on cue. He swooped around the table, bowed to Cleo and Danielle, kissed Leona Casell's cheek, shook Martinelli's hand and patted Tyler's shoulder. Eyeing the two empty places left at the table, he commandeered the chair at its head.

"Now," he said crisply, "would someone please fetch the goblets so we can drink a toast to new friends and the start of a great adventure."

"Goblets! You did say *goblets?*" Tyler asked in mock dismay. "Sorry, old man, but you'll have to make do with plastic cups."

"Ah well," came the cheerful reply, "It's the spirit that counts, isn't it?"

Tyler spent the following morning with the local liquor distributor. Returning to the cabin, he discovered that its communal area had been transformed by Avery: a trio of delicate Oriental silk hangings covered the bare walls and a pair of ornate candlesticks, set of slim leather volumes and foot-high bronze of Diana, the Huntress, graced a corner table. Preston emerged from his room rubbing his hands with satisfaction:

"How do you like it, old man?"

"Looks great, Avery. Say, where'd you find the table?"

"You'd be surprised what miracles can be wrought for ten American dollars. The foreman for the construction crew - Forbes, I think he said his name was – 'found' it. I didn't ask where. Useful man to know, that Forbes. By the way, my stereo should be arriving soon, and I thought it might look well over there," he pointed to an empty space. "What do you think?"

"Guess you're not used to roughing it."

"Just because this island is an outback of civilization doesn't mean I plan to live like a savage."

Three more containers arrived that afternoon and every available man in the compound was enlisted to help with the unloading. Beneath a canopy of merciless sun, the gruelling task was begun. Before long the entire forecourt of Belle Jours was littered with discarded wooden crates, cardboard and packing material. The debilitating heat took its toll in sweat, aching muscles and frayed tempers. As the sun began its swift descent, the men were dismissed. Tyler stumbled back to his quarters determined to find out why Preston had not joined them. The New Yorker was lounging in a chair on the porch, book in hand, the remains of a papaya on a plate beside him.

"Where the hell were you, this afternoon?"

"Reading a book, my good fellow. What does it look like?"

"We needed all the help we could get. Who exempted you?"

"Scranton, old man, I was hired for my brains, not my brawn. Sorry, but lifting heavy boxes is not my thing." To signal the end of the matter, he turned a page and resumed reading.

For two cents I'd kick your smug ass from here to Singapore.

The next three days were spent helping Caswell, Cleo and Danielle sort and mark for dispersal the hundreds of items spread across the reception room floor. The barman rose early, took his meals on the run, and fell into bed past midnight, avoiding contact with Preston completely.

"Tyler, old man! Been looking everywhere for you. Our new fridge has arrived!" He waved a bottle of *Chivas Regal* in the air. "Let's celebrate in style."

My, aren't we laying on the charm. Kiss-and-make-up time. What the hell, we're stuck here together for the duration.

"Where'd you find the hootch, Avery? That's not Scotch, it's nirvana."

Preston ran his tongue along his bottom lip, pleased at the civil response. "Quite frankly, I was beginning to feel like a bit of a pariah, everyone working his bum off and me unable to get into my cubby hole until it's done. I took a cab into town this morning to look for a few odds and ends. The *Chivas* comes under the heading of 'odds,' because the odds of finding my favorite Scotch in this god-forsaken hole are about 100 to 1."

Emboldened by a second drink, Tyler asked the question that had puzzled him since Preston's arrival. "Tell me, Avery, what made you decide to come to Lutigua?"

The New Yorker took a thoughtful sip of his drink before answering. "I suppose it's as simple as waking up one morning and deciding city life was becoming a bore, that a change of venue was in order. Years ago, my Uncle Willard courted Laura Foster-Jones. He was quite smitten. To no avail, I might add. They kept in touch over the years, annual Christmas cards, that sort of thing. He told me she was planning to reopen the hotel and I wrote immediately to see if she needed a bookkeeper. She cabled me to come ahead. Of course, I only promised a year max, no more. My firm was very good about it, said my old slot would be waiting when I return."

He leaned forward with a lewd smirk and slapped Tyler on the knee. "Adventure, old man! Adventure! Who can tell what romantic thrill lies ahead in this tropical backwater? A nice piece of fresh, black meat maybe, eh?"

Scranton's countering wince registered immediately. Preston stiffened and sat back. With the false air of a penitent who gets caught with his hand in the cookie jar, he said, "Sorry, old man. I do get carried away sometimes."

CHAPTER V

Time became the staff's common enemy.

A perspiring, cursing Martinelli spent half his days on the telephone threatening, cajoling and begging parts from errant suppliers in the States. In the kitchen, an autocratic Corbin led his crew through the the intricacies of souffles and sauces, curries and flambées while Tyler drilled his small team in the complexities of a dry martini, sloe gin fizzes and frozen daiquiris. Every morning young James, Wash's son, appeared unbidden to run errands and make himself useful. The carpenters, who worked a 10-hour day, no sooner finished an area when the painters took over. Farrell Cafferty arrived at dawn and could be heard bellowing orders long after dark. Each day brought a new set of crises – missing machine parts, delayed shipments, petty thievery, shortages, even injuries (one local fell off the roof and broke his back). Tempers flared and egos were rubbed raw. Only Wash managed to keep his equanimity. Beneath the chaos a silent undercurrent of excitement raged: Laura Gallon Foster-Jones, the Mistress, "de white lady boss" would be arriving soon.

The afternoon of her scheduled return to Lutigua found everyone restive and on edge. Leona left for the airport immediately after lunch to welcome her employer back to the island. For the third time that day, Danielle made a careful check of the guest quarters and dining room; she paused at the threshold of the recently completed public room adjoining the reception area and gave it her full attention. It had been transformed into a masterful blend of elegance and comfort: the settees and armchairs were covered in a cheerful English floral chintz; a handsome gilt oval mirror graced the wall above a polished antique mahogany sideboard and Aububonesque prints of birds and flowers indigenous to the Caribbean were scattered about the walls. A brilliant bouquet of flowering red ixora and amarylis, white jasmine and spider lily provided the final theatrical touch. Only the hemp rug was missing, and the local women commissioned to weave it promised the rug would be ready in time for the hotel's official opening. She glanced at her watch noting that the arrival party was forty minutes overdue.

At that moment the staccato beep of the taxi's horn sounded in the driveway. Danielle nervously patted her hair before walking swiftly towards the front entrance to join Wash, who had stationed himself there to greet his Mistress. On her way she met Tyler and Avery, both freshly shaven and dressed for the occasion. With an air of expectancy, they lined themselves up on the steps at the entranceway and watched as Darius Owen emerged from behind the wheel to open the door on the far side of the car for Leona Caswell. Tyler took in the scene: *All that's missing is a fanfare of trumpets.*

Wash opened the door facing them and offered his arm to a tall slim woman dressed in white. Placing a hand delicately on his sleeve, she turned to the elderly Lutiguan, a smile of genuine pleasure suffusing her features, "My dear Wash, how lovely to see you." She spoke to him in a voice barely audible to the onlookers. "Tell me, how's your family? Is Mrs. Wilson keeping well? And your sons, they must be grown young men by now?"

The old man beamed. "Yes, Mistress, de boys all done wid their schoolin'. Mrs. Wilson, she send her regards."

Focusing her undivided attention on the old retainer, Foster-Jones barely glanced at the others as the two mounted the steps of the hotel and disappeared from view.

Caswell, her face damp and grey from the exertions of the trip, hurried around the front of the car and breathlessly cautioned the group on the steps. "Mrs. Foster-Jones is extremely tired from her long journey and asks that you please forgive her for not stopping to introduce herself this afternoon. Scranton, will you and Preston see to the luggage. Owen will help you. Wash has his own instructions. Mrs. Foster-Jones will meet with each of you tomorrow ."

Keen to air his opinion of the day's events, Preston cornered Tyler later that same evening: "You know, old man, last year my uncle and I attended a reception for the French ambassador at the White House - black tie, Marine Band, the works - and this afternoon's little 'do' almost matched it. Have you ever seen such a fuss over a nobody? I mean, it's not as if she had a title or were related to royalty."

Tyler decided it would be unwise - *no, buddy-boy, just plain stupid* - to gossip about his new employer with Avery.

In a flash the barman recaptured his impression of the woman who would be central to his life as long as he remained on the island: the rectangular-shaped face with its fine underlying bone structure, aquiline nose and arresting grey-green eyes; thin lips, slightly downturned; chords tautly stretched under a firm chin and tell-tale wrinkles on the swan-like neck; her light brown hair dappled with grey was worn in a truncated French twist. He'd noticed that her outfit, the white linen jacket and slacks with matching handbag and pumps—all bore the earmarks of being couturier-bred.

"You have to admit, she's got style," was all he would say.

In another part of the island, Danielle faced her father across the kitchen table.

"Mrs. Foster-Jones arrived today," she told him, "but she was weary from her journey, and we did not speak."

"Word passin' like de October winds she's back on de island."

"Remember, Daddy, you promised to tell me the rest of the story ... what happened after her husband was killed in the war?"

"So I did, Dani. Lemme see now ... Must've been 1944, when Mis Laura come home...just 'fore Christmas.

"All dis time passin' en Mistress Alice, she's keepin' to her bed. She never did come 'round after de last stroke. Your great aunt Jessie say she can hardly move, don't talk neither, but her eyes let you know she still have her wits 'bout her. Poor lady was holding tight to life, just waitin' to see her sweet girl's face onc't more. Wid Mis Laura home at last, de house is fixed up real fancy, like before de war, wid candles in all de windows en poinsettas bloomin' in every corner of every room.

Ole Bessie, de cook, she know it's a special Christmas for de Gallons en she fixes up a fine dinner for de family ... sorrel en fish cakes, roast pig, yams... cou-cou ... peas en rice... more fancy dishes than I can remember. Dessert was Bessie's famous black fruitcake. (That cake been soakin' up de rum since All Hallow's.)

Mis Laura en her Daddy take their meal wid de Mistress, right in de room where she's lyin' so still. Jessie tellin' how Mistress Alice's eyes are swimmin' wid tears of joy, en a hundred years drop from Gallon's face since his little girl's return. Only now she's a growed-up lady. At dinner Mis Laura's sayin' how brave de folks in London was, ebben when de bombs was fallin'. She tellin' funny stories, too, 'bout bein' a driver for a high Army officer en how all de time she's gettin' them lost; en how de air raids was always interferin' with what she has a mind to do, like takin' a hot bath, or 'bout to bite into a piece of toast with *real* marmalade, marmalade bein' scarce as duppies in a churchyard. Her stories set her Daddy to laughin', but her eyes held a sadness that don go away."

On Boxing Day, the day after Christmas, Laura invited a small group of her mother's closest friends to afternoon tea; it was to be a surprise. But that morning when Jessie went to wake her Mistress, the figure on the bed was still. 'Time to wake up now, Mistress,' Jessie coaxed, her heart in her throat as she tried to rouse her.. ...Later, she said she'd never seen a grown man cry like Gallon when they told him his wife was gone. Laura tried her best to comfort him, "but tears fallin' like rain from her eyes, also. Sorrow lay round that house like a blanket of moss from de sea."

A few weeks after the funeral, guests - some of whom had stayed at the hotel before the war - began to trickle back to Belle Jours for the winter season. Paralyzed by grief, Gallon retreated into a world of his own leaving Laura the responsibility of managing the hotel. She welcomed the excuse to be busy; when Bessie came down with dengue fever, Laura took over the added burden of preparing meals until the cook recovered. Then her father contacted the dengue, and the fever left him weak and apathetic. His daughter fussed over him, preparing his favorite food, insisting he walk every day to regain his strength. One afternoon Gallon hiked as far as Rainbow Reef and was caught in a sudden downpour; it was a struggle to make his way back to the hotel where he immediately had a relapse. The fever returned, quickly developing into pneumonia. Laura nursed him herself, catching snatches of sleep in a chair at his bedside but hers was an uphill battle: George Gallon had lost all interest in living. He died within the week.

"For sure, de trouble tree don't bear no blossoms. Poor Mis Laura. Her Mummy and Daddy both gone, en she not havin' time to bear her sorrow, what with the hotel open en guests to be looked after. Her Daddy's friends come round and tell her to close Belle Jours, to put it up for sale, but she sayin', 'No, I plan to keep it ... it's all I've got left now. '

"For de longest time Mis Laura tendin' to things like she's walkin' in her sleep, draggin' through the days... on en on ... 'til one fine morning folks notice she's her old spirited self again. Come summer's end, she shut down de hotel, hired painters en workmen to put in de pool, fixed up de rooms and such like, makin' de place as fresh en sweet as a newborn baby. When de hotel is ready for guests once more, Wash come to work for her."

"Mr. Wilson never say he's been at Belle Jours before!"

"Jeremiah Wilson, he's a man who knows how to keep things to himself. Like your Granny always, 'de tongue ain't made to tell everything.' En Mis Laura, she was wise enough to know Wash wouldn't go bruisin' her personal affairs in every rum shop in de parish. After a time, you see, there was enough gossip to make a busy-body's jaw ache."

Word quickly spread of a small jewel of a hotel by the sea where the service was friendly, the food delectable and guests graciously welcomed by its personable owner. Reservations for the next winter season came flooding in. Early in February, a Canadian artist whose work was admired on two continents, checked into Belle Jours saying he expected to stay for some time. Within a matter of weeks Laura Foster-Jones was seen everywhere in the company of a lean, attractive man with carrot-colored hair and beard. Those who knew her family history were happy for her; after so much sorrow - losing a young husband, then both parents within a few weeks of each other - it was a pleasure to see her enjoying herself again. As one Lutiguan put it, 'After all de pain she bearin', must be de Lord took pity en make her more beautiful than before. Besides, it ain't natural for one so young en sweet to be sittin' under de mango tree alone...'

The artist became a familiar figure on the island, seen everywhere with his easel and paints, filling canvases with the beauty of its natural scenery, the faces of its local denizens. (A rumor began circulating that he'd painted Laura in the nude. No one actually saw the painting, but they were positive it existed.) At the end of April, he left to prepare for an exhibit of his works in Boston. As soon as word of his departure made the rounds, a continual stream of escorts materialized, eager to be Laura's dancing partner, squire her to parties. This did not sit well with the local women; the gossip was fierce. Laura, who must known people were talking about her, didn't seem to care. Like a caged bird beating its wings against the bars, she continued to dance the night away with whomever she pleased—a hotel guest, a cruise ship officer and on occasion, a man sporting a gold ring on his left hand.

When the artist showed up again, she sent them all away.

He and Laura were together constantly. Often she accompanied him on his painting excursions, spreading a blanket on the grass close to his easel, not speaking, but content to fill her eyes with the sight of him. She never counted the days, the number of times his long sensitive fingers roamed her body, moving her to a level of passion she barely dreamed possible. Friends noticed a special glow about her, the rapturous look of a woman who has opened her heart to love... The incident at 'Bellaire' changed everything.

'Bellaire' in St. Thomas, a handsome coralstone 'great house', was erected a few years after the original house on the site was destroyed by the vengeful hurricane of the 1830's. Surrounded by 14 acres of magnificent gardens and parkland, it sits on a hill several hundred feet above sea level with breathtaking vistas of the parish. Each year a great ball was held at the plantation in August, a tradition begun in the early 1900's, and, save for the two World Wars, faithfully honored by succeeding generations of the family. It was a gala renown for its lavish food, generous supply of spirits and music performed by some of the finest musicians on the island. Invitations to the ball were highly prized. One of the few names added to the guest list that summer was 'Mrs. Edward Foster-Jones.'

Laura and her escort were among the last guests to pass through the receiving line. "So dreadfully sorry we're late," she said to her hosts, "but we had a small crises at the hotel. One of the guests cut her foot rather badly and we had to send for the Doctor." (In truth, she and her lover had spent the afternoon together in bed, forgetting about time, forgetting about everything but the mutual pleasuring of their bodies.)

When the couple made their appearance moments later on the front portico where cocktails were being served, they became the cynosure of every eye. Resplendent in a white silk evening gown with a motif of seed pearls decorating the bodice and along the hemline, a spray of white orchids artfully arranged in her upswept hair, Laura was the envy of every woman. As she moved with singular grace amongst the partygoers, her lover at her side, each man present silently wished he could trade places with the tall, bearded artist.

Tables were spread across the lawn under the stars for the guests to enjoy the elaborate buffet; afterwards, they drifted back to the house, drawn by the music wafting through open French windows. The great hall of the house had been cleared to make room for dancing, cleared of all encumbrances save a wooden platform at one end for the band. Under the benign glow of two glittering crystal chandeliers, Laura stepped into her partner's arms and they glided onto the floor. A bar had been set up in the adjoining library and from it emerged 'Bo' Mottley, the dissipated heir of one of the oldest families on the island. As usual, Mottley had waived the temptation to partake of food for the greater allure of the rum pot. Surveying the dancers from a corner of the room, his eye was arrested by a familiar figure. Laura Gallon. It had been years since he'd last seen her. With a lopsided grin of optimism he made his unsteady way across the dance floor.

"'Lo, Laura darling. Wonderful to see you again. Sorry, frien', ish my turn with the lady," he slurred, tapping the artist on the shoulder.

Recoiling from the reek of liquor on his breath, Laura quietly demurred, "No thank you, Bo. Some other time." But Mottley was not to be denied. Raising his voice he again demanded his turn, attracting the notice of several of the dancers, who paused to watch, curious to see what would happen.

"The lady said 'No,' sir."

Accustomed to having his way, Mottley put his beefy hands on the artist's shoulders and tried to push him away. "Shuffle along, boy. You don't own her," he bellowed. Noting the man's inebriated condition, Laura's partner tried to deal with him calmly, but Bo stubbornly repeated "You don't own her." (By now, even the band had stopped playing.) Mottley drew back his fist to take a punch at his rival, but Laura grabbed his coat tails, crying out, "Stop this instant, Bo! Stop behaving like a spoiled child. This is my fiancé. We're engaged to be married!"

Mottley dropped his fist, suddenly conscious of the scene he'd created. Without another word he turned on his heel and shambled out of the room heading straight for the bar. The band woke up to the fact they'd been hired to perform and swung into a lively fox trot, but Laura's escort seemed oblivious to it all. Briefly he stood clenching and unclenching his fists, his face by turns deadly white and beet red, before grabbing Laura's hand, pulling her off the dance floor and out of the room. "The party's over, dear heart," he muttered rebelliously, "we're leaving."

As they waited on the gravel driveway for Owen to bring the car around, heated words were exchanged:

"How dare you treat me like this in front of my friends! How dare you drag me off the dance floor! I'm not ready to leave yet."

"*And how dare you lie and announce to everyone we're engaged!* Damnit, Laura, I've told you from the beginning, my work comes first. I don't plan to be tied down.... now, or in the foreseeable future. Get that into your pretty little head."

With eyes ablaze, her face bearing equal parts rage and pain, Laura reached up and slapped him hard across the cheek. At that moment the taxi slowed to a stop beside them. Before her lover could move or speak, she wrenched open the passenger door telling Owen as she stepped inside, "Take me home. The gentleman won't be coming with us." The next morning, soon after the diningroom opened for breakfast, the artist and his belongings were gone from the hotel.

The guests at 'Bellaire' who had witnessed the contretemps on the dance floor and heard Laura's ringing declaration, weren't privy to the events *outside* in the driveway; the surprising news of her engagement, however, provided conversational fodder for the remainder of the evening. Two or three days later when word seeped out that the fiancé had hurriedly left the island, the air was rife with gossip and speculation. Stubbornly refusing to acknowledge her hurt pride, Laura ignored the maelstrom of spiteful talk and carried on as if nothing untoward had happened. *"He'll be back. I know he'll be back."*

As the days slipped by, she was like a condemned prisoner awaiting word of a pardon – listening for an overseas call that never came, hoping for a letter that was never posted. Affairs at the hotel received desultory attention and she withdrew from her friends, shunning all social contact. With Wash the only witness to her unhappiness, the wounded woman retreated to her rooms where increasingly she turned to the rum bottle for succor. She was brought her to her senses by an incident involving one of the hotel 'regulars', an elderly American widow, a particular favorite of Laura's who'd been coming to Belle Jours for many years. While taking a late-afternoon swim, the woman suffered a stroke; only the alertness of another guest saved her from drowning. When the gardener was sent to 'fetch de Mistress,' he'd been unable to rouse her from an alcoholic slumber. Since it was Wash's day off, the responsibility for deciding a course of action was dumped on the shoulders of the frightened young receptionist on duty. A hastily whispered phone call to an older sister for advice resulted in the island's sole ambulance being sent for; it showed up an hour later. The American woman died on the way to the hospital. That evening when Laura, fully awake and wanting solid food, sent for a light supper she was told the disturbing news.

"Why wasn't I informed immediately?" she shouted at the waiter who brought her tray.

"Mr. Amos, de gardener, he tried wakin' you, Mistress," he replied, shifting miserably from one foot to the other.

"I'll fire that stupid bloody girl first thing tomorrow. Why didn't she call the Doctor! Everyone on this island knows you can't depend on that damn ambulance in a real emergency."

Leaving her plate untouched, she paced back and forth. The reality of the hapless waiter's indictment slowly sank in: she'd been drinking all afternoon and must have passed out. *Oh dear God.* With an overwhelming sense of guilt and shame, Laura knew she had no one to blame but herself.

The early hours of the morning found her standing at the wrought iron railing encircling the patio, eyes lifted towards the heavens, chin tilted defiantly as she made a silent vow: *No man will ever humiliate me again. Not ever.*

Stung by the horror of the tragedy, Laura resumed an active role in managing the hotel, foreswearing those afternoons of solitary drinking and the attendant anguish over her lover's desertion. To signal her intention of continuing to participate in the island's social life, invitations to dine at Belle Jours were delivered over a period of several weeks to select members of what passed for the upper echelons of society in Lutigua as well as embassy officials and prominent businessmen. The gatherings were purposely kept small, never more than a dozen at a time and of course, wives were included. Eager to see for themselves how 'that woman' will behave after publicly being made a fool of, no one dreamed of declining.

Aware of their prurient curiosity, Laura outwitted them by acting the perfect hostess—all smiles, small jokes and charm. The drinks flowed like spring water and heaping platters of food were served to suit the most discriminating palate. Word spread rapidly of Mrs. Foster-Jones' stylish and elegant *soirees*; her invitations acquired a certain *cachet* and became much sought after. In time, whenever the owner of Belle

Jours name came up in conversation, people ceased alluding to her fiancé's defection. Moreover, it was noticed that Laura arrived at functions and left without an escort... no more indiscreet late nights, no more behavior to titillate the scandal-mongers. This bland state of affairs lasted a year or so until, as Mapp would relate, "Trouble poke its head round de corner again."

At the behest of the Foreign Office, Arthur Anderson was posted to Lutigua as acting head of the British Consulate for the entire Caribbean. Upon his arrival his predecessor, Burney Dean, hosted a large cocktail party to bid a personal farewell to the islanders and introduce his replacement. An old hand at ingratiating himself in new surroundings, Anderson immediately captivated the Lutiguans, particularly the ladies, with his debonair good looks, courtly manners and dry sense of humor. New faces were warmly received in this insular part of the world and after Dean's party the Consulate was deluged with invitations. Anderson's wife was in England, awaiting the end of the school term before she and their two sons would join him. Once the local ladies heard this, they fairly tripped over themselves volunteering to show the handsome newcomer around the island and help him hunt for a house. The Englishman was the center of attention wherever he went, including a *soireé* held in his honor at Belle Jours. If his hostess seemed unusually animated that evening, no one thought much about it. Anderson had that affect on women.

But soon the Consul was showing up at the hotel for drinks and dinner with Laura alone; on other occasions he'd arrive late in the evening on his way back from an official function. Of the regular staff, only Wash was on hand to serve them. Their growing attraction to each other remained a secret for a long time, in part because Anderson boldly parked his car with its diplomatic plates and telltale Union Jacks adorning the front bumpers in Belle Jours' driveway; anyone who noticed the sleek white Mercedes assumed he was there in an official capacity.

One night when the moon was full, shedding its ethereal glow over the entire island, the owner of a popular rum shop took his usual shortcut home, a footpath running parallel to the sea. As he strolled along he spied a couple holding hands and walking barefoot at the tideline. Being curious - most sensible people stayed clear of the beaches late at night for fear of being robbed or assaulted - the man hid in the shadow of a casurina tree. He saw the man draw the woman to him, watched him cover her face and neck with kisses. Moments later they had shed their clothing and were making love on the beach, acting as if the whole universe belonged to just the two of them, with only the moon privy to their ardor. The shop owner had never seen the man before, but he recognized Laura; he'd known the Gallon family since before the war. He left his hiding place and hurried along the path, eager to tell his wife all he'd witnessed. The next day his wife repeated his story to two of her neighbors.

Rumours that the British Consul and Mrs. Foster-Jones were having an affair spread like a dry bush fire .

The news hit the white community like a bolt of lightning causing an immediate reaction: most agreed that Laura had gone too far this time, that her carrying on with a married man in his position would would reflect badly on the entire island.

Just when it seemed the pot would boil over, that some sort of showdown was inevitable, Anderson's wife arrived from abroad with their boys, two bright-looking, well-mannered youngsters. Everyone sighed with relief, believing this would end the sorry business.

Emily Anderson was a pleasant, unpretentious woman; she was tactful and kind, perhaps a bit too anxious to please, but so accustomed were Lutiguans to the cool, distant manner of British consular wives, they warmed to her at once, going out of their way to make her feel welcome. Despite his family's presence on the island, the besotted Anderson refused to end the affair and continued seeing Laura on the sly.

What started casually – a group of Laura's old friends dropping by – on Sunday afternoon for drinks on her private patio-over time became a weekly affair.

Dubbing themselves 'The Society of Tipplers' (SOTS), they consumed a fair amount of their hostess' liquor supply in return for trading gossip and amusing stories. On this particular Sunday, to cover their embarrassment at being privy to the scandal, they drank more than usual, talked louder, laughed harder. In the midst of their merrymaking, Wash appeared and quietly spoke to Laura: "Mistress, a lady's at Reception askin' to see you."

"Tell her that I'm entertaining, Wash, to come back tomorrow. Better still, invite her to join the party."

"I think de lady have it in mind to speak wid you alone." The disquiet in Wash's tone seeped through the haze of liquor.

"Who is it, Wash?"

"She don't give no name, Mistress." Wash would never lie. Yet he couldn't bring himself to say he guessed whom the visitor might be.

Laura scrutinized the face of the trusted Lutiguan, taking note of his his apprehension, of an unaccustomed nervousness, and resigned herself to seeing the caller. "While I'm talking to this 'person', whoever she is, bring another round of drinks for my guests," she said sharply and left the patio.

Her friends ignored the interruption; they were accustomed to Laura's occasional absences due to hotel business. However, when their hostess reappeared a few moments later, they were taken aback by the parchment-white pallor of her skin, the hard, tight line of her mouth.

"My dear, whatever is the matter? You look as if you'd seen a ghost."

"It's nothing. Just someone, who ...Oh, nevermind. I need another drink. Where's Wash?"

At that moment a small woman, her fair hair disheveled, fists clenched at her sides, stormed onto the patio.

"Why did you walk away from me, Mrs. Foster-Jones? I hadn't finished what I came to say." The refined voice was taut with repressed fury. One of the guests recognized her immediately. *Oh my God, it's Anderson's wife.*

Laura whirled around. "There's no law requiring me to stand and listen to some stranger make disgusting allegations against me."

"I may be a stranger to you, but my husband is no stranger...to *your bed.*"

"You're deranged if you think ..."

"I don't 'think' anything." The voice rising now, straining in an effort to keep control. "*I know for a fact.* Arthur confessed to me last night. He had to, you see, after the cable came from the Home Office. Arthur is being recalled. Back to London. His career in the diplomatic service is over. And all because of you! Not only does everyone on this bloody island know what's going on, word got back to England, too."

"Don't blame me for decisions made three thousand miles away. Besides, how do you know his career is 'over', as you say? You're just overwrought!"

"Overwrought ... Is that what you think? That I'm 'overwrought?'" She threw back her head, her pretty mouth distorting into a rictus of laughter. The sound emanating from her lips was so chilling in its despair, those witnessing the confrontation shivered inadvertently in the warm afternoon air.

"You are incredible, Mrs. Foster-Jones. Absolutely incredible! Poor Arthur. He thinks he's in love with you! He doesn't know about the others, yet. And there have been *many* others...I know that for a fact, too. But no more." She was sobbing now as she fumbled with the handbag strapped across her shoulder. "You're never going to destroy another marriage, ruin another man's career because ..." With a shaking hand she withdrew a small revolver and pointed it at Laura .

"Bloody hell," one of the men in the party exclaimed. "Mrs. Anderson, you don't want do that!"

But she didn't hear him or the others who murmured their alarm but were unable to act, paralysed by alcohol, by the swiftness of the unfolding drama. It was as if Anderson's wife was submerged under water, drowning in her anguish, her need for revenge. With tears streaming down her face, she took a jerky step backward and aimed the gun. In a stillness electric with shock and disbelief, the sound of the trigger being pressed back and released was deafening. Nothing happened. She pulled it again ... again, and again, howling now in frustration.

"Look like de gun need fixin'. Here, Miz Anderson, why don't you give it to me?" a calm voice entreated. Wash emerged from the shadows, his arm outstretched in supplication. Those present held a communal breath as he moved slowly and cautiously towards the distraught woman, continuing to plead with her in soft, reasonable tones. At last, he managed to place himself between her and his Mistress.

"Come now, Miz Anderson. It's time to go home. Your children waitin' for their supper."

Like a giant tidal wave, details of the lurid incident washed over Lutigua and right up the steps into the Governor General's House. It was the biggest scandal since an aggrieved field hand hacked his master and the plantation manager to pieces ten years previously. (He hung for it, too.) There were pockets of agitation among the locals, some wondering why the police weren't called, why a white lady can point a gun and threaten to kill someone and not go to jail. But among those who knew her, knew about her husband's philandering, there was an enormous swell of sympathy for Emily Anderson. It took the British Consul and his family three days to pack and then they were gone.

But the business wasn't over yet. The Governor General took it upon himself to pay a call on Laura, bringing with him two distinguished citizens: the Dean of the Cathedral and Ian Greenidge, patriarch of one of the oldest families on the island. The meeting was private, but the gist of its content soon reached the rumor mongers. The three men pleaded with Laura to take a long holiday, to give the scandal a chance to quiet down. She refused, saying, 'I'm not running away just because some hysterical woman points a gun at me. I have a hotel to run, gentlemen'. The Governor wasn't happy with her decision, but he couldn't force her to leave. Laura was convinced that with the Andersons' departure from the island, life would return to normal...Events proved otherwise: the first inkling of trouble was the disappearance of the sign from the front of the hotel ('Sign like dat cost a good six month's pay'); next, when cartons containing the hotel's weekly liquor supply were opened, all the bottles were found smashed; a week later three guests arrived at the pool for a pre-breakfast swim to find dead fish and garbage floating on top of the water. The ugly incidents continued until the morning Laura found a dead cat hanging from a rope on the balcony of her private suite . That very day, she dismissed the staff and sent them away, everyone except Wash. He helped her close down the hotel.

"Remember now, Dani," Mapp recounted in a weary voice, "all this happen 'fore Independence... 'fore we movin' out from under de crown's thumb. Not many hotels on de island back then, en none of them as fine a place as Belle Jours. Folks with money stayed there in de wintertime, en they gets to thinkin' of Lutigua as a second home ... wantin' to help out our people. Like when de hospital was being built, guests at de hotel, they raised a pile of money for beds en de like, same with de library. It was in a sorry way 'til they donated new shelvin' en books. You think this is a poor island now, but it's a paradise compared with how things were back then.

"When Mis Laura shut down Belle Jours not only de folks workin' for her was hurt, but in a hun'red different ways it hurt de whole island. En while I don't hold with gamblin', I'd wager a gold sovereign piece that's exactly what she had a mind to do."

CHAPTER VI

"Do you wish Mr. Bhagwan's name to be included, please?"

"That rascal. Absolutely not! Now then, is that the entire guest list?"

"Yes, Miss Caswell. The invitations come from de printer only yesterday, late in de afternoon. I will try to see that they are ready for posting before night falls.

"Good. If there are any problems, send one of the boys to find me."

The arrival of her employer and Miss Caswell had lead to a turbulent period of adjustment for Danielle. In her first interview with Mrs. Foster-Jones, she had been told that Miss Caswell would make all final decisions regarding the running of the hotel. (The heavy woman had appropriated the Lutiguan's desk, relegating Dani to a small wooden table in a corner of the office.) Not a word of thanks or appreciation had been offered by either woman in recognition of the myriad tasks thrust upon her shoulders before their arrival.

The staff, unaware of this new arrangment, automatically turned to Danielle for guidance. Once Caswell realized this, she made no attempt to hide her annoyance. "Inform the staff they are to come to me," she said coldly. Swallowing her pride, the young woman did as she was told. But it wasn't long before she realized that Leona made only those decisions which suited Foster-Jones, that the owner had no intention of relinquishing the reins of power.

Invitations to the two social events to be held before the official opening of Belle Jours brought the matter to the fore: the first affair was to be a lavish formal dinner for the Prime Minister, officials of his government and their wives along with prominent members of the local community; the day following, a cocktail party for travel agents, airline reps and others who directly or indirectly could affect the fortunes of the hotel.

Working from a list of names supplied by Leona, Danielle and Cleo were in the midst of addressing invitations when Wash appeared at the office door.

"De Mistress say for you to bring de guest list to her suite."

After a late lunch, Caswell happened to pass by the table where the two young women were at work and glance down: "That name's not on *my* list. Who told you to include it?"

"The Mistress, she gave it to me."

A deep flush spread over the stout woman's face as she caught her breath; she left the office without another word.

Lord, help me to keep my temper in my pocket. Two bosses living under de same roof spell trouble for sure. Miss Caswell, she act like we back in de old days of slavery, not a sweet word to anyone with black skin ... The Mistress, I study her all de time. She's not half so vexing, still she's a puzzle ....Like why does she wear only two colors, black and white? And why is she sweet to Miss Caswell some days, and other days snap at her like a clap of thunder? ... Mr. Wilson say we must call her 'Mistress.' But that word ...it sticks in my throat... Lord, I beg you. Help me to know what I needs to do to please these two ladies.

The afternoon of the formal dinner found Tyler tense and restless. Seeking to divert himself from worry about his crew's part in bringing the evening to a successful conclusion, he decided to make a leisurely circuit of the hotel and grounds.

Pausing at the threshold of the recently completed public salon, he marveled at its transformation from the barren, uninviting space it had been on the night of his arrival. *Looks great. Classy.* He sauntered on, through the archway and past the meticulously landscaped area around the pool with lounge chairs and gaily striped yellow and white umbrellas encircling it, on down to the wrought iron fence bordering the beach. He stopped and smoked a cigarette as he gazed out to sea. *This is the life, buddy – boy.* He inhaled deeply and felt the tension begin to dissipate.

The American returned by way of the dining hall to find a small circle of waiters gathered in a corner near the kitchen door awaiting the signal to set-up tables. Osbert Marshall, the tall, patrician Lutiguan who had been lured away from a hotel across the island to be the hotel's *maitre d'*, was discussing the seating arrangements with Danielle: "Sixteen at de head table," she said, checking off a list, "and five tables of eight. I will see to de place cards later."

"Yes, Miss Danielle."

"Tyler! There is a problem?" she asked as he strolled into the hall.

"No problem," he grinned. "I just took a quick tour. Everything looks terrific! You deserve a medal." The unexpected compliment caught Danielle off guard; she appeared flustered, but quickly regained her composure and returned his smile. Then, remembering how crucial the coming evening was to them all, she said soberly. "There is much to do before de guests arrive. With God's help, all will go well."

It was past two in the morning, the last guest had departed and the staff, relieved of their duties, wandered wearily off to their beds. Tyler lingered on at the bar to help Sam, the brightest and most responsible Lutiguan on his team, lock up the liquor supplies.

"It was a fine party, Mister Tyler."

"First rate, Sam. Everything went like clockwork. The only foul-up was mine. I assumed the islanders would prefer rum, but those ministers grabbed for the Scotch like drowning men and the women avoided the punch bowl like it was poison. I won't make that mistake again."

"No, sir."

"Go on home, Sam. I'll dump the ice and take care of the lights." With the last of these chores out of the way, a sudden surge of adrenalin overrode his fatigue. *What the hell. One more for the road.* He poured himself a nightcap and moved to a chair by the side of the darkened pool.

The events of the evening danced before his mind's eye like scenes from a De Mille extravaganza, its soundtrack a blending of the soft calypso provided by a local trio, the sprinkling of laughter, clink of glasses and rising murmur of appreciation as the waiters marched into the room bearing Corbin's dessert flambé. Formal dinner parties were still a novelty to members of the fledgling government – the early years since Independence being devoted to arranging elections and struggling with the problems of setting up a Parliamentary system of rule – and the wives took the occasion seriously. Their home-grown creations of satin and tulle, lace and taffeta, vividly evoking every color in the rainbow, embellished with ribbons, sequins, tiara's and bejeweled combs totally eclipsed the understated attire worn by their counterparts from the white plantocracy and business community. Tyler found the entire spectacle fascinating. Other details of the evening were equally vivid: the anxious look of a young waiter as he gingerly poured a glass of wine; Preston, his piscatory mouth in perpetual motion, surrounded by a laughing trio of women; the Prime Minister's absorbed expression as he listened to his hostess, who was resplendent in a white silk gown with a silver-sequined jacket. There was a moment when his own eyes swept the room and he experienced an enormous sense of pride: *I'm part of this.*

But then he remembered a darker, more disquieting side to the scenario.

Hell, it wouldn't have killed F-J to include Danielle and Cleo at the dinner. Well, Danielle, anyway. She's got enough poise to carry it off. Not that they expected an invitation ... still, those two broads did all the work . Goddamn 'colonial mentality' on this island ... it sucks. Caswell has it, too. She high-handed as hell with the help ... But not me. She's really decent around me. I think the old girl's lonely. She certainly looked miserable this evening.

F-J ignored her completely when cocktails were being served ... didn't introduce her to a soul... Funny, when they first came, she acted like they were old buddies. Still does, when it suits her... Poor Leona, stuck with that stuffy prick Wilkinson and his wife. Did F-J deliberately set that up, I wonder? Maybe not. Still I wish I could figure out what makes my boss-lady tick. She was cordial enough at that first interview ... doesn't seem to care how the bar is run as long as she gets her 'usual' when she asks for it. She's at the bottle early enough in the day. Must have a wooden leg ... Got to hand it to her, though. Not a hair out of place after a half-dozen rum and sodas. And she can charm the birds out of the trees when she sets her mind to it ... that guy from the Brazilian consulate and the one from Canada, they were falling all over each other to get her attention...What time is it? ...Hell, I better hit the sack ... plenty to do before the cocktail party tonight.

Unable to sleep, Preston was forced to listen to the night sounds of the island; two in the morning was not a suitable time to be playing Bach Preludes. His expectations that Laura Foster-Jones would ignore his position as a member of staff and treat him as a welcome addition to the island's social life and hers had not come to fruition. Mention of his Uncle Willard - he'd brought the name up several times - had not provided the access he'd counted on. Naturally, he'd been included as a guest at the dinner party, but she'd made no effort to intercede on his behalf with some of her more distinguished guests. He smiled to himself. Nevermind. He'd done all right on his own.

Surprised you, didn't I, dear Laura... you didn't realize how utterly irresistable I can be. Lady Ward seemed to think so anyway. 'A few of my friends are coming to tea next Sunday. Would you care to join us?' Bet your sweet ass I would. And that couple who own the brewery ...what's their name? ...Watkins? No, Wilkinson. That's it. Wilkinson ...said I'd be hearing from them soon. You can tell they've got taste, breeding. My sort of people...Light years away from those Ministers and their wives. Especially the wives. No class at all. No savoir faire. An utterly primitive lot. Well, what can one expect, only a generation or two removed from the jungle?.... Poor, Leona. She looked perfectly wretched the entire evening. Serves her right. If she'd just do something about her weight... fat people are such a drag socially... Sounds like Tyler's come in. Wonder what he thought of the party?

On the heels of their success the previous evening, the cocktail party went off without a hitch; or so the staff believed until Leona Caswell's curt announcement as they were in the midst of cleaning up in its aftermath:

"Tomorrow morning at eight sharp, there's to be a meeting in the dining hall. I expect each of you to be present."

At eight precisely, she arrived wearing the predictable turban and a flowing gown of a heavy material totally unsuitable for the tropics; her face was a flushed, stony mask as she waited for the room to quiet down.

"Good morning. Thank you for being here promptly as I requested." She referred to a sheet of paper clutched in her hand. "This is a list of errors committed by the staff at last night's affair and the formal dinner party." Flinging words like 'careless,' 'unprofessional,' 'inexcusable' at them, she tackled a wide range of blunders, from soiled cuffs on a waiter's jacket to "a table that remained uncleared for 15 whole minutes, I timed it myself."

"She doesn't miss much, does she?" Preston whispered to Tyler.

"I wish to bring to your attention another, extremely serious matter ... You understand, I'm sure, that single men and women, traveling in groups or alone, will be among our guests at Belle Jours. It is a maxim of the tourist business: romance sells more rooms than *haute cuisine* and travel agents like to stress the romantic aspects of a Caribbean holiday. Unfortunately, a lady or gentleman arrives at his destination to discover the hotel is full of *couples* not a single member of the opposite sex in sight. Still, it's a holiday, they're far from home, and who's to care if they end up under a palm tree with a waiter or a room maid?"

She must have caught the act at the bar last night. Tyler was thinking of the bold, sallow-faced girl from Liverpool, one of the airline reps at the cocktail party who'd sashayed up to the bar early on and plunked herself down in front of him. "Hey, luv," she said in a loud voice, "where you been hiding yourself then?"

He'd seen her kind a hundred times: on the prowl for anything in pants and not shy about it either. When they had too much to drink, it became even messier. A few painful episodes during his first job at a lodge in Vermont had taught him how to defuse a situation before it got out of hand.

"Mrs. Foster-Jones has asked me to warn you," Caswell continued in a strained voice, "the co-mingling of guests and employees at this hotel will not be tolerated and will bring instant dismissal. It is your responsibility to see that word is passed to the others not present here this morning." She crumpled the notes in her hand. "I believe that's all for the moment. Thank you." The hall was deathly still as she made her exit.

When she was out of earshot, Avery wiped mock tears from his eyes and blubbered, "Oh dear! Think of all those luscious damsels who'll be deprived of my fair white body." The tension in the room collapsed like a burst balloon and there was a scattering of applause. He fell into step beside Tyler as they left.

"Avery, you're wasting your talent. Hollywood would go crazy over the likes of you."

"Oh, I've had offers, but you know how it is, old man, finding loopholes in the tax laws is much more fun."

"Is that why F-J's wooing the Minister of Revenue?"

"My lips are sealed. Look, can I ask a favor of you, Scranton? Would you mind bouncing a few packages to the post office in town for me in that derelict station wagon? They'll be late as it is, but I always say, 'it's the thought that counts.'"

"Late?"

"Packages for Christmas, old man It's only 12 days away you know."

"I'd forgotten. Christmas seems unreal in a place like this."

"You have a point. But I have my uncle to consider, a lively soul and I'm his only nephew. Then there are a few friends ... we always exchange presents at the Finley's annual bash on Christmas Eve. It's the highlight of the season, the party, I mean. Can't believe

I'll be missing it... first time in seven years. Ah well, such are the vicissitudes, etcetera, etcetera."

"Sure, Avery. I'll plan to leave around noon."

"Thanks, old man. It's a drag not being able to drive, but owning a car in New York City is like selling ice to the Eskimos, an anachronism of the highest order."

Leona Caswell was mid-way to her room when she felt the gorge rise in her throat. Cupping her hand over her mouth, she bent her head low and prayed she wouldn't meet anyone, that she would reach the safety of her bedroom before the rising bile became untenable.

The door! She'd forgotten to lock her door! This rare oversight was emblematic of her panic when she'd left the room earlier. In this case it proved a blessing. She couldn't have managed the key. With her entire body convulsing, she vomited the remains of a light breakfast into the sink. As the spasms slowly subsided, she reached for a towel to bathe her face and neck.

Afterwards, feeling lightheaded and faint, she sought refuge on the bed.

Damn Laura. She knows bloody well how terrified I get speaking to a large group ...she knows I'd do anything to avoid it... Half those notes she wrote herself and then insisted I deliver them... knowing ...knowing...Such an unbending dictum. If the staff didn't dislike me before, they dislike me now. I can live with that.

What I can't abide is how much Laura's changed since we came here. One day her old self, the next so thoughtless ... so cruel. What happened to the endearing Laura I once knew? I'd have done anything for her when we were at 'Clove Hill', she knew that and still, she never imposed. Now ...now it's so humiliating .... treated no better than a lackey in front of everyone. Why?

Why did I ever agree to come with her to Lutigua?

CHAPTER VII

"Why the hell should I feel guilty?" Tyler asked himself as he waited in line at the post office. It was not the first time he'd pondered the question.

On the ride from Belle Jours to St. James, he found himself preoccupied with thoughts of the past, of his brother Neddie and Myra. He assumed he'd perfected the art of not thinking about any of it, especially his mother.

After mailing Avery's packages, Tyler impulsively decided to send a few Christmas cards himself. As he wandered the streets of the island's capitol in search of a place that might stock them, he was caught up in the festive spirit of the approaching holiday: coloured lights and tired ropes of tinsel swayed above the thoroughfares as Christmas carols, some with a calypso beat, blared at the passing foot traffic from hidden microphones; traditional symbols of Yuletide - many bearing the scars of age - were on display at the government offices and more prosperous shops. Ribbons and homemade ornaments embellished the vendors' carts and even the meanest storefront made an effort to adorn itself. At one street corner a dark perspiring face peeked out from under Santa's hat as a young coconut seller, his machete smashing down again and again, tried to keep up with the demand for the refreshing waters inside the green shells.

Eventually the American found a selection of cards at a pharmacy, on a shelf next to a cache of dust-caked linament bottles. Printed in England, the cards depicted landscapes and picturesque villages under a blanket of white, carollers in mittens and scarves. He purchased several: one for Herbie, the night manager at the *Sheraton*, another for a district manager and his wife in upstate New York who'd befriended him when he was a sales trainee, and one for Lyle, an old classmate still living in Thompson. He would have bought one for Erly-Mae, but he didn't know Jocko's address and didn't dare send it in care of Miz Annie.

On the last card, an etching of the Salisbury Cathedral with the word 'PEACE' printed inside, he scrawled a few dutiful lines to his mother:

Lutigua is a beautiful island. The job is fine but it keeps me busy. Merry Christmas. With love from your son, Tyler.

* * * * * * * * * * *

Like a company of recruits honed to readiness and itching to prove their mettle, who storm the beachhead only to find the enemy has withdrawn, the official opening of Belle Jours in mid-December proved anti-climatic. Between them, the booking agent in New York and the one in Miami had been able to fill only 11 of the 24 rooms. "Reservations won't start picking up until after New Year's," they advised.

In essence, the hotel was only half full. "*Half empty* is the way I look at it," Preston said caustically. "One has to watch the balance sheets: we need to fill 20 rooms every day of the year just to break even, and a full year of a full house before the hotel can recover the cost of refurbishing."

To honor their status as Belle Jours first guests, a complimentary magnum of iced champagne and a basket of fruit were placed in each room, eliciting a delighted, "They're treating us like it's the maiden voyage of a luxury liner!" from a new arrival. The group departed, tanned and mellow after their scheduled week in the sun and the news that seven rooms had been re-booked for the following year swept through the hotel like a bracing gust of wind, taking some of the sting out of a drastic drop to a six-room occupancy through the first of the year.

For the two Americans, far from home and emotionally jarred by the incongruity of climate and place, the holiday spirit was illusory: when the station wagon arrived from St. James with mail and packages for every-one, the only greeting Tyler received was an off-color card from Herbie with the news he'd been promoted and was leaving Atlanta for New Orleans; Preston hung a string of colored lights across the cabin porch, and quietly proceeded to drink himself into a stupor by four in the afternoon of the 24th.

Laura took charge of the arrangements for Christmas Eve dinner herself, fussing over the menu with Corbin, telling Danielle what decorations were needed for the tables, instructing Tyler in the recipe for Lutiguan *coqui* a drink consisting of two kinds of rum with coconut cream and spices, not unlike egg nog.

"We'll serve *coqui* at the punch table before dinner. Those who insist, can have the hard stuff later. I don't want anyone too inebriated to appreciate Corbin's cooking."

Because so few rooms would be occupied, Tyler decided to take over the bar himself from the 24th through Boxing Day, parceling out a minimal three-hour shift among his men so they could be with their families.

"It don't seem right, Mr. Tyler, you workin' so much straight time en de rest of us bein' on short call," Sam offered when Tyler came to relieve him early in the afternoon of Christmas Eve.

"If the hotel were full, Sam, it would be a different story. As it is, I'll probably have a hard time keeping busy."

"Yes, sir."

"Besides, I'm not as big-hearted as it looks. Come Thursday, I'm taking off. You'll need a search party to find me."

"Yes, sir. Good afternoon, Mister Tyler ... en Merry Christmas!"

"Merry Christmas, Sam."

He watched his senior barman leave, then made a random check of his domain; everything was spotless and in place. *Well, here you are, buddy-boy. Forty-one years old, and all you have to show for it is a space in a rented storage unit filled with J.C. Penney 'sale' furniture and a stereo with speakers that cost $400 in 1975.* He chose to forget that during the five years he'd been tending bar, both in Vermont and Atlanta, his schedule was such that not a spare moment was left over for either reflection or reaction to a season weighted with sentimental pitfalls. So absorbed was he in a litany of self-pity, he didn't hear the soft footfall approaching the bar. A hesitant tug at his sleeve caught him by surprise.

"Mr. Scranton? You all right, please sir?"

"What? Sorry, Wash, you startled me. Sure I'm o.k. I'm *fine*. What've you got there?"

The elderly Lutiguan carefully placed a gallon jar of clear, ruby-red liquid on the countertop, then stepped back a pace, suddenly overcome with generations of inbred reticence.

"It's called sorrel, a drink we folks makin' special for de holidays. Mrs. Wilson, she all de time worryin' - truth to tell, dat woman's middle name is *worry* - she sayin' to me, 'Dat nice boss man James MacArthur's got, here it's Christmas en de poor man's far from his home en family.' She sendin' this for you, Master Scranton, wid kindest wishes for a happy Christmas."

Coming at the moment it did, the graceful gesture was too much for Tyler. He turned his head and blinked rapidly to stem a rush of emotion which threatened to get out of hand.

"Tell you what, Wash," he said clearing his throat, "how about sharing a toast while I have my first taste of sorrel?"

James MacArthur volunteered to trade places with the man scheduled to help Tyler at the bar that evening, freeing the other to sing in the choir at his church. The young Lutiguan customarily wore a short-sleeved white shirt and black pants for his duties as busboy, but to honor his temporary elevation, he'd borrowed a waiter's jacket and bow tie. When he presented himself, Tyler was impressed: *This kid could be Belafonte's double. It won't be long before the girls discover him ...his Mama will have to beat them off with a stick.*

"You're looking snappy tonight, James. Don't let that outfit go to your head."

"No, sir, Mr. Scranton."

"Good. Remember, when I give the signal you're to uncork the burgundy so it can sit for a while. In our country it's called 'letting the wine breathe.'"

"Yes, please."

At a few minutes past six, the American strolled to the edge of the open dining hall where he found Danielle arranging place cards. The room was bathed in the luminescent glow of candlelight abetted by cheerful islands of poinsetta and anthurium; a medley of familiar carols sung by the Robert Shaw Chorale wafted softly into the air from a hidden tape player. Eye-catching centerpieces at the tables - circles of red and silver ornaments set-off by dark green cordia leaves - added an additional celebratory note. At each guest's place lay a small package wrapped in bright red foil and tied with silver string; a modest pile of gifts awaited the only youngster at the hotel.

"Bravo! Danielle," he called to her.

At the sound of his voice she lifted her head and looked around as if seeing the room for the first time. "Truly, it is the Mistress who has made everything so sweet."

Tyler's reconaissance came to a sudden halt as he remembered Preston's condition. *He shouldn't miss this.*

"Duty calls. See you later," he waved as he turned to leave the room.

"Wait, please, Tyler." From the pocket of her skirt, she withdrew a dainty package. "For you, Tyler. The sewing is as my auntie taught me." She responded to the look of astonishment on his face with a smile. "Not to worry. It is our custom to give small gifts at this season. Merry Christmas!"

Embarrassed by the unexpected offering, the American stammered his thanks along with reciprocal wishes and left the dining hall. *First Wash, then Danielle. Can't beat these Lutiguans when it comes to making an outsider like me feel welcome.*

At the bar he found Wash's son arranging punch glasses around a large, cut-glass bowl.

"Here. I'll finish that, James. I want you to run an errand for me. On the double. Go to the kitchen – for heaven's sake, don't get in Corbin's way! – and ask one of the boys for a tray with two pots of hot black coffee and some sweet crackers. Take it to my cabin and see if you can persuade Mr. Preston to join the party."

An hour later Belle Jours' guests began gathering at the punch bowl; they included two young couples, who'd planned their trip together, a divorced father with his 10 year old son, an elderly pharmacist and his wife, a college professor in his mid-forties and two matronly sisters. Despite incongruities of age and perspective, the spirit of the holiday acted as a magnet, drawing them together in a tacit resolution that no one should feel left out or neglected. The miracle was its spontaneity. Conversation had warmed to a lively tempo when Mrs. Foster-Jones made her entrance clad in a deceptively simple evening gown of black chiffon; a choker of diamonds and pearls was at her throat, a matching bracelet on one slim wrist. She made the rounds, addressing each visitor by name, wishing them 'Merry Christmas' and saying she hoped they'd have a pleasant evening.

"Will you be joining us for dinner?" the professor asked. (None of the guests had ever seen her in the diningroom at mealtime.)

"I'm terribly sorry, I have other plans," she responded graciously. Moments later Leona appeared, dressed in a sumptuous Mandarin-style robe of plum satin with matching turban.

"My dear Miss Caswell, don't you look lovely!" the pharmacist's wife exclaimed. The heavy woman turned to her gratefully. "Thank you Mrs. Stein. I do my best." Her employer slipped unobtrusively away from the gathering; out of the corner of her eye, Leona watched her disappear and sighed bitterly. Laura had been invited to a party at the Brazilian consulate but her English friend had not been included. *She could have arranged it, if she wanted to. There must be something about this place, this island, that makes her so bloody-minded.* Sensing the Englishwoman's unhappiness, the group opened ranks and enveloped her in their communal celebration.

As James and Tyler circled the room filling wine glasses, the American was pleased to note that the young man seemed his serene, good-natured self once more. When he'd returned from the cabin there had been a distinct edge of belligerence to his announcement: "Mr. Scranton, sir, Mr. Preston say to tell you he's not in a 'party frame of mind.'"

"Thanks, James." *Damnit, when will I learn? I'm not Preston's keeper.*

Shortly after midnight, the guests began dispersing to their rooms. Caswell wearily climbed the stairs to the second floor wing of the main house where she and Laura shared adjoining suites, hers being the smaller of the two. Since she was unable to tolerate either hard liquor or wine, during the evening she'd confined herself to glass after glass of soda water laced with bitters. At the top of the steps Leona paused, feeling a bit queasy after all the rich food and drink.

Since a light was always left burning in the suite, she immediately caught sight of the enormous package resting against her favorite chair; its elaborate wrapping and size defeated her. *Tomorrow. It can wait 'til tomorrow.* She disrobed slowly, each movement costing an enormous amount of energy. When, at last, she faced herself in the vanity mirror, she unwound the turban and began removing her makeup. Leona Caswell was completely bald, a condition - as was her weight - caused by an imbalance of hormones which had overtaken her in her mid-twenties. By the time she was thirty, she had come to accept that no male would ever desire her, that church records with the word 'spinster' next to her name would forever bear that barren description.

Titus Caswell, her father, a tenacious, unimaginative man, owned a dry goods shop in a hamlet near Exeter; Leona, his only child, had been an unwelcome surprise arriving as she did when his wife was in her early forties and had long since despaired of having children. Still, her parents did their best by her, sacrificing the few luxuries they'd looked forward to in their old age so she could attend a good public school. When she was ten they'd borrowed money from the bank to buy a second-hand upright piano and for several years Leona dutifully took lessons. Then one day she rebelled, declaring 'I *hate* Mozart'.

In her teens Leona was obliged to help her ageing father in the shop and missed out on the giddy activities of her peers. (Her mother's expectations that daily contact with Mr. Caswell's customers would give the shy, awkward girl a measure of self-confidence were never realized.) At school Leona had one 'best friend', a brash, brilliant tomboy named Gemma Witham, a scholarship student who was snubbed by her classmates at the public school because her father managed the stables on a large estate: '*Not our sort, you see.*' To Leona's dazzlement and awe, Gemma ferociously employed both a tart tongue and rapier wit to combat their snobbery. These two incongruous souls, each lonely and in need of companionship, became inseparable. When school ended, however, despite aggressive attempts on Leona's part to continue the alliance, they went their separate ways.

The Caswells died within a year of each other; they left no debts, but neither were there sufficient funds for their daughter, then in her early twenties, to maintain herself indefinitely. Leona wisely used part of a modest legacy to enroll in a secretarial course. She completed her training at the top of her class, but securing a suitable position was another matter. A distant cousin of her mother's came to the rescue, recommending her as a secretary/companion to an elderly widower, the first in a succession of similar posts that led her to Laura Foster-Jones' doorstep.

The exhausted Englishwoman settled herself in a cocoon of mosquito netting and lay back with a sigh. But sleep was elusive; her thoughts kept returning to the provocative package in her sitting room. *Oh dear, I won't be able to rest 'til I open that bloody box.*

Without stopping to don slippers or robe, she returned to the next room in her bare feet, seeking the comfort of a chair as she painstakingly removed the wrapping. Inside the box, tidily folded, were four measures of elegant polished cotton, each of a different pattern and color. She beamed with pleasure at the familiar handwriting on the enclosed card:

My dear friend, Merry Christmas! I hope you will forgive my presumptuousness in ordering the enclosed from Simpson's. (I couldn't help but notice how unsuitable your lovely wardrobe is in this intemperate climate!) My dressmaker is at your disposal and can whip up any style your heart desires. Have I told you lately how pleased I am you're here! Love, Laura.

As she reread the message, the depression and melancholy of the past several days vanished: *How dear of Laura. How thoughtful! Imagine, sending all the way to London for a gift for me!*

Back at the cabin, Tyler was slipping his blue linen jacket onto a hanger when he noticed the slight bulge in its lefthand pocket. *Danielle's present! How could I forget!* Impatient fingers tore at the wrapping to reveal a single white cotton handkerchief, its borders a hand-sewn continuum of tiny stitches; in one corner, in brilliant scarlet, were the initials TS . He stood there, biting his lip, trying to hold back the moisture in his eyes that welled up and threatened to overflow. The American couldn't remember the last time anyone cared enough to give him a present they'd made themselves.

CHAPTER VIII

Traditionally, the month of December heralded the beginning of the Caribbean's most effulgent season, the moisture-laden heaviness of November giving way to hot, sun-gilded days and dry, crisp evenings. The rain, when it came, washed down in small volleys just before dawn, as if someone had turned on a sprinkler; one woke to find the tropical foliage freshly laundered, decorated with sparkling drops of moisture. On Tyler's scheduled day off he rose with the distant cock crow and slipped soundlessly from the cabin, reaching the creamy sand of the shoreline just as golden arms of color were spreading from the east across the sky. He returned from his swim to the wakeful chirping of birds and the distant whining of black belly sheep.

With beer and ice stowed away in a borrowed cooler on the empty seat beside him in the station wagon, he studied the old map Wash had loaned him the day before. Tyler decided on a route that would take him to the eastern side of the island, to the Atlantic coast, where he had never been. From there he would move inland and explore Lutigua's mountainous area, try to find Watu–Kai, the waterfall shown at its center.

Watu–Kai. What a funny name. But then so are some of the others - Celestine's Knot, Sidon, Rose Hall, Lapi-Lap, Bethlehem - sort of a mixture of English, Biblical and what? Creole? He soon discovered that the route to St. James from the hotel was one of the island's better roads. As the American headed east towards Bethlehem, (shown as a dot near the ocean), he was forced to drive at a snail's pace around pot-holes and rock-strewn roads, narrow passageways with barely enough space for two cars. In the rural areas he passed tiny enclaves, patchwork groupings of unpainted chattel houses, their drabness offset by brilliant clumps of poinsettias and hibiscus, their corrugated roofs and fences looking like broken teeth. Time and again he was to notice the two essentials to life in these remote villages —the communal water spigot by the side of the road and the rum shack, its walls plastered with weathered signs, its dark interiors occupied by a handful of faithful imbibers.

Untethered sheep wandered across the road at random, and strutting cocks ignored the bleep of his horn, moving sedately out of his path at their leisure. The islanders stared as he wended his way past their houses, past women stoically clearing a small patch of ground, motionless old men and aimless children. He threaded the car between fields of growing cane, cane so lush and tall it made visibility a nightmare when the road curved.

An hour later he labored up a steep incline in second gear; when at last he reached the top, Tyler's reaction was an awed: "Christ, will you look at that!" Below him, stretching as far as the eye could see was the Atlantic, a magnificent slate-blue mass of crashing waves and rolling white caps around massive boulders of rock straddling the shoreline. He parked the Ford off to the side of the road on a rough shoulder of crushed rock, reached beside him for a beer and emerged from the car, grateful for a chance to stretch his legs. The wind was master here, flattening trees and bushes against the contours of the land, snapping at Tyler's body and clothing; the temperature on this coast felt a good ten degrees cooler than on the Caribbean side of the island.

He gazed down the hillside, saw the torturous route to the bottom, with the road continuing parallel to the sea but protected from it by a narrow strip of beach. From where he stood the village of Bethlehem, consisting of several houses and a church, looked like miniature pieces in a game of 'Monopoly'.

It would be hell getting down there, to say nothing of getting back up. He decided to stay where he was and enjoy the view from a fallen tree trunk he'd spotted about 15 yards below the crest. He'd no sooner seated himself than two small boys, shirtless and shoeless, scrambled down from the path above. Tyler guessed the older one to be about eight, the younger one no more than five or six.

"We watch de car for you, mistah" the older one said.

"Why does my car need watching?"

"Robbers, dey bad round heah." The youngest nodded in dumb agreement.

"How bad?"

"Dey mean, dose robbers. Mebbe your car gettin' scratched, mebbe a rock hittin' it."

"How much will you charge to guard my car?"

"A dollah," was the quick response.

"One whole dollar?"

"You gets two to watch it for dat one dollah."

The barman shook his head with amused resignation and reached for his wallet. Emboldened by the success of his first transaction, the boy said in a rush, "My sistah, she got conch shells for sale. Nice shells for de man. Only two dollah."

"You're some businessman, kid. No thanks, no shells today. Just watch the car." He handed the bill to the boy, who folded it carefully and stuck it in the pocket of his faded shorts; then he turned and motioned to his younger brother, "Come."

That's the last I'll see of those two monkeys. He turned his attention once more to the scene before him. He would like to have lingered for the rest of the morning - the cooling breeze itself was a welcome change - but he was unsure of the route from the east coast to the mountains, and he particularly wanted to see the waterfall. He finished the beer and reluctantly rose to retrace his steps up the hill.

"Well, look who's here."

Squatting together on an outcropping of rock a few feet from the Ford were the two boys. They jumped up at his approach.

"We watch for you. No robbers come," their spokesman said proudly.

"Tell you what," Tyler replied, "you've done such a good job of keeping those robbers away, you deserve a bonus." He dug out a handful of change from his pocket and handed each of them fifty cents.

"Thanks, mistah," the older one beamed at him. The smaller one seemed glued to the spot; he clasped and unclasped the tiny brown fist holding the coins, staring at them as if some trick of magic had placed them there and at any moment, they would disappear.

Tyler braked and switched off the ignition. For the past half hour he'd been creeping along a rutted two-wheel track he'd picked up at a junction in the road where a wooden signpost with arrows pointing in three directions contained the legend: Blue Hill, 3 kil. According to Wash's map, the waterfall lay at the northern tip of this mountainous area, but the road ahead seemed to disappear in a tangle of brush; he didn't dare press on in the car.

Looks like I'll have to hoof - it from here.

It was past noon and the heat of the day pressed upon him with cruel zeal. He retrieved another beer and noticed the ice was melting. *This will have to hold me for a while. Damned stuff makes me sweat and I don't need to be any hotter than I am right now.* He filled the first empty bottle with water from the cooler, deciding it might come in handy later. From force of habit, he locked the car and gamely started along the trail, which soon contracted into a single foot path. *This would be a breeze if only the damn bugs would leave me alone ...I'd make some Boy Scout. No compass, no canteen, no bug repellent.*

Tyler was so absorbed in following the path, in swatting tenacious gnats and mosquitos, it was some time before he was aware that the sun was no longer beating directly upon him. While he paused to get his bearings a magnificent purple-throated bird with black plumage and metallic green wings swooped down from overhead and circled slowly before flapping out of sight. Tyler shifted his gaze upward, to the towering canopy of trees which shut out the sun. There must have been a dozen species, but somehow they all looked alike, their trunks centuries' thick and coated with smooth grey bark; at their bases enormous buttress roots dipped like curved arms out of the soil. Below the canopy was another layer of trees, hundreds of herbaceous plants, leaves and flowers–all in fierce competition for the sparse sunlight. He remembered photographs he'd once seen of a rain forest in South America and was struck by the similarities between those scenes and his present habitat.

The path was easy to follow, but the deeper he penetrated the copse, the more uneasy he became about finding his way back to the Ford. Patches of verdant fern made a welcome contrast to the somber palette of lichen and moss which coated the dead limbs and rocks surrounding him, but a carpet of wet leaves on the ground made the going slippery. Overhead the air was rife with chattering monkeys, screeching birds and the grunt of tree toads.

Tyler was too fascinated to be afraid, but he was nagged by the thought that he might inadvertently stray from the path. Just as he was deciding it was time to turn back, his ears picked out a low, distant rumbling. *It must be the waterfall* . Immediately he plunged ahead, only dimly aware that with each step he was moving farther from the lush, protective shelter of the rain forest. With only the resonant throb of falling water to guide him, he pushed aside tree limbs and heavy vines blocking his way, scrambling and stumbling over hugh rocks, driven by an urgency he sensed but did not understand. Panting for breath, he broke into a clearing and stopped, mesmerized by the sight of cascading sheets of water falling from on high, descending in a roar of silvery, glistening power and defiance. A shimmering rainbow gracefully arched above spray caught in a beam of sunlight. So perfect was the beauty and majesty of the place, for a moment the American thought he must be dreaming.

Tyler lost all sense of time. At last he moved hesitantly forward to the edge of a large, flat grey rock which overhung the falls. Looking down at the pool of clear, bubbling water below, he fought off an impulse to strip and dive into its inviting crystalline depths, to immerse himself in its cool embrace.

A tearing screech close to his ear interrupted his reverie and so startled him he nearly lost his balance. From somewhere in the dense thicket behind him an enormous mottled white owl swept down close to his head, dipped and circled above the pool then settled itself on a small outcropping opposite the flat rock to watch the intruder through slitted eyes. Instinctively Tyler shuddered, "You're an evil-looking little bastard."

The arrival of the winged creature broke the enchanted spell. All at once Tyler couldn't wait to get back to the car. Without a backward glance, he retraced his steps. A short distance from the clearing loomed a boulder twice his height, a landmark he remembered because the footpath had ended on its far side. He was within arm's length of the boulder when a figure stepped from behind it blocking his way, a presence so unexpected, Tyler froze and couldn't speak. A toothless black man, barefoot, and with a long, dirty tangle of beard and hair stood before him. Trembling with rage this Apocalyptic vision shook a stick at Tyler, shouting a torrent of indecipherable words which he repeated, again and again. The old man's shirt was a tattered rag, his torn and filthy trousers held at the waist by a piece of rope. Spittle dribbled from the corners of his toothless mouth and the venom in his watery eyes pinned Scranton to the spot. As the angry words spewed from his lips, Tyler finally grasped the few that mattered: "Don't ... belong ... here ...go."

"Don't worry mister," he hollered as he turned to flee, "wild horses couldn't keep me."

He reached the station wagon as the first drops of a late afternoon shower splattered across the windshield. The storm gathered in strength and followed him all the way back across the island. He drove automatically, unable to shake a lingering pall of fear and revulsion.

"I'll remember that old man's face 'til the day I die," he thought grimly. "What the hell was he doing there? Why'd he try to fighten me away?"

It was pitch black when the headlights shone on the lighted sign with its familiar green scroll: **HOTEL BELLE JOURS**. With a sigh of relief he turned into the driveway.

I need to find Wash. Maybe he can explain it all. But first, damnit, I need a drink.

CHAPTER IX

"Folks here don't hold wid goin' to Watu-Kai no more. They has their reasons. It all happenin' long 'fore you were born, Mister Scranton, in de days when we still belongin' to England, en de King, he's choosin' a Governor to rule us. Dis Governor, he's charged wid keepin' de laws en settlin' disputes, but my Mummy sayin' de ones in her time mostly liked to dress up fancy for parades en give grand parties.

"Back then, all de Governors stayin' at a big white house wid a monkey-bread tree in de yard. They callin' de house 'Villa Carib' en it sit at de top of All Saints Hill. (Villa's gone, now. Nuthin' left to see of it but de chimney stones standin' watch against de sky... but de name's there still, on a ole marble pillar covered wid moss at de bottom of de drive. De year our James Mac Arthur is born, a fire come sweepin' down All Saints Hill wid flames so fierce it eat up de whole house 'fore dey even get to hitch de donkeys to de water carts.

'Course de monkey-bread tree, it sits there still, its limbs bowed down wid de passin' of de seasons.)"

Tyler and Wash were seated at the far corner of the deserted dining hall, their only source of light a fat, yellow candle which sputtered in the evening breeze. The storm had passed and one by one the stars emerged from hiding. Two quick Scotches and an omelet had done wonders for the barman's equilibrium; as he poured a teaspoon of sugar into his coffee, he was abashed to remember how intimidated he'd been by that deranged old man.

"Tell me, Wash, do you know who the old guy was, the one who shouted at me this afternoon?"

"Yes, please. Dat's Simon. He don't mean no harm, Mister Scranton.

It's just dat his brains are rattlin' round in his head en not settled right. Truth to tell, he's not been de same since ..." The gentle Lutiguan's voice trailed off.

"Since what, Wash?" Tyler prompted. "Finish your story."

"I was mebbe six, seven years old when de King send along a new Governor. (Simon, he older den me, mebbe 14.) De white folk calls him 'Lord Dunham', but we called him 'Big Master.' He's a fine gentleman, en de Mistress, she's a kind en sweet lady; it don't take a wise man to see they has a lovin' for each other true as de morning star.

"They sailin' from England wid their daughter en a boy baby. De sailors tellin' how de seas is rough en de Mistress and de little one is sick de whole crossin'. De Mistress, now, she gets to feelin' better, but de angels come en carry de baby away soon after they come to de Villa... a sad beginning to settlin' in a new land.

"De Dunham's daughter now, she takes her schoolin' in England en only comes back at de Feast of Our Lord's birthday. She don't come in summer. In summertime lots of de white folks leave from here. Heat layin' heavy over de whole island, en wid de heat come mosquitos en de dengue.

"While Big Master is our Governor, de folks here wearin' a happy face. He has a wise head en a just hand, not like de ones dat come before. En de Mistress now... she's speakin' in de same sweet way to one en all, be they field hand or Bishop... Folks rememberin' how she always cookin' up a broth by her own hand en carryin' de broth to old folks in de parish en ones that is sick. Come market day, Mistress Dunham don't send de cook like de other ladies; she picks out de yams, en christophene en such like herself. She even go down by de wharf where de fishin' boats come in to buy fresh fish for de Villa. (Those docks' smellin' somethin' fierce, en most white folks, they won't go near de place...) Just like de high wind dat finds where de old fence stands, trouble come sneakin' in through de back door one year at Crop-Over time.

"We celebrates Crop-Over, Mister Scranton, at de end of every harvest. It's a time we give over to thankin' our Lord for blessing dis island wid de richness of de cane. Everything is shut down tight ... 'ceptin' de rum shops—*dey never close*. A big parade wid steel bands en tuk bands march from de harbour down Lord Nelson Street to de main square. De rum pot passin' round en folks dance en carry on 'til de moon catch up wid de sun.

"On de last day of Crop-Over, Mistress Dunham takin' to her bed wid a high fever (some sayin' it's spoilt meat she et, some, dat a scorpion bit her); three days passin' en she's gone. All Lutigua has de misery, feelin' such a sorrow for de Governor. Come de funeral day, all de houses empty out. Every movin' body, young en old, dey at de church; even ole Aunty Nedda, who's been a cripple since she was born, dey carry her in a donkey cart.

"My Mummy tellin' how she dressed me in my Sunday suit en took me along to de church, but I don't recalls it. She tellin' how Big Master's eyes are dry, but his heart's broke in little pieces. 'Anyone wid eyes to see could see that,' she sayin'.

"After they puttin' de Governor's lady in de ground, a message of sympathy arrive from de King sayin' Dunham can quit his post en come back to England if he has a mind to. But Big Master, he say, 'No, my work's not done here.'

"Along come summer... de flamboyant trees' showin' off like painted ladies, snapper en kingfish plentiful in de marketplace, but 'Villa Carib' is still in mourning. De long days en nights weighin' like a stone on Big Master, so he send for his daughter to come stay wid him in de big white house. They sayin' what a pretty thing she is en quick, like a hummingbird, en how she lookin' just like her Mummy, but she's not disposed like Mistress Dunham. De daughter now, she wants to have her way en she has a temper dat boil over like an unwatched pot when she don't get it. Still, she is sweet en loving wid her Daddy, en Big Master, he's pleased to have her company.

"Like always, most of de young white folks' gone from de island, en when de Governor must tend to his duties, de daughter's left to her own self. Seein' how lonely she is, her Daddy does his best; most days 'fore he goes to town, they rides over de hills together in de sweet morning air, she on her Mummy's favorite chestnut mare. He ebben has folks to tea, though de mourning time's not over yet... One day a message from de King come to de Villa; he orderin' all de governors from de colonies to meet wid him in Bermuda, an island 'bout two days' sailin' from Lutigua (dat's supposin' de weather's fair). Big Master can't say 'No' to de King, so he sail away leavin' his daughter all to herself in de big white house wid no one 'cept Cidrene, de housemaid, to pass de time of day wid.

It's true what they say, Mister Scranton, 'Idle hands is de debbil's workshop.'

"One morning while her Daddy's away, de daughter come back from ridin' alone en pass by de orchard at de back of de house. It's there she sees Marshall pickin' limes. Now Marshall, he's young same as her, en very beautiful. Marshall's Mummy, she does all de cookin' at 'Villa Carib.' Folks sayin' her stew pot en cou-cou's de sweetest on de island.

"'Fore a guinea bird can open his mouth, de daughter takes to passin' by de orchard two, mebbe three times a day ... always lookin' for a reason to be where Marshall is at. She don't take no notice of de gardeners or stable hands; they watchin' her wid de cook's boy, seein' how she tease him en try to take his mind offin' his work. Soon lips is beatin' behind hands en spreadin' de word 'bout Marshall en de Governor's daughter. Marshall's Mummy, she hears de talk goin' round en she gives Marshall a good whuppin' wid a stick, but nothin' he can do. She's followin' him still. Den one day he's gone from de orchard.

"Now Simon, he works at 'Villa Carib' also. He sweep de yard, clean out de stables en de like. Simon, he's got no home, no one to claim him, so he makes his bed in a dry spot 'neath de kitchen porch. One night very late Simon hears voices comin' from de garden. He pulls de sleep from his eyes en - quiet as a cat lick his ear - he creeps up to de garden wall en looks over. What he sees is de cook's son wid Big Master's daughter. They holden on to each other en talkin' in voices low. When she throws back her head to laugh, Simon say it sound like church bells pealin' 'cross de cane fields. Marshall, he say 'Hush, hush,' but she just shake her head en laugh again like it's some game they playin'. Den Marshall kisses her on de mouth to stop her en Simon, he don't want to look no more. He leave de way he come en he don't tell of it, what he's seen. He knows Marshall en de white girl are doin' wrong, en he don't know why but he's afraid.

Simon hears them in de garden three maybe four times more en always when de night is half over. But he don't go to look, he's too scairt. He knows if Big Master finds out, trouble will boil like a cohobblepot, en if cook finds out, Marshall will get licks ebben harder than before.

My Mummy used to say: 'If you throws dirt long enough, some will stick.' No one can say how he findin' out, but when Lord Dunham come back from his meetin' wid de King, he hear 'bout dis business.

"Come a morning when de air's so still, not even de sugarbird's whistlin'; Big Master send for his daughter in de room they callin' a 'study' en shuts de door. (They tellin' how de walls in dat study are covered so high up wid books, it makes a man's eyelids ache to think on it.)

Seems like de clock took sick en stopped, de two of them in dat room so long. Like thunder crackin', Big Master's voice is soundin' through de house, Simon say. Ebben wid de door shut tight, his voice carry clear to de garden, en folks hearin' it is struck dumb. Big Master, he never raised his voice like thunder in his own house before. De daughter's voice is raised up also, but it sound more like tiny stones against a chattel door. Them dat hears her have de shame for one so young to be settin' up against a wise man like her Daddy.

"The daughter, she leave de study, de door slammin' after her like de debbil oiled de hinges. She marchin' up de stairs to a room she call her own en fix de lock herself to be shut in. De whole day long, no one sees her shadow. Folks workin' at de Villa, dey worry so it hurts their bones."

Wash closes his eyes and sighs, the burden of his tale almost too much to bear.

"After ... Simon, he don't tell de white folk all he seen dat night. He just tells what he has to when they asks him ...words dat has no color.

"Come time for dinner en Lord Dunham send Cidrene to fetch de girl, but she won't come. She's leavin' her Daddy to eat alone. They tellin' how later, when it's time for him to carry hisself up de stairs to bed, his head's bowed down clear to his chest.

"Dat night de moon is full, en folks believe when de moon's full you lookin' to see a pot of rain en a piss of trouble. Simon tellin' how he toss on his mat like a mill sail en can't sleep when he hear sounds like chickens scratchin' for their meal. So he gets up en lets his feet take him round de Villa to where de noise is comin' from. By de moon's sweet light he sees Big Master's daughter climbin' out her window. Simon holds back en watches her go to de garden where de cook's boy is waitin'.

"When she see Marshall, she runs to him, tears flowin' from her eyes like an open spigot. De boy he comfort her en after a time de tears stop. Den Marshall, he takes her hand en leads her away from de garden.

Simon, bein' a young fool, he followin'.

"They walkin' on, payin' no mind to de road passin' under their feet, en Simon, he's one step behind. (Simon tole how he feel just like a fish hooked to de end of a long line: he don't want to be there, but de hook's too deep to wiggle free.) Marshall, he all de time whisperin' sweet words to her. Once't he stops to kiss her hair, her cheek... en she kissin' him back. (De moon's so bright, Simon see it all.) Marshall reaches up and breaks off a flower to put in her hair ...Later, Simon see that flower for hisself ... we calls it 'lady of de night.'

"Time is runnin' like a thief en they keep movin' on ...across de cane-fields en gullies, by old orchards heavy wid fruit; suddenly a dark cloud come along en cover de moon like a cloth for mourning. In de pitch black, Simon can't see, en he's so scairt his shit freezes. But he's more afraid of bein' alone in de dark, so he keeps followin' de sound of their voices until he hear de rushin' of water en knows Watu–Kai is near . (In de old days, folks is packin' up Sunday lunches en goin' up de mountain; they don't come to bathe at Watu–Kai, they go there just to study de sweetness of de place. My ole granny is tellin' how de Waterfall is like all God's tears has come together in one place.)

"Close on to Watu-Kai, de water soundin' like a tin roof in a storm, makin' such a racket Simon can't hear their voices, can't see them neither, but he know they there. Den de moon pushes back de cloud covers to show its face, en everything is bright like before. Simon, he looks round to find a place to hide. Same rock you saw him by today, I'm guessin'.

"He peeks out from his hidin' place en sees de two of them near to where de water's fallin' from on high, pourin' down de mountain like liquid silver from a pitcher. Marshall and de girl are standing on a stone wide as a beggar's hand en flat as a mealie cake. They're clingin' to each other en kissin', but sad-like, Simon say, as if de troubles of de whole world are sittin' on their young shoulders.

"What come next, he's not believin', so he rub his eyes hard to be sure it's not some dream he's dreamin'. But a pain starts deep inside his belly en dat pain tell him he's awake for sure. Big Master's daughter, she pulls off her clothes, easy like but wid no shame, as if she were in some dream of her own. She never move her eyes off from Marshall's face en he never turns from her. When she's done, she stand dere wid her arms loose at her sides en her face carryin' a look like she's in church. Marshall, he don't say a word, just nods like he's bewitched en starts unbuttonin' his pants. Soon he's naked as a newborn, just like her. Simon say it tore his heart to see them, they're so beautiful together....de cook's boy, dark en strong like a piece of fine mahogany ...de girl, white en pink like a conch shell from de bottom of de sea. Lord Dunham's daughter, she move into de shadow of his young arms en close her eyes, en he lean down en touch each bud on her sweet breasts wid his lips. When she lifts her face up at him en smiles, Simon say it's 'like a room wid a thousand candles all lit at once.' Den she take Marshall by de hand and tugs it gentle-like en Simon, he's still so dumb with lookin' at de beauty of them, he's not understandin' what happen next. They on dat rock, then they gone.

"Simon, he start to shake. Dat boy shake so hard his teeth is knockin' into his head. His legs, they turnin' to piss-water en he falls to de ground like a kite on a day when de wind goes still. De clock has no hands to tell how long he's layin' there ...Simon say a tug of war is goin' on inside hisself, his head tellin' his feet to move en his heart sayin', 'No, not me.' But his head wins. Simon drag his feet along to de flat rock where last he seen de two young lovers, en make hisself look down to where de water come to rest after its long fall from de mountaintop. All he seein' is water whirlin' round en round. He starts to feelin' better, studyin' as how maybe an Angel come along en snatched those two up in his hands en carried them away. Den he looks down again, en what he sees dis time is de flower Marshall give to de girl... there ... floatin' on top of de water is ... 'lady of de night'.'

"Once't more de church bells toll. De Governor, he's so bowed down wid de weight of misery, he can hardly walk to de church. De island folk, they come also, their hearts bruised en sore, their eyes so full of water they can't hardly see de coffin restin' at de foot of de altar under de cross of Our Lord. Frangipani en lily bells ... jasmine white as a wedding veil ... cover de coffin... It don't even look like a coffin, more like a spot of garden for angels to rest in. When de service is over, they carry de coffin down de aisle en out to de churchyard where they sets it down wid gentle hands next to where Big Master's lady's lyin' in de ground, her resting place so new de grass ain't fully growed over it. (Ebben now you can see de two stones, side by side in de shade of a tamarind tree at de cemetery behind All Saints Church. Course with no kin livin' here to care for them, de weeds is high en de names hard to study, but they there.) Before de priest can say de final blessing, a cloud heavy wid rain pass over de churchyard en drop a bucketful of water on every living thing. But folks don't stir. They stay on to keep Big Master company in his sorrow, en de rain en tears, they all mixin' in together.

"Marshall's Mommy, now, she's too shamed to show her face. While folks are gathered at de church, she's followin' behind her sister's two grown boys as dey carry Marshall in a box up Wishbone Hill to de old slave cemetery. En where de tulip trees are growin' tall, dey puts him in de ground... just she en those two boys to mourn. She's sayin' all de prayers herself, en all de while her heart is torn to pieces because Marshall, he's her only chile. After she come home from buryin' her sweet son, she don't go back to 'Villa Carib' to cook no more. She close de shutters en shut de door en keep to herself. All de day en night long, folks what live close to hand hear de noises of her sorrow. It never stops.

"'Fore he leaves de island, Big Master takes some niggers from de cane field en carries them up de mountain in a wagon to Watu-Kai. He givin' out orders to pick up all de big stones they sees en pile them high across de path leadin' to de waterfall (de same path what carry Marshall en de girl). Those niggers haulin' rock 'til de sun goes down en build a wall so high en thick, folks can't get to Watu-Kai no more.

"Next morning, Lord Dunham leave de Villa in a fine white uniform, de one wid shiny gold buttons. On his head he wearin' a white helmet wid feathers red to match de braid. From de stables they bring round de horse he fancies most, Ebony Prince. (They tellin' how de onliest time dat horse act like a gentleman is when de Governor is in de saddle.)

"Big Master look just like a storybook picture sittin' on that char-black stallion as he ride down from All Saints Hill in de morning light. He en dat horse has to travel a fair ways to find de house where Marshall's Mummy's livin' at. Soon's he gets to her house, he leave Ebony Prince tied to a tree en go knockin' at de front door. (Folks livin' close to hand gather quick as a pickpocket's fingers when they sees dat stallion.) A voice from inside call, 'Come, if you've a mind to,' so he open de door en steps inside. No tellin' how long he's stayin', but those buzzards outside, they're as restless as a flea wid no dog in sight: they can't see nothin', can't hear neither.

Lord Dunham come out from de cook's house carryin' his helmet under his arm. His eyes are locked in like de spirit's on him en his face bears such a look of pain, those standin' round drop their eyes en turn away.

After he's gone, they tellin' how Marshall's Mommy, she's lookin' to be at peace, en de noises of her sorrow, they're heard no more."

CHAPTER X

At the end of his tale, the old Lutiguan closed his eyes and heaved a barely audible sigh. Unexpectedly moved by the tragic narrative, Tyler had trouble rousing himself from its spell. "That's one helluva story," he said at last. "And you say it's true? It really happened?"

"Yes, Mister Scranton."

"Look, it's late, Wash, and I know you're anxious to be on your way, but tell me, how come there was no stone wall blocking my way this afternoon?"

"True. De years passin' en folks forgettin' about Watu-Kai, 'til that white man come here from London." He went on to tell about an Englishman named Elliot, who appeared on their shores one day in the late sixties claiming a star-spangled reputation as consultant to the British travel industry, a whiz at promoting tourism. A discreet hint was dropped that with a little persuasion, Elliot might find time in his busy schedule to help Lutigua establish an image that would draw tourists from all over the world. The recently installed government did handstands in their haste to hire him; nevermind that his salary, to be paid over in pounds sterling, was roughly equivalent to a quarter of the newly independent island's gross income.

"This gentleman from England, he all de time fillin' de air wid sweet speeches, talkin' big plans for Lutigua. Mebbe too big for this small island."

One of his more practical schemes called for turning Watu-Kai into a showplace.

"So de government, they gets busy takin' down de wall, cuttin' a path to de waterfall from de main road en puttin' fancy signs up all over. You'd see pictures in de paper of Mister Elliot width his arm round a Minister en de two of them smilin' like monkeys squattin' on a ripe banana tree." The only way for visitors to get to Watu-Kai was by taxi and to a man, the drivers refused to go up the mountain.

"They don't say why, they just sayin' 'No.' One by one de signs disappear. Folks stealin' 'em for firewood. Soon de bush growin' back up, heavy like before." He shook his head, "They pays Elliot all dat money, but de tourists never come."

"And Simon? What's he doing up there?"

"Soons that wall come down, Simon, he takes it 'pon himself to guard Watu–Kai, to keep folks away. Poor crazy old fool. He thinks Marshall en de Governor's daughter will be comin' dat way, en he plans to stop them this time."

* * * * * * * * * * *

With so few rooms occupied, Preston suggested they run an ad in the local paper inviting people to celebrate New Year's at Belle Jours. When he spoke to Laura, hoping to persuade her to let Danielle book a steel band for the occasion, she immediately corrected him: "In this part of the world, Avery, we don't say 'New Year's Eve,' we say '*Old Year's Night*,'" enunciating the last three words with deliberation. "You and Scranton need to remember that."

Ignoring her condescending tone, he pushed ahead with his plan: "We can add fifty per cent across the board for every drink served, *plus* an entertainment tax . People won't mind. They *expect* to pay more on a traditional night for partying. Besides, my dear, think of the extra cash it will generate!"

Despite his optimistic forecast, the New Yorker was not at all sure what kind of response they could expect. Danielle scoured the island for paper hats and horns, and the staff pitched in to put up decorations. At ten p.m., the published start of the gala evening, the band faced an empty dance floor. In an agony of suspense, Preston stationed himself at the end of the main bar so he could watch for new arrivals. Leona Caswell padded into view and singled out Tyler, who was checking the supply of mixers.

"Do you have enough help?"

"Yes, ma'am. I drafted two boys from the diningroom to stay on for a couple of hours and there'll be three of us here at the bar to fill orders."

She turned to Avery, "Don't fret," she said kindly. "I'm sure people will show up. No one's ever on time on this island. Good luck! If anyone needs me, I'll be in my room."

An hour later cars started swinging into the driveway, disgorging party-goers from all over the island.

Tyler checked his watch; it was after three. He longed for the comfort of bed. The band had packed up and left an hour ago and he let his men leave with them after admonishing Sam, "You'd better have two boys here at seven to clean up. This place is a pig-sty." A few diehards still lingered: a boisterous party of six at one table, a querulous couple at another and a single drinker at the end of the bar who was having trouble staying upright on his stool. *I better cut him off.* The room was littered with silent tokens of the evenings' festivities —crushed paper hats, half-empty glasses, overflowing ashtrays and confetti, like colored snowflakes, scattered everywhere.

He reached in his pocket for a cigarette and was about to take a drag, when the Buddha-like silhouette of the Englishwoman appeared at the edge of the dance floor.

"Miss Caswell! What are you doing up at this hour?"

"I saw the lights from my room and decided to come down and find out how the evening went. Jolly well, I should judge," she said glancing around. "Avery must have been relieved."

"Can I get you something to drink?"

"If you've any coconut milk and nutmeg on hand, I'd love a glass." She sat down at a nearby table to wait. When the American brought her drink, she asked, "Won't you join me? I can't manage the bar stools and perhaps those night owls will take the hint when they see you've left your post." Tyler groaned inwardly. *Just what I need. A late night tête à tête after working my balls off.* But he felt rather sorry for her. F-J was off again, leaving Caswell to handle any emergencies that might arise at the hotel.

"After all the booze this lot has swilled, I wouldn't count on them being up to anything as subtle as a hint."

He excused himself and went to tell those who still lingered that the party was over.

"Tell me, Tyler," Caswell began when he'd returned to the table with a nightcap, "Were you born knowing how many drops of Angostura bitters go into a Manhattan?"

"Do you mean have I been a bartender all my life? No, ma'am. My first stretch behind a bar was at a ski resort in Vermont; then I moved on to the *Sheraton.* Before that, I was a salesman. A jobber for a glass manufacturing company."

"A salesman? How interesting. What made you give it up to become a ...a ...bartender?"

The way she says 'bartender', it sounds one step lower than a pederast.

"Look, Miss Caswell. I did o.k. as a salesman. I wasn't a 30-day wonder, or anything like that, but I did pretty well. What got me finally was the kind of life I was leading. I woke up one morning and all at once I couldn't stand the thought of one more night on the road, one more depressing motel room, one more plastic meal."

He'd made variations of this same speech a dozen times without ever disclosing just how precisely incised in his memory were the details of one particular episode at the *Holiday Inn* on the outskirts of Albany ... how, when he finally got the courage to sit up in bed, the back of his neck ached and the inside of his bruised mouth tasted like rotting leather from too much booze and a sexual romp that resembled an Olympic free-for-all. Or how the gorge rose in his throat when he glanced at the sleeping figure on the other side of the king-size bed. A pickup from the bar across the street. Mary? Marie? Did it matter? She lay sprawled on her side, mouth open, saliva oozing down her chin; her hennaed auburn hair was scattered across the pillow like dried weeds. But above all, it was the rank, female smell of her - so pervasive it over-powered the lingering scent of her cheap perfume - that sent him stumbling into the bathroom to be sick.

"No more," he swore to himself when the retching finally stopped, "so help me." But as he stood gargling with tap water to vanquish the sour taste of bile, a cynical inner voice prophesized, 'not 'til the next time.'

Tyler didn't believe in Fate but he did believe you were a horse's ass to ignore the obvious; thus, some 36 hours later when he heard the mellifilous voice of the announcer on the car radio purr, "Tired of your present job? Ready for a change of pace?", he pulled right over and jotted down the address and phone number of the Rawson School of Bartending. He checked out the school, found it to be reputable and gave notice to his employers. Since he had an essentially benign view of the human race - Tyler genuinely liked most people - he took to his new vocation immediately. He also appreciated the luxury of being able to stay in one place for as long as it appealed to him, of moving on when he got the urge. *I can kiss those one-night- stands goodbye.*

"Oh my dear Tyler, I've offended you," the heavy woman looked stricken. "I didn't mean ...to denigrate your profession ...please believe me. It's just that you've done such a fine job of training your men ... of dealing with the local suppliers ... you seem capable of so much ..." she stopped in embarrassment.

"Forget it. You're not the first to ask . Tell me now, are you enjoying it here? This climate must be a big change from what you're used to."

She paused before answering, unwilling to reveal the depths of her disillusionment, of the wounds inflicted by Laura Foster-Jones' cavalier treatment. *We were so close those last few years in Clovelly.* 'It's a change, I'll admit that," she answered gamely, "but I'll muddle through, I expect."

He woke at noon in a foul mood. "I've got to get away from here for a couple of hours before my shift starts. I hope too hell no one's taken the Ford." He threw on a pair of old khaki's and a shirt, grabbed his swim trunks and headed for the door of the cabin, so intent on flight he didn't notice his cabinmate, who was playing a game of Solitaire in a corner of the porch.

"Busy night?" Preston asked solicitously.

Tyler halted and turned to him, "Bet your sweet ass it was. But you'll be pleased to know we raked in a pile."

"I heard you come in. Must have been about four."

"I didn't know I had a 'Nanny' clocking me in."

"Sorry, old man. It was just an observation.

"My fault. I didn't mean to bite your head off."

"As the natives here are so fond of saying, 'not to worry.'"

"Well, see you later, Avery. I've got to make a quick check of the bar to be sure the cleanup crew showed this morning."

As he hurried down the path he came abreast of James balancing a tray of covered dishes on his shoulder.

"James. Hello. Wait a sec, what've you got there?"

"Afternoon, Mister Scranton. It's Mr. Preston's lunch, sir."

"Why the devil are you delivering it? The boys from the dining hall are supposed to take care of all food orders."

The handsome young Lutiguan stared down at his feet. “Mister Preston told Mr. Osbert I was to carry de tray to him.”

“Well I’ll be damned.” He was both puzzled and annoyed. “I’ll check into this later.”

“Yes, sir.”

When Danielle handed him the keys to the station wagon, she gave him a searching look: “Is something de matter?”

“Nothing that a few hours away from this place won’t cure.”

CHAPTER XI

As he steered the Ford around the circular drive and away from Belle Jours, Tyler toyed with the idea of returning to Watu-Kai. Ever since Wash's tale of the two young lovers, he'd been unable to shake off a morbid fascination with their fate. They were alive to him ... that dark boy from the island, the fair girl from England. He pictured them standing naked and unashamed before one another, a luminous moon casting its benediction over their embrace; afterwards, their unspoken agreement to fling themselves into the waters below. He saw it as a metaphorical act of a passion as profound as it was pure: death not as a tragedy, but a touchstone, a symbol of enduring love.

Suddenly he was immoblized by a searing revelation. He pulled over to the side of the road, jammed on the brakes and turned the motor off, letting his hands slide from the wheel: *All except the ending. Ours sure as hell had a different ending.*

A Pandora's box of memories locked away in a corner attic of his mind flew open with heartrending ease. *Julie.* How many lifetimes ago? Sunlight tracing the soft down on her cheek ... a tiny mole hidden in the curve of a breast ...the delicate taste of salt on warm skin as his lips brushed her shoulder. The scent of her hair, the feel of her small, delicate body against his—as familiar once as his own breath. How many lifetimes ago that afternoon? Tears washing down her face like a hard spring rain against the window pane. The hibernal desolation of her voice ...

"Tyler, you promised." Softly, softly, tearing his gut apart, "*you promised!*" Afterward, the shame. The crushing self-awareness that he had been exposed for what he was, a coward.

"I'll never leave you, Julie. Nothing can keep us apart. We'll be together always."

And what happened? I let them take you from me. I let them. It was easy. They knew exactly which buttons to push.

"Tyler, please. I *want to.* Please."

For an answer, he pushed himself off her body, using his hand to give himself leverage, then turning sideways, half-kneeling to grope for the discarded cashmere sweater and brassiere on the floor.

"I promised Macy we'd have the Chevy back by eleven, remember?"

She sat up slowly, thin arms enfolded across her bare chest in a consoling hug.

"I thought you loved me."

"You know I do." With eyes averted he pushed the clothing into her lap and fumbled for the chrome door handle. Once outside he stood with his back to the maroon Chevrolet inhaling generous gulps of cold night air, his shoulders shaking as he zipped up his pants.

On the ride back to town from the reservoir she sat mute and rigid, her body pressed against the door on the passenger side as if he were contagious. Gliding to a halt by the yellow hydrant a block from her parents' house, he switched off the radio.

"Meet me after practice Monday?" In the dim light of the dashboard, he saw the imperceptible shake of her head.

"Julie. Don't be that way. Listen, it wasn't easy back there. I want it as much as you do." He pulled her toward him, whispering against her hair, "Come on, baby, kiss me goodnight." A warm tear slid onto the back of his hand.

"You make me feel so *cheap*. Begging for it like that."

"Cheap?" He wrenched himself upright. "Cheap! That's the last thing ..." He slammed the steering wheel with his open palm. "Can't you understand? *Not in the back of Macy Squires' smelly ole Chevy!*"

At seventeen, save for some fleshing out of shoulder and thigh, Tyler Scranton's physique denied his years. Green eyes flecked with brown in a face that was a composite of straight lines and planes conspired to give him the petulant good looks of those male fashion models in *Vogue* and *Harpers Bazaar*, the perfection marred by a chipped front tooth, token of a misadventure on roller skates when he was 12. By his Junior year at Thompson Central High, Tyler had acquired a modest reputation on the track field and a minor one as a ladies' man (girls had been in hot pursuit since fourth grade). Because National League batting averages held more allure for him than possessive nouns and logarithms, his scholastic average was mired in a C. The yearbook described him as 'The Running Man.'

The accident in the middle of his Sophomore year - it was mentioned in news reports as far south as Harrisburg - threw a transitory spotlight in his direction.

"Scranton? Was that *his* brother?"

In Thompson, like any small town with symbiotic ties, the sudden and tragic death of one of it children was cause for communal grieving. The morning of the funeral service at the Presbyterian Church every seat was filled; floral tributes covered the front of the church, spilling over into the aisle. For several weeks afterwards wherever Tyler went, someone would approach to pat his shoulder, or grip his arm briefly in an expression of sympathy. Older women, inquiring after his mother, became teary-eyed.

The death of his younger brother, Neddie, robbed Tyler of the only well-spring of warmth and affection in his personal universe. He avoided the oyster shingle house with its intaglio of memories, shrivelled at the sight of his mother's raw-scrubbed, swollen face, eyes dulled by grief with their silent, wounding accusation: "Why Neddie? *Why not you?*"

Desperate for human contact, he found a modicum of comfort in the eager arms of a steady stream of compliant girls; emboldened by the ease with which favors were bestowed, he quickly became adept at snaps and buttons, at easing past restricting nylon and elastic. When his favorite site for amatory excursions, the balcony of the old Loew's Theater, was torn down to make way for a parking lot, he continued his explorations at the drive-in in the back seat of cars borrowed from classmates.

His conquests were confined to saucy girls with painted faces from his side of town, the exception being

Mary Ellen Scobie, the funeral director's daughter. The Scobies, like the rest of Thompson's established gentry, lived across the tracks in an austere, turn-of-the-century mansion, its original lines marred by the 20th century addition of a flat, concrete building which housed Mr. Scobie's business. To compensate for myopia and a wavering chin, Nature had been kinder to Mary Ellen in another way. As Tyler's best friend, Lyle, observed wonderingly, "She's got the biggest tits on the Eastern seaboard." Her breasts became Mary Ellen's ticket to the transient, lubricious attentions of half the boys in the Junior class and a few Seniors as well. Tyler, his eyes tightly shut, laid her twice on the grounds of the State Park near the reservoir. Whatever remorse he might have felt quickly vanished when he plied open her thighs with his knee and felt her anticipatory wetness.

With a sense of ennui he couldn't shake, Tyler rode out the ragged end of his Junior year with barely passing grades. Escape from Thompson became all that mattered. Drawn to a notice on the school bulletin board listing jobs available for the summer, he applied for and was hired as a counselor at a boy's camp.

"The pay's lousy," he told Lyle, "but at least I'll be away from this place for two months."

Camp Devon for boys and its sister camp, Aurora, were located alongside the fertile east bank of the Susquehanna River some two hundred and fifty miles south of Thompson. Traditionally the two camps shared the same water facilities, small fleet of canoes and a large, drafty, wood-beamed rec hall, site of joint amateur theatricals and weekly square dances. On the first Saturday of the season when both camps converged on the rec hall, Tyler experienced a jolt of recognition when he glanced across the room and saw a face from home. *I know her. That's Julie Waterman, Judge Waterman's granddaughter.*

He observed with interest the tanned, lithe legs beneath white shorts, the slim body and small chest, slightly rounded shoulders and sunburned nose above pale, pink lips. Her carmel hair, pulled back from her face in a pony tail, accented its heart-shaped contours and fine bones. At school she belonged to a small coterie of students whose parents were the acknowledged aristocracy of Thompson. These were the heirs presumptive, the young men and women who moved with the ease and assurance of those whose passage through life has been chartered and subsidized from birth. For some, it meant leaving public high school at the end of Sophomore year and enrolling at Shipley or Farragut before drifting on to a junior college in the south or Midwest. The brighter ones completed Central High and continued their education at colleges and universities of stature. A select few marched soberly onward to graduate school, returning home to work in Daddy's law firm or establish a medical practice in the front parlours of one of those gabeled Victorian dinosaurs on Church Street. When the time was right, they married each other; the periodic arrival of new faces, new bloodlines from somewhere outside the magic confines of Thompson's city limits kept it from being incestuous.

Attentive now, he watched Julie coax two shy campers onto the floor to join the other dancers, while a trio of local musicians, two fiddles and a banjo, tuned up. He waited until the first set of Virginia Reelers were swinging through their paces to make his move.

"Hi! As they say in the funny papers, 'small world.'"

"Sorry?"

She doesn't know me from Adam. Stung by the snub he'd brought upon himself, Tyler rattled off his name, adding that of Thompson's star basketball player for good measure. "Yeah, well Lyle's a good buddy of mine."

"Of course," she said, recovering gracefully, "I remember now. You were in Somerset's homeroom."

Wrong. It was Hatcher's. But he didn't correct her. After all, he'd gotten what he crossed the room for: she was talking to him.

Usually Tyler regarded the girls who aroused his interest as accessories after the fact of his own physical pleasure, and because they made it easy for him to have his way, he'd become cocky and not a little conceited.

But from their first awkward exchange, he sensed that this time the scenario would be different. Despite marked incongruities of background and upbringing – Julie's father was an attorney, well-known in legal and political circles across the State, her mother involved in numerous civic and charitable enterprises, a past president of the Junior League, all this in contrast to Myra, who worked the 7 a.m.-3 p.m. shift at Al's Diner – whatever self-consciousness he once harbored about Thompson's inbred social demarcations had dissolved after the interlude with Mary Ellen Scobie.

Freed from the tangible barriers and intangible taboos of their home town, Tyler Scranton and Julie Waterman circled each other with wary curiosity. The young woman's initial response to his casual pursuit was one of caution: still smarting from the recent break with her steady boyfriend of two years and the humiliating news that he was dating her best friend, she resolved to avoid any serious entanglements her last year at Thompson High. But her wounded pride called out for succor, and Tyler Scranton was clearly very good looking.

In that bucolic setting along the banks of the Susquehanna, a mutual attraction took root and flourished, like the early crocus pushing its way through the damp earth to burst forth at the first warm breath of Spring. For Tyler, whose emotions had been on hold for so long, it was a revelatory journey into sunlight and freedom.

He told her everything.

For Julie's part, once the amenities of the courting game were past, once she broke through his fortress of deceptive nonchalance, became sensitive to his neediness, his vulnerability, she forgot her resolve and fell in love with an aching, tender possessiveness that astonished her.

The summer sped by, propelled by the demanding routine of camp life, the tension of being in sight of one another without being able to touch (they adopted their own, private semaphores) capped by lively Saturday evenings when the two camps joined forces. In the midst of a press of milling, adolescent bodies, they traded small talk and laughter, but had eyes only for each other. Periodically they arranged to meet down at the waterfront after 'Taps.' Under a patchwork quilt of stars, they sat on the dock and exchanged whispered confidences punctuated by honey-sweet kisses and feverish embraces. Swamped by emotions completely alien to him, Tyler was content to honor the innocence of their pleasures.

Their idyll ended on a soggy, rain-ladened morning in late August when the two camps officially closed for the summer.

With the aid and sympathy of a tiny network of confederates - she told two close friends, he confided in Lyle - Tyler and Julie managed to be together the autumn of their Senior year. Safe from the prying eyes of a social hierarchy too formidable to be broached, they exchanged intoxicated kisses in borrowed cars, held hands and talked in the privacy of a booth at a roadside tavern on the outskirts of town. If Tyler resented this arrangement and all it implied, he was too humbled by the fierceness of her attachment, too grateful for her love to protest. Besides, he was only too aware of what it was costing her to betray her parents' trust, since the entire burden of devising elaborate evasions and petty deceits fell to Julie. Secrecy and subterfuge added another dynamic to the relationship, so that bone and flesh quivered, cried out to be joined. They began to quarrel. Tyler, displaying unaccustomed self-control, insisted: "Wait. Wait 'til we can spend a whole night together. Someplace where we'll feel free, where time won't matter."

He got his wish. The Waterman's accepted an invitation to visit old friends in Philadelphia at the end of January. For two days and nights he and Julie made love in her pristine bedroom on the second floor of the imposing house on Water Street, the only witness to their union a scruffy Pooh bear with one button eye missing. He had to bite his lips to keep from crying when he realized she was still a virgin.

It was early April, that 'cruellest' of months, when she told him she was pregnant.

With the grim relish of one who painstakingly arrives at the solution to a bitter, elusive equation, he understood now why he had never let another living soul come close. *First Neddie, then Julie.* The grief and scars were still there, buried deep in the marrow of him.

Tyler stared, unseeing, out of the car window, oblivious to a fiery sun which beat down savagely on the metal body of the car, turning its interior into a harbinger of Hell. The stabbing horn of a taxi swerving by broke his reverie. Later he was unable to remember how he found the small deserted cove hidden in a curved pocket of shoreline miles from the hotel. He swam until his limbs ached, then walked slowly up and down the narrow strip of sand willing himself to forget the past.

CHAPTER XII

"They're like a plague of locust," Leona Caswell sighed.

"More like throwbacks to Neanderthal man, if you ask me," Avery offered. "Cheap bastards. Free room and board and they have the nerve to bring along their own booze."

"And raise hell with my boys about the cost of mixers," Tyler added, "but we have a little ploy of our own: a 20% knock-up on everything the bar serves."

"Mrs. Foster-Jones, does she know of this?" Danielle asked.

"Not to worry," Tyler reassured her with a grin, "I checked with her first. When she heard that four of them were nosing about the kitchen early this morning, she had a fit. Corbin was trying to get out the breakfast orders and they made him so mad, he threw his chef's hat on the floor and stomped on it."

"True. Corbin come running to the office angry like a boar hog."

"And they carry those bloody check lists everywhere!" the bookkeeper interjected. "Snoop-poke-check. They could show the graduates of Moscow Centre a thing or two."

Like a band of early settlers heading West through hostile territory, the senior staff were gathered in the office for mutual protection and comfort. A maurauding contingent of travel agents had descended on Belle Jours and the hotel's owner made no bones about the importance of their evaluations. "They can make or break us, "Foster-Jones had warned at a special meeting, "so be on your toes, everyone."

Avery rolled his eyes mischievously, "Anyway, thanks to Tyler, Westchester County is all sewn up."

"What do you mean by that crack, Preston?"

"My dear man, one would have to be blind not too notice the enthusiastic bids for attention being thrown your way by a certain Miss . . Miss . .."

"Adams," Danielle prompted with a smile.

"Ah yes, the endearing Miss Adams. Managing directoress of the 'Sunshine Travel Tours,' a chain of local travel agencies spread across fashionable, filthy-rich Westchester County. *The* Miss Adams of the baby-doll voice, peroxide streak and size C cup. Or maybe it's a D. Hard to tell these days." He assumed a falsetto voice: "'Such a mah-vu-less island' the well-endowed Miss Adams croons. 'The natives are too mah-vu-less. So colorful, don't you agree?'"

"She said that?" Caswell asked incredulously.

"Well something like that. The adjective 'mah-vu-less' takes a terrible shellacking from Miss Adams. In any case, the lady is positively ga-ga over Lutigua, but more ga-ga I think, over our handsome Mr. Scranton."

"Lay off it, Preston."

"I wouldn't dream of intruding on your territorial rights, old man."

"Gentlemen! Remember, there are ladies present," Caswell admonished to forestall further bickering.

"Please to excuse me," Danielle said, "it is Cleo's lunch time and I must take her place at Reception." She paused at the doorway, "Our people have a saying: 'The night still come though the day be long.' In four days the travel people will be gone, then all will be sweet again."

"She's right. We're going to have to grin and bear it."

"I leave the grinning up to you, old man," Avery shot back. "I can hardly bear it."

Tyler followed Danielle out into the corridor. "Sometimes I could wring Preston's neck."

"He likes to tease, but I do not think he is happy to be teased back."

"You don't miss much, do you lady?"

"There is another saying of our people: 'He 'ent got no hind claws.'" She giggled, then clapped her hand to her mouth like a small child who has spoken out of turn. "You are understanding?" she asked, struggling to regain her composure.

"No, but it'll come to me."

In the weeks following his arrival at Belle Jours, a relaxed bond of comaradarie had developed between the American and the beautiful Lutiguan. Because he didn't dare admit to himself how lonely he was, Tyler welcomed the change. But the more he was around this graceful, discerning woman, the greater became his compulsion to move the relationship onto a more intimate plane. Her casual tolerance of his flirtatious signals - a quick squeeze of the hand, a light brushing against her bare arm - baffled him and whetted his appetite. Admittedly, he was spoiled. For most of his adult life, few women had put up more than token resistance to his overtures. On balance, however, he rarely pursued a woman he didn't instinctively know would eventually acquiesce. Winning them over meant getting them into the sack as quickly as possible. If the sex was good and the woman undemanding, the relationship might last for months. At the beginning, usually after they'd made love the second or third time, he would caution, "Listen, I like you a lot, but I'm not interested in being tied down."

But the nesting instinct, a biological compulsion as old as time itself, eventually betrayed the women. Tyler was adept at divining the signs: the moment his monogrammed initials appeared on any item, be it cuff links, robe, or cocktail shaker, he knew it was time to blow the whistle. He tried, not always successfully, to be kind. Rare were the instances when familiarity bred a dawning recognition of his hedonism, when a hasty retreat was beaten ahead of *his* timetable.

But Scranton was experienced enough to know the old rules of the game didn't apply in his new surroundings. His impatience to win over Danielle was tempered by an inner prudence, and like the Lenten penitent who embraces his abstemiousness in expectation of a richer reward, he was careful to hide his mounting desire for her.

Sounding as casual as possible, he said, "I'm free tonight after seven. How about letting me take you to dinner at the 'Belvedere'?"

The unexpected invitation robbed Danielle of her usual equanimity. Tyler spoke rapidly to bridge the uneasy silence that followed. "Of course, if you're busy, we can make it another time." His adroit pulling back seemed to compound her confusion.

"Please to forgive me, Tyler. My thoughts are with Cleo, who waits for me. I will speak with you later," and she fled from his sight.

Well, that's that. Nothing ventured and all that malarkey. But he was disappointed all the same.

* * * * * * * * * *

It was the beginning of the school holiday; classes wouldn't be resuming until after Easter. In the kitchen Danielle finished wiping the last of the breakfast dishes. The cassava would soon be done and she would be free to join her friend Jolie and Jolie's two older sisters for an outing at the beach. She was alone in the house; her Daddy had gone to town to pick up lumber for a new porch railing and Jacob was at the cricket field with his school chums. She'd be leaving herself as soon as the baking was done. As Danielle put the clean cups away on a shelf above the sink, tears suddenly welled up and splashed down her cheeks. She wiped them away with the back of her hand. Barely a year had passed since cancer had taken her Mother from them, and not a day went by that the ten year old didn't miss her, grieve for her. This was her first attempt at making biscuits by herself and she made them from memory, from countless hours spent watching her Mother peel and grate the cassava root, sift the flour, scoop fresh coconut from a shell. She knew that her brother Jacob was partial to their Mother's cassava, that he was missing her, too. It was important to the child that the biscuits turn out just right.

She was in her bedroom at the back of the house when she heard a scratching at the door. It was Mr. Maycock.

Rufus Maycock lived in a shack patched together from salvaged timber, tin and coconut fronds in the hills behind the Mapps' house. He and Danielle's father were the same age, had once attended the same school, but Maycock's father had hauled him out after a year to work in the cane fields. The family was always in need. What became of them was of little interest to Josiah Mapp, who was privy to appalling tales about Rufus' brutish father and slovenly mother. Suffice to say he was not pleased when Rufus had shown up on their doorstep three years ago to pay a call on his 'old mate.' Danielle's mother took pity on him and invited him to supper. Later, she and Josiah had one of their rare quarrels: "That man is not welcome in my house. Please to see that you never invite him again." His wife protested, alluding to the Lord's Commandment, saying that Rufus Maycock was now their neighbor and while they certainly didn't have to love him, it didn't hurt to share a meal with him. "He looks so hungry, so poorly," was her compassionate defense.

"I don't want him near to you or my children," Josiah said quietly. Danielle's mother saw a look of such implacable hardness on her husband's usually benign face, it took her breath away. She quickly acquiesced, "I'll do as you ask, Mr. Mapp."

After that evening, Rufus showed up regularly once or twice a month, always with the excuse of needing to borrow one tool or another (he was punctilious about returning whatever he took). Mrs. Mapp never strayed from her husband's mandate, but she made sure that before Rufus left their yard, he carried with him a dish of leftover cou-cou or stew meat. The day of her funeral while the family was at church, Maycock left a home-made wreath of flowers on the porch steps with a pencilled note: *'Sory. Rufus M.'*

"Your Daddy home?"

"No, Mr. Maycock. He's at de lumber yard."

"I was wantin' to borrow de pancart to haul some rocks."

"He'll be back 'fore dinnertime. You can ask him then."

"Say, what's dat you cookin', girl?"

The child didn't much care for their neighbor, in fact she was a little afraid of him. His breath was rank and he was never clean. But her Mummy always said she must respect her elders, so she swallowed her misgivings and answered without hesitation: "I'm makin' cassava biscuits for my Daddy and Jacob," she said proudly. "They're 'bout done. Would you like one to take home? Please to wait here, I'll see if they're ready."

As she entered the kitchen she heard the screen door open and shut.

Her mind refused to acknowledge what happened next. But imbedded in her unconscious was a memory of utter helplessness, of searing pain ... more pain, and fear (*If you tells, girl, I comin' fer you en chop you to pieces wid my cutter*) and afterwards, shame. Permeating the convergence of these horrific emotions was the indelible odor of burning cassava.

Josiah Mapp saw smoke coming from the kitchen window and jumped down from the back of the lumberyard's truck. He ran into the house and angrily turned off the oven, calling as he did, "Danielle! Dani! Where you keepin', child? You tryin' to burn dis house down?" he roared. There was no answer. He stomped from room to room calling his daughter's name. The door to her bedroom was shut. Irritably he pushed it open to be transfixed by the sight of her slight figure buried under the bedclothes, blood on the sheets, traces of blood on the clothing strewn across the wooden floor. Hearing him enter, she burrowed more deeply under the covers. Softly now, "Dani? Baby, what happened here?"

He sent for his older sister, Dorothea. "She's mighty young for that woman's business. Maybe it come en scared her. I'm thinkin' she'll talk to you."

Dorothea finally emerged from the bedroom wiping tears from her cheeks, "It's not what you're thinkin', Josiah. Lord have mercy, that poor child's been interfer'd with."

"What are you sayin'? You tellin' me some nigger interfered with my baby?" His brown face turned ashen. "Who did it? Just tell me de name of de scoundrel en I'll ..." he shook his fists in helpless rage.

"She's not sayin'."

"*I'll make her tell!*" His sister caught him by the arm as he stalked off in the direction of Danielle's bedroom.

"You'll do no such thing, Josiah. Leave her be! The child's in such a misery . . " and her tears started afresh.

"I'm fetchin' de police."

"You're not doin' that either. They'll send some young constable still wet behind de ears who will ask a lot of fool questions. No, brother. Listen to me. I'll take care of Dani. You've got to understan', more den her body's been hurt ... inside her head, it's hurtin' also. She's so afraid, she can't speak."

Gradually responding to the gentleness and warmth of her aunt's ministrations, the ten year old regained her willingness to talk. But when asked by Josiah to name her attacker, she covered her ears and ran screaming from his sight. As driven as he was to find and punish the man who raped and sodomized his daughter, the questions ceased when he saw the anguish they were causing the child.

Several weeks later during their evening meal Mapp remarked to his children, "Haven't laid eyes on that pest Maycock for a while. You seen him lately, Jacob?"

A glass of mauby slipped from Danielle's fingers and spilled across the table, her chair falling to the floor as she jumped up to rush from the room.

"Dani, what's vexing ..." Mapp never finished the sentence. Slowly his eyes assumed a dangerous glitter as realized the significance of her flight.

Two days later a neighbor reported seeing thick black smoke up in the hills, coming from the area where Rufus Maycock lived. The two constables sent to investigate found the house a smouldering ruin and no sign of its owner . Maycock was not seen in the parish again, and since he was known to be a strange fellow, one who kept to himself, he wasn't missed.

In her late teens the young girl blossomed; when she reached an acceptable age to start dating, young men clustered around, vying for her attention. But Dani's response to their overtures was one of diffidence and apathy. Eventually, word got about that she was 'cold as yesstiday's stewpot', and the young men looked elsewhere. Sadly, her father recognized that the trauma she'd suffered made it unlikely his daughter would allow any man to become intimate, indeed, that she might never marry.

* * * * * * * * * *

In the midst of handing out room keys and mail, Danielle's thoughts centered on Tyler's invitation . She was rarely invited out. A friend of her brother's had taken her to a dance sponsored by the church, but that was months ago.

This American... he and I, we have become friends. I like to hear how he speaks. Sometimes de funny words he sayin' make me laugh ... No harm can come to spend an evening with him. Besides, how sweet to dine at 'The Belvedere'! For such a fine place I can wear de dress aunty stitched up for me last Easter.

The 'Belvedere Arms' was a hundred year old plantation house on the outskirts of St. James. In the mid-forties an enterprising Englishman had converted it into a guest house, and for many years it was the only commercial lodging available in that part of the island. Later it was sold to a wealthy Trinidadian, a man of business acumen and zeal who refurbished the guest rooms, enlarged its meager dining facilities and established a reputation for serving excellent cuisine, thereby insuring its popularity with the locals and tourists alike.

"What will you have to drink, Danielle? Scotch? Gin? A rum concoction?"

"A Coca-cola, please, Tyler."

Scranton gave the waiter their order and sat back to examine his surroundings. The room was bathed in candlelight, lending it a soft, intimate atmosphere; thick coral walls of creamy-white - the only traces of its previous incarnation - were vestiges of an era of construction nearly extinct. Dominating the center of the restaurant and lending it a rather bizarre charm, was a copy of a Roman fountain brazenly painted turquoise to match the ornate corner modillions and border of rococo molding. On the far side two archways opened out onto a dramatically lit tropical garden, lush with orchids, jacaranda, amherstia and giant yellow-toothed philodendrum. He took note of the crystal chandeliers, damask linen and ornately carved mahogany sideboard . *Someone's put a pile of dough into this place.*

Danielle, sheathed in a dress of soft lavender material, a string of white coral beads at her throat and matching earrings, sat stiffly opposite him. Tyler was aware of the covert glances of admiration that followed them to their table. His companion had been subdued and tense during the ride into town, dampening all his efforts at conversation. He'd counted on liquor to loosen her reserve, to relax her so they could fall back into their old pattern of easy familiarity. At the moment he was having trouble absorbing the idea that this woman who had acted with such intrepid assurance ever since they met, now seemed totally intimidated. *She has me tongue-tied, like some kid on a first date.*

As if sensing his thoughts, she offered a weak smile. "Please to forgive me, Tyler. My head, it spins like a kite in de blowing wind. For me, it is a thing of wonder to be at this fine place. You are understanding?"

He reached across the table to take her hand. "Relax, Danielle. I've never set foot in this place before tonight, either. If it makes you feel any better, just pretend we've never left Belle Jours, that we're in our own diningroom."

She flashed him a look of gratitude and gently withdrew her hand. "Thank you, Tyler. I will be easier now. And shall I tell you a secret? Coming here, it was so worrying to me I could not touch one bit of food! Now my stomach, it is crying with emptiness." She smiled her enchanting smile, "So you see, Tyler, your money will not be wasted. I will swallow every bite."

He was non-plussed: *She's worried what it's going to cost me! Lady, there are a few American broads I know who could take a lesson from you.*

It seemed to Tyler the meal was over almost as soon as it began. In response to his low-key prodding, Danielle revealed the outlines of her life away from the hotel: she was the youngest and sole girl in a family of four; her two older brothers had emigrated to Canada, but she and Jacob remained at home . "I wished to go to University in Toronto - my brother, Noah and his family are living there - but with Mummy gone, I would not rest easy being so far from my Daddy. He sent me to Jamaica to study how to be a secretary and keep a proper ledger; when I returned, I see that he is eating poorly and de house is in a sorry way, so I am happy I did not leave home."

The Mapps traced their roots on the island back to the late 1700's a time when slavery still prevailed; and although emancipation was proclaimed on paper in the mid-1800's, whites were still the sole landowners and maintained the reins of power, leaving the native Lutiguans no better off than before. The reversal of their fortunes was pathetically slow to materialize; finally, in the 1940's, by dint of factors both economic and political (including bloody strikes and protests), the island embarked on the road to becoming a more democratic society. When Lutigua became an independent state within the Commonwealth, a parliamentary system of government was initiated. The first elected Prime Minister was black as were many members of the new Assembly. Admired and respected by his peers, Josiah Mapp's appointment as Minister of Agriculture in the first Cabinet was greeted with widespread approval. Mapp retired from active politics when his party lost the next election, relieved to be freed from the endless pettiness and bickering.

Several hundred feet from the main building of the 'Belvedere' was an old stable which the owner had recently converted into a nightclub. "It's too early to go home, Danielle. Let's look this new place over. I'd like a nightcap anyway." She studied the gold watch on her wrist, "The hour, it grows late..."

"*Pretty please*, with sugar on it?"

"Pardon?"

Her perplexed look made him laugh. "It's only another crazy American expression. Come on," he urged with boyish enthusiasm, "just a peek. Just to please me!"

In contrast to the elegance of the main house, informality was the keynote here: the narrow room with low ceilings was dimly lit; a five-piece band occupied a raised platform at the far end and a scattering of tables and chairs were arranged in a semi-circle around a miniscule dance floor. As they were being led to their table, Tyler recognized the music, a medley of Broadway show tunes. *Wonders never cease. Rodgers and Hammerstein alive and kicking on the isle of Lutigua.*

"Care to dance, Danielle?"

"No please. I'm happy just to listen."

Beginning of the ninth and two strikes against me. Must have left my all my persuasive charm back in the good ole U.S. of A.

He ordered a double Scotch. The band played decorously for twenty minutes, then swung into a Latin beat sending three sedate white couples on the dance floor hurrying back to their tables. With frenzied abandon the quintet finished their set with a new calypso from Trinidad that was sweeping the island. The perspiring musicians retired to the bar, the lights dimmed and all conversation came to a halt as a single spotlight heralded the star of the evening. A tall, willowy black girl with saucer eyes and dazzling white teeth glided up to the microphone. Her soft, breathy

"Good evening. My name is Annette" was greeted with partisan enthusiasm.

"She is from our island," Danielle whispered, a look of rapt anticipation on her face.

By the end of her second solo, Tyler was squirming in his seat. *God, she's awful. A third-rate imitation of Diana Ross.* He was about to pass his opinion on to Danielle when she turned to him, eyes shining, "Is she not wonderful, Tyler? One day Annette will be a big star. All Lutigua will be proud." He sank back in his chair and took a large gulp of his drink. *Saved by the bell.*

It was well after midnight when they strolled hand-in-hand across the lawn of the 'Belvedere' to the parking lot. "The Minister of Finance, did you see him, Tyler?" Danielle chatted merrily, all traces of her former reticence gone. "In the corner, near to de bar? And de lady with him? Did you see her? She's not long from de schoolroom. I do not think she is his daughter."

As her words floated past him in the fragrant night air, Tyler struggled to pay attention. The drinks he'd downed, one after the other, gave him a feeling of being encased in cotton candy. He was conscious only of the faint scent of Danielle's perfume, of her warm hand in his, of those enticing breasts, rising and falling to the rhythm of her breathing . When they reached the Ford, the idle chatter ceased and she said earnestly:

"Tyler. Please to forgive my asking, but will de driving go well? You have taken many glasses of strong drink tonight."

"Don't worry about it, babe, I'm fine. He fished in his pocket for the keys. "Ah, here we are. Allow me." She was directly behind him as he bent to unlock the door on the passenger side and their bodies collided as he jerked it open with more fervor than he intended. "Sorry about that." ... The American turned suddenly and placed both hands on her shoulders pushing her gently against the car. His mouth sought hers and while the Lutigan did not respond to the light pressure of his tongue to open her lips, she did not struggle. Emboldened by her passivity, he tightened his grip and pushed his body hard against hers, feeling the tautness of her nipples, the inviting curve of thighs imprisoned in his. He renewed his efforts with his tongue and when she resisted, removed a hand from her shoulder placing it on her hipbone where he began kneading roughly with his fingers.

She jerked her head back, "No, Tyler! Please!"

But he was drowning in the taste and touch of her, all peripheral sight and sound lost to him. Danielle's body stiffened automatically when she felt his erection against her, but all efforts to free herself from his demanding and despotic hands and mouth only intensified their probing. With a single despairing motion she sank her teeth into his cheek. He dropped his arms and staggered back.

"What the ...why the hell did you ...?"

Danielle was aghast when she saw the tiny drops of dark blood against his ashen face. "Dear Lord, dear Lord," she moaned softly, "I am not meaning to hurt you, Tyler. Please to forgive me." She stepped back, half turning from him so he would not see her tears.

Damn her. I'll probably get rabies. Can you get rabies from a human bite? My face hurts like hell. Shit. His ears were ringing with the pain and for a moment, he was afraid he'd pass out. He took a deep breath and held out a hand to steady himself against the car. When his head cleared he became aware of the girl, of the tremors that shook her body as she stood with her back to him fighting for control.

"Danielle?" He reached out a hand to offer reassurance, then quickly withdrew it. *I really blew it this time.* "Look, I'm sorry, kid." But she did not answer. A great weariness overtook him. "Come on. I'll take you home."

"I wish to be taking a taxi," she whispered, her back still to him.

"Look, don't be difficult. I promise I won't touch you. Get in the car."

"There. Up de gap... the house with de porch light." The first words she'd spoken since leaving the 'Belvedere'.

He switched off the motor. "Listen, I'm really sorry I spoiled your evening." She refused to look at him, replying austerely as she eased out of the car. "Please to see to your face. Iodine, it is good for broken skin," Her final words through the open window made him wince.

"What you have spoiled this evening, Tyler, is my trust."

As he turned in his sleep, a piercing javelin of pain drove through the tissue and bone of his face to the top of his scalp. In a panic, Tyler stumbled out of bed, fumbling his way in the dark to the bathroom. A cry of disbelief escaped from his lips. The face that stared back at him in the mirror - its one eye a slit, its cheek a swollen angry red with pinpoints of purple where the teeth had left marks - seemed to belong to someone else. *My God, it's infected.* For a long moment he continued staring at his reflection, paralyzed with shock. *Hot water. I've got to soak it in hot water ... and after . . where the hell did I put that antiseptic stuff I brought from Atlanta?*

His fear made him clumsy, but it also gave him the courage required to keep applying the water-soaked towel to the wound. It was an agonizing chore. A half hour later he sank back on his cot and directed an anguished petition to the ceiling: *Please ...please. Don't let it get any worse.* Eventually he fell into a restless sleep on his back, willing his subconscious to wake him if he started turning over.

It was close to noon when he woke again to the strains of Bach, a composer his cabinmate seemed inordinately fond of. For a time he lay stiff and apprehensive, unwilling to face the mirror. Gingerly he let his fingers roam the parameters of his face, relieved he could do so without pain. Eventually he pulled himself off the bed and checked his reflection: the swelling had subsided, his eye looked almost normal. Weak with relief he conscientously reapplied the hot towels, dabbed *Polysporin* over the injured area and covered it with a gauze square held in place with scotch tape. *Looks like hell, but it'll have to do until I can borrow some adhesive from Caswell.* He prayed to be spared Preston's tart, inquisitive tongue.

Over a period of time a certain routine had evolved on Sundays at the cabin; Tyler liked to sleep in late, skipping breakfast and starting the day with instant coffee which he made from tap water. Whereas Avery rose early, took a taxi to the cathedral and returned after services to listen to his records until one, when the main meal of the day was served. (Despite a few complaints from guests, the hotel abided by its policy of serving a light buffet on Sunday evenings so the regular kitchen staff could have the time off.) After tending to his wounded cheek, Tyler washed down three aspirin with a half-tumbler-full of Scotch, followed by strong black coffee. At last the music stopped, the screen door banged shut and he was alone. He remembered that Danielle had this Sunday off. *Thank heaven for small favors.* He certainly wasn't up to facing her.

He spent the remainder of the afternoon before he was due to take over the bar nursing his injured face and wounded pride. In the wake of the fear and pain he'd suffered earlier, Danielle's reaction to his advances - he'd been damn careful not to rush her, hadn't he? - triggered a litany of self-justification.

So I didn't behave like a perfect 'gentleman.' What the hell, she's no kid anymore, she knows the score. Sex, with a capital 'S' is what it's all about. What's so terrible about two, normal healthy adults getting it on together, doing what comes naturally? From what I can see, that's all they do in Lutigua...Where the fuck does she get off making me feel like two cents worth of dog shit just because I made a pass? Acting like I was trying to assault the Virgin Mary? Venting his spleen provided Scranton with a modicum of satisfaction which lasted long enough for him to calm down; but in retrospect he recognized that his outburst was an excuse, a way of protecting himself from the obvious: *There you go again, buddy-boy. So much easier to blame her when the signals were all there from the beginning. Danielle never once gave you the come-on ...never once indicated she thought of you as anything more than a co-worker, a friend. But as usual, you let that horny prick of yours take over and spoil things.*

Late in the afternoon he left the cabin and went in search of Leona Caswell. As he passed the pool area he noted that several of the travel agents were taking a break from their labors: A few lay sprawled on the lounge chairs under thick coats of suntan oil while a small group frolicked in the pool, tossing about a red plastic ball.

"Yoo-hoo! Hello! Mr. Scranton!"

Miss Adams. Just what I need. Tyler quickened his pace and didn't look back.

"How's it been going, Brian?"

"It's quiet now, Mister Tyler, but lunchtime was busy."

"Where's James? Isn't he supposed to be helping you today?"

"True. But James call to say he's not comin' in."

"You mean you've been on duty by yourself since eleven this morning?

"Yes, sir."

"Is James ill? Why didn't he get someone to cover for him?"

"He didn't say he was sick," Brian's face registered his discomfort with the subject.

Tyler was visibly irritated. *Time I started pulling in the reins around here.* "O.K. Brian, scoot. I'll take over."

As he went about checking supplies, his fingers absently patted the new bandage on his cheek. Leona had changed the dressing with quick, capable hands, her only comment when she saw the wound, a quick intake of breath. She asked no questions, but then Tyler had counted on that traditional English reserve .

"Mr. Scranton?"

"Hello there, Miss Adams. Can I get you something?"

"A rum punch would be mah-vu-less. I've developed quite a passion for them."

Arriving at the bar from the pool, she'd thrown a beach top over her bikini, a lightweight, gauzy affair which did nothing to hide the sturdy figure crested by firm, generous breasts. The sun had lightened her hair and the tan spread evenly across her body enhanced her looks.

"It's Tyler, isn't it? I heard someone call you 'Tyler.'"

"Yes, ma'am."

"I hate formality, don't you? I'll call you Tyler if you promise to call me Marie."

"My pleasure. Enjoying yourself, Marie?"

"It's been mah-vu-less. I shall hate to leave. You have no idea how refreshing it is to discover an unspoiled island in the middle of the Caribbean. And of course, the kind of clients I handle will love Belle Jours. It's classy in a quiet sort of way, just like the people I do business with."

"Mrs. Foster-Jones will be pleased to hear it."

They had the bar to themselves and for the next twenty minutes she plied him with questions about the hotel. Despite a heavy sprinkling of 'incredible,' 'mah-vu-less,' and 'divine,' it was obvious that beneath those fashionably-styled peroxided locks was a penetrating mind. He enjoyed himself thoroughly.

"Hey, fella', a man could die of thirst around here."

Marie slid from her stool and said winsomely, "You're wanted. Besides,it's time to change for dinner. Shall we continue our little dialogue later?"

"Sure thing. Sundays are usually slow and we shut the bar down early, but since it's my turf, I can do as I like. How about a night cap, say around 9:30?"

"Mah-vu-less. See you then."

She appeared as promised. Tyler took one look at the gown she was wearing and decided it had been designed with debauchery in mind.

"You look fantastic, Marie."

"Why thank you, Tyler. I'll have that drink you mentioned earlier. You'll join me, won't you?"

Over their second cognac, he said, "Tell me about yourself, Marie. How did you get into the travel business?"

She glanced at the clock behind the bar. "It's nearly eleven. Can't we continue this conversation somewhere else, around the pool or on my patio?"

"Sorry. No can do. The hotel has a firm rule about employees and guests mixing it up... and I like my job."

She pouted for a second, then proffered a resigned grin, "Let's have another round then. Incidentally, Tyler darling, has anyone ever told you what a divine body you have? Don't laugh, I'm serious. But do wipe that smug look off your face."

"Compliments like that, lady, can lead to serious trouble. By the way, you more than hold your own in that department."

"My last husband - number two, that is - couldn't keep his hands off me. He was an Italian Count, terribly gallant *outside* the bedroom; his title came with a broken-down palazzo surrounded by acres of fallow vineyards and ten thousand greasy, garlic-chewing cousins. It was a disaster. Luckily I took precautions and there were no little bambinos to add to the confusion." She had resumed her maiden name, she told him, as soon as she got back to the States. "I was dead broke after the divorce ... no marketable skills, but I'd had lots of experience booking international flights. Ergo, the travel industry. And now that you've heard my life story, how about yours?"

Tyler mentioned a few of the salient points.

"You mean you've never been married?"

Once. Briefly. So briefly, it doesn't count."

"You're not a fag or anything are you?"

"What do *you* think?

"I think we'd better call it an evening, Tyler darling, much as I hate the thought. An all-day trip around the island is planned for tomorrow and the bus leaves at an ungodly hour. Tuesday, of course, we fly on to St. Maarten's"

"I'd like to see more of you, Marie. Preferably when I'm not stuck behind this bar."

"What did you have in mind? Something terribly physical, I hope. But not in a car, darling. I'm too old for that."

"What would you say to checking out of here tomorrow night? The government operates a small motel near the airport where I could meet you. The motel's not fancy, sort of a sub-par 'Day's Inn' without TV, but we'd have the night together and we could always liven things up with an X-rated movie of our own. You can catch up with your group later."

"The lady says 'yes.' Absolutely! Just so long as there aren't any roaches. Roaches spoil my sex drive."

"I can't promise about the roaches, but I'll try to keep you too busy to notice."

Late the following evening, Tyler rapped on the door of Room #8, the number given to him by the night clerk.

"Tyler, is that you?"

"Hi, babe." He stepped inside the softly lit room, his eyes drawn immediately to the seductive figure lounging on top of the counterpane. "I brought some booze and ice, but I forgot the popcorn."

"To hell with the popcorn. Fix me a drink, and guess what, darling? I'm not wearing a thing under this negligee."

"Let's skip the formalities then, shall we Miss Adams? Just spread those gorgeous legs. I'm coming in for a landing."

CHAPTER XIII

"What's your excuse for not showing up on Sunday, James?"

"No excuse, Mister Scranton."

"A reason, then? You must have a reason." *Come on, kid, make up something if you have to. Don't force me to throw the book at you.*

"No, sir." The young Lutiguan stubbornly refused to look at Tyler. Uncharacteristically, he stood with his hands jammed in his pants' pockets, an expression of barely concealed defiance etched on his fine features.

"Listen, James. You can tell me. Is there a problem at home? Get some girl pregnant? What?"

The boy's lips tightened, barricading words behind lock and key.

"Damn it all, James, you know I can't let you get away with this."

"No, sir."

"O.K. then. You're grounded for a week, off the payroll 'til next Tuesday." *Am I crazy? He actually looks relieved.*

"Can I go now, Mister Scranton?"

"Yeah, beat it. No! Wait a minute! There's something you need to hear." Wash's son obediently retraced his steps. "Look, James. I *know* you. You're smart, you're a good worker. I haven't a clue why you're behaving like this, but you'd better remember: I never let my personal feelings interfere with running the bar."

Tyler watched the retreating figure with a sense of unease. *Something's up. Something fishy, but I'll be damned if I can figure out what it is.* He'd like to sound out Danielle, discuss it with her, but their relationship was at an impasse. *After the fiasco at the 'Belvedere' she works as hard at avoiding me as I do her. Too bad we can't erase the raunchy parts and start over.*

Last night his male vanity, more deeply wounded than his cheek, had been refurbished and restored, his sexual appetite sated after his fling with Marie Adams. In the past, an evening of carefree and unrestrained sex with a woman left Tyler ready to take on the world, the act of copulation unleashing untapped reservoirs of energy along with a euphoric sense of well-being. But on the early morning drive back from the motel to Belle Jours he'd been overcome with a pervading sense of lethargy and depression. *These one night stands sure as hell ain't what they used to be.* Unwillingly, his mind wandered back to the evening with Danielle, to the sight of her in the parking lot, shoulders shaking as she tried to stem her tears after his brash and tactless assault ... her concern for his face in spite of it all. *That's one helluva gal. God, I behaved stupidly. She didn't deserve it. If only ...* All at once he had a terrifying vision of the future, a future of moving restlessly from job to job, of having one brief affair after another until there was no place left to go, no woman who would have him. The yawning emptiness of that vision staggered him. Had he been so busy guarding his independence, keeping himself removed from any lasting and serious commitment that he'd missed the boat? By-passed a chance for a real relationship with someone whom he could love and trust, who would love him in return? *Someone to come home to ...* A pang of loneliness engulfed him, he felt rudderless, like a stranger in a hostile land wandering its mean streets in a hopeless quest for comfort and sustenance.

Shaken to the core, he gripped the steering wheel in silent protest.

Tuesday marked the beginning of a new month, time to tabulate receipts and inventory and report to Mrs. Foster-Jones. While he cross-checked bills from suppliers, a spasmodic twitch reminded him of that panicky moment in the midst of lovemaking when the bandage had come unstuck. He'd fumbled for it blindly and somehow managed to smooth the tape back into place without Marie ever noticing.

"Coming to lunch, old man? You look like you could use some nourishment."

Tyler sat hunched over an untidy mass of papers, so absorbed in checking figures he hadn't heard the bookkeeper come onto the screened porch. Luckily, his bandaged cheek was hidden from view. Preston lingered, his hand on the door knob.

"Big night on the town?" he asked with a smirk.

"It was o.k."

"Well, are you coming or not?"

"No thanks. I'll send for a sandwich later. I'm not moving 'til I get these damn sheets to tally."

An hour later he sat back and rubbed his eyes, conscious that the side of his face was throbbing painfully. Wearily he went about resoaking the wound and changing the dressing, his mind preoccupied by what he now knew was a major discrepancy in inventory. *F-J is not going to be happy when I tell her we're short: three Scotch, four gin, two brandy.* He looked at his watch: just enough time to grab a bite to eat before their monthly meeting in her private suite.

"It's unfortunate, Tyler, but these things happen," the hotel owner said calmly, thrusting aside a magazine. "The point is, what do you plan to do about it?"

"I thought you might have some suggestions on how to handle it. I'm a little out of my depth."

The woman was slow to respond and when she did, all signs of geniality had evaporated.

"What you're really saying,Tyler, is you don't want to make a scene—'rock the boat' as they say these days." Her look was frigid. "See here. I hired you to *manage* the bar. Preventing theft is just one of the requisites of being in charge. And while we're on the subject, I've been meaning to speak to you about your attitude. You seem to encourage a 'buddy-buddy' relationship with your men." Her eyes narrowed as she snapped, "I'm here to tell you it doesn't work. You're not running for public office, you're running a bar. You have to be tough with these Lutiguans or they'll rob you blind! Being tough may not make you 'popular,' but it will get their attention, maybe even their respect." She picked up the magazine.

"Anything else?"

"I docked Wash's son. A week off without pay. I hated to do it, but he's been damn irresponsible lately."

"I heard."

"You heard? It only happened this morning."

"Tyler," she said drily, "when are you going to realize this hotel is a very small, inbred community."

Needing time to sort things out, to shake off the sour aftertaste of her censure, those scornful words adding to his disconsolate state, the American drifted down to the comforting solitude of the beach. He was chastened by the older woman's perceptive indictment. She was right. He'd spent a lifetime avoiding direct confrontations, preferring always to smooth things over, look the other way, a conditioned reflex he'd learned in order to survive those traumatic encounters with his mother. *You've just been told off by a pro, buddy-boy. But then she never came up against my old lady. A real scrapper, that one. And with Myra, you could never win.*

Warm sea water nipped at his bare ankles, a lone sandpiper skittered companionably ahead as he paced up and down the shoreline, haunted anew by memories of his mother's flailing tongue,

They began, those scenes, innocently enough: muddy footprints on the kitchen linoleum, a bike left out in the rain overnight, tar on his school pants. *Over fucking nothing at all.*

"What you got to say for yourself?" she'd ask with sinister calm. After being smacked across the mouth a few times when he stammered to explain, he learned never to answer back, no matter how unjust the accusation. Afterwards, as he stood biting his cheek to hold back the tears, she'd leave him with a withering, "You'll be the death of me yet, boy. Just like your father. Think a pretty face excuses everything." He was plagued with guilt and remorse for crimes he never understood, knowing the bike, the mud, were not the issues.

Clinging tenaciously to the life raft of hope, he doggedly sought ways to placate her. A cologne called *Nuit de Paris* cost five dollars at Woolworth's, a staggering sum to an eleven year old. Tyler determined to buy it for Myra's birthday; surely a gift of such extravagance would win her over! He hoarded dimes and quarters earned from odd jobs in the neighborhood. *Shovelled so damn many walks that winter, my ears nearly fell off from frostbite.* Like a faded lithotint his mind's eye recaptured that bitter birthday eve: his mother at the kitchen table in a house dress, *the grey one with the pink cabbage roses.* Chapped, nicotine-stained fingers carefully remove the dark blue bottle from its silver box and raise it to the light. "My, my, Tyler," she says approvingly. His heart pounds with excitement as she uncaps the top and leans forward to sniff its contents. Her nose begins to crinkle the way it does when she suspects a stray cat has relieved itself on the back porch. Silence, broken only by the tick-tock of the kitchen clock.

"It's a pretty bottle, son," she says at last, replacing the cap, "but no self-respecting woman'd wear a scent like that."

Neddie was the only one she loved. But then Tyler loved him, too. Neddie, with his oversized head attached to a leprechaun's body, so skinny the veins in his arms and up the back of his legs were like ribbon streamers. Unblinking grey eyes under a stubble of lash and a lopsided smile to charm the angels. Neddie.

Barely three and toddling after Tyler from room to room, thumb in mouth, free hand clutching a dirty, yellow blanket. At five, attentive as a small sparrow, perched on the front steps, eyes following Tyler as he mows the lawn, tinkers with his bike. The wiry seven year old, tagging after Tyler and his friends.

"Can'tcha do somethin' about that kid brother of yours, Tyler?"

"Go home, Neddie. Beat it!" The momentary retreat then reappearance of that familiar, spare frame. Always at a distance, always within sight.

"Neddie, I tole ya. Beat it!"

One of the boys picks up a rock and flings it lazily in Neddie's direction.

"Cut that out! You don't need to go throwin' rocks at him."

"Well do somethin' then, Tyler. After all, he's *your brother.*"

Loyal. *Stubborn as a damn mule.* Neddie, whose dogged devotion to his older brother was the one spark of warmth in that otherwise bleak household.

What the hell. Can't use Myra as an excuse forever. Time to cut the umbilical cord and move on.

In response to a terse notice on the bulletin board, Tyler's staff gathered before breakfast in the dining hall. The men were baffled by the peremptory summons and spoke of it amongst themselves in low, guarded tones. An awkward hush fell across the room as the American moved briskly forward. He spoke for a half hour. His parting shot to them, "Don't forget, theft of property is a crime and will be dealt with accordingly." The men filed quietly out of the hall, sobered by the uncompromising tone of his remarks. Tyler pulled his head barman aside.

"Think they got the message, Sam?"

"Yes sir, Mister Tyler. They knows you ain't foolin' around."

* * * * * * * * * *

A succession of spectacular Lutiguan days - the sky an inimitable pale blue backdrop to spun-sugar clouds, an affable sun with trade winds keeping the humidity at bay - did nothing to lighten Tyler's spirits. For days he avoided conversation with members of the staff and when his shift ended at the bar, sought the solitude of his own room where he spent his waking moments sipping whiskey and immersing himself in one paperback thriller after another.

Hurrying to drop off the weekly bar tabs at the office, the American paused at the sight of a group of new arrivals clustered in front of the Reception desk; nearby Colin, the bellhop, stood guard over a mound of luggage. *How did we get so lucky? Get a load of those beauties checking in, especially the blonde in the navy pants' suit. 'I pass' on the tall, skinny one with the weird haircut, though.* He felt his spirits lifting.

Thinking of the evening ahead, Tyler spent an extra few moments checking his appearance in the mirror, adding an extra splash of *Brut* before leaving the cabin;

he was keen to start his shift and get a closer look at the newcomers. At the sound of women's voices, he looked up from the daiquiri he was mixing to see four of them engaged in animated conversation as they headed his way.

"Hi," said the one with freckles and an engaging smile, "we're here to collect our complimentary rum punches," holding aloft white cards from the hotel.

"Welcome to Belle Jours, ladies. Four rum punches coming up."

"Make that five. Sarah will be along in a sec."

"Right." A quartet of faces bearing the glowing pink of initiation to the Caribbean sun sat in rapt attention as he lined up the glasses and set to work.

"What's that you're sprinkling on top?" asked the tall, skinny one with black laquered hair in the shape of a helmet. (Up close he saw she was older than the others.)

"Nutmeg from Grenada. Freshly ground."

"Are you from the States? You *sound* like an American?"

"Yep, born and raised in the fair state of Pennsylvania."

"Philadelphia?" the blonde asked languidly, shoving a lock of hair back from her face with a practiced gesture.

"Sorry. Not even close. By the way, the name is Tyler," he said with a grin directed at them all, but meant particularly for the blonde.

"Glad to meet you, Tyler." Freckle-face was like an eager puppy. "I'm Marcy." She pointed down the line of bar stools and introduced each of her friends .

While sipping their punches, the foursome aired enthusiastic comments about the island and their accomodations, then switched to discussing plans for the following day. "Do you think Sarah will want to take a tour of the island?" one of them asked in hushed tones.

"Oh I hope so. This trip couldn't have come at a better time. She needs to get her mind off ..."

"Shush. Here she comes."

The missing member of their party, the one they called Sarah, was greeted with noisy affection. (Since he couldn't help overhearing the conversation, Tyler assumed someone close to the young woman had recently died. He took note of the ovoid shape of her face with its fine, small features, the toffee hair streaked by the sun and the oversize glasses perched on a sunburnt nose. She had the look of a sombre owl. A sad, fragile owl, nonetheless.)

In the ensuing exchange of banter Tyler learned that they all were on term break from their teaching posts at a private school for girls in Greenwich.

"I'll have you know, sir, *Miss Pringle's* is a veddy veddy superior school," Marcy explained, imitating a voice familiar to her companions who hooted with laughter.

"Veddy, veddy superior."

"Actually, it's a haven for the social register's messed-up *enfant terribles,*" the skinny one added scarcastically. "Spoiled little bitches who can't tell a geometric mean from a Chinese take-out menu, and could care less."

"Oh, come on, Ann. They're not all that bad!"

"Wanna bet, Sarah? Remember hon', this is your first year of teaching. Wait 'til you've been at *Pringles* as long as the rest of us."

"Look, I didn't come all this way to talk about school!"

"Hear! Hear! Let's make a pact right now: no mention of *Pringle's* or its inmates for the rest of the vacation!" Marcy's words were greeted with vigorous applause.

By the end of their second round of rum punches, the names belonging to the other two faces were wedged in Scranton's memory: the one called 'Freddie' had a ski-slope nose, a birthmark on her right cheek, and an extravagant pair of knockers, and the spectacular blonde with the spectacular figure was Stacey.

Before going into dinner, they plied Tyler with questions: Where was the best place to snorkle and could they rent equipment from the hotel? Would he recommend they take a tour of the island? Where could they buy souvenirs? Their presence was like a breath of star-spangled American air and when they dispersed for the evening meal, the barman experienced the first pangs of homesickeness since coming to the island.

Hoping to wean Stacey from the others, he was chagrined to find that the young women stuck together, pursuing every activity en masse. On his half-day off he volunteered to show them around the island, an invitation they accepted with alacrity. He paid particular attention to Stacey on the outing and was rewarded by her insistence on sitting next to him on the way home. ("Freddie, you go in the back. It's my turn to sit up front with Tyler.")

When a rainy day spoiled their plans to go snorkeling, they begged him to join them in a new board game called 'Trivial Pursuit.' ("Five's an uneven number, "Ann explained, "we need you to make up the second team.") He cleared with the front office, commandeered Brian to take his place, and before joining them in the Lounge changed into a *LaCoste* shirt the sales' girl told him matched the green of his eyes. After the first few questions, he knew he was in over his head.

"Come on, Tyler, don't you even know the capitol of North Dakota?" Stacey could scarcely hide the scorn in her voice. Their team was losing badly.

"So what?," Freddie said in his defense. "Teaching French hasn't helped you much when it comes to Science and Nature."

"Let's get on with it," said Marcy, the peacemaker, "no need to take this personally. It's only a game."

The barman couldn't wait for it to be over. Except for Sports, he'd fluffed too many answers; when Ann suggested a second round, he begged off, pleading the need to return to duty. Mumbling, "Catch you later," Tyler bolted to his cabin where he hastily downed a double Scotch before relieving Brian. *Well you've gone and done it, buddy-boy, Made an absolute ass of yourself.* Certain that he'd been the object of derision as soon as he left the Lounge, he wasn't looking forward to the cocktail hour. *Only two days left before they pull outta here. Might as well chalk up trying to score with Stacey ... a dead loss after the fiasco this afternoon.*

Ann and Sarah were the first of their party to arrive at the bar. Both women were smartly turned out in anticipation of the special barbeque with entertainment by a steel band, always a popular evening with guests and locals alike. The diningroom was fully booked and the bar was buzzing like a beehive but they managed to wedge themselves in at the far corner.

As he served their drinks, Tyler noticed that mousy Sarah had been transformed: dressed in a melon-coloured silk pants' suit with ropes of beads at her neck, her toffee hair in a becoming upsweep, she was suddenly quite appealing. Even Ann, whose taste in clothes did nothing to mollify her string-bean figure, was benefiting from her choice of a flowing chiffon gown of buttery yellow. They greeted the barman like a long lost friend, not some-one they'd been with a few hours before.

"You two look great. You'll have to beat off the men with baseball bats once the music starts ."

"What men?" Ann asked sarcastically. "The only male specimens I've seen since we arrived are three old married goats, one with a twitch, one with a paunch the size of Yankee stadium and a bald, skinny one with a cane."

Tyler laughed. "Don't be such a cynic. The evening's young."

The rest of their group strolled into the bar and not a few heads turned as they made their way to their friends. Stacy, of course, outshone them all, her skin-tight black sheath catching the appreciative eye of every male present, young or old.

"Sorry, we took the last seats," Sarah said. "Do you mind standing, or do you want to move to a table and have our drinks there?" Stacey was all for moving on, but she was outvoted and they remained clustered at the end of the bar happily chatting amongst themselves, unaware that their presence was causing a stir.

As the waiters were clearing the dessert plates, the band broke into its opening number and within minutes, Stacey was being led onto the dance floor; Marcy and Freddie soon followed. No one, it seemed, was asking Ann to dance; turning away several prospective partners, Sarah loyally stayed at her friend's side. From his vantage point at the bar, Tyler had a clear view of their table as well as the dance floor. *Damn nice of Sarah to stick with her buddy. God, I wish I were free to ask Stacey to dance.*

Business at the bar picked up again and there wasn't time to monitor the comings and goings of the quintet. Close to midnight, however, as the flow of drink orders slowed to a trickle, he glanced at their empty table and then over to the crowded dance floor where he saw Ann gamely being twirled around by a man a head shorter than she; seconds later Stacey glided into view. Her blonde head was resting on the shoulder of her partner, who held her possessively in his arms. Not for the first time, Tyler wished like hell he'd chosen some other occupation.

On his way to the front desk the next morning, he started along the pathway at the far side of the pool, but detoured when he saw Stacey lying on a deck chair by the deep end. He couldn't believe his luck: she was by herself. *If I play my cards right, maybe we can get together when my three-week break comes up this summer.*

"Good morning, Stacey."

She pushed her dark glasses up over her forehead and struggled to a sitting position. Her entire body, except for parts covered by a scant bikini, was a toasted, golden brown, her hair bleached by the sun. His loins ached as he struggled to keep his eyes from resting on the enticing curve of her breasts, the tiny V of her bikini. The thought crossed his mind that she'd make a perfect *Playboy* centerfold.

"Oh, it's you, Tyler." She seemed genuinely glad to see him.

"Sorry. I didn't mean to disturb you. Where're your buddies?"

"They went charging off in a taxi to look for souvenirs, but not me. I'm not going to miss one second of this glorious sun."

He squatted down next to her chair. "Enjoyed your stay at Belle Jours?"

"It's been o.k. A lot quieter than I expected, if you know what I mean."

"Try to imagine what it was like before you came! Your crew really livened this place up; you even made me forget how far from home I am. I'll be sorry to see you leave tomorrow, Stacey. Do you think you might come back some day?"

"Who knows? There's so much of the world to see. Returning to the same place year in and year out, that's what old fogies do, don't they?"

He laughed. "If you say so! How about it, can I buy you a drink?"

"No thanks. Too early in the day for me. But don't run off. Stay and keep me company." She sighed disconsolately. "I was just lying here thinking how much I dread having to go back and face those teenage monsters."

"You teach French, right?"

"That's what I'm paid to do, but the only French those snotty kids are interested in is the kind you find on a wine list or a menu." She sighed and laid back again in her chair. "Be a love and hand me that bottle of suntan lotion, would you, Tyler?"

He watched in silence as her long, painted fingers applied thick cream to her chest and stomach. *Another minute of this and I'm going to get a hard-on.* "Why are you teaching, since you obviously don't like it?"

"Believe me, I'm out of *Miss la-de-da Pringles* come June. That's when my boyfriend will be finished at Grad School. We plan to get married, you know, next September."

"No. I didn't know."

The young Americans were due to leave on an early flight Saturday morning. In a fit of pique– he couldn't believe how badly he'd misjudged his chances with Stacey - Tyler decided he'd had enough. *I'm not sticking around for the 'goodbyes.'* "Look," he told Sam, "I'm off to St. James. Take over my shift and don't bother to tell me you can't, because I don't want to hear it."

"Yessir, Mister Tyler."

He took the keys to the Ford from Danielle with a preemptory, "Thanks" and was out of the office before she could speak. She shook her head, *Tyler look like a man what just took a bite of a sour akee.*

CHAPTER XIV

"Miz Danielle! Miz Danielle! Hurry. We needs you en Miz Caswell to come." The voice, with its undercurrent of hysteria, belonged to Mike, a young dishwasher on the kitchen staff.

"Miss Caswell's not here, boy." She stared in consternation at the sixteen year old's appearance, at the white apron and pants plastered to his body, drenched in a gummy orange substance from which emanated the familiar odor of fish.

"What's the trouble? Why are you looking so?"

Wiping his hands distractedly on the soiled apron, the youth was on the verge of tears.

"Oh Miz Danielle, it's Mistah Corbin. He gone crazy. He turned over de soup pot ...en he's throwin' things... Annie, she's locked herself in de cooler en Esther ...Esther, she's lyin' on de floor with blood all over de place ...Oh mon, I tellin' you . . "A sob prompted by uncertainty and fear broke from his lips.

"Hush now, boy. You're too big to cry." She pushed past him and hurried across the lobby in time to hear a salvo of bloodcurdling shrieks and a high-pitched wail in the direction of the dining hall. As she quickened her pace, she barely missed colliding with Wash, who was rounding the corner with a tray of sandwiches and drinks. The startled old man hung on in grim bewilderment as plates and glasses slid alarmingly to one side. He called out to the retreating figure, "You needin' me, Miss Danielle?"

"No please, Mr. Wilson. You take care of de guests," several of whom were sunning by the pool and called out to her as she passed by:

"What's going on?"

"Is someone hurt?"

"Has there been an accident?"

Like bloodhounds drawn to the scent of prey, guests, waiters and hotel maids were congregated in a jostling knot around the entrance to the kitchen. Tyler, with Sam at his heels, thrust his way through the milling bodies, yanked open the door and stepped inside. He was back out in a moment, pulling the door firmly shut behind him.

"All right, folks," he said calmly. "Move back, please. There's nothing to see. Hotel personnel, return to your stations at once!"

"Did somebody get murdered in there?" shouted a heavy-set man with a Kaiser Wilhelm mustache and a sunburned paunch.

His allegation caught the crowd's fancy: "Murder! Did he say '*murder*'?"

"No one's been murdered, I assure you." *Stupid bastard. I'd like to wring his fat neck.* "There's been a slight mishap in the kitchen and some of our people are upset. Now please, step back."

They ignored his plea and remained intractably in place, eyes focussed on the kitchen door. What dissuaded them finally was the barman's stare, the challenging thrust of his chin and implacable stance, like a guard at the palace gate. With shrugs and sighs of disappointment, they slowly dispersed. Over their heads Tyler saw Danielle wading through the tide of disengaging bodies.

Once inside the kitchen with the door shut and bolted, Tyler, Sam and the woman mutely surveyed the surrealistic chaos that greeted them. Gobs of thick orange - pumpkin soup with bits of crab, tomato and kingfish - dripped from the walls and lay in oily fetor on the floor. Potatoes and onions, skillets and saucepans were scattered everywhere. Broken pieces of china mingled with particles of food lay heaped in a sickening mound on the floor at the end of the serving counter. Three terrified kitchen helpers could be seen huddled against a wall in the passageway into the food storage area. Someone had rescued Annie from the cooler and the heavy, middle-aged Lutiguan was leaning against the large double sink moaning into her hands. Esther lay in a fetal position under the wooden cutting table; as soon as she realized she had an audience, her wails turned to whimpers: "I dyin'. Dat man's kill't me wid his knife."

"I'll be damned," Tyler said softly, "will you look at this. Sam, go tell Osbert to send two of his waiters to help clean up this mess. Danielle, you'd better see to Annie. I'll have a look at Esther. I wonder where that rascal Corbin is?"

The story, when they finally pieced it together, was fairly simple: Corbin had been moody and irritable all morning; the kitchen crew, only too aware that his petulance signaled trouble, was nervous and on edge. Annie and Esther shared the task of dicing and chopping ingredients for individual salads; every few moments, Corbin would pass by to inspect their progress, each time berating them for their slowness: "If you two don' wear out, you 'll rust out." The women became more and more flustered. On his last march past them, the Master Chef snatched a meat cleaver from its hook and smashed it bladeside down on the cutting table within inches of Esther's hand. Both women jumped back in alarm and Esther inadvertently cut herself with her own chopping knife, but in her panic she was convinced the chef had mortally wounded her with his cleaver. She dove under the table and began shrieking, adding fuel to Corbin's rage . He grabbed the tureen full of soup and hurled it at the door where a luckless Mike was beating a hasty retreat. Screaming an indecipherable 'Yah! Yah! Yah! interspersed with curses, he completed his handiwork.

The gardener was recruited to drive Esther to the hospital and Annie was sent home by taxi. Sam plied the frightened kitchen workers with cokes and cajoled them into staying on to help with dinner while a team organized by Osbert scrubbed down the walls and floor. Between them Danielle and Tyler worked at restoring order. 'Thank-goodness-Foster-Jones-and-Caswell-were-invited-out-to-lunch' became their mutual mantra as they skirted fetid orange puddles to pick up the crockery that was salvagable and make a cursory inventory of what remained. They were able to assemble enough ingredients from the well-stocked larder to make up a simple menu for the evening meal.

"Now, the $64,000 question–who do we get too supervise the cooking?"

"There's a lady we call Aunty Roo who was de cook for our Prime Minister 'til her back gave her so much pain, she had to leave. Aunty isn't able to work a full day, but she will come to help out at Belle Jours if I ask her."

"Your Aunty Roo sounds like a gift from the gods. We may need her for more than a day, but that's up to to Foster-Jones to decide, not me."

"Please tell me, Tyler, what shall we do about de guests? Bad news, it travels by de fastest post. Such tales will hurt de hotel."

"Right. I've an idea. Let's throw a party this evening and ply everyone with rum punches on-the-house. After a few drinks, they'll forget about the uproar this morning and hopefully, they won't care what's served for dinner, either."

She flashed him a look of wondering approval. "What a wise plan, Tyler. Mrs. Foster-Jones will be pleased."

"Not so pleased when she hears about this little fiasco. By the way, has anyone seen Corbin?"

"Mr. Wilson has gone to look for him."

"I'd better get a move on. Plenty to do before tonight." But he was reluctant to break away. The crises had brought them together and the coolness that had characterized their relationship since the incident in the parking lot had evaporated.

"Hey, lady," the American said softly, extending his hand, "friends again?"

"Yes, please," she said, gripping it firmly with a smile, "friends."

The next morning Wash came by the office and whispered to Cleo from the doorway, "Mister Corbin's back."

"He stayin'?"

"Seemlike. De Mistress en Miss Caswell were shut up wid him a long time. Den Miss Caswell en Corbin go to de kitchen en she's tellin' all de folks there that everything is sweet again, not to worry. She give Corbin a poke in de ribs en he say he's 'sorry', but he's not lookin' too happy 'bout it."

"You think Mr. Wilson, maybe de trouble in de kitchen is over?"

"I prays so, chile. I prays so."

The following week James appeared at the start of his shift, sponging off tables with an air of conscientious grimness which Tyler found disconcerting. *Wish I knew what was eating him. I'd like to talk to Wash, but James would never forgive me.*

Dry winds blew across the Atlantic from Western Africa and settled over the island, a rare phenomenon during the winter season; the winds turned the grass and vegetation a bleak, greyish brown. Along the beaches giant waves pummeled and clawed at the sand like avenging spirits and the accompanying undertow made swimming in the sea a prohibitive risk. Unappetizing blankets of kelp from the ocean floor covered the shores at low tide filling the surrounding air with a harsh, metallic stink. The island's water supply dropped precipitously forcing the government to declare a state of emergency. Voluntary rationing was instituted and when that failed, the police were ordered to arrest offenders.

Foster-Jones had an exasperating conversation with the Minister of Agriculture on the phone, her plea to exempt the hotel from the ban eliciting only his 'sympathy' and 'regret.' She sent Caswell by taxi to the Minister's office with three hundred U.S. dollars in an unmarked envelope. He called within the hour to say "I been studyin' your problem. Not to worry, now. You take all de water you needs."

Many of the paying guests at Belle Jours took the unseemly weather as a personal affront; they clustered around the pool and bar, drinking heavily and snapping peevishly at the innately sunny Lutiguans who served them. Late one night a woman guest, member of a charter group from Munich, set the bed clothes on fire when she fell asleep with a burning cigarette in her hand. Smoke was discovered billowing through the air vent by Neville, the night watchman, at about the same moment the woman herself awoke. Panic-stricken howls in a Teutonic tongue pierced the heavy night air causing pandemonium among those who were still awake. The glass door on the woman's patio was locked, forcing Neville to smash it with a coral rock; he reached his hand inside and was able to unlatch the door, but the woman was so confused and hysterical, she refused to leave. Fortunately, two men from her party arrived and addressing her sternly in their native tongue were able to coax her to come outside.

Lionel, the other Lutiguan on duty, ran to fetch Tyler and Avery. By the time they arrived at the scene most of the guests were huddled together on the parched grass under the palms. With only a skeleton staff on hand and water pressure so low it rendered garden hoses redundant, the two men organized a bucket brigade manned by willing guests to siphon water from the pool; their timely efforts prevented the fire from spreading.

Shortly after dawn, Mrs. Foster-Jones, pale and obviously shaken, appeared at the dining hall where the four exhausted hotel employees were drinking coffee. "You have saved my hotel," she said feelingly. "I am deeply grateful." She singled out the two Lutiguans, praising them for the courage and quick-thinking; when they rose to leave, she escorted them to the driveway, an unprecedented gesture on her part.

Tired and begrimed from their labors, Tyler and Avery trudged up to the cabin.

"That stupid woman! Imagine, smoking in bed!"

"Mrs. Schmidt isn't the first, Avery. She won't be the last, either. It's why insurance rates are sky high and why hotel owners get ulcers."

Spurred by the lure of generous overtime pay, the local workmen eschewed the national mania for putting off until tomorrow or the day after what should have been done weeks before, and the damaged rooms were made habitable in record time.

CHAPTER XV

Dat chile o'mine. God never made a sweeter boy en He save him up for last. Never a day's worry is he givin' his Mummy en me...after Mister Scranton take him on, a prouder boy on dis island you wouldn't find. Den it seem like de devil creep in de window one night en steal all my James' sweetness away. Dis mornin' his eyes is heavy wid sorrow, like a widder at de graveside, his body wound tight like a cherry too long in de sun en 'bout to bust its skin... Lord! Lord! ... all dis worryin' makes my head to beat like a drum . ... en we all know de trouble tree don't bear fruit.

* * * * * * * * * * *

"A good-looking fellow like you, James, I'll bet the girls don't give you a moment's peace."

"No, sir, Mister Preston."

"Come now, don't tell me you haven't got a steady girl?"

"True. Got no time, no money neither."

"Don't we pay you enough here at Belle Jours?"

"Yessir. But de money is passin' to my Mummy. She en Daddy is gettin' old now. Time's soon comin' when my Daddy can't work no more."

"What have we here! The Fifth Commandment, alive and viable on Lutigua! I'm impressed. You must understand, James, in the United States fellows your age aren't as conscientious about their filial responsibilities."

"Yes, please."

"You haven't the faintest idea what I'm talking about, do you?"

"No sir. Will that be all?"

"Yes, for now." James had gained the screened porch when Avery called, "Wait! Just a minute." The New Yorker reappeared from the back of the cabin with a tan calfskin wallet; he deftly withdrew several bills and thrust them toward the young Lutiguan. "Here, James. I'm a great believer in rewarding virtue. It's damn hard come by these days."

"I can't take money from you, Mister Preston."

"Surely you can accept a gift from a well-wisher?"

"There's no cause for you to be givin' me money."

"You've humbled me, James," Preston said with a mocking air. "I should have guessed. With you, virtue is its own reward. A most commendable attitude. Certainly a rare one on this fair island." He replaced the money in his wallet with a preoccupied air. "Well trot off, now. I'm sure you're needed in the bar."

* * * * * * * * * *

"James, Mister Preston called on de house phone to say de kitchen forgot to send along butter wid his roll. Get it en take it to him, boy."

"Mister Osbert, I saw de butter on his plate!"

"Don't mout me, boy. Just do it."

"Can't Walter or LeRoy carry it to de cabin?"

"Mister Preston send for *you*, boy. It don't do to cross a man like Mister Preston. You've got to dance to the drumbeat, James, if you wants to keep your job." *That man, Preston, he's like a snake lyin' on his belly, waitin' in de marsh grass for a tasty morsel. Him, wid his tongue too big to fit, all de time callin' here en orderin' me to send that boy. Why James, I asks myself? Then I catch that white devil givin' Wash's boy a look. His evil eye give him away. When you see a man like that in de daylight, you don't need a candle to know him at night.*

* * * * * * * * * * *

"Put the tray on the table by the window, James, then come help me with this extension cord. Tell me if it's long enough to reach the socket." Avery was standing on a borrowed stepladder adjusting the last of the Christmas lights he'd strung across the front of the cabin.

"Plenty of cord to reach de socket, Mister Preston."

"Good. Plug it in, will you?"

Avery stepped down from the ladder to admire his handiwork. "Well, what do you think, James?"

"Lights look fine, sir."

"My little contribution to the Christmas spirit around here."

"If that's all ..."

"Ah, but it's not. Don't leave yet, James. I'll be right back."

Gritting his teeth in exasperation, Wash's son muttered to himself, *What's he wantin' now?*

The bookkeeper reappeared, hands clasped behind his back, lips expanded in an anticipatory smile. "Three guesses what I have here, James."

The busboy shook his head.

"Oh my, how serious we are! Come now, let's see a smile. After all, tomorrow *is* Christmas." He unclasped his right hand disclosing a slim gift-wrapped box. "For you, James." With his eyes devouring every line and curve of the embarrassed young Lutiguan's features, he added, "Merry Christmas!"

Later that same evening at Tyler's behest, James returned to the cabin with hot coffee and biscuits. Feeling dignified and manly in his borrowed jacket and tie, he whistled as he crossed by the pool and followed the footpath. His good humor reflected the unexpected thrill of owning the latest model AM/FM transistor radio. He'd hardly been able to believe his luck when he tore off the wrapping and opened Preston's present.

"Mister Preston?" Silence. He knocked twice more, puzzled about what to do next; he had been given a specific message for the bookkeeper. With his free hand he pushed the porch door open and crossed the communal area to the darkened interior, the string of colored lights behind him providing the only illumination.

Louder now, "Mister Preston, you here, sir?"

"Is that you, James," came the muffled response from behind a door to his right.

"Yes, please. Mister Tyler send me." Silence.

"I'm in here. The door isn't locked."

Eager to be on his way, the youth turned the knob and entered as bidden. As he struggled to focus, to make sense of the scene before him - a towel had been draped over the bedside lamp - his nostrils were assailed by the acrid odors of whiskey and human sweat mingled with the cloying scent of incense. An empty bottle of Scotch lay on the floor and another, half-full, stood like a sentinal beside a finger-smudged glass on the night table. Nearby, a lazy spiral of smoke rose from an ornate brass receptacle atop a chest of drawers.

Nervous now, his eyes were drawn like magnets to the unmade bed where Preston lay sprawled, naked save for a pair of undershorts, his skin white and lubricious as the underbelly of a fish. The New Yorker's hair was plastered to his skull, a day's growth of beard darkened his cheeks and chin and glassy eyes gazed at the youth with shameless intensity out of two swollen pouches . With an effort he propped himself against the pillows and began to massage his bare belly, the palm of his left hand moving in lazy, concentric circles.

"Well look who's here. If it isn't my young friend, James. How 'bout a drink, young friend James?"

A fat, ugly slug ...dat's what he look like. A drunk one, too. An involuntary shiver coursed through the youth's body and beads of perspiration appeared on his brow. *Best be movin' outta here.* "No please, nuthin' to drink."

His epicene lips pouted. "Don't be such a spoilsport, James. It's Christmas Eve, remember? '*Deck the halls with boughs of ivy'* ...oh shit." Groping for the bottle with his free hand, Avery clumsily knocked over the glass beside it. In desperation, James mumbled hurriedly, "Mister Scranton send this tray for you, sir. He asked me to tell you to please come join de party."

"Screw your 'Mister Scranton.' Tell him for me I'm not in a party frame of mind."

"Yes, please. I'll tell him," he pacified, glancing wildly around the darkened room in search of a place to deposit the tray. "I'll leave this for you in de front room, Mister Preston. I best gettin' back to work now."

"What's your hurry, James? I don't eat bus boys for breakfast. Put the damn tray anywhere you like and bring me another glass."

When he came back into the room Avery motioned him to the bedside: "Hold it for me." Shakily he poured himself a dollop of Scotch and polished it off in two greedy swallows.

"There. That's better." Once more his eyes skewered Wash's son, but as he spoke, the abrasiveness was gone from his voice. "I know ...I know you'd like to beat it out of here. But stay a while and keep me company, James. Here I am, thousands of miles from home. No family. No friends. A man shouldn't be alone on Christmas Eve.

...And she brought forth her firstborn son, and wrapped him in swaddling clothes and laid him in a manger

Quite remarkable, you know, when you think about it. In a wretched stable surrounded by a handful of dumb animals, a young virgin gives birth to a baby, and nineteen-hundred-and-some-odd years later, half the world still drops to its knees in celebration." He paused, stirred by memories of other times, other places. "You have no idea how isolated I feel ... how lonely I am. Does it surprise you James to learn that 'Mister Preston, sir' has feelings, too?" Overwhelmed by alcohol and self-pity, his eyes grew misty. Brusquely he rubbed his fists against them in a gesture familiar to any mother of a small child.

Preston's erratic behavior and maudlin confession caught the young Lutiguan off guard. He felt a pang of sympathy for the man. *You're one sorry cockroach.* The bookkeeper marked the softening look on the boy's face and moved with cunning swiftness. He snatched James' arm and moved him closer to the bed, his grip so febrile the boy was bent almost in half. Drawing his pale, unwashed white face close to the alarmed black one, he whispered huskily, "Can't we be friends, James? You and me?"

Goaded to action by the pervasive stench of whiskeyed breath and sour skin, the disquieting note of intimacy in his tormentor's voice, James jerked his arm free and bolted for the door. As he sped along the darkened path toward the cheerful, beckoning lights of the main building, the name 'Gumby' came tumbling into his mind.

* * * * * * * * * *

"What does 'buller' mean, David?"

"Where'd you hear that word, James? Mummy catch you sayin' it, you get a lickin' for sure. If'n Daddy hears it, you won't sit for a week."

"That's what Luther's callin' Mr. Gumby, a 'buller'."

"No fleas sittin on Luther's big mout', that's for sure. You best be forgettin' you ever hear *that word*, boy. You're too little to pull out your belly en stuff it wid that kind of trash."

"Ah David. You en Charlie are always treatin' me like a baby. I've grow'd up, you just don't take no notice."

"Lissen, James. You put seven years on de seven you got, then you comes to your big brother en he'll tell you all de bad words you're wantin' to know."

"Lightnin', you know what de word 'buller' means?" Rudy 'Lightnin' Barker lived four chattel houses below the Wilsons.

"Course I does, don't you?"

"It means your eyes is crossed, don't it?"

"Who told you that?"

"I hear folks talkin'. They say Mr. Gumby, he's a 'buller.' But de funny way they sayin' it ... don't sound like crossed eyes to me."

"It's not. Look, if I tells you, don't be chewin' your mout where you hears it from, lessen you want a rock to your head."

"I'm not tellin, Lightnin'. A horse got no tongue en I got none either."

"And I'm not givin' away somethin' for nothin', boy. Go get me a mango offin' Granny Tilden's tree."

For all his twelve years, Lightnin' was finding it difficult to select the right words to describe a sexual aberration he was none to clear about himself.

"It's like dis, James," he pontificated between careful bites of succulent fruit, "most men wants a woman to fool wid. When de foolin's done, de babies come. Happen all de time. Looka my sister, Gemstone. She's not passin' 19 en has herself two babies already. Then there's de other kinds of men, ones dat don't look to women for their fun. That's what a 'buller' is. A buller only has eyes for other men. Boys, too. De older a buller gets, de younger de boys he goes after. Ole Gumby, he's dat kinda' man. You best look out, James. Once't a 'buller' casts his evil eye on you, boy, you're gone."

The secret was safe with James. His neighbor might have been conjugating Latin verbs for all he understood. He forgot all about Gumby until a few years later when he overheard his parents talking late into the night.

"You hear de news, Mr. Wilson?

"I hears it, woman. It's passin' like brush fire all over de island."

"Praise de Lord his Mummy's not alive to hear it. They tellin' how his body is layin' at de bottom of Eagle Hall gully all cut to pieces. Do they knows who did it?"

"The police ain't sayin', but theys plenty to chose from. I'm guessin' de list's as long as de road to salvation. In truth, that Gumby was next-o-kin to de Devil."

"Shame on you, Mr. Wilson! Speakin' ill of de dead. Murder's a sin in de eyes of de Lord."

"Mebbe this time God turned his head so as not to notice."

On his way to school the next morning, James learned from his classmates of the murder of 'buller' Gumby. The body, which lay at the bottom of a steep ravine, was sighted from the main road by a passing workman. Closer examination by the police showed it to be covered with multiple stab wounds, the scrotum hacked to pieces.

* * * * * * * * * * *

"Dis come for you, James." One of the boys from the kitchen slid a parcel wrapped in brown paper onto the bar.

"Your feet must be where your eyes is. Nobody's sendin' me a package."

"See for yourself. Miz Cleo send me to give it to you. Got your name on it, look ...J A M E S W I ..."

"Here. Lemme see."

"You gonna open it?"

"Later. I'm busy now." James made a great show of wiping the counter top. "They don't pays me to be tendin' to my private business when I'm workin."

During the holidays the busboy had been a knot of misery, dreading the summons that impelled him to face the prurient attentions of the white man; but there had been no more calls since that harrowing encounter on Christmas Eve. By mid-January, he began to relax. If he saw Preston at all, it was when the bookkeeper passed through the bar on his way to the front office and James, with the antennae of the hunted, managed to make himself invisible for the second or two it took him to cross the tiled floor. Now this.

It's from him. En for sure, everybody at de hotel knowin' a package come for James Wilson 'fore de sun passes. Making certain he was unobserved, he slipped away to the gardener's storage room and shoved the unopened parcel behind a bag of fertilizer.

"What's in your package, James?" Cleo teased. "Someone send you a million dollars?"

"Sure could use de money, Miz Cleo, but truth to tell it's from a friend who likes playin' jokes . He wrapped up a old box en stuffed it with newspapers. Guess he was hopin' to fool me." Without a qualm he told variations of the same story to everyone on the staff who asked, and many did. Packages arriving by mail were an event on Lutigua. When Wash waylaid him later in the day - "How's it your Daddy de last to know a box come for you in de mail?" - he repeated the story with lowered eyes. James had never lied to his father before.

When his shift was over, the young man sidled warily up to the shed to retrieve the box, but the shed was locked for the night. He didn't dare abandon it, much as he wanted to. Another day passed before James felt it was safe to move the parcel away from the hotel grounds. With the unwelcome burden under his arm, he searched until a found an abandoned field of rotting cane stalks. After assuring himself there was no one about, he ripped off the wrapping and drew from the box a dove grey shirt with the initials 'JW' stitched in blue on the breast pocket. The material was silk, as smooth and delicate to the touch as a frangipani petal. A small white card fluttered to the ground and he leaned over to pick it up: 'To my friend, James' it read, in bold, block letters. There was no signature. The word 'buller' came to mind as he held the gift against his body. "It fits, for sure. Don't matter. I'm not keepin' a shirt from dat cockroach." Angrily he yanked the fabric with both hands, and when the material refused to give, pounded it with a shard of coral until the collar and sleeves were shredded. At the end of a row of cane stalks he found a natural hollow and shoved the shirt into it, covering the place with earth and stones. When he was done, he felt calm and light-headed.

"Just let him ask me where de shirt got to. Just let him!" he hooted in triumph.

In the hushed, sultry interlude before dawn, James tossed restlessly on his pallet, the elation of a the day before giving away to deepening depression. He was overwhelmed by a dilemna new to him but familiar to any black man emerging from under a 300-year-old shroud of colonial rule. Wash's son prized his job. Innately intelligent and ambitious, he desperately wanted to prove himself, to show he was worthy of the trust implicit in the happy circumstance of being hired by 'Mister Scranton.' In despair, he pounded his fist into the pillow. The spectre of Preston pursuing him at every turn - the bookkeeper seemed no longer at pains to hide his intentions - was repellent to this unworldly youth, and yet to openly defend himself against the New Yorker's advances was an option foreclosed to him: Preston was white, James was employed at a hotel owned by a white woman, a white man was his boss. He ached to confide in someone, but he was too ashamed.

His brothers would accuse him of making it up as an excuse to quit working and laze about ('You one spoiled boy, James. Mummy en Daddy has lost their heads over you.'). He'd be open to ridicule and suspicion from his friends ('A 'buller' after you, mon?

Must be you gave him de goobie eye.') His mother would have told him to hand his problem over to God (Mrs. Wilson's penchant for tossing all her troubles into the Almighty's lap, including finding a husband for an unmarried sister, was viewed with reserved scepticism by her family.) And his father? "Daddy'd tell me not to be passin' wicked tales 'bout a white man." He had nowhere to turn.

The remainder of the month passed without incident. No allusion to the silk shirt was made by Avery, and on the few occasions when James was required to serve him at the cabin or office, the bookkeeper's manner was entirely impersonal. But the gratuitous gift of the shirt forced the young Lutiguan into a state of perpetual vigilance. From the moment he entered the hotel grounds, he was on his guard, his stomach in knots, each nerve and muscle coiled like a tightly wound spring; he returned home at the end of each day in a stupor of exhaustion.

On an overcast morning with clouds chasing each other across a darkening sky, James attended to his first chore of the day—collecting clean glasses from the kitchen to replace those used at the bar the night before. To the contrapuntal murmur of breakfasting voices in the dining hall, the young Lutiguan was bent on finishing his task before Sam arrived to open the bar.

"Ah! Here you are! Just the fellow I was looking for." James scalp prickled in alarm: the voice was all too familiar.

"A good morning to you, James," Preston cast a dubious glance at the sky, "though not so 'good' if those clouds overhead turn to rain. Frankly, I'd welcome a respite from this damn chamber-of-commerce sun." Sharply now, "What's the matter? Cat got your tongue, James?"

"No sir. I'm busy wid my work."

"Rest assured, I wouldn't dream of interfering, but the fact is I have something I want you to look at. A magazine. Friend of mine sent it from the States."

"Don't have much time for readin', Mister Preston."

"Ah but James, you've never seen a magazine like this before, I promise. Besides, it's mostly photographs. Some very creative photos, I might add. Should be an education for you." He pushed a thin manilla envelope across the bar in the youth's direction. "Take your time looking at it, but I'd like it back when you're done."

Midway across the tiled floor he hesitated and returned to the bar. "A word of advice, James. This magazine is not meant for the great unwashed. The material is unique, to say the least. I don't think your friends would understand."

Whatever else he was expecting, it was not a request to read a magazine. Puzzled as he was by Preston's remarks, he was dizzy with relief to see him walk away. Not until his shift ended and he was trudging up the hill to his house did the young Lutiguan begin to have doubts. *That low-belly's got somethin' up his sleeve.* But then he reminded himself, *Can't be much mischief in a old magazine.*

He had the house to himself: Wash was at Belle Jours, his mother visiting a cousin in another parish, his brother David was rarely home before dark, and to his parents' displeasure Charlie, the eldest, had moved in with a woman . ("Don't know what come over you young people today," Mrs. Wilson lectured. "If de girl's sweet enough for you to hand over what you earns at de garage every week, why not marry her, Charlie? You think our Lord's blindfold to your sinnin'?") A spasm of hunger drove James straight to the kitchen where he knew his dinner waited on top of the stove. He carried a tin plate with its cold chicken, rice and peas out onto the porch, and after seating himself on the top step, plunged his fingers into the food. When the leg bone was picked clean, he went back into the tiny kitchen for a cold glass of mauby. Carefully wiping his fingers, he picked up the manilla envelope and brought it back with him to the porch.

The magazine, *Men Friends*, immediately fell open to the centerfold, a full-color spread depicting a male trio, all of them nude. The one in the middle, his head languidly propped on one elbow, lay stretched across the length of the two pages; he looked not much older than James. Behind him a mustached blonde had reached over to caress his taut penis; the man on the right, held the central figure's other hand over his scrotum. They were smiling at the camera.

James stared at the picture for a long time. It was his first exposure to pornography. His mouth was dry as he idly turned the other pages. When he came to a section of black and white photos of a very fat man and several children, his stomach rebelled. A few seconds later he was at the back corner of the yard retching against the galvanize fence.

The next morning his mother surveyed her youngest child with undisguised concern. James had barely touched his breakfast, yet seemed unwilling to leave the table.

"You sick, boy?"

"No, Mummy."

"It's time for work. Best be on your way, son."

He sighed tremulously and rose. "I'm leavin'," he said listlessly.

"Mind yourself, son," she said softly, following him onto the porch and watching until his shambling figure disappeared. *What's vexin' James Mac Arthur? He ain't eatin' enuff to keep a yellowbird alive. Don't look to me like he's sleepin' much either, en never before did that chile take it 'pon himself to burn de trash without bein' told.*

Down and road and out of sight of the house, James veered to the left and took a path leading away from Belle Jours.

* * * * * * * * * *

A disconsolate group of physical therapists crowded around the bar. Moribundly they'd watched each day of their conference-cum-tropical holiday dissolve in a wash of heavy rain. A local steel band, hastily hired for the evening to enliven the group's sagging spirits, called to report a large stretch of the road from St. James was flooded and they'd had to turn back. The announcement of the cancellation at dinner had been greeted with resigned shrugs and a general stampede to the bar. Sam and James were the only two on duty to cope with the conflux of aggrieved guests.

"They behavin' like puppies wid fleas. If dis rush keep up, I'm callin' Mister Tyler," Sam whispered to James as he picked up a trayful of drinks. Just then the house phone rang and James overheard the barman say, "We jammed up, Mister Preston, but soon's we're clear, I'll send up your order." He called impatiently after his young helper, "When you finish wid dat order, boy, carry gingerale en ice up to de cabin. Mister Preston's laid low wid a bad stomach. I'm callin' Mister Tyler to come here on de double."

The busboy knew it was pointless to argue. The harried bartender would fire him on the spot if James asked him to send one of the waiters from the dining hall. The rain let up just after dinner, but dampness and humidity pressed down on the island like a millstone. En route to the cabin Wash's son found a measure of comfort in repeating over and over, "I'm not sayin' a word. Don't have to say one word to dat white slug."

He mounted the steps with a heavy tread, his face set in unbending grimness, and rapped sharply on the screen door.

"Who's there?"

The youth flung open the door without answering. *He open his mout 'bout dat magazine, I'm throwin' dis tray at his ugly face.*

Preston emerged from the back of the cabin in time to see James set the tray down on a table. He was dressed in an Oriental robe of heavy green silk, a sinuous red and gold dragon across the front panel. Below the hemline, from the knees down, his legs were bare.

"What the hell's the matter with you, James? Why didn't you answer me?"

With great dignity, the youth stared straight at the bookkeeper. Flustered by the raw hostility of his glance, the older man fumbled with the sash at his waist in an effort to stall for time and reassert his dominance.

"You're being intolerably rude, James. You owe me an apology," he blustered, but the black boy remained mute, his eyes spitting defiance. Preston stepped back nervously and held his hand up in a gesture of appeasement. "Let me guess. The magazine. You didn't like it. Come to think of it, boy, it was three weeks ago that I loaned it to you. Why haven't you returned it as I asked?" On surer ground now, he said acidly, "I'll bet you sold it to those simple-minded friends of yours. Probably auctioned it off to the highest bidder."

Stung by the unfairness of the allegation, James forgot his resolve. "No one seen it. I burned it. Dat's what I did, I burned it wid de trash!"

"Well now, I'm sorry to hear that. The magazine didn't belong to you. But since destroying it seems to have made you feel better, let's just drop the matter. Forget all about it, shall we? You see, James, I don't want anything to stand in the way of our friendship. We are friends, aren't we, James?"

Hypnotized by a growing awareness of the depravity underlying those sweet, reasonable words, the young Lutiguan recalled the exhortation of his minister, of his warning to the congregation, 'The Devil has many faces, many disguises. You must always be on guard!'

Dis man's de Devil himself, come to swallow me up. The revelation terrified him. He remained rooted in place, incapable of either speech or flight.

In the ensuing silence, Preston studied Wash's son. He moved forward and grasped him by the upper arm. "James. My dear boy, you look absolutely terrified. For God's sake the last thing in the world I want is for you to be afraid of me! Whatever else you may think, I never wanted to harm you." He shook James' unresisting arm. "Come on. Snap out of it! Haven't I told you a hundred times what your friendship means to me? ... I like you James. Do you hear me," he whispered huskily, "I like you *very much.*" He moved his fingers lightly down the boy's arm and took his hand. "I want to show you how very special are to me. Feel my heart, James," he commanded softly, "see how it beats. It beats like that every time I see you." With his other hand Avery released the sash and the silk robe slid open, revealing his nakedness. Slowly he guided the boy's black hand down his hairless chest to his waist, down ...James shuddered, the trance broken as he wrenched his hand from the man's grip with all his strength.

"Keep your hands offa me, you white Devil," he sobbed, shoving him out of his way with both hands. The bookkeeper fell to the floor with an indignant yelp of pain, but James was past caring. He sprinted from the cabin and down the path, oblivious to everything but his terrible need to thwart his tormentor.

"I gettin' de cutter. I gettin' de cutter en fix that white Devil for good."

CHAPTER XVI

At the far end of the dining hall Osbert Marshall was distracted from his nightly task of checking the dinner receipts by a flash of movement on the periphery of his vision. Half rising in his chair, he caught a glimpse of a dark figure racing across the hotel grounds.

"That rascal's up to no good, for sure." Pushing the pile of papers to one side, he retrieved a flashlight from the bottom drawer of the sideboard and embarked on a search of his own for the intruder. Moving cautiously in an ever-widening circle, he was poking the beam of light into an overgrown thicket of cassia when a piercing shriek followed by another and another punctured the night air. The screams came from the direction of the cabin housing Tyler and Preston, a several hundred yards to his left. Despite the drawbacks of age and a balky knee, the patrician head of the diningroom raced to the building, vaulted up the steps and flung open the porch door. The sight that greeted his eyes made his stomach turn.

Huddled against the wall in a passageway between the two bedrooms, arms enfolded protectively over his head and bare legs jerking spasmodically on the planked floor, was Avery Preston. The exposed parts of his face and head were covered with blood; deep red stains, like a child's fingerpainting, were smeared across the wall and floor. Standing over him, a raised machete in his hand, was Wash's youngest son. With the monotony of a scratched record the busboy chanted, "I cuttin' you for good, white slug. I cuttin' you for good."

The bookkeeper's howls had turned to whimpers. "Don't ... please ... *please* ..."

Praise de Lord, he ain't dead yet.

"Put de cutter down, boy! You don' want to be killin that man!" But James, imprisoned in a sound-proof cell of rage, continued to stand over his victim.

He's gone en lost his mind. Cautiously the older Lutiguan moved to the younger one's side. "Easy now, boy. Easy. Give Osbert de cutter. That's it. Now, James, go sit on de porch. Sit there en don't move.

Hear me, boy? Don't move! Soon's he's able, Osbert bringin' you a drink of water."

Once the the significance of the *maitre de's* presence surfaced in Avery's consciousness - he'd been rescued, if not from certain death, certainly from mutilation - he lapsed into uncontrollable hysteria.

I needs Miz Caswell to come in a hurry.

Osbert's terse message alarmed the Englishwoman. Transcending the dual handicap of soaking terrain and heavy girth, she moved faster than she dreamed possible with the aid of an unfurled umbrella which served as a walking stick; she arrived at the cabin with heart pounding, her breathing, painful and erratic.

"Dear God," she whispered, transfixed by the carnage. It took every ounce of self-discipline not to turn and flee. "Marshall, telephone Reception. Tell them to find Mr. Scranton and ask him to come here immediately ."

She knelt beside Avery and spoke to him in a calm, reassuring voice; eventually, he quieted down and allowed her to make a cursory examination of the damage. She discovered at once that most of the blood came from a deep cut on his left hand - *I can bandage it to stop the bleeding, but he needs to see a doctor* - and two superficial wounds on the upper arm. An ugly welt on his right thigh would heal in time. *No other cuts that I can see. The robe saved him.*

At the sound of feet pounding up the wooden steps, Leona turned her attention from Avery in time to see Tyler enter the room and come to a dead halt, a spontaneous 'what the--,' emanating from his lips as he surveyed the scene. She said briskly, "Quickly, now. Help Marshall carry him into the bedroom." There'd be time for questions later.

The two men eased their burden gently onto the cot. Preston, his eyes shut, his face the color of undercooked pasta, lay back on the pillows. His breathing was shallow and from time to time his plump body twitched convulsively, but he was calmer. Tyler went to fetch a glass of water and two aspirin, the only pain killers in his medicine chest.

"Here, Avery, take these. I'll bring you a brandy in a sec, but first, tell me, what the hell went on here tonight?" (In the darkness, neither he nor Leona had seen James slumped in the far corner of the porch .)

Avery opened his eyes and fixed his cabinmate with a look of undisguised contempt. "I should think it was perfectly obvious, old man. That damn nigger tried to kill me. I want the authorities notified. I'll swear out a warrant. Whatever it takes. That boy belongs behind bars, he's a goddamn menace."

"Easy now, fella. Relax."

Mystified by Preston's accusation, Tyler returned to the room so proudly decorated by his cabinmate to find Caswell making a desultory stab at cleaning blood off the walls and floor:

"The maids shouldn't see this."

He took the towel from her protesting hands, "Sit down, Leona. I'll finish wiping up later. I know you don't like liquor, but you look as if you could use a stiff drink." Noting the grave-faced Lutiguan standing nearby he added, "You've earned one, yourself, Marshall. Thank God you got here when you did. Look, please don't leave until we get a chance to talk."

"Yessir, Mr. Tyler. Do you mind if I takes James a drink of water? He's waitin' on de porch."

"James? *James MacArthur?* What the devil … You mean James is the one who attacked Avery?" The other man nodded. "He'll need something stronger than water when I get through with him!"

"Mr. Tyler," there was an edge of steel in Osbert's deferential manner, "I needs to speak with you. I needs to speak with you *before you has words with James.*"

"Christ!" Tyler murmured. "No wonder the kid went after him with a machete." He took a long swallow of his drink, then spontaneously reached over and gripped the islander's shoulder. "Thanks, Marshall. I know it hasn't been easy to talk to me about this. I appreciate your frankness. Don't worry about James. We won't notify the police. What happened here tonight is just between us. If word ever gets around, it would kill his father. Just damn luck Wash worked the early shift today."

"If you'll allow me, sir, I'll take James home with me. My youngest can go 'round to his folks en tell them James Mac Arthur took sick. My house is close to here."

"Fine. Keep him there for a day or two if you can."

Moths courted the light from the single lamp, a lone cricket droned tenaciously, while up above dark clouds tumbled furiously westward as if pushed by a giant hand, clearing the night skies for the emergence of a single, winking star. The American took Leona's arm protectively as they left the cabin.

"Avery was asleep when I looked in on him. Saved me from having to be civil to the bastard. Talk about being blind *and stupid!* All these months and it's been going on right under my nose."

"Stop blaming yourself. None of us guessed. Laura will have to be told, of course. It must wait 'til the morning, though, I just couldn't face her now. Do you think we made the right decision, Tyler? Not calling in the police, I mean?

"Believe me, Leona, once Avery knows we're on to him he won't dare press charges. From what Marshall told me - *his pauses were more graphic than his words* - he's been chasing James for months. I still can't believe it. Not the fact that Preston's a queer, but all this time we've been sharing the same cabin and I never tumbled to his vicious game. When I think of the hell he must have put that boy through ...Son-of-a-bitch. I'd like to break every bone in his body."

"Oh Tyler," she said wearily, "thrashing him won't solve a thing." They parted by the pool; the barman returned to the cabin, remaining awake and on guard for the rest of the night.

Leona dozed fitfully, unable to shake the sordid melodrama from her mind. Aware that her friend was an early riser, she knocked at Laura's door shortly after dawn. A shudder of revulsion crossed Laura Foster-Jones' features as she listened to her English companion describe the incident at the cabin. When she finished her account, there was a long silence. Straightening her shoulders, the Mistress of Belle Jours said, "Leona, this is what I want you and Tyler to do." She issued her instructions in a cold, rapier voice.

An hour later, Tyler pounded on Avery's door. Without waiting for a reply, he pushed it open.

"Get up, Preston, and start packing. Just your clothes. The rest of your stuff will be shipped C.O.D. I'm driving you to town to the doctor and when he's finished fixing your hand, we're heading straight for the airport. Caswell is booking your flight. We're shipping you back to the States, you bastard."

The bookkeeper opened his mouth to protest, but Tyler didn't give him a chance. "Not a word, Preston. Do you hear me, not a word! Or so help me, I'll finish the job James started last night."

When the Ford wagon pulled up to the departure wing of the airport, Tyler shifted into 'park,' but left the motor running as he reached across the still figure at his side and unlatched the door.

"Your ticket's at the *Eastern* counter. Now move it! Get the hell out of my sight!"

He drummed his fingers impatiently on the steering wheel as Preston, still groggy from a local anesthetic, cautiously edged himself off the seat. He signaled a porter with his good hand and when the last of the elegant luggage was unloaded onto a cart, he turned to follow but seemed to have second thoughts. He strolled back to the idling car with its passenger door still ajar and gave the metal a vicious kick, slamming it shut with such force, the entire car shook. Leaning down so his face was parallel with the open window, he grinned like the Cheshire Cat.

"Up yours, old man."

Leona was waiting when he pulled into the hotel driveway.

"He's gone?"

"Gone and good riddance."

"Thank heavens." She looked at his drawn face and smiled. "Bless you, Tyler. We couldn't have managed without you."

"The main thing is we got Preston out of here before he had a chance to shoot his mouth off. No one saw us leave, did they?"

"No, I don't think so."

"Good. I'm off to check the bar schedule and get someone to cover for James."

"Laura says you're to take the rest of the day off. You *do* look exhausted, my dear. A nice, long nap will do you good."

"Thanks. I could do with a little shut-eye."

Sprawled in undershorts on top of the unmade bed, he swigged the last of a cold beer and was asleep before noon. An hour later the room maid's rapping at the porch door roused him from a heavy torpor. *She can't come in here! I haven't finished cleaning up the blood on the walls.* He sent her away and rolled back over; the latent tensions of the past 12 hours soon made themselves manifest in his dreams:

Tyler is standing under the gnarled branches of an ancient mahogany tree by the side of the road. It is hot and he's thirsty. He longs for a cool drink but is unable to move. A group of barefoot school boys comes running down the road. He calls to them, "Water! Please, I need a drink of water!" But they ignore him and disappear over the horizon. Time passes and his thirst grows. At last he spies a figure approaching at a fast pace. As the runner draws near, Tyler sees that it is James and begs him to stop. "Can't stop, Mister Scranton. He's after me ..." Tyler is frightened now. The heat and his thirst are unbearable and no matter how much he struggles, his legs remain rooted to the earth .

A bell sounds in the distance. He recognizes it at once. "It's Neddie, on his bike!" He peers down the road, overjoyed to see the familiar profile of his younger brother. "Neddie!" he calls, "Neddie, it's me, Tyler!" Without a glance in his direction, the boy pedals by at a furious pace, pursued by an ominous cloud of thick, grey dust. At the center of the cloud is a

Mephistophelean vision in a swirling black cape, a black mask covering the upper half of its face. One hand holds two monstrous white wolf hounds on a silver leash, the other wields a sinuous leather whip. The whip smashes down across the dogs' backs again and again, driving them into a frenzy of speed. The figure in the mask is familiar.

"It's Avery. He's after Neddie ..." Tyler makes an agonizing effort to break free. "I can't move ...someone help me. Help me!" He starts to sob, "Help me!"

With pulse pounding, the American wrenched himself awake. The jumbled, hallucinatory images of Preston, James and his brother fade but do not leave him. Sluggishly he disentangled himself from the encumbering sheets and stumbled to the shower, unable to shake a lingering pall of despair and sadness.

He was in no mood to see anyone, but knew he must speak to Marshall and find out about James' condition, and since Danielle had taken a bad fall in the laundry room two days before, he owed it to Leona to offer a helping hand if it were needed. *She's been through the wringer, too.* Reluctantly he left the sanctuary of the cabin.

He was unprepared for the sight of Danielle sitting placidly at her desk in the front office, a pair of wooden crutches propped against the wall nearby.

"Welcome back. How's the ankle?"

"God has been merciful. De bone did not break, it is only a bad sprain."

"Have you seen Miss Caswell?"

"Yes, please. Miss Caswell is in her room; her eyelids's look so heavy, I tell her to rest, that I will call if there is a need."

"Look Danielle, if anyone asks for Avery, tell them his 'aunty' took sick and he had to leave in a hurry." (He and Leona had concocted this alibi several hours before.)

"I am sorry to hear it. Will Mr. Preston be back soon?"

"No. The bastard's gone for good." His vehemence caught her by surprise. The Lutiguan glanced at him sharply, opened her mouth to speak, then seeing his grim expression, changed her mind.

The following morning a slim, nervous young man, impeccably attired in a dark blue suit, cream shirt and maroon knitted tie, presented himself at Reception.

"Excuse me. My name is Yousuf . I have an appointment to see Mrs. Foster-Jones. Will you tell her please that Mr. Kissoon, the accountant, is here."

A week later the only physical evidence of Avery Preston's disruptive stay on the island were the six large wooden packing crates stacked against a wall in the common room of the cabin.

"How long's that stuff going to sit there?" Tyler asked Leona.

"The local agents won't ship a thing until Avery cables a money order. The inventory and insurance forms were forwarded to New York last Friday, but you know how the mail is here." She glanced at her wrist. "I must watch the time. Kissoon's requested I go over the new billing system he's set up with him."

"How's he doing?"

"Kissoon? He seems very conscientious, very eager to please ...and he's a genius at figures. I checked his references before he was hired. He graduated with honours from a second-rate school, you know, but after he came down, one of the oldest accounting firms in London offered him a place, which says volumes about his ability. It's very rare you see, for a man of colour, an *Indian,* to find that kind of position in my country nowadays. The only reason he came back to Lutigua is illness in the family. (The Kissoons own two large furniture outlets here on the island.) His father has cancer, I'm told. Very sad for him, but lucky for us with Avery gone." She shook her head, "Do you realize, Tyler, not one person has mentioned Avery? It's as if he never existed. I find that kind of indifference rather chilling. Of course he was an odious man, but *they* don't know that!"

"Be fair, Leona. People like Avery Preston are never missed."

"Please, God, nothing else goes wrong. I could do with a little peace and quiet."

"As the locals say, 'not to worry.' I'm sure the worst is over."

But he was wrong. An episode would transpire that became a permanent part of the island's folklore, and because of the role she played, Leona Caswell- 'dat English lady round as a sow 'bout to drop a litter' - would be remembered by the Lutiguans with affection and respect.

In the weeks following their New Year's gala, Belle Jours became a popular alternative to the old 'Belevedere'; moreover, it had acquired a cachet as a preliminary setting for seduction among a few of the hornier local males. The most notorious of the island's philanderers was its Police Chief, Rupert Haynes, a hulking scoundrel with mean, porcine eyes, who shaved his head and eyebrows for affect and strutted about in flamboyant, locally-made uniforms inspired by the Douglas Fairbanks' epics of the late 30's.

Haynes had a habit of sweeping into the hotel sans reservations on Friday evenings, drawn by a menu featuring filet mignon flown in from Omaha and a popular steel band; table bookings were made well in advance. Others might be turned away, but never the Chief and his entourage. Although it was public knowledge that Haynes had a common-law wife and a slew of children, he brought with him a parade of pubescent girls, none of whom was over eighteen, most still virgins, and all of them clearly terrified of their escort.

"How does he get away with it?" Tyler asked Sam. "We have laws in the States to protect minors from bastards like him."

The two had just silently witnessed a particularly repulsive interlude: halfway through the meal, Haynes, who always drank heavily on these occasions, roughly pushed his hand up the skirt of the chubby moon-faced girl beside him (she barely touched her dinner). As his fingers slid under the elastic of her cheap cotton panty to begin their languid probing, the child jerked back in shock. Her elbow hit a glass of water, tilting it over and dumping its contents in the bully's lap. Barely able to conceal his outrage, the Chief jumped up to wipe his trousers and in the heat of the moment, overturned his chair. Conversation in the room petered out and all eyes turned in his direction with undisguised curiosity. The mortified girl seized a napkin to hide her face and ran from the room. Haynes' indignant roar, "Get back here! You! Come back!" went unheeded.

"That should dampen his ardor," the American said with disgust.

The following day, quite by chance, Tyler discovered that Haynes' bills, forwarded to his office at the end of each month, were never acknowledged. He took his wrath out on Danielle: "It's bad enough we have to let that child molester on the premises. Now I find the s.o.b. doesn't even pay his bills!"

"True, she said softly. "I am bringing it to Miss Caswell's attention, but she says Mr. Kisson will handle it when he is more settled."

"To hell with that. I'm telling my boys to cut Haynes off 'til he pays up."

"Please do not do this, Tyler. Chief Haynes, he can make wicked things happen and no one dares to point a finger. Last month our neighbor, Mr. Layton, he told de Chief to stop fussin' round his daughter, Elizabeth. Poor Mr. Layton. He was beat up so bad, he's in hospital still. And before that, a fire at de rum shop up by Sugar Hill. It burned down in de night soon after de owner told Chief Haynes, 'No more rum on credit.'"

"If you think I'm going to let some half-baked Idi Amin free-load at my bar, you're crazy." He left the office angrier than she had ever seen him.

Danielle turned to Cleo, "This 'Idi Amin' Mr. Scranton speaks of. Do you know him?"

Tyler's orders to the Lutiguans staffing the bar were received in stunned silence. None of the men dared argue, but an impromptu meeting away from the hotel was hastily organized.

"Mebbe we could just tear up de Chief's bill."

"Burnin' it would be better."

"You got breadfruit for a brain, boy? You knows Mister Tyler, he countin' every ounce."

"True."

"We could mebbe poison his rum."

"En hang for it? Not me."

"A dead man can't run from de coffin, en I'm better off broke than dead. *I 'm payin' for his drinks myself.*"

"Hey, mon! Yeah! Dat's sweet." Several voices were raised in assent.

"I 'm not payin' for no drinks for dat fucker."

"Dat's right, 'Choo-Choo,' you ask de Chief for his money," Brian winked at the others. "Comes your funeral, we'll pass de hat for your Mummy."

Haynes reappeared a few nights later in the company of three junior officers. Brian, who was preparing to lock up for the evening, marked their progress across the tiled floor with dismay. The Chief had been drinking alone since noon in a rum shack across from Police Headquarters and, eager for companionship, had commandeered the trio as they were coming off duty. He walked with exaggerated care and his speech was voluble but slurred. Haynes slid a chair out at one of the tables and gestured to the others to seat themselves.

"You there, boy! Take care of my frens."

He's been at de rum pot for sure. The Lutiguan came out from behind the bar and approached the group with misgivings. "Will you be wantin' de usual, sir?" he asked Haynes, remembering the Chief favored a double rum with tonic.

"None of dat local piss-water, boy. We're drinkin' Scotch tonight. De best you got. Put de bottle right down here," he commanded, slamming his fist on the tabletop with such force that the startled bartender accidentally dropped his order pad. Clearly pleased with himself, the massive black man winked broadly at his sober companions, who lowered their heads in embarrassment.

Several rounds later, all inhibitions had vanished in a 90-proof vapor. A second bottle of Scotch was rapidly disappearing and Brian panicked, guessing they would want a third. *Take half my life to pay for dat imported stuff.*

He debated furiously with himself about what to do, eliminating each option save one. Quietly, he eased himself out from behind the bar and made a beeline for Leona Caswell's room.

"Do you realize what time it is, Brian?" she asked crossly.

"Sorry to wake you, Miz Caswell," he said abjectly to the opaque figure behind the partially opened door," but dis load's too heavy for me. De gentleman's here wid his friends, de one Mister Tyler sayin' we're not to serve. They been drinkin' for a time en ..."

Mortified to be caught without her turban and in a state of *dishabille,* Leona interrupted sharply, "If Mr. Scranton gave you orders not to serve him," she hissed, "why are you bothering *me?*"

"Miz Caswell, de gentleman, he's de *chief of police,*" Brian added desperately.

Still groggy with sleep, it was a second or two before the import of his words registered.

"Yes, I can see that would be a problem. All right, Brian, I'll see what I can do. Go back to the bar and make up the Chief's bill. I'll join you shortly." Leona's equanimity deserted her as soon as the door closed. She hurriedly dressed, her thoughts in a turmoil: *What am I going to say to that dreadful man?*

A patch of darkness at the edge of the dance floor hid her from view as she studied the unruly group. *Just look at those hooligans ... so intoxicated, they're capable of any kind of behavior ... What will I do if they get ugly? Dear God, I can hardly breathe my heart is pounding so ... This will never do. I must get a grip on myself.* The temptation to retreat to her own quarters was overwhelming. Clenching her fists to steady her trembling, she whispered, "One for the money . . two for the show ...go, Leona, before you change your mind."

With his head resting on the table, arms dangling at his sides like a puppet's, Chief Haynes appeared to have passed out or fallen asleep. His companions, their collars loosened and shod of their heavy boots, resembled the tawdry remnants of a retreating army. As the Englishwoman emerged from her hiding place, a young constable slapped his thigh in glee, having reached the punchline of a bawdy tale. His two cohorts hooted with laughter and Haynes raised his head to reward the storyteller with a wide smile. But the smile dissolved as he became aware of the massive figure advancing in their direction. Something about the woman—an air of rectitude, the way she moved despite her size, made him sit up. Alert now, he watched Leona's progress through narrowed, bloodshot eyes. *What's dat white bitch doin' here?*

"Good evening, Chief Haynes. I don't believe we've been introduced. I'm Leona Caswell, acting manager of Belle Jours. I was making my rounds when I saw the lights on over here. I'm afraid I must ask you and your party to leave. The bar should have shut down an hour ago."

Remembering his manners, one of the young officers started to rise, but without taking his eyes off the woman, Haynes seized his arm rudely and shoved him back into his seat.

"Me en my boys, we're not done drinkin'" he glowered, expecting an immediate retreat.

"I'm sorry to hear that, but I must insist. The bar shuts down at one a.m. during the week. It's a hotel regulation."

"Lady, I makes de rules on dis island."

"May I remind you, sir, this is private property," came the soft but firm rejoinder.

Haynes blinked, unable to believe his ears as he slowly rose to his feet—all 265 pounds of muscle and flesh. His nostrils flared and a small vein near his left eye bulged. An offending chair was sent crashing to the floor. Caswell paled, but did not flinch. The three constables, their alcoholic fog pierced by the sound and fury of this unorthodox confrontation, were frozen in place: their Chief's temper was legendary. Watching helplessly from the sidelines, Brian broke into a sweat. *Lord, Lord, he's gonna break Miz Caswell in a hun'red pieces.*

Two menacing steps brought the brute within inches of Leona. His hamlike fists opened and closed erratically as if they had a life of their own. The sour stench of animal heat and perspiration mingled with alcohol assailed her nostrils, and for an anxious moment, she felt faint. *I mustn't. I shan't!* She inhaled deeply and held her ground, her gaze never wavering from the figure towering over her.

"And before you leave, sir, please be so kind as to settle your bar bill. The hotel can no longer extend credit until your account with us in paid in full." Having dared so much, she willed the earth to open up and swallow her.

The woman's courage and audacity added fuel to an already combustible situation. The silence which descended on the heels of her ultimatum was inflammatory. Shaking his head like a wounded animal, the Chief's lips closed over bared teeth and a snarl.

The mesmerizing tableau was interrupted when a constable's errant sleeve brushed against two glasses on the table sending them skimming to the tiled floor where they shattered like a pistol shot. With inordinate presence of mind, the young officer leapt to his feet.

"Le's go, Chief," he cajoled. "dis place's not fit for cockaroaches. Big man like you don't wanna be wastin' time wid dat old white cow." He touched Haynes tentatively on the shoulder. "Come. They got better places to drink den dis heapa dung ." The other two scrambled to their feet echoing his derision, "Heapa dung for sure, Chief."

The white woman had triumphed and Haynes knew it. To save face, he stuck a fist into his pants' pocket and, ignoring Leona completely, turned towards Brian at the bar.

"Come, boy. Come gets your money." Brian came to respectful attention in front of the Police Chief.

"Open your mout, boy." Without thinking, the barman obeyed. "Here!" Haynes shoved a wad of bills into the open cavity and cackled with glee as the barman started to gag.

"Just so you keeps it to mind, boy," all traces of levity had disappeared; he was facing Brian but the warning was meant for Leona: "It don't pay to be messin' wid Rupert Haynes. You better take care." He snapped his fingers at his men, turned and stomped noisily from the bar; trailing after him, boots in hand, were the three constables in stockinged feet.

"Brian! Your lip is bleeding. Are you all right?"

"No problem, Miz Caswell. He just scratched me."

"What a cruel, disgusting man," she said in a strained voice.

"You fixed his wagon, for sure!"

The exuberant Lutiguan executed an impromptu jig while holding aloft a fat wad of rolled bills for her inspection. "Looka! De Chief left us half de Treasury. Wait 'til I tell de boys! Their faces gonna drop in a ditch." But his elation shifted to concern when he saw the woman sink like a rag doll onto a chair, hands shielding her face, her enormous frame shaking uncontrollably.

"Miz Caswell? Miz Caswell ...somethin' wrong?"

She shook her head, incapable of speech. Tears of relief from tension and fear spilled through her fingers.

The tears were too much for Brian. *Here she's gone and whupped de meanest man on dis island, so what's she cryin' like a baby for?*

CHAPTER XVII

As she walked from the main road to the hotel, the still air presaged another sultry oppressive day prompting Danielle to quicken her pace, the sooner to gain the comfort of a fan-cooled office. Addressing the girl on night duty, she asked, "Celene, did you leave any worries on my plate?"

The chubby, young Lutiguan soberly read aloud the items she'd made note of during her shift:

"They callin' from de bar round midnight to say de ice-machine's broke again. En de Kimballs in Room 114, tellin' how de window's stuck en they frettin' 'bout mosquitos, so I send Lionel to fix it. ... . That's all, 'cept a call come from a lady in Antigua, a Miss Locke. She askin' if we has any single rooms available. I tells her to come right along since five are empty. She sayin' how she was a guest at Belle Jours once't before."

Danielle frowned, "It's a name I'm not recalling, but I will check the old registration records. When is Miss Locke arriving?"

"By de first flight she can get out of Antigua, she say."

Striding along the path near the pool, Tyler caught a glimpse of a woman in a lounge chair under one of the striped umbrella's who appeared to be completely absorbed in the book she was reading. He'd seen her somewhere before, but he couldn't place where or when.

He ducked into the office previously occupied by Avery and spoke with Kissoon about a large unpaid bar tab left by a guest who'd already checked out; with that business settled, he paused by the Reception desk to chat with Danielle. "By the way, I saw a woman at the pool just now who looks familiar. Has she been here before?"

"That would be Miss Locke, one of the school teachers from America. They were our guests last winter."

He snapped his fingers. "I remember now. Sarah. The mousy one. How long's she been here?"

"She arrived from Antigua three days ago."

"Oh. Well, I'm off. Are you free for coffee later on, Danielle?"

She looked at her watch. "Yes, please. Cleo is taking over de desk in an hour."

"See you then."

"Hello, Sarah. Thought I recognized you when I passed by a while ago."

"Why, Tyler. How nice to see you!" She closed the book, using a finger to hold her place.

"My spies tell me you've been here for a few days. How come I haven't seen you at the bar?"

"I'm only here because so many of our students came down with chicken pox, they called off classes and sent everyone packing. Marcy was supposed to come with me— you remember Marcy, don't you— but at the last minute she had to rush home. Her Mom collapsed and was taken to the hospital."

"That still doesn't explain why you haven't come by to say 'hello'."

"To be honest, there's something about a single woman in a bar that ... *you know.*"

"Come on, lady, you're kidding! This isn't sin city, a wicked place like New York or L.A. This is the li'l ole island of Lutigua, remember?"

"*I prefer not to frequent bars alone,*" she responded with a defiant lift of her chin.

He realized she was serious, that it wasn't an act.

"Sorry. I didn't mean to give you a hard time."

Her obstinate expression melted; with a weak smile she pushed her sun glasses over the top of her forehead and squinted up at him . "That's o.k., Tyler. Guess I sound like a real stick in the mud. But really, I'd be most uncomfortable by myself in a bar ... anywhere, anytime."

He squatted down alongside her chair. "Tell you what. It's been sorta slow here at the hotel; cocktails before dinner is about the only time we're busy. After that, who's ever on duty just stands around twiddling his thumbs 'til closing. Why not mosey in around ten? I can leave my station and join you at a table. That way you won't be alone. How about it, Sarah?"

"Thanks, Tyler. I think I'd like that."

"Evenin', sir."

Startled, they both looked around to see two women with mops and buckets in hand, part of a team hired to clean all the public areas of the hotel while the guests were sleeping.

"Holy cow, what time is it? Two a.m.!". Scranton scrambled to his feet. "Sorry, Sarah. We were so busy talking, I forgot all about closing down the bar. You'll hate me in the morning for keeping you up so late. By God, *it is the morning!*"

She rose quickly, "I promise not to think poorly of you, Tyler. I've had a lovely time."

"I'll get Lionel to see you to your room."

"That's not necessary. I'll be perfectly fine on my own. After all this is the safe 'li'l ole island of Lutigua' isn't it?" Her eyes sparkled with laughter as she threw his words back in his face. "Good night." Her heels clicked a lively tattoo across the tiles as she disappeared from sight.

Back at the cabin, Tyler found sleep elusive; as he lay staring up at the ceiling his thoughts centered on Sarah Locke, recalling how her face lit up when she laughed, how, when she was pondering the answer to a serious question, she ran her thumbnail back and forth under her two front teeth. He decided she wasn't the type to bed casually, if at all; but she was damn good company. He liked her.

"If you don't mind my asking, how come you decided to return to Belle Jours?"

"For starters, I've made up my mind to leave Miss Pringle's at the end of the school year. Before rushing into another job, I need time to sort things out, decide what I want to do next. You see, I've always wanted to teach. I know it sounds corny, but inspiring young minds seems like such a challenge! After six months in Greenwich, I want no part of the 'young minds' we have at Pringles'—spoiled suburban brats, most of whom aren't a bit interested in getting an education. Designer labels and the 'in' thing to wear are what turns them on, not art or literature or history."

"I remember your skinny friend, what's her name ....?"

"You mean Ann?"

"That's right, Ann. I remember she sounded-off about the place, but then Ann was always sounding off about something, so I didn't pay much attention."

Sarah smiled. "Actually, underneath all that 'sounding off' as you put it, lies a genuine, caring person. I'm not happy at Pringles', but it's my first job and I was afraid if I left I'd look like a quitter. Ann's the one who's encouraging me to take the plunge. I'll always be grateful to her for that."

"I heard you flew in from Antigua."

She didn't respond immediately. "My, word does get around .... Yes, it's true. I didn't much care for the hotel," she added, "*or* the island. Belle Jours is much nicer. So here I am, with only eight days left to enjoy this beautiful island."

A handful of guests were clustered around the bar as Sarah passed by on her way to dinner. She waved a casual 'hello' to Tyler, who motioned her to come over. She hesitated a moment, then reversed direction and moved to the end of the counter where she waited 'til he was free.

"Sorry. That's no way to get a lady's attention, but as you can see, I've got my hands full. Did you have a good day?"

"Perfect. This afternoon I took a long walk away from the hotel grounds. It gave me a better feel for the *real* Lutigua".

"Will you come by for a drink later?"

"Oh Tyler, thanks, but I can't. I've put off writing some important letters far too long, and I promised myself - come heaven or high water - I'd start on them tonight after dinner. Maybe another time?"

"Sure. Another time." The ensuing sting of disappointment caught him by surprise.

"Morning, Sarah. Scranton here. I hope I didn't disturb you?"

"Disturb me, Tyler? Heavens no! I was up early to finish off those letters I mentioned."

"Look, I have the afternoon off. Would you care to go for a drive? I checked with the office and the Ford is free."

"Sounds wonderful. What time?"

"Why don't we plan to leave around eleven. I'll meet you out in the courtyard."

When the station wagon pulled up, Sarah hopped into the passenger side. She was dressed casually in pale green slacks and a lemon shirt knotted at the waist, her toffee hair pulled back and held by a matching lemon ribbon; the combination of colors accented the burnished tan on her face and arms. As soon as the door shut on her side, Tyler rammed his foot down on the accelerator and they sped out of the driveway.

She turned to him laughing, "Why the rush? I thought the idea was to take life easy on this island. That's what that darling old man, Wash, told me: 'Mistress, 'tween de sun en de rum, folks here takes life easy, one breath at a time. You lives longer that way.'"

Tyler returned her smile with one of his own. "The old guy is something, isn't he?" He didn't add that the less the staff had to gossip about, the better. Nor had he forgotten the stricture about employees getting too personal with the guests.

Sarah seemed to read his thoughts. "Now that I think of it, not much escapes notice in this place. No need to start tongues wagging when there's nothing to wag about. ... Tell me, where are you taking me?"

"It's a secret." He'd already decided to drive over to the Atlantic side of the island, to the east coast where the two small boys had 'guarded' his car. "Holler if you get thirsty. There's a cooler in the back with plenty to drink."

Sarah quietly studied the scenery and people they passed on the road while Tyler concentrated on his driving. *Fucking road. Same pot holes as the last time.*

It was a clear, bright day, the harvest season would begin soon, a time when men armed with machetes cut down the ripe cane; they were accompanied by women of all ages who stacked the rich stalks into piles to be hauled away by truck or donkey cart to one of the four major sugar factories on Lutigua. At the factory not a bit of cane is wasted: the raw stalks are chopped and pressed, cleaned and boiled, and in the process the cane becomes molasses and sugar, fertilizer, feed for chickens, and last but not least, a golden rum.

They drove past a plantation where a group of women wearing colorful head scarves and straw bonnets to protect themselves from a burning sun, were digging up yams.

"Look at those women working in the fields! And it's so warm today! Poor things. It's disgraceful...no one should have to work under such awful conditions."

"No one's forcing them to work, Sarah. It's their livelihood."

She turned a stricken face to him. "You're right, I suppose. But this is the *twentieth century*; what I see out there looks more like a throwback to the the seventeenth or eighteenth."

"Lutigua is still a Third World country. I don't see that changing for a long time, if ever. Let me give you an example: about 10 months ago, the government opened the island's first tv station. Know how long they stay on the air? Three hours a day! And the few Lutiguans who can afford it, pay astronomical prices for a crummy set from Korea or the Phillipines. You don't see *Magnavox* or *Panasonic* around here. Other struggling wanna-be's dump their unsalable trash all over Latin America and the Caribbean!"

"I didn't realize things were that primitive," Sarah murmured, "but then I've seen so little of the world. Did I tell you, Tyler, I'm thinking of joining the Peace Corps?"

"The Peace Corps? You're outta your mind!"

All conversation ceased as he shifted gears and the old wagon started its sluggish ascent up the steep hill to the crest, where Tyler had his first memorable view of the coastline.

He turned off the engine and they sat in silence, captivated by the scene below them, by hugh waves, moving in white lines like marching armies, to crash against the massive rocks, coming to rest along a ribbon of sand which stretched for miles.

"Oh, Tyler! How beautiful! I've never seen anything like it!"

You hit the jackpot, buddy-boy. The lady approves!

After locking the car he glanced around hoping the two youngsters would reappear, but the place was deserted. He'd wanted Sarah to meet them. With the wind whipping at their backs, they scrambled down rocks and across ditches, over turf and pieces of old, dried timber from ancient wrecks until at last they gained the beach. Sarah immediately took off her sandals and holding them aloft in her outstretched arms, danced and whirled across the sand with unrestrained delight.

Losing all sense of time, they rambled along the shoreline in their bare feet, inspecting shells, old bottles, the mysterious sea life clinging to partially submerged stones and the detritus tossed up by the sea.

"Isn't it odd," Sarah said casting her eyes upward, "I don't see any sea gulls, do you?"

"Sure don't. Listen lady, my stomach's giving me fits. Let's get some-thing to eat."

"Around here?"

"We passed a rum shack a ways back. We can probably pick up a light lunch there, beer and cutters."

"What's a cutter? It sounds lethal."

"It's what they call a 'sandwich' here. You'll see. Come on, let's make our way back to the car."

The next time he looked at his watch, it was close to four. "Oops, duty calls. I'm due back at six." He helped her to her feet. "What happened to the time? It sure as hell passes in a hurry."

She grinned at him, "Like the wind. I hate to leave."

"We can come back again, if you like."

"I'm going to hold you to that promise!"

During the next several days they managed to spend a few hours together: a deserted cove within walking distance of Belle Jours provided an inviting place to swim and afterwards, they sat in the sun and were entertained by a family of sandpipers skittering along the tide line. At Sarah's initiative they looked up old churches in the area and explored the neglected cemeteries on their periphery, stopping to peer at headstones and vaults, some dating back to the late seventeeth century; a grove of mahogany trees on the mountainous part of the island near the old clay factory was the setting for a picnic lunch until a sudden shower sent them racing for the car. After their second outing Tyler made an appointment to see his employer.

"I know the rules, Ma'am, that's why I need to speak with you. We have a guest at Belle Jours, an American.

Sarah Locke's her name. I met her when she was here with a group last January. Since things are pretty quiet at the hotel, I've been driving her around the island when I'm off duty, showing her the sights, that sort of thing."

"I heard you were keeping company with one of our guests."

"Miss Locke and I are *friends*. That's all. There's no hanky-panky involved, I assure you."

"I'll take your word for it, Scranton, but fair warning ... there's something about a tropical island that defeats the best intentions, that leads people to behave in quite extraordinary ways. Don't ask me to explain, but I can assure you it happens more often than not. Just remember," she added tartly, "'amorous' activities involving a guest and member of staff are forbidden at this hotel. There are no exceptions. Do I make myself clear?"

"Yes, Mrs. Foster-Jones. Thanks for seeing me." He had all he could do to control his temper. *Bitch. Sarah doesn't deserve those innuendos.* He flung open the door of

Laura's suite and was half-way through it when she called him back.

"Scranton," she said in a mellower tone, "I'm sure Miss Locke is grateful to you for playing tour guide. Just be careful, that's all."

On his way back to the cabin, indignation fueled his pace: *I don't know why everyone assumes just because you take a girl out a few times, the two of you have to be fucking away like dogs in heat. I haven't laid a hand on Sarah, nor do I plan to. Why do people automatically make something sordid and dirty out of a simple friendship?*

Figuring '*What's the point?*', Tyler never kept track of the days, a habit he'd fallen into since coming to Lutigua; after all, he was locked into a two-year contract. Sarah's announcement during a late-afternoon swim, caught him unawares.

"I'm really going to miss all this. I can't believe I've got to leave in the morning."

"Whaddya mean, 'leave in the morning'? Don't tell me it's time for you to go back to the States?"

"I'm afraid so, Tyler."

"You're not serious? You mean your eight days are up already!"

"I'll take that as a compliment," she said, smiling as she dried herself off.

"Will I see you for a drink later?"

"I can't promise. My plane leaves early and I need to finish packing."

When she hadn't shown up by ten that evening, Scranton phoned her room: "Please come over and let me buy you a farewell drink, Sarah!" An hour later she appeared. With the exception of a middle-aged couple who were into their third round of rum punches, they had the bar to themselves.

"Hi! Thanks for coming by. What can I fix for you?"

"Just a gingerale, please, Tyler."

While filling her glass, he suddenly felt tongue-tied as a schoolboy. Since they'd parted that afternoon, he'd rehearsed a little speech about hoping to see her again, wanting his request to sound as casual as possible. Now he found he badly needed assurance that when she left

Lutigua, there was still a chance they'd see one another. She seemed to sense his unease.

"Is something the matter?"

"No ... *no.*" He grabbed a wet cloth and began wiping the bar, unable to meet her eyes. "Look, Sarah, don't most schools let out around Easter-time? ... I seem to remember, we always got a spring break."

"Of course, though I imagine the school will lop off a few days to make up for this unexpected furlough. I've promised to spend a weekend at home, then Ann and I talked about going into New York ... to shop, see a few plays."

"I don't suppose you'd consider forgetting New York and coming back here to Lutigua? There's so much of the island you still haven't seen."

"Tyler, why don't you stop that?"

"Stop what?"

"Rubbing so hard. You'll wear the finish right off the counter-top."

He looked up at her with a weak grin. "Right. As I was saying ..."

"Look, Tyler. I'm really flattered you enjoyed my company enough to want me to return. Let me think about it ... I'll let you know, I promise. Now, sir, *goodnight.* It's high time I was off to bed!"

Before Sarah left the bar, he asked her to write down her address and phone number.

* * * * * * * * * *

Turning to face his flock at the Bethel Methodist Church, Superintendent Eastmond waited patiently for the final verse of the opening hymn to end. At his side stood the new Minister of the Circuit, Peter Callender, whom Eastmond would introduce to the congregation later in the service. Callender, a widower in his mid-thirties, had arrived the week before from his island birthplace, Grenada. Once again, the newcomer silently thanked God for calling him to Bethel, for allowing him and his young daughter Tamika a chance at a new life, one far from the setting of his wife's painful, lingering illness.

Callender's eyes swept over the congregation and choir. Briefly they came to rest on the face of one particular woman amongst the choristers, the gleam of her gold-hammered earrings having captured his attention. Her almond-shaped eyes and distinctive features elicited an admiring: *Ah, now there is a face to give a man pause.*

CHAPTER XVIII

The rebirth of the S.O.T.S (Society of Tipplers) came about gradually. On a Sunday shortly after the Christmas holidays, two members of the former group arrived at Laura's suite hoping to re-establish old ties, reminisce and proffer the latest gossip. Their hostess greeted them with obvious pleasure. Word spread quickly amongst the original circle and the following week, their ranks slightly reduced, they came trickling back to Belle Jours, gratified to have a destination on what was universally agreed was Lutigua's longest and dullest day.

On successive Sundays new faces were enlisted, and occasionally a hotel guest whom Laura particularly fancied was invited to join them on the patio. Attendance at the gatherings fluctuated; at her insistence, either Wash or Tyler served the group, drawing drinks from the small, well-stocked bar in the adjoining sitting room. In time the American found himself absorbed in the personalities and foibles of a few of the regulars.

Sir Edmund Hawkes, O.B.E., was descended from a distinguished line of landed gentry in northwest England. An Oxford graduate with a degree in Economics, he was attending to his government's trade interests in Eastern Africa when war in Europe broke out. Hawkes became a member of Montgomery's staff during the Egyptian campaign and was knighted for bravery after Alamein. At the end of the war he returned home to a loyal wife, four year old son (a squalling infant when last seen by Hawkes) and the job of managing the family estates, an activity which soon palled. In the early fifties he re-applied at his old Ministry and, to his relief, was posted to Lutigua as an adjudicator-sans-portfolio, handling trade and economic matters for British possessions scattered across the Caribbean. Hawkes was gratified; the assignment freed him from a wife who increasingly bored him and the daily minutiae of raising a brood which now numbered three. In addition to inherited income,

Hawkes received a generous salary enabling his family back in England to enjoy a comfortable lifestyle, a fact that greatly eased his conscience. As further penance for his decampment, Sir Edmund sequestered himself in a cramped two-room flat on the outskirts of St. James.

For several years after assuming his new duties, Hawkes dutifully spent the Christmas holidays and his annual leave in Northumberland; as the children grew older, however, he found excuses to stay away. He'd been invited to one of Laura Foster-Jones' soirees shortly after his arrival on Lutigua and was immediately attracted to the striking, vivacious woman; the attraction was mutual. Laura, captivated by Hawkes' aristocratic bearing, his charming manner and the glamour of a title, singled him out as her next bed partner. But Hawkes was cautious by nature and by the time he made up his mind to fuck her, Anderson arrived on the scene and beat him to it.

The ensuing scandal appalled Sir Edmund, particularly since it involved a member of Her Majesty's government; he had a hard time accepting that a man as worldly as Anderson would be so indiscreet.

Thanks to Laura's frequent invitations to her dinner parties in those early days, Hawkes met members of the reigning social set and high government officials, contacts which proved invaluable in his work. After she fled the island, he sorely missed the liveliness and intimacy of those gatherings at Belle Jours, and while he never joined the Sunday afternoon circle on a regular basis, how annoying that the option no longer existed! During the intervening years, in a half-hearted attempt to assuage an ubiquitous sexual appetite, Sir Edmund had affairs with several women who were on the periphery of his social circle ...none of them serious, none lasting.

In the mid-seventies, a woman who would change his life dramatically was amongst the guests invited to a reception at the Venezuelan Embassy. As a rule, Sir Edmund abhorred large receptions - the press of people, the necessity of indulging in superficial exchanges of pleasantries - but he dutifully accepted most invitations because the Home Office expected it of him. After attending so many, he evolved a game plan for escaping as quickly as possible without appearing rude. The requisite hour at the Embassy was nearly up and he was about to duck out when an acquaintance hailed him: "Sir Edmund, someone wants to meet you. May I introduce Mrs. Mona Forde," indicating a short, rather plump lady in a flowered chiffon dress and large straw hat. After the usual banalities, Hawkes was on the verge of excusing himself when she pointedly asked, "And you, Sir Edmund, do you find these receptions as tedious as I do?"

He was about to demur, to lie and say he rather enjoyed them, but her conspiratorial wink totally disarmed him. "Yes, they are rather tiresome," he blurted, in spite of himself.

"Good. We agree. I'm not surprised. You see, I've been studying you from across the room. I couldn't help but notice how detached and uncomfortable you seemed, and I thought to myself, 'Mona, you must meet this rare and sensitive soul.'"

"Sensitive! Me?" He laughed at the absurdity of the appraisal, but her frankness intrigued him. Refocusing his attention on the face beneath the hat he observed the smoothness of her *cafe au lait* skin, the delicate nose and mouth, the dark liquid eyes which sparkled at him from beneath long lashes. Abandoning the formal manner he affected with most strangers, Hawkes impulsively invited her to join him for a drink away from the embassy.

An expatriate from Guyana, Mona Forde left her impoverished and benighted country for the stabler political climate of Lutigua after her husband died. The beguiling Mrs. Forde represented everything Sir Edmund desired in a woman: poise, intelligence, a tacit senuousness and a delicious sense of humor. More to the point, she was available. There was, however, one grave drawback: her colour.

Edmund Hawkes belonged to that strata of British society where family name, school ties, religion and race mattered. His upbringing, the social milieu he selected (given a choice) consisted of people of his own class and background. Since his original posting on the island, Britain had dissolved her legal grip on Lutigua and he'd been forced to deal with a civil service that had changed overnight from white to black. It had not been easy for him. In conversations with his white friends, he spoke disparagingly of 'they' and 'them,' of 'their' lack of education and manners, of 'their inbreeding.'

True to his nature, Hawkes embarked on his relationship with the widow from Guyana with caution; but as the weeks passed, his growing appreciation of Mona Forde's uniqueness coupled with a consuming urge to appropriate her body, became an unceasing dilemna. His farewell kisses at her door moved up the scale from pecks on the cheek to ardent explorations of her mouth and neck with his tongue. Exerting a wrenching self-control - he always pulled away before he lost himself - cost him many a sleepless night. It was Mona herself who brought the matter to a head.

They'd established a certain routine on Saturdays: an excursion by car to some point of natural beauty on the island, afterwards returning to Mona's tiny cottage for afternoon tea. Seated on her verandah after a leisurely ride along the East Coast, Hawkes sighed with contentment as he swallowed the last bite of homemade lemon cake and reached for a cigarette. In a subdued voice Mona said, "Edmund, I have something to say to you. It is a delicate matter, so please bear with me." She drew in a breath. "You have told me about your wife in England, but I do not think you care very much for her or she would be here with you now and I would not. It's obvious, is it not, that we are mutually attracted to one another? We are adults, Edmund, and as such you and I are prey to the hungers of the flesh, which is normal in a man and a woman. So I ask myself, 'Why does he not make love to me? Why?' It has taken me time to arrive at the answer ...but in some matters it seems, I am very naive. Forgive me if I express myself awkwardly.

"When we first met at the reception and you whisked me away, I thought to myself, 'Well, this is certainly not your typical Englishman, the God-Save-the-Queen-and-Empire type I have so often met. And for a time, I admit I was flattered like any schoolgirl that you singled me out. Blinded, too. But during these past, very pleasant weeks, I have come to know you well, Edmund ..."

"Darling, Mona ..."

"Hush, let me finish. Being conscious of my colour and unable to accept it is inbred in men like you, my dear. And I understand that one cannot erase overnight a prejudice that has been reinforced for generations and is as natural as the air one breathes. I don't expect you to change, Edmund, but neither can I change who I am, or where I come from—nor do I want to!" She pinched the flesh of her forearm, "Look! This is me, Edmund Hawkes. *This is who I am!* ... My family has a long and distinguished history in a country that I will always love, but because of the political climate, can no longer abide to live in. Amerindian and Portugese and East Indian blood flow in my veins, Edmund, and I am proud of it!" The recalcitrant look in her eyes and set of her mouth forestalled any effort on his part to deny the truth of her declaration. In the gentlest manner possible, she asked him to leave and not come back. "It is better this way," she murmured, reaching on tiptoe to kiss his cheek, "you'll see."

A fortnight later Mona retired to bed early, willing herself to become so immersed in a new novel she'd be able to ignore the storm now raging aross the island. Lightning terrified her and had ever since, as a child, she'd seen it split a tree in her family's orchard and kill the laborer sheltering beneath it. A few chapters on, she became aware of a dull, persistent banging and assuming it to be a shutter loosened by the wind, ignored it. But the noise continued and was distracting. Reluctantly, she rose and moved cautiously toward the front of the cottage where the sound was loudest; as she did, she realized it was no loose shutter, but someone at her front door. *Out in this storm. How dreadul!* Quickly undoing the latch, Mona pulled the door open to find a water-logged Sir Edmund, his London 'brolly' having proven unequal to the task of protecting him from the torrents of rain washing down from the the sky.

"Hello, Mona. I remembered how frightened you are of lightning and I didn't want you to be alone in this ghastly storm ... besides, I've been damnably miserable without you. May I come in?"

Uttering a gasp of pleasure at the sight of him, followed by rush of concern, she shooed him into the kitchen and demanded he shed his wet garments while she fetched him a towel. When he emerged a few moments later with a towel cinched round his waist, he held out his arms to her and she came to him without a word.

Hawkes' prudent nature - an invaluable asset in his job - unfortunately carried over to his lovemaking. That night, their first in her bed, Mona Forde not only managed to break through his habitual reticence, she awoke in him a latent, reckless carnality that carried him to amorous extravagances. In her deft and delicate hands, in the soft and welcoming curves and crevices of her body, he experienced release and gratification beyond his wildest imagining.

Like a desert wanderer, he drank greedily and often at this oasis of pleasure, returning to his rooms after a night in her bed happily counting the hours 'til their next meeting. He mentioned her to no one.

After several weeks, it came as something of a shock when she gently chided him: "Edmund, we can't go on like this, hiding ourselves away from the world, not seeing anyone. Every week now, three or four nights of lovemaking! Neither of us is young anymore, my darling. You are wearing me out! I have been thinking, there is this lovely new restaurant in St. Thomas. Won't you please take me there to dinner this weekend and perhaps, invite a friend to join us?" By then he knew he was deeply in love with Mona Forde, and while he was not insensitive to her wish to add a semblance of normality to their lives, his first priority was to protect himself from scandal.

Deeming it unwise to be seen with her alone in public too often, Hawkes managed over a period of time to introduce her to a few local acquaintances and a smattering of overseas residents–individuals with no ties to his colleagues in the service. (When Laura returned to Belle Jours and the Sunday group resumed gathering on her patio, he came by himself.) Mona gradually tumbled to these convoluted arrangements and learned to accept them. She knew Edmund Hawkes loved her and that was enough.

Tyler silently concluded Sir Edmund was the most urbane member of the group, an Englishman who liked his Scotch neat and who, when paying for his round of drinks, never forgot to slip him a tip. *Different as night from day to that cheapskate Schultz.*

Dieter Schultz spent the duration of the war in the safe harbor of neutral Switzerland, acting as caretaker for his aunt's property in the village of Frutigen near the Jungfrau. In 1947 his aunt returned from abroad (she'd fled to Canada the day after Hitler invaded Poland) and finding her house and lands in less than prime condition, immediately accused her nephew of indolence and threw him out.

Before the war Dieter had studied engineering, but his ambitions were thwarted when the Germans goose-stepped across Europe. When the war ended, he decided he was too old to go back to school and instead, carved out a modest living by representing a dealer in Bern whose specialty was decorative porcelain figurines and cuckoo clocks. One morning Schultz awoke and decided it was time to find a wife, preferably a rich one, and settle down. He took to heart the advice of a friend who claimed that cruise ships were fertile hunting grounds for unattached females; after a year of rigid self-denial, Dieter saved enough to afford passage on a ship touring the Mediterranean. His third evening on board he finagled an introduction to Daria Cospopolous, who according to shipboard gossip, was the daughter of a wealthy Greek exporter of olive oil. Daria was one of Nature's less generous gestures, burdened as she was with the a barrel-shaped figure and the kind of coarse features no makeup can hide. (A sunny disposition and warm heart made up for these shortcomings.) Her family had long since abandoned hope for her future, so when the tall, self-possessed Austrian (several years her junior) with a nut-brown mustache and impeccable manners presented himself to Daria's father and asked for her hand, he was greeted with open arms. (Mr. Cospopolous, however, took the precaution of setting up an elaborate conduit for his daughter's money so that he controlled its outflow and she its dispersal.)

After the honeymoon Dieter and his wife settled into an apartment in Paris, but spent much of their time travelling from one exotic locale to another aboard luxury liners. He continued to make a desultory effort at selling figurines and clocks, not only because it allowed him some precious hours of freedom, but lent him he felt, a certain 'respectability.' (Dieter recoiled at the notion people would think him totally dependent on his wife, which, of course he was.) When Daria suffered a second miscarriage, she gave up her dream of having children, much to his relief. (A constant change of passengers and scenery on shipboard made the marriage tolerable; a child would certainly limit their peregrinations.)

During a winter cruise of the Caribbean, Lutigua was one of the ports-of-call; after two days spent exploring the island, Daria fell under its spell. The following year they rented a villa on the West Coast and were introduced to Laura Foster-Jones and her Canadian lover at a party. Schultz immediately seized on the importance of entertaining this woman who was so well-established and cajoled Daria into inviting her to a lavish dinner party; other invitations followed.

The Shultzes faithfully returned to Lutigua every winter until Daria's untimely death from a heart attack. Dieter, an attentive husband albeit un-fettered by sentiments of love (he prided himself on never having cheated on his wife) was chagrined to learn that the bulk of her estate would go to a niece and two nephews. In addition to some personal items, he was bequeathed a lump sum of 50,000 pounds, a handsome amount in those days, but who could tell about the future? In a panic, he decided to invest it all and live on the interest, thus waiving his accustomed style of living. He elected to remain on Lutigua year round where his money would stretch farther than on the continent, with enough left over to travel from time to time. Dieter had been frugal before his marriage; after his wife's death, he became a died-in-the-wool tightwad.

Schultz never gave up the hope of marrying another woman of means, one who would consider a man in her bed more important than the cost of his upkeep. What better place to reconnoiter than Belle Jours? Aside from his punctual appearance on the Sabbath at the start of the drinking hour (he'd disappear to 'the gents' when it was his turn to buy a round), he dropped by for cocktails during the week as often as he dared. With soulful looks he'd allude to his 'lonely life', and Laura, out of sympathy for his plight, invariably invited him to stay on as her guest for dinner.

For a time Dieter gave serious thought to courting another faithful Sunday attendee, Marianne Pharr, an American from the Midwest who originally came to Lutigua on assignment from UNESCO; when her task was completed, she'd resigned her post and moved to the island permanently. Coldly assessing her handsome house on a cliff overlooking the Atlantic, her jewelery, her penchant for exploring the world - Marianne took a three-month holiday every year - Schultz decided the woman must be affluent indeed. He invited her to dinner at the 'Belvedere' justifying the cost to himself as an 'investment', but the evening ended dismally: Marianne found him to be an unctuous boor, and he concluded she was another typical American—opinionated and lacking in refinement.

Plain of face, friendly and outspoken, Pharr was one of Laura Foster-Jones' few good women friends. They'd met when she stayed at Belle Jours in the early days of her work for the U.N. Laura admired her independent spirit and treasured her discretion: Marianne had been among those present the Sunday Arthur Anderson's wife had threatened the hotel's owner with a gun. Pharr rarely indulged in gossip and when society turned its back on Laura after the Anderson affair, she remained steadfast and loyal. Little was known about her personal life, except that she came from St. Louis, had worked for a time at the State Department and had a cousin from Cincinnati who accompanied her on those yearly jaunts. As far as anyone knew, she'd never married and seemed totally at ease with her single status.

The Shelbys of Dugan Hill were among the oldest families on Lutigua, having arrived from England in the late 1700's. The first settlers established a successful sugar-cane plantation, but after two severe droughts, sold the land and moved to a steep, hilly area later known as 'Potters Mount' drawn there by large deposits of clay-rich soil. After a long struggle, a crude factory for the manufacture of clay bricks began its operations and the Shelbys' fortunes were established for the next several generations.

Jean Shelby Gardner and her husband Philip were among the regulars at the Sunday afternoon drinking parties. (Laura's mother was related to the English branch of Shelby's, and Jean was a distant cousin.)

During the war Philip Gardner, the son of a village schoolmaster in Tunbridge Wells, rose to the rank of Captain in the BEF; afterwards, he came to view this turbulent period of history as the richest and most rewarding of his life. His peacetime employment as a Loan Officer for *Barclays Bank* in London offered no such challenges. When the bank posted an opening overseas, he jumped at the chance to leave the stifling confines of a country where he would forever be marked by his humble beginnings.

Before embarking for the Caribbean, Gardner had engraved calling cards printed with the title 'Captain' alongside his name. He spent two years at *Barclays* in Jamaica before being promoted to Assistant Manager and transferred to its offices in the capitol of St. James. He met Jean Shelby a few months after his posting to Lutigua and they were married within a year. Jean, whose bland, pretty looks would fade by the time she turned 35, was timid and self-effacing; her husband, who insisted on being addressed by his military rank, never lost the habit of barking orders at his subordinates in the bank or any native West Indian who crossed his path. Having married into a family whose name was respected across the island conferred on Gardner a deference and social status far beyond his grasp in England. But this was no marriage of convenience; Philip Gardner adored his wife, and for all his blustering and pomposity, her quiet word carried the day.

Gardner eventually became the Bank's Manager; he retired before Belle Jours reopened. With the clay factory no longer in Shelby hands, he passed his days serving on the boards of charitable organizations and his evenings with a rum bottle at his elbow, recounting stories of the war to anyone he could corral.

Tyler referred to the Gardners as Tweedledum and Tweedledee.

Among the other Sunday habituees were Gideon Moss and Bill Howard. Balding and pudgy, Moss, who had grown up with Laura, was the scion of prominent family from the old plantocracy; his forebearers successfully farmed hundreds of acres of prime land, but over the years their fortunes had dwindled (Gideon's father had been an unrepentant gambler), and he now spent his days in a frantic scramble to eke out a living for his two unmarried sisters and himself. He was divorced and his only son, at his urging, had left the island to start anew in Canada. Moss wore a black patch over his left eye to hide its loss in a freak accident when he was a young boy. His relaxed demeanor, the continual stream of weak jokes and puns he never tired of telling were Gideon's way of shielding from the world a grim battle to satisfy the debts he'd been forced to assume due to his father's profligacy. Tyler, who dubbed him 'The Iron Man,' was awed by Moss' ability to down one rum punch after another and remain seemingly unaffected.

Bill Howard, representing the third generation of a family who owned the island's sole jewelery store, showed up at Belle Jours whenever he could manage to dodge his nagging wife. Having met the over-bearing Mrs. Howard, Laura sympathized with his need to escape from her sharp tongue. Silent and morose, Howard absented himself from the group's lively discussions, preferring instead to settle in the lounge chair in a corner of the patio imbibing one rum drink after another until he sometimes became too intoxicated to drive. Gideon Moss or one of the others usually volunteered to take him home.

Late on an oppressively warm Sunday afternoon early in March the regulars were on the patio arguing the merits of the government's latest scheme to raise money by slapping a prohibitive duty on all imported electrical equipment - uncharacteristically, Gideon and Dieter had nearly come to blows over the matter - when the house phone rang inside Laura's suite.

"Scranton, answer that for me, will you? And take a message."

CHAPTER XIX

Tyler returned to the patio and leaned down to whisper in his employer's ear: "It's Reception. An unexpected arrival wants to pay for his room with a check. Cleo told him about the hotel's policy of not accepting personal checks without a prior reservation. The fellow was very irate and created a scene, said he 'knew Mrs. Foster-Jones personally,' that you'd vouch for him. What do you want her to do, Ma'am?."

"Oh dear," Laura sighed, "one of *those.* Did Cleo say what his name was?"

"Scully, I believe she said. Claims to be a famous artist, something like that."

To Tyler's amazement, Foster-Jones jerked back in her chair, her body becoming as taut and unyielding as granite. When she turned to look up at him, all the color had drained from her face.

"Are you certain she said *Scully?*" her voice barely above a whisper.

"Yes, Ma'am."

She sighed deeply, raising her hands to her lips in an attitude of prayer, then slowly removed them. "Cleo's to tell the gentleman I'm busy at the moment and ask him to wait in the Lounge." Turning to her guests, she signaled for silence and addressed them in a strained voice, "My dears, a matter of some urgency has just arisen. Forgive me but I must ask you all to leave as quickly as possible."

The peremptory manner in which Laura delivered her request penetrated the various stages of her guests' insobriety. If they doubted her words, they had only to look at her face. Hastily putting aside their drinks and murmuring muted farewells, they emptied the patio. Before going their separate ways, however, they gathered in the driveway to speculate about their hostess' astonishing behavior.

Expecting a phone call, Gideon separated himself from the others and headed for the main lobby. As he approached the Reception desk he observed a gaunt, bearded man pacing back and forth under one of the arches. The stranger, clad in white with a navy jacket slung across his shoulders, wore a Panama hat which obscured his features. The pacing figure stirred a memory, but Gideon couldn't place it. He ignored the man and spoke to Cleo: "Any messages for me, Cleo?"

"No please, Mr. Moss. No messages come this afternoon."

With the patio to herself, Laura instructed Tyler to get in touch with Reception again: "Tell Cleo she's *not* to send the gentleman along until she hears from me. When you're finished clearing up, you may go. I won't be needing you. Just leave a bucket of ice and fresh glasses out on the counter."

She rose slowly from her chair and with the uncertain gait of a sleep-walker, moved towards the bedroom to freshen her makeup. Tyler was non-plussed. *Whoever this Scully character is, he sure as hell isn't your every-day Joe Blow. I've never seen F-J so rattled.*

"Come in."

The door to the suite swung open. The man stood for a moment at its threshold before sweeping off his hat in a grand theatrical gesture, "Laura, darling. It's me! Lawrence!" He walked smartly across the room to where she sat - her chin at a hostile tilt - and bent down to kiss her cheek.

"It's wonderful to see you again, Laura. You look beautiful ... as always."

Before he could embrace her, she raised her hand in a gesture of demural and said huskily, "Lawrence. Is it truly you? After all these years? Step back. Let me look at you."

Outside, the shadows of evening crept across the sky as they sat across from one another; in an awkard effort at bridging the permutations wrought by time, they exchanged the bare outlines of their lives since parting. He: 'I live in the States now, along the Gulf coast in Florida, but I've kept my Canadian citizenship; She: 'I inherited Edward's family place in England and lived there for a time, but I missed the island.'

"May I fix you another drink, my dear?" he said springing up and stretching out a hand.

"No thank you, Lawrence. I'm still sipping this one. (*His third gin in less than an hour. In the old days, nothing would do but Scotch and then, only the best.)* Tell me, what brings you back to Lutigua after all these years and how on earth did you know I would be here at Belle Jours?"

"Actually, it was a root canal that led me to you! Honest to God, Laura, that's how it happened! Last Fall I was thumbing through a travel magazine in my dentist's office, when the words *Lutigua* and *Belle Jours* leapt off the page...some article with a sappy title, like 'Hidden Gems of the Caribbean'. The writer described the island as 'breathtaking and upspoiled' and added that a small luxury hotel was due to re-open in December, to be 'managed by its original owner.' A nice, short history of Belle Jours followed; they even mentioned your father's name. Didn't you see it?" She shook her head. "After the New Year kicked in, I got my old, restless urge for a change of scenery - that's not news to you, is it, my darling? – and hopped aboard a ship bound for Rio to visit old friends in Sao Paulo. Then I thought, 'Why not stop off in Lutigua on my way back home?'" Scully was careful to omit the fact that the journey to Rio was made aboard a freighter because it was all he could afford. Nor did he describe 'the old friends' in detail. In reality they were a wealthy Brazilian couple he barely knew. Many years before, when Scully's name was a by-word in New York and London art circles, the husband had paid cash on the spot for six of his oils at a reception given by his 57th Street gallery. He could hardly refuse the couples' invitation to cocktails the following day in their suite at *The Plaza*. During the first round of drinks, the husband was suddenly called away on business; several drinks later, Scully backed his voluptuous and accomodating wife up against the livingroom wall, lifted her skirts and serviced her with gusto.

The gallery continued to send engraved invitations to Sao Paulo whenever there was a new exhibit of Scully's work, until the year it severed ties with the Canadian. ("Sorry, Lar', but you know how it is. The public are such fickle assholes. Newman, Still, deKooning - *that bunch* - they're all the rage nowadays.")

As his words floated across the room – the Scotch burr she once found so endearing softening the edges of his consonants – her keen eye observed the soiled yellow silk ascot, the frayed cuffs and the poorly-trimmed beard with its traces of red amidst white and grey. Only his strong hands with their long, delicate fingers which had once explored her body with such sensitivity and passion seemed untouched by the passing years.

To think of it ...this unkempt man with his pale face and hollow body is a person I once loved to distraction... this same man, the one who invaded my thoughts, my mind and my body like a conquering army laying siege ... making bloodsport of my infatuation, smashing and pillaging my dreams of our future together, then moving on, leaving behind the scarred, broken landscape of my heart. She bit her lip to stifle a rising sob. *Well, Lawrence Scully, you miseerable bastard, you won that war. No other man has ever managed such a complete victory. Since you deserted me, have I given my body in lust? Yes, of course, many times . . In love? Never.*

Silence fell, he was staring at her now, hurriedly trying to conjure up the right words to soften the expression on her face, to mitigate the coiled tension of her demeanor. "I had to come back. I had to see you, Laura darling," he said softly. "You were...*are*... the one great love of my life, you know. I'm just sorry things ended the way they did."

She dropped her eyes and studied her hands, which were clutched tightly in her lap. The stillness of the room was broken by the sound of muffled voices rising from the hotel diningroom. Laura did not respond, but he noticed with relief that her ramrod posture had slackened a bit. She picked up her glass again and emptied it.

"Fix me another, Lawrence, while I call Reception and ask them to send up a light supper." He overheard her tell the Lutiguan on duty, "take Mr. Scully's luggage to room 107. He'll be staying on for a few days as my guest."

Laura visibly relaxed over their meal and he responded by entertaining her with stories of his past travels and misadventures; here and there he'd drop the names of former patrons: the Italian countess ("She was built like the *Hindenburg,* so I shaved fifty odd pounds off the finished portrait, and she was so pleased she paid double the standard commission!"); a famous British actor ("Queer as a three dollar bill and on the make. Kept insisting if I slept with him, it would give me a richer view of life, make me a better artist"); a paranoid American multi-millionaire ("Before every sitting, he'd send two of his bodyguards to search my flat. It was damn cheeky, but what could I do? One morning, the sight of one of his muscle men on his hands and knees looking under my bed just cracked me up. I laughed 'til I cried, and after that I didn't mind.") He didn't mention that his paintings were no longer in demand, but Laura had already guessed as much; that the new wave of Op and Pop Art had eclipsed his popularity in the marketplace and he'd fallen on lean days, reduced to producing kitsch seascapes for a gift shop in Pensacola in order to pay the rent.

He was astute enough not to try any amorous moves when it was time for them to part. She walked him to the door of her suite and surprised herself by saying, "It's been such a lovely evening, Lawrence. I'm glad you came back."

He put his arms around her lightly and drew her to him, brushing her hair with his lips. "Sleep well, my darling . Tomorrow can't come too soon for me. Shall we spend the day together?"

For Laura, sleep was out of the question. She fixed herself a nightcap and returned to the patio to stare unseeing at the night sky. The hours slid by as she retrieved the past, retrieved from wilful and resolute burial, memories of halcyon days of laughter and lovemaking. When at last she rose to go to bed, she sleepily recognized that she was once again under Lawrence Scully's spell.

Scully stepped from the shower, towelled himself off and padded across the room to bed, too exhilarated to sleep. He folded his arms under his head and lay back against the pillows with a sigh. For the next few days at least he wouldn't have to worry where the next meal was coming from. The trip to Sao Paulo had been a fiasco from start to finish. When he'd called ahead from Rio, the maid asked him to repeat his name three times and his reason for wanting to see the *dueno*. (The call itself had cost him a small fortune.) Lugging an unwieldy folio of recent paintings, the artist arrived at a dazzling mansion on the outskirts of town at the agreed upon hour only to be kept cooling his heels in its marbled terazzo foyer. As he sat waiting, a matronly woman accompanied by a three jabbering young children came from the interior of the house and passed by him without a glance on her way out the front door . With a shock of recognition, he realized that this matriarch was the same woman who once provided him with an interlude of extravagant carnal pleasure. *She doesn't even remember me.*

The husband's reception was courteous but brief: he looked at Scully's work with an air of impatience, said he was sorry but he'd just returned from purchasing several new pieces of sculpture in Rome and wasn't interested in acquiring anything more at the moment. Having counted on a warm welcome, and being offered the hospitality of the house - neither was forthcoming - Scully skulked back to Rio on an ancient, exhaust-spewing bus. *The bastard didn't even offer me a drink.* At the waterfront he cajoled his way aboard a filthy trawler bound for Guyana where he was laid up with dysentery for three days before continuing his journey to Lutigua.

I'd have known Laura anywhere, though I could tell she wasn't too pleased to see me. But I can fix that. All I need is a little time. He had to admit that she'd weathered the years better than he'd any right to expect. *God, what a beauty she was, still is, in a way. And what a little spitfire back then! Fantastic in bed, too.* He smiled with satisfaction at the memory of that eager, responsive body, yawned in spite of himself and closed his eyes.

Tyler stopped by the office after a late breakfast. "Danielle, hi! Would you please put dibs on the wagon for me this afternoon? I just checked the schedule and my shift doesn't start 'til four. I'll pick the keys up about one."

"Good morning, Tyler." Her greeting was tepid. She didn't like having to disappoint him. "I am sorry, but de wagon, it is gone for de day. Mrs. Foster-Jones has taken it."

"The boss-lady's using the car? I didn't know she could drive. She usually calls Owen when she wants to go somewhere."

"Her guest, Mr. Scully, he comes for de key. Will this cause a problem?"

"No, it's not 'a problem.' I just counted on getting away for a while. Thanks. See you later." He left, mulling over this tantalizing turn of events. *Well, there goes your excuse, buddy-boy. Can't run away from those messy drawers and closet any longer. Time for a cleanup... dispose of that pile of old magazines and paperbacks.*

He was mid-way through the chore of getting his personal belongs in order when the sight of a shirt that needed laundering reminded him of Sarah. He'd worn it the day they'd spent together on the East Coast. Thinking of her, recalling the sight of her holding aloft her sandals and dancing barefoot in the sand, brought a smile to his lips, and reminded him of how empty the days had been since she left. *Shit! Forgot all about promising to write. Mail's so slow outta here, I'd better send a cable.*

Leona Caswell was tired and out of sorts by the time she arrived at the office, having spent the morning with the head housekeeper preparing the monthly inventory of linens and towels. She scanned the list of new arrivals as she did daily, noting that whereas there had been three empty rooms the day before, only two remained.

"Danielle, what's going on here? The two couples from Boston arrive late this afternoon and I planned to put them next to each other, in 107 and 109. I see by the register that 107 is filled. How is that possible?" she asked crossly. "No advance booking was made."

"True. Cleo tells me a gentleman arrived without notice yesterday afternoon and de Mistress requested he be put in 107."

"Where's the registration form? I don't see it in the pile of 'New Arrivals.'"

"No, please. The Mistress says he is to be 'her guest.'"

It was on the tip of Leona's tongue to say, "She didn't tell me she was expecting anyone," but the heavy woman caught herself in time. "I'm going up to my room now, Danielle. You can reach me there if I'm needed." *But I'm never needed around here, unless there's some boring or unpleasant task to be done.* Caswell rarely indulged in self-pity, but the fact that her friend never told her she was pre-empting a room rankled. Assigning rooms was one of the responsibilities Laura had thrown her way in the beginning: *'Leona, dear, so much depends on matching up the rooms with the right people. I just can't trust the staff to do it properly. Be a dear and look after it for me, will you?'*

Later that same afternoon Leona knocked on Laura's door, anticipating with pleasure the ritual of sharing a cup of tea while discussing hotel affairs because it meant she had her old friend to herself for an uninterrupted interval. When there was no response, her sense of aggrievement returned. Retreating to her own suite, she saw a note had been slipped under the door:

Leona, Forgive me, I shall have to forego our usual chat. An old friend is back for a visit and we expect to be gone all day and most of the evening. I want you to meet Lawrence! Please join us for cocktails at sunset tomorrow in my suite . L.

Promptly at six Leona, who had dressed with meticulous care for the occasion, was admitted to Laura's suite by Wash.

"De Mistress is waiting for you on de patio Miz Caswell."

In the fading light a tall, lean man rose from his seat, but before he could be introduced, Leona had a quick glance at Laura's face. 'Radiant' was the only word to describe it.

"Leona, my dear. I want you to meet Lawrence Scully, a famous artist and a dear friend of mine from the past."

He moved towards her with his hand extended, "Miss Caswell. I've heard so many wonderful things about you from Laura (her name having been mentioned only seconds before). It is a pleasure to meet you at last."

Leona hated him on sight.

An hour later the Englishwoman excused herself saying one of the new guests was demanding a special diet and she must smooth the way with the kitchen staff. Scully gallantly saw her to the door and when he regained his seat observed, "Don't think you're lady-friend likes me much."

Laura leaned across the table and squeezed his hand. "Don't be ridiculous, my dear. How could she not? You were utterly charming to her, much nicer than she deserved considering how cooly she behaved.

But that's Leona. It takes her a while to adjust to things. I'm certain she'll end up adoring you, just like every other woman who crosses your path."

"Don't bet on it. I have the distinct feeling Miss Caswell doesn't take kindly to competition. She wants you all to herself."

"Oh, Lawrence, that's an asinine thing to say," she replied heatedly.

"I've known Leona for years. There's never been the slightest hint ..."

He leaned across the table, "Dearest Laura. The matter in question is not worth arguing about. I won't have anyone or anything upset you while I'm here."

She smiled. "You're right, of course. Shall I have Wash fix us another drink before we order dinner?"

Scully eyed the empty glass in his hand and set it down; it wouldn't do to drink too much in front of Laura. She had a way of noticing these things. It was late; a light rain shower had forced them to move indoors. Wash disappeared as soon as he'd poured their after-dinner brandies. They were seated on the the antique settee in Laura's sitting room, her head resting on his shoulder. He knew it was time to make a move, but he was bone tired. *Too much fresh air and sun and too many drinks. This old grey stallion ain't what he used to be. Best I wait 'til tomorrow night anyway. Mustn't rush these things.* He summoned the energy to invest their parting with a foretaste of what lay ahead.

Idly, his finger traced the outline of her face, moving slowly down her neck and stopping at the cleavge between her breasts. He leaned over and kissed her eyes, her lips, the hollow behind her ear, while his practiced fingers gently pushed below her dress, finding and caressing her breasts, squeezing a nipple, feeling it hardened under his touch. "Laura, my darling," he murmured. He heard her breath quicken, felt her body lean into his as he pushed the top of her gown off her shoulders and gave his full attention to those pearly appendages.

With a show of reluctance, he carefully restored the straps of her dress and sat upright.

"Look, sweetheart. It is very late and you look a bit bushed." He laughed. "I know I am! All the walking we did today! But tomorrow I want you all to myself—for the entire day, if possible. I thought perhaps a picnic at Rainbow Reef, then later I want to take you out to dinner. You pick the place. Afterwards . . to be blunt about it, I hope we can spend the entire night making ferocious love." He kissed her quickly. "Don't move. I'll see myself out. By the way, before we leave for the Reef, can Owen take me to a barber shop in town? I could use a trim."

The next evening they dined by candlelight at a new restaurant on the Atlantic side of the island. With a half moon rising up over the horizon and waves crashing against the rocks below, it was a romantic setting straight out of a George Stevens movie set. The only sour note was the meal they were served (Scully blanched when he saw the prices)--everything was either overdone, undercooked, or swimming in some unpronouncable sauce.

"Lawrence, darling, I'm so sorry I dragged you here," Laura said in a stricken voice. "But everyone raves about the place!" He reached for her hand. "Forget it, my sweet. It's only food. Besides, you're looking so absolutely ravishing tonight, I hardly noticed."

She smiled across the table at him, silently approving the near miraculous changes the past two days had wrought: gone, the seedy scarecrow look of their first encounter. Tonight his face was ruddy with tan, his hair and beard neatly trimmed and his body seemed to have filled out, though she knew that wasn't possible. He looked like the same handsome, debonair artist she had fallen madly in love with so many years ago.

"Nevertheless, tomorrow we're dining on my patio, and I'm going to fix your *favorite dinner* myself! ... Correct me if I'm wrong: Mr. Scully's favorite dishes are curried lamb with rice and mango chutney, yams, and plantain soaked in rum and coconut milk and fried in butter," she said triumphantly."

"You are a wonder, my darling. Imagine! After all these years."

"I need to get something in my room. Be back in a jiff." He turned away as she unlocked the door to her suite. Fix me a nightcap, will you, darling?"

"Don't be long, Lawrence," she called after him. *I cannot bear to have you out of my sight. Oh, Lawrence, if you only knew how often I dreamed you'd come back ... how I waited and waited and when I finally accepted it would never happen, a part of me shrivelled up and died.* Her father's blind admiration had led her to expect the same from all men, and while she had truly loved her husband, Edward, she had loved him with the indiscriminate intensity of the very young. Their time together had been too brief for her to learn the give and take of a mature relationship. Wilful and headstrong, accustomed to to having her own way, she was unprepared to have her plans for the future destroyed by the capriciousness of one man. It was a humbling lesson. Having given of herself so completely to Edward, she vowed never again to allow any man to capture her heart. Then Lawrence Scully had come into her life, and in the scorching heat of their love affair, her vow had turned to ashes.

When the months sped by and he did not return after the incident at 'Bellaire', she sought revenge in the arms of others; like the sirens of mythology, she lured men to her bed with enticing words and blandishments. Coitus became her weapon and she used it skillfully and with hedonistic pleasure; those who enjoyed her favors never forgot. Years later, whatever their circumstances – wives, children, fame, even mistresses - their brief intimacy with Laura Gallon Foster-Jones remained a burnished memory; unconsciously, they measured other women against that memory and found them wanting.

After her flight to England, Laura continued to have affairs with men who crossed her path. But she gradually discovered that Englishmen are better lovers away from their 'sceptred isle'. Was the damp, bone-chilling climate to blame? The water supply? The stullifying caste system? She had no answer. (Anderson, upon learning she was living in Devon, made a furtive trip to see her. In less than an hour Laura decided he'd lost all his *joie de'vivre* and become a terrible bore; she coldly ignored his stilted hints at resuming their liason and sent him stumbling down the path at 'Clove Hill' a confused, unhappy man.)

On one of her shopping trips to London, she engaged the attention of a wealthy Lebanese businessman who gazed with admiration at the elegant woman sipping tea at an adjoining table in *Brown's Hotel.* When her purse slid off the chair onto the carpet, he retrieved it and introduced himself. After a long, animated conversation they abandoned their tea and took a taxi to his hotel suite in Mayfair where Laura remained for three days. On the train journey back to Devon, feeling luxuriously sated, she acknowledged to herself that the chances of her meeting another man as skillful and prodigious were rare. *You certainly couldn't call it 'making love.' Just pure, marvelous sex. Better to stop now than be disappointed.* And while she still made every male who met her feel that he was charming and clever, 'the wittiest and most intelligent in the whole tiresome universe,' she kept them out of her bed.

But now that Scully was back, she could hardly wait for him to touch her intimately, to plunge deep inside her, feel his warm semen on her thighs and smell the lingering essence of him on her sheets.

When he let himself back into the suite, she was waiting for him in her favorite dressing gown, the serenity of her welcoming smile belying an inner tremor of anticipation . She noticed at once the rolled cylinder he carried in his hand.

"What have you there, Lawrence?"

"Something special to show you, darling."

She was about to say, 'Can't it wait until tomorrow?' but the gravity of his voice, the look on his face changed her mind.

He stepped closer to a nearby lamp to take advantage of the light and unrolled the cylinder.

"I meant for you to have this thirty years ago, but I left in such a hurry, it got mixed in with my other paintings."

She caught her breath as she gazed at the figure of herself painted three decades earlier, naked and stretched out like Ingres' *Odalisque* on the very same settee where she was now sitting.

"Oh, Lawrence!" was all she could think of to say. It took every ounce of self-control to hide her outrage: *How cruel and insensitive! To show this to me now, just before we are to make love. I will be exposing a body that cannot possibly compete with the one in that painting. What can he be thinking!*

"Marvelous, isn't it? You have no idea how many offers I've had to buy it, but I said to my dealer, '*Listen, this painting's not for sale and that's final!*' I want you to have it, darling. It belongs with you."

Waking from a light sleep, Laura peered across the somnolent body lying next to hers to the clock on the bedside table and saw that it was after four in the morning. Scully's futile attempts to show off his prowess in bed had proved disastrous. Having deftly aroused her, he was unable to sustain the momentum to bring her to satisfaction; ejaculating quickly, he mumbled a muted apology and fell back on the pillow pleading exhaustion. *Dear God, what a fiasco.* Tears came unbidden to her eyes. This was not an evening to savor for the rest of her life. Gone forever, the virile, ardent lover enshrined in her memory. Worse still, his performance reminded her of the one subject she resolutely avoided. *We are both getting old. How I hate the thought of it!* At that moment, she fervently wished he'd never returned to Lutigua.

In time, the tears stopped. She consoled herself with the words he'd spoken the first night they were together: '*You are the one great love of my life.*'

Lawrence was brimming with good cheer when he awoke; he turned towards her on the bed and said, "Wasn't it wonderful last night, darling?" Giving her a quick hug, he rose and hurried from the room saying, "It's not fair to subject a beautiful lady to a half-day's growth of stubble." She waited for him to finish his ablutions, torn between the hope he would come back to bed so they could make love and fear of being disappointed again. Scully shouted from the bathroom, "I'm absolutely famished! Can we have breakfast here, sweetheart, or would you prefer me to leave after I'm finished dressing? I don't want to be the cause of any gossip."

"Of course you can stay." Laura phoned the diningroom and ordered breakfast for two to be served on the patio; with a sigh of resignation, she reached for her slippers. <u>To hell with what the staff thinks. Let them gossip.</u>

Seeming blissfully unaware of his companion's subdued air, her unresponsiveness, Scully's expansive mood continued during breakfast. Over their second cup of coffee Laura told him he would have to amuse himself until after lunch because she was going to have Owen take her shopping: "I plan to scour the entire island for the sweetest lamb and the freshest vegetables for our dinner tonight."

"Are you sure you want to bother, darling?"

"Of course, Lawrence. I love cooking for you. Don't you remember?"

"Of course... *Of course I do!* By the way, Laura, who's that young lad in the photograph? The one I saw on your dresser? Don't tell me you have a son somewhere."

"No, I never had children. That's Ian. His mother used to deliver eggs to 'Clove Hill.' The poor boy was born with a deformity and I was able to see that he got proper medical attention in London . . . it's a long story, one you'd find terribly dull." Laura lapsed into silence as a vivid mental image of that brave endearing boy flashed before her eyes. "I was very fond of Ian, that's all," she said quietly.

"I know what you mean," he said, matching her mood. "A kid can really get under your skin. It damn near killed me when Eve walked out on me and took Thea with her. For months I was out of my mind trying to trace them. The bitch finally wrote from some podunk town in Australia to say they were fine. She runs off to fucking Australia with my daughter! I'll strangle her with my bare hands if I ever get the chance."

Laura stared numbly at him across the table. *I can't believe ... Lawrence ...married? I must have misunderstood.* "A daughter, Lawrence? You have a wife ... a daughter?"

"Past tense, darling. The operational word here is *had.* Like Peter, the pumpkin eater. *Had* a wife and couldn't keep her. I'm sure I mentioned it." One glance at her face and he knew he hadn't. "Sorry, meant to. It's not a secret. Eve walked out on me about 15 years ago, when Thea was 10. The divorce papers arrived by post 2 years later."

"So ... you married soon after you left here." *You bastard. You rotten, lying bastard. After swearing to me you could never marry, that your work came first.*

"Not 'soon after.' Maybe three or four years later. Something like that."

"Tell me about it. Tell me about Eve," she implored. Hidden from sight by the table, Laura dug her nails into her thighs to keep from rising and smashing her fists against his chest. *He gave her his name. She bore his child!* It was an unbearable offense to her pride.

"Laura dear, you don't want to listen to my sour old tale."

"Oh but I do, Lawrence. I do!" she replied with a bright smile. She needed to hear about her rival, if only to punish herself for the tears, the heartache, those long lonely years of misplaced devotion.

A friend in New York, he told her, had recommended Eve as a model. "And as soon as she showed up at the studio, I understood why. Eve was Venus incarnate, a living, breathing composite of a hundred masterpieces: thick, flaming red hair, skin and features that Titian would have killed for. One look at her and I was like a man possessed. I must have made dozens and dozens of sketches of her, and the paint would be barely dry on a canvas she'd posed for when it was sold. The funny thing is, during all those months we barely spoke." He stopped and turned his face from her, his thoughts a thousand miles away. "Then I had to be in Paris for a couple of months for a show my dealer had set up, and when I got back ...well, we sort of got together." He cleared his throat noisily and took a sip from his cup.

"After we were married, Eve didn't want to pose anymore. That was o.k. with me, I'd exhausted her as a subject and I needed to move on. Then we had Thea ...God, Laura, she was such a beautiful baby! I mean, people on the street, in the park ...everywhere... they used to stop and admire her. We were happy in those early years ...Then, I don't know. *Does one ever know?* My stuff was selling well and I had to travel a lot and when I was home, I was cooped up in the studio working. I guess Eve was lonely. But she never said a word... I came home one night and all of her and Thea's things were gone. Nothing else was missing, except my favorite study of Thea, one I made when she was five or six. Eve nicked that ... There *must have been someone else* ...but I never found out who he was. Australia's such a fucking big continent, how could I ever find them? It's hopeless. I don't care about Eve, but, goddamnit, I would like to see my daughter again."

'I don't care about Eve.' (mimicking his voice to herself.) What a liar! He still loves her. It's as if I never existed.

With her purchases on the seat beside her, Laura directed Owen to drive across the island to Turtle Grove, a tiny enclave barely touched by modern civilization. There, amongst the scattered shacks hidden in the hills - most without running water and electricity - lived an old woman known to the islanders as Alceena, the Queen. Like her mother and her grandmother before her, Alceena was said to possess extraordinary powers: she could put a hex on your enemies, lift a neighbor's curse from your household, cure anything from colic to impotence with her magic salves and potions. Owen broke out in a sweat as the taxi drew near the small community; along the way he'd had to stop and ask for directions. When Alceena's name was mentioned, a look of superstitious dread and fear crossed each face; shaking their heads, they turned away. At last, a bare-chested young Rastafarian pointed to a dirt road hidden from view by an overgrown patch of dead banana trees. At the end of that narrow, rutted lane stood a crude wooden fence; the cabdriver braked to a halt. "Can't go on, Mistress." Laura heard the apprehension in his voice and said calmly, "That's all right Darius. I was here once before, years ago. I can find my way." She returned a half hour later gingerly holding in her hand a small pouch tied with string.

"I'd forgotten what a marvelous cook you are, darling! The lamb, the plantains ...all done to perfection."

"Thank you, Lawrence. It's a pleasure preparing a meal for you. Reminds me of the old days. Would you like another helping of rice and curry?"

"I'd love some. And would you pass the chutney? Fabulous stuff! No one makes chutney like they do here on Lutigua, I know, I've tried them all." He helped himself to several spoonfuls of the dark, savory relish. "How about you, darling? You haven't had any. How can you resist?"

"The last time I ate mango chutney, I broke out in hives ...and I haven't touched it since!"

"Too bad. You don't know what you're missing."

"Lawrence dearest, shall we take a walk along the beach after our coffee? It's such a lovely evening."

"Sounds fine to me. Besides, I've made a pig of myself and need to work off some of your superb dinner!" He grinned knowingly at her, "Let's have a nightcap when we get back from the beach, and after that ... Damnit, Laura, I can't wait to get my hands on you again!"

Scully was mid-way through his snifter of brandy when Laura saw his sudden grimace.

"Is something the matter, Lawrence?"

"No, I'm fine. Probably just my stomach punishing me for being such a glutton."

Five minutes later, he was doubled over in agony. Laura phoned Reception and ordered that two able-bodied hotel workers be sent to her suite immediately. "Mr. Scully has taken ill and needs help getting to his room."

She remained at the artist's bedside the rest of the night, wiping his brow, offering sips of tepid gingerale after each violent siege of vomiting; nothing, however, seemed to ease the spasms of pain contorting his body. At dawn, she called the Doctor.

"Poor fellow, he's had a bad time of it."

"What's the matter with him, Dr. Harcourt? Is he going to be all right?" The two were having a whispered conversation in the corridor outside Scully's room.

"Looks like food poisoning to me. But I can't be sure unless I run some tests. And you know how it is here: all the blood and urine specimens have to be flown to the lab in Miami and the results can take up to two weeks. Look, Mrs. Foster-Jones, my suggestion to you is that you put your guest on the next plane to–night. Where's he from?"

"Florida. A town in Florida."

"Right. He needs to get back to his own doctor. I'll give him a sedative now so he can sleep, and if you can get him a seat on the late afternoon flight, he ought to be able to make it on his own. I'll leave some pills to help ease the flight."

"Food poisoning! I don't understand it. We both ate the same dinner last night. It must be something he had earlier in the day."

From the top step at the entrance to Belle Jours, Laura blew a kiss and waved at the ashen figure huddled on the back seat of Owen's taxi. As soon as the cab disappeared from sight, she calmly returned to her suite, locking the door behind her. From the back of a closet shelf she pulled out the jar of mango chutney and flushed the remains down the toilet. Withdrawing a pair of heavy scissors from a drawer in the bedroom, she returned to the sitting room and retrieved the rolled-up canvas leaning against the wall. When she was done with the scissors, she dropped the pieces, one by one, into the waste basket.

With a sigh, she picked up the telephone and asked for an outside line:

"Marianne! It's me, Laura. Are you free tonight? Good. Come have dinner with me. I just got rid of an extremely tiresome guest and I want to celebrate . I'll call Gideon and see if he can join us."

* * * * * * * * * *

Hoping no one would notice, Peter Callender wiped his moist palms on a handkerchief as he waited for the choir to finish. It wouldn't do for anyone to guess how nervous he was. Today he would be giving his first sermon at Bethel Methodist, and with every ounce of his being he prayed it would go well. *She was here last Sunday, but I don't see her here today.* He struggled to overcome a pang of regret as he searched in vain for that special face amongst the singers; illogically he'd counted on her being there.

Thanks to the members of Bethel's Women's Fellowship, Callender and his daughter were now settled in a cozy chattel house within walking distance of Tamika's school and the church. A few treasured items from his former house had been shipped from St.

George's and the churchwomen diligently set about furnishing the rest. They also arranged for him to interview two ladies for the position of housekeeper: he ruled out the first, who was more intent on admiring her recent manicure than answering his questions and hired Mrs. Linton, a buxom older woman who affirmed she 'liked children', had raised three of her own, and shyly admitted to being 'a passable cook.' Not only had she been too modest in describing her culinary skills, but he was pleased to learn her family had been one of the founding members of the Church, that Mrs. Linton knew by heart the names and history of every congregant.

CHAPTER XX

The morning after the Scully debacle the kitchen crew was alarmed to see the Mistress enter their domain shortly before the diningroom opened for breakfast. Laura was attired in what she flippantly referred to as 'my working clothes'—impeccably tailored black linen slacks, white cotton blouse cinched at the waist by a wide black leather belt and black thong sandals. Silently she toured every inch of the area, inspecting the contents of the three hotel-size refrigerators, peering into the freezer, running her finger idly along the countertops and stove to check for greasy spots, randomly picking up a plate, a cup, a tray, a piece of cutlery, and giving it her full attention. Suddenly she was aware that the entire food operation had come to a halt and that her conduct was the focus of every eye.

"Please, continue with what you're doing. I don't wish to interfere with your routine." Corbin stomped in at that moment, his broad hands holding an outsize metal bucket full of fish fresh from the docks. "You there, Dewey, get off that mutha-fucking ass a'yours en give me a hand ..." his voice died when he saw his employer in a corner by the chopping table. While the chef's mind rapidly assessed what his next words should be, the hapless Dewey slipped the bucket from his grasp and moved out of sight. Stalling for time - *What she doin' in my kitchen?* – the Barbadian leisurely wiped his hands on the corner of his apron as he strolled over to where she stood.

"Morning, Mrs. Is there somethin' we can do for you?"

"Good morning, Corbin. I'm here to see how you and your staff are coming along. Very nicely, as far as I can tell, but there are a few items that need attention. Please plan to attend the meeting at four this afternoon in the office. We'll discuss it then." She nodded and walked serenely past him and out the door.

"Well I'll be a duppy's uncle. What's tearin' her shirt?"

Like a whirling dervish, Laura appeared unannounced at all the major service areas of the hotel (by the time she left her next stop, the grapevine had warned the others) including the gardening shed where she caught a maid and one of the kitchen helpers in a torrid embrace. She stood by the open door of the shed until they became aware of her presence; hastily moving apart, they expected to be sacked on the spot, but all Laura said was, "Get back to your duties immediately!"

The last to hear about 'the Mistress' inspection' was Leona Caswell.

The meeting that afternoon lasted for some time. The hotel's owner had gone over every inch of her property with the finesse of a Dress-Parade Sergeant and nothing, it seemed, escaped her keen eye. Only Osbert Marshall and the head gardener remained unscathed. (The couple in the shed were never mentioned.) Before dismissing the group, Laura warned, "I shall be checking to see that these lapses have been corrected in the very near future."

Marshall and Tyler fell in step alongside each other on the way back to their respective stations.

"Congratulations, Marshall. You got away with a clean slate."

The elder Lutiguan shook his head admiringly: "De Mistress, she's not missin' a trick. I've been at some fancy places in my time, but her eagle eye beats 'em all."

"I thought Corbin would explode when she got to the part about the floor in the cold food storage area needing a scrubbing. ... Not that my bar won any Oscars. I'm going to have to knock a few heads together, especially after she mentioned dirty ashtrays lying around and the habit my boys have of rinsing used glasses in cold water. But damnit, that crack about the barman's unpolished shoes was sort of gilding the lily, don't you think?"

"De details, Mister Scranton. 'Tention to details. That's what runnin' a good hotel's about," Marshall said with a grin as they parted.

It had been a long, tiring day, but her expended efforts gave Laura a keen sense of satisfaction. Better still, not once had she thought of Lawrence Scully. Helping herself to a generous rum and soda at the small bar in her sitting room, she slipped off her sandals and padded barefoot onto the patio to watch the sun go down. Sinking gratefully into a lounge chair, she reviewed the events of the day. Three familiar raps on the door interrupted her reverie. *Oh damn. That will be Leona. She's probably cross because I didn't tell her about the inspection.*

"Come in."

* * * * * * * * * *

To Leona Caswell, life consisted of one losing battle after another. As a child she'd been plain and shy; in her early twenties at a time of life when most young women could count on attracting a husband or a lover, physiological problems manifest themselves in an unseemly weight gain and loss of hair. Nor were financial ease and comfort to be her lot. After completing a commercial course, she had moved from one dreary secretary /companion position to another— her diligence unappreciated, her personal feelings ignored.

The ugly reverberations from her affair with Anderson had driven Laura to England, to 'Clove Hill', a house inherited from her late husband's family and sited on the outskirts of the quaint fishing village of Clovelly on Devon's western coast.

Leona was introduced to Laura Foster-Jones at a church fair in Clovelly; they met again in the village several days later. Laura was picking over the display of fresh fruit in front of *Bolton's*, the green grocer, when Leona spoke to her. In the midst of exchanging pleasantries, Foster-Jones peered sharply at the heavy woman, "Excuse me, Miss Caswell, but is something the matter? Are you unwell?"

Leona was so taken aback by the question that in spite of herself she blurted out, "I'm fine, thank you ... No. No, I'm not! Everything's so bloody awful," and to her everlasting shame, burst into tears. Laura guided her across the cobbled street to the village tearoom and over a cup of that restoring brew, Caswell hesitantly confided the details of her difficult life: her employer, she related, was a querulous widow, a chronic hypochondriac whose demands were unceasing and unreasonable. ("Two doctors have already washed their hands of her. The one she has now encourages her mythical aches and pains so he can pocket the fees. I am at my wit's end.") She didn't mention the woman's scorching tantrums, her vindictiveness, but Laura had heard enough.

A month later a taxi deposited Leona and three bulging suitcases at 'Clove Hill,' a handsome Georgian-styled 'cottage' with a lilacs in lush bloom at the library window and primroses climbing over the doorway. She was installed in the unused maid's quarters, two smallish rooms, freshly painted, on the second floor at the back of the house. With furnishings from the attic which she selected herself and new curtains from *Selfridges*, it evolved into the most appealing sanctuary the Englishwoman had ever known.

In the beginning her secretarial duties at the large, comfortable house in Devon took up so little time that she eagerly volunteered to take on more responsibilities. Under Laura's patient tutelage, Leona learned how to select the freshest fish, where to place an oyster fork, appropriate wines to be served with each dinner course, how to discreetly check whether Millie, the daily, or Mrs. Dorsey, the cook, were helping themselves to provisions from the larder and other practical matters. After a few months, Caswell was not only handling Laura's correspondence and bills, but had taken over the running of the household as well.

The seasons dissolved, one into the other, and Leona Caswell had never been happier. She was totally devoted to Laura and earnestly believed her to be 'the cleverest, most attractive, and (despite occasional displays of temper) kindest person in the universe.' She would never forget the day when her employer said casually, "I think it's time we dropped the formalities. Call me 'Laura' and if I may, it will be 'Leona' from now on." Once she'd gained the privacy of her own small suite, the unloved woman wept with joy.

When she was finally settled, with the rooms decorated and re-arranged to her satisfaction, Laura made contact with distant cousins on her mother's side;

she was particularly taken with a niece, Mary Farmington, a spirited girl in her mid-twenties who became a familiar presence at 'Clove Hill'. She also wrote to an aunt of Edward's, inviting her to come for a visit. A reply was received by return post:

Dear Mrs. Foster-Jones,

Thank you for your kind invitation, which in good conscience I cannot accept. What possessed my brother to change his Will and leave 'Clove Hill' to you, I do not know. I can only surmise that being a a sentimentalist at heart, he meant it as a gesture to the memory of his only son, my dear nephew Edward.

'Clove Hill' has been in our family for six generations. It seems to me a marriage that lasted at best a few weeks, hardly qualifies you as 'family,' particularly since you and Edward had no children. The property should have passed to my daughter, Elizabeth or her younger brother, James.

However, what is done is done.

Yours truly,

Daphne Foster-Jones Williams

The virtues of a tranquil life in a small English village had no appeal to Laura, who preferred to surround herself with people who were bright and amusing . (It was noted by the ever-curious locals that the males who crossed her threshold far outnumbered the females) While she refused to be drawn into 'good works' and what passed for 'ladies' activities' in Clovelly, she was astute enough to invite the village patriarchs and their wives, the vicar and his lady and the local doctor to high tea from time to time. Old friends from University days and the war years in London arrived in a steady stream to spend a weekend at 'Clove Hill' during which liquor and laughter flowed in generous proportion and the downstairs' rooms were ablaze with light long after midnight; her dinner parties became as legendary as they had been on Lutigua.

Every month or two Laura would go up to London by train for a few days, returning with a designer tote-bag full of food. Shooing Dorsey out of the kitchen, she would spend the next several days preparing West

Indian dishes with exotic names like *coo-coo, sofrito, callaloo, pudding & souse.* Afterwards, when the food was gone, she was pensive and irritable.

The episode involving the crippled Harden boy further endeared her employer to Leona. It had its modest beginnings when Mrs. Dorsey, the cook, asked to have a private word with Laura. Nervously shifting from one foot to the other, the stolid countrywoman said, "If it's agreeable, M'um, could we buy our eggs somewhere else besides *Bolton's*?"

"What an odd request, Dorsey. Is there something wrong with Mr. Bolton's eggs?"

"No, M'um. They're always fresh as the day they was laid. But it's like this, M'um." As she began to speak about the Harden family, tenant farmers on an estate two miles north of the village, Mrs. Dorsey's agitation evaporated . The Hardens, she related, had five children, the youngest "a baby still in her nappies." The father had recently sustained serious injuries in an accident at the farm and would be unable to work for a long time, if ever. His two oldest boys and wife carried on as best they could, but they were having a hard time of it.

"What has this got to do with eggs, Dorsey?"

"I'm getting to that, M'um," was the stout reply.

When he became aware of their plight the landowner offered to let the boys handle the sale of eggs produced at the farm instead of using his customary wholesaler. "It were a fair offer, M'um, but then Mr. Aldrich, him what owns the land, he's a fine gentleman. Said they could sell chickens, too. Not the whole lot, of course, but enough so's they'd have some extra come the end of the month. So I was hopin', M'um ..."

From that day forward, the Hardens supplied the household with fresh eggs and chickens.

The weekly order was handed over to the cook at the kitchen door and it wasn't until Dorsey was laid up with the flu that Mrs. Harden met her benefactor. On a raw, windy October afternoon with rain clouds hovering in the distance, Laura was in the kitchen setting out the ingredients for a soufflé when she was interrupted by a light tap at the door. She opened it to find a woman in a black rain slicker standing on the lower step, a basket of eggs on her arm; her face, sallow and pinched, was old before its time. Behind her in the gloom, Laura caught a glimpse of a child of indeterminate age sitting swathed in blankets in a hand-made wooden trundle.

"Oh, you must be Mrs. Harden."

"Yes, M'um. Come to bring the weekly order."

"Tell me about that child in the cart who came with Mrs. Harden" Laura asked Dorsey when she returned to work.

"Oh, that would be Ian, the middle one. Poor little lad, he was born like that. Both legs bent like a wishbone, and them with no money to fix 'em."

"How old is he?"

"Ian must be all of nine years now."

"But surely they've applied to the National Health?"

"I hear tell in the village it took years before the Missus could persuade Mr. Harden to register Ian with the local board, him havin' his pride and all. Now they must wait their turn. Could be another year, maybe more before his name comes up."

The next time Mrs. Harden appeared with the weekly order, Laura made a point of meeting and speaking with the boy. Something about his sweet countenance, his cheerful acceptance of his disability, touched her deeply. Thereafter, she not only saw that he had a steady supply of puzzles and books ordered from *Foyles* in Charing Cross Road, but she embarked on a search for an orthopedic specialist who would accept Ian as a patient. Because it was impossible for his mother to leave her family when the time came for the boy to go up to London for an examination, Laura hired a taxi and took him herself. She remained at his bedside after surgery and during the long stay in hospital, and when they returned to Clovelly, arranged for a physical therapist to oversee his rehabilitation.

The plight of this unspoiled, crippled boy - Laura called him 'my brave little soldier' - triggered a profound emotional response from the childless woman: untapped reservoirs of patience, selflessness and love were lavished on Ian during the long days of his convalescence.

Watching the subsequent stream of bills emanating from this largesse only served to strengthen Leona's devotion.

When she first discovered a man had spent the night with Laura, had actually *slept in her bed,* Leona's sense of shock and betrayal was underscored by a tinge of jealous pique. Other paramours succeeded him, of course, and eventually Caswell came to view these sexual forays in a different light. Those pre-mating rituals of flattery and flirtation - enacted before her eyes and anyone else's who happened to be at the house - were merely a game to Laura, she decided, her seductive power over men affording her a vicarious thrill, a preverse pleasure. Having convinced herself that this accounted for the careless turnover in bed partners, the Englishwoman relaxed.

Lawrence Scully was another matter entirely.

A period of dark moods and despondency descended on the Devon household; Laura stopped inviting guests to 'Clove Hill', took no interest in what she wore or how she looked, and was by turns testy and unapproachable. Nothing Leona did seemed to please her. Finally, alarmed at her deterioration - she, who always took such pride in every aspect of her appearance - the Englishwoman mustered the courage to suggest Laura seek medical help.

"You haven't been yourself for a long time," she said softly, dreading the tongue lashing she was sure would follow this effrontery. But to her amazement, Laura agreed.

"Thank you for your concern, Leona. I know these past few months haven't been easy for you, but I don't need a doctor to tell me what the problem is, I know myself: I miss Lutigua. I miss my island. I want to go home."

A week later they boarded a flight to the Caribbean; Laura's spirits lifted with each passing mile that carried them closer to the place of her birth. She seemed like her old self again. After assessing the condition of Belle Jours, she announced plans to give up the house in England and return to Lutigua as soon as possible to reopen the hotel. Shortly after their arrival back in Devon, she made legal arrangements to deed 'Clove Hill' over to Edward's cousin Elizabeth.

Later Caswell would remember that she was never asked if the move to a tropical island suited her; Laura took it for granted that wherever she went, the dedicated woman would follow. One afternoon at teatime as she and Laura were discussing details of closing down the house in Devon, the heavy woman timidly voiced her reservations: "Perhaps it would be better if I didn't go to Lutigua with you. I've absolutely no experience of running a hotel, you know. I'd only be in your way."

"Nonsense, my dear. Of course you must come with me! You know how much I depend on your judgement ... your good common sense." Flattered by this admission, Leona was content to let the matter rest.

But Lutigua had been a mistake. She could see that now. Not only did the climate on 'this bloody primitive island.' sap her nerves and energy, making it a struggle each day to leave the sanctuary of her cool rooms and face the relentless heat, but it was as if the woman she had known and revered had peeled off a mask and assumed another darker personality. Whereas Leona had been treated with a measure of respect and intimacy in Devon, nowadays she felt on a par with the locals whom Laura ordered around like a medieval monarch.

Little by little, Leona watched her authority undermined to a humiliating degree, but like a ship-wrecked sailor she clung to the hope, "Tomorrow will be better. Tomorrow she'll be like the old Laura."

Then Lawrence Scully had appeared on the scene. One look at Laura's animated face the afternoon Leona met him was enough. Later that evening, the Englishwoman broke down and wept tears of bitterness and defeat. But as she paced the floor, smoking one cigarillo after another, the tears gradually gave way to stirrings of rebellion. *There's nothing to keep me here. Laura doesn't own me.*

Scully's sudden illness took her by surprise, as did the detached look on Laura's face as she made arrangments for his departure from the island. But it was too late, her mind was made up.

"If you're not busy, Laura, I need to speak with you."

"Of course, my dear. Come, sit down. Would you like me to send for anything? A cold drink? Cup of tea?"

"I haven't time," she replied coolly. "One of the new maids is causing a problem and I'm needed in housekeeping."

"Look, if you're upset about my inspection this morning and the meeting, let me explain ..."

"You don't owe me an explanation, Laura. Besides, it has nothing to do with that." She paused, marshalling the nerve to utter the words she'd rehearsed a dozen times over. "I'm here to give you notice. I want to return to England as soon as you can find a replacement for me. I can't stay here any longer."

Stung by this unexpected news of desertion, "What do you mean, *you can't?*" she snapped back.

With grim satisfaction Caswell sensed panic underlying the angry words. *She's upset. Well that's too bloody bad. Did she expect me to be at her beck and call forever?*

Instantly regretting her show of temper, Laura calmly probed for the cause of Leona's decision, but seeing that her mind was made up, perversely refused to beg her to stay on. Minutes later as she stepped from the suite, carefully pulling shut the door behind her, Leona's shoulders sagged. What should have been her moment of triumph was instead the dull, stabbing ache of irretrievable loss.

CHAPTER XXI

The note was under Caswell's door when she returned to her rooms after lunch:

Leona, Please stop by my suite late this afternoon.

There are several matters I need to discuss with you.

Laura

Not 'Dear Leona' ... not even 'Love.' As if I were a stranger. Probably what I deserve ... after all, I'm jumping ship. Still ... She sighed deeply and slowly began unwinding her turban.

Promptly at five, she rapped on Laura's door, bracing herself for an unpleasant interlude. As she entered and crossed the room, the sight of the customary tea tray on the patio caught her off guard.

"Oh, I wasn't expecting ..." she bit her lip, fighting back the temptation to show surprise.

"But, of course, my dear. Don't we usually take tea at this hour? Come, sit down," Laura offered graciously. "Pour us both a cup, won't you?"

Still smarting from their last encounter, the heavy woman remained subdued as her hostess chatted brightly about minor hotel matters. Laura paused finally and putting down her cup, leaned forward. Holding the Englishwoman's gaze in hers, she said softly, "I'm sorry you will be leaving, Leona. I shall miss you terribly. You must understand that your announcement, coming as it did, was quite a shock. I apologize if I took the news badly. I've had time to think about it over these last few days and realize that returning to Lutigua is what I wanted - *it is my home, I belong here* - but it may not suit you at all. You have every right to wish to move on, and if I can be of any help, if there is anyone I can contact about a position back in England, please don't hesitate to ask."

Caswell was grateful for the apology, grateful that that there would be no more fuss over her wish to leave.

Still, if that despicable Scully hadn't shown up, I might have stayed on. Perhaps it's all for the best.

"Thank you, Laura. I appreciate your offer."

"Now Leona, I need your advice on the best possible person to take over when you leave. Yesterday I jotted down a list of all the responsibilities you have shouldered here at Belle Jours. It's a very impressive list! So impressive, in fact, I've decided to give whoever succeeds you the glorified title of 'Assistant Manager.' Since the pay won't be much, the title ought to help. I was thinking I might offer the position to Scranton. After a somewhat uninspired beginning, he seems to have the bar running quite well. What do you think, my dear? Should I ask Tyler to step in?"

"Oh dear, I wish you hadn't asked. Don't misunderstand, Laura, I'm very fond of Tyler. Remember what a tower of strength and diplomacy he was during that dreadful mess with Avery? And yet ..."

"And yet, what? Please speak frankly."

"Well, I've always wondered. Here's an attractive, personable man with no ties, nothing to hold him back, and what's he doing at the age of 40? He's running a bar for someone else. Of course, there's nothing wrong with that, or wouldn't be if Tyler were not very bright. But he *is bright*. So what does that suggest?"

"Perhaps no one's taken the time to notice his potential."

"Could be, but in my experience the people who get ahead don't wait around to be noticed. No, I don't think it's that simple."

"You're hesitating again, Leona. *Please*. I value your opinion."

"You're very kind. But remember now, it's my intuition speaking ... a far cry from cold, hard facts." She took a moment to concentrate on selecting the precise words to express herself:

"I've come to suspect, Laura, that underneath that agreeable facade of Tyler's is an incurable adolescent ...someone unwilling, perhaps unable, to persevere when matters get difficult. He may be magnificent in a crises, but I don't think he can sustain it. Most disturbing of all - and you must have observed this yourself - the man will go to any lengths to avoid a confrontation or any unpleasantness. The business with Avery is a perfect example. Before the flare-up, before James was driven to defend his manhood the only way he knew, there had to be a dozen different signs as to what was going on. I believe Tyler chose to ignore those danger signals rather than face up to a scene with Avery. Then, when the whole thing came crashing down and he could no longer ignore it, he had to act. And of course, he acquitted himself beautifully. The job of Assistant Manager at a resort hotel is a demanding, thankless task with all of the headaches and none of the glory. And Tyler's been here long enough to know it. I think he'll turn you down."

"You can't be serious! It's a wonderful opportunity. Of course he'll take it. He'd be a fool not to. I'm not naive enough to think he'll want to stay on here forever. But think of how the experience will embellish a resumé when he returns to the States!"

"What about Danielle? She's an extremely capable young woman."

"*Danielle Mapp?* A native girl? I wouldn't dream of it. No, sorry, but that won't do at all."

Scranton was summoned to Laura's suite the following morning.

"Miss Caswell is leaving us."

"I'm sorry to hear that, Ma'm. She'll be missed."

"I'm telling you this in confidence. For the moment, no one else on staff is to know."

"I understand."

"The point is, I need someone reliable to replace her, an Assistant Manager, if you will. The job has tremendous possibilities because along with taking over from Miss Caswell, the person must be willing and able to assume responsibility for managing the entire operation on his own should the need arise. And while I'm making this change, I also plan to clear out the deadwood. It won't hurt if word gets around that the hotel expects a full day's work for pay. Decide if you want to make any changes in your bailiwick and do it soon because severance notices need to go out at the end of next month."

"I'll give it some thought, Mrs. Foster-Jones, but off hand, I can't think of anyone who isn't pulling his weight."

"How about Sam?"

"Sam's first-rate. He could run the bar with one hand tied behind him"

"Good. He may have a chance to prove it sooner than you think." She flashed him a warm smile. "How would you like to be Belle Jour's new Assistant Manager, Tyler?"

"Me, Ma'm?"

"I don't see anyone else in the room, do you?"

"But I've had no experience..."

"I underestand that." Struggling to overcome his astonishment, Tyler missed the exasperated edge in the woman's voice. "There's a school in Miami, runs a crash course in Hotel Management. I'd be prepared to stake you to it if you decide you want the job."

"I guess I need a little time to think it over," he said lamely. Increasingly of late, Tyler had begun to fantasize about the future, certain that given half a chance, he would meet the kind of woman he would want to spend the rest of his life with. Instinctively he knew that staying on in Lutigua for an indefinite period would foreclose any hope he might have of finding a safe harbour, of writing *finis* to his free-floating lifestyle. Yet Foster-Jones' offer was tempting: he liked his job, liked the Lutiguans and the tempo of life on a tropical island; he never tired of Lutigua's natural beauty, nor its agreeable climate—both exerted a powerful magnetism. But he wasn't sure it was enough to make up for the hassle of running a hotel.

"You do that, Scranton. Take 24 hours to sleep on it. I want your answer by noon tomorrow."

He left the suite and slowly trudged back up to the cabin, his thoughts in a turmoil as he debated the pros and cons of his employer's offer. As Tyler pushed open the screen door he saw the letter. *Reception must have told someone to stick it under the door.* He picked up the envelope. *It's got a Greenwich postmark, must be from Sarah.*

Dear Tyler, It was a toss-up between seats for 'Evita' (tenth row center!) and rum punches on a sandy beach on Lutigua.

Guess which sounded the most tempting??!

Flying in the Monday after Easter. Please ask Danielle to hold a room for me. Sarah

"You'll need to order four dozen beach towels, six cases of hand soap, three dozen pillow slips," Leona looked up from the list in her hand and said, "Laura, I've been meaning to ask, have you spoken with Tyler? Did he take you up on your offer?"

"No. You were right. He didn't want the job. I've considered contacting an employment agency in London, but only as a last resort. I keep hoping I might find someone here."

"This may sound a bit far-fetched, but what about your niece?"

"*Mary? Mary Farmington?* She's so ...so young ... and she doesn't know a thing about running a hotel!"

"But Mary's terribly bright, and you could teach her, Laura. Besides, she's family. Someone you know and can trust. Mary wasn't all that keen on her position at that publishing house as I recall. She might jump at a chance to come to the island, of facing a challenging job."

Laura gazed at the heavy woman with admiration. "Leona! You're a... It's a wonderful idea! Worth a try, anyway, Mary can always say 'No.' I'll send a cable this evening."

* * * * * * * * * *

Several weeks later, the following notice was posted on the bulletin board:

To: All Staff and employees of the hotel

From: Mrs. Foster-Jones

Miss Caswell will be leaving Belle Jours at the end of the month to return to her home in England. We have been fortunate to have Miss Caswell with us. Her contribution to the successful re-opening and smooth running of this hotel cannot be over-estimated. I know you wish her well, as I do.

Miss Mary Farmington is to be our new Assistant Manager, assuming many of Miss Caswell's duties. I count on you to give Miss Farmington any assistance she may need. Your full cooperation is appreciated during this changeover in personnel.

None of the hotel employees attached any significance to the appearance of a young woman with a clipped British accent and a milk-maid complexion who arrived on one of the bi-weekly flights from Heathrow and asked to be directed to the hotel owner's quarters . (In response to her niece's enthusiastic acceptance of 'a trial run' as Assistant Manager, Laura had written: "To get you started off on the right foot, I'd like to keep our relationship from the staff for as long as possible, so do forgive me if I welcome you in the privacy of my suite." She added a postscript: "Of course, nothing stays a secret for very long on this island!")

Mary threw her arms around her aunt and hugged her, "I can't believe I'm here. Don't wake me up if I'm dreaming," she said breathlessly.

"Stand back. Let me look at you."

"I'm a proper mess from the long trip. But once I've had a washup and settled my hair, I'll look so dignified and professional, you won't recognize me," her voice teased, her hazel eyes flashing with merriment. Copper-coloured bangs and straight hair framed a moon-shaped face with its creamy alabaster skin and rosy cheeks, the kind of complexion associated with so many denizens of the British Isles.

Laura gazed at her with affection, "If you truly mean to look professional, my dear, I suggest you leave that skirt you're wearing in the closet. It's ... well, let's just say it's a bit provocative for Lutigua."

"But Aunt Laura, it's what everyone's wearing in London ..." her voice drifted off as she looked down at the expanse of shapely leg showing below the hem of her mini. "You're right, of course. Sorry."

"As the Lutiguans are so fond of saying, 'Not to worry,'" Laura answered blithely. "I have a wonderful dressmaker. We'll get you fixed up in no time. Come, let's sit on the patio. I've ordered dinner to be served up here so we can talk. I want to catch up on all the news."

Dreading the moment when she must take leave of the only person she has truly loved, Leona nonetheless threw herself into the task of preparing Laura's niece to take over her duties. She was fond of the young woman, had come to appreciate her outgoing personality and keen mind during her stays at 'Clove Hill.' Belatedly, Caswell discovered that the very qualities that made Mary outstanding in her own surroundings, might prove a liability on Lutigua. For one thing, there was Mary's accent, hallmark of an expensive education and an upper-class milieu . Since gaining their independence, Lutiguans were trapped in a love/hate relationship with their former colonial masters. They liked the funds Britain dutifully sent upon request to improve the infrastructure, were grateful for their favoured-trading status, their British-trained police force, and the excellence of the parish school system established by an Anglican priest sent over by the mother church. The Queen's picture graced the Lutiguan currency, and so wedded were the islanders to the trappings and rituals associated with royalty and the British judiciary, they were emulated at every opportunity.

But as the black political structure grew in sophistication and power, a reaction to their former masters set in; they would retain the pomp and ceremony, but privately they resented any symbols that reminded them of the past, embracing instead burgeoning relationships with the U.S. and Canada. Moreover, the young people, born after Independence, were openly distainful of anything - be it products or people - that bore the hallmark, 'Made in England.'

In contrast, as the years rolled by the white plantocracy clung more desperately to the the images and tokens which signified their former status. Amongst themselves they mocked the pretentions of the new government and made fun of the civil service. The prospect of an educated, prosperous, black middle class was frightening.

On Leona's last evening at Belle Jours, Laura hosted an elaborate dinner party in her honor, inviting those who had gone out of their way to befriend the Englishwoman: Sir Edmund, Gideon Moss and Marianne Pharr from the Sunday group, Dr. Harcourt and Mary. (Remembering Tyler's kindness to her, the obese woman had asked that he be included, but Laura, still smarting from his rejection, said he was 'too busy.') Hot canapes, mock turtle soup, roast beef and Yorkshire pudding (two of Caswell's favorites) and one of Corbin's special desserts, cherries jubilee *flambé*—all this, accompanied by generous helpings of vintage wines and champagne, highlighted the evening meal. When the last guest had departed, trailing in his wake 'good luck, Leona', the two women were left to themselves.

"Oh Laura, it was a lovely evening! Perfect in every detail! I can't thank you enough."

"Nonsense, my dear. No more than you deserve. *You're the one* who deserves thanks... for your loyalty, for the order and tranquillity you provided in my life."

Leona's eyes swelled with tears; she groped awkwardly in her pocket for a handkerchief and dabbed at them.

"None of that, now Leona," Laura said with mock severity, relinquishing her brandy glass and rising to her feet. "When I come back, I don't want to see a trace of tears!" She disappeared into the bedroom and returned a moment later bearing a small, elegantly wrapped package. "Here. This is for you, my dear."

Slowly the Englishwoman untied the silver bow, pushed aside the tissue-paper hiding a black velvet box bearing the legend, *Harrods*; with trembling fingers she lifted the cover to find a fine Swiss watch imbedded in a gold locket.

"I don't know what to say ... it's so beautiful ..." As Laura looked on in dismay, tears started afresh, dampening the cheeks of the unattractive woman.

"You don't have to say anything. Just think of me when you wear it."

* * * * * * * * * *

A few weeks prior to the hotel's official opening and with a half-day off to squander, Tyler had driven to the island's capitol city one afternoon to wander aimlessly along its byways looking for diversion. In an alleyway near the harbor, nestled between an abandoned police station and the skeletal remains of a warehouse, he discovered *The Bristol*, a loving replica of that backbone of the British Empire—the local pub. As he sat nursing a cold beer at the bar, he looked around its dimly-lit interior and marvelled at the beautiful old mahogany beams and the tattered Union Jack prominently displayed on its white-washed walls. In a corner at the back of the room he spied a darts board and next to it, a door with GENT'S LOO in peeling painted letters. The bar was a long slab of wood, its surface nicked and blackened with age and use; the sole occupant of a bar stool at its far end raised his head at the advent of the newcomer, then turned back to his drink, ignoring him completely.

As Scranton paid for his beer, he asked the bartender, "Is this place always so quiet?"

"No, mon. When Mister Robertson's in port - he's de boss - dis place's jumpin' like a party of crapauds. Truth to tell, there ain't a sweeter sound than him callin' to me, 'Isaiah, set 'em up, I'm back.'"

He'd headed straight for the *Bristol* the day the American teachers went back to the States, but once again, the pub's elusive owner was absent. He hung around anyway and drank too much, but instead of feeling better, he drove back to Belle Jours more depressed than ever.

Third time lucky, maybe? was his optimistic conjecture as he headed for the *Bristol* once more. Sarah would be arriving in a few days and he was on edge, caught between his impatience to see her and a nagging skepticism. *Am I making too much of this? Getting too worked up over a casual couple of days together? What if she gets here and decides she can't stand me... or worse, I can't stand her?* It was only after he'd parked the station wagon and was walking in the direction of the pub that he noticed an unorthodox stillness pervading the entire city: the shops were closed and there wasn't a vendor in sight. He stepped across the street to read a small sign posted on the door of a dry goods emporium: *Closed for the Easter Holiday.*

Well I'll be damned.

On Easter Sunday morning the Bethel Methodist Church was full to over-flowing, its congregation a sea of rainbow colours, the women's dazzling finery overshadowing the men in their sombre suits (usually the only suit they owned, reserved for weddings and funerals and attendance at weekly worship.) Their exuberant voices claimed "He Lives" as the choir, dressed in robes of Wedgewood blue, moved sedately down the aisle. As head usher and a Leader in the church, Josiah Mapp stood at the rear, happy to see his beloved daughter amongst the singers; there were many Sundays when Danielle's duties at the hotel kept her away. Peter Callender saw her too, and felt a rare quickening of his pulse.

CHAPTER XXII

For three weeks, with British school 'hols' beginning and ending a few days before spring break in the States, every room at Belle Jours was occupied. Mary, who had her hands full, commented sourly, "From the looks of it around here, you'd think we were running a summer camp, not a hotel." With the exception of a short hiatus on Good Friday, Tyler worked continuously over the weekend, carefully arranging the bar schedule so that once Sarah was in residence, he'd have plenty of time off.

So few major airlines flew into Lutigua on a regular basis that the islanders knew by heart their schedules, except, of course, during the 'high' season, when a growing number of charter flights unloaded visitors from various parts of the world, all seeking escape from the bane of winter. Since Sarah had neglected to mention what airline she'd be on - there being a four-hour difference in the arrival times of the two major carriers from the U.S - Tyler had no choice but to wait for her at the hotel. By four p.m. he knew she'd missed the flight out of Miami and had taken the later one from New York.

He kept checking his watch: *Sarah should have been here two hours ago... She'd have let me know if she couldn't make it.* At 10:30 he started trying to get through to the airport; the line was busy for over an hour. When a voice answered at last he was informed that the flight had been delayed by weather in New York, and wasn't due in until mid-night. His sense of relief was palpable. *It'll be one in the morning before she gets here.* He helped Brian close down the bar, then posted himself on one of the steps at the entrance by the circular drive, smoking one cigarette after another, oblivious to the soft caressing breeze, the riot of stars blanketing the night skies.

At last he heard the sound of a car approaching, saw two stabbing headlights move down the drive from the main road. He rose quickly and waited as the taxi circled the drive, braking to a stop in front of him. He seized open the passenger door and after a quick glance at the figure pressed into a corner of the back seat, offered a cheerful, "Welcome, Sarah. Welcome back!" She clasped his hand for support and jumped lightly to the ground. While the driver circled around to retrieve her suitcase from the trunk, Tyler scrutinized her face, noting its ashen pallor, the grey smudges of exhaustion behind the glasses.

"Wait here, while I take care of the driver."

"But you don't ..."

He ignored her protest and handed the driver the fare along with a generous tip. The Lutiguan smiled, offered a tentative salute along with his thanks and sped away. Tyler picked up Sarah's bag and took her firmly by the arm leading her into the hotel. "Thank you for taking care of the driver," she said so faintly, he could hardly hear her. When they reached the Reception Desk he put the bag down.

"Sarah, are you o.k.? You're so pale ..."

"I'm fine. Really. It's just that mother and I sat up talking 'til after mid-night, and then I had to get up at five this morning to make the connection in New York ... I'm so tired I can't think!"

"Good evenin' Miss Locke," Celene said brightly. "It's nice to have you back wid us. Would you please sign in."

"Sign in?" she asked in a dazed voice.

"You have to register, remember?" Tyler said softly. He took the room key from the Lutiguan and led Sarah to her suite, unlocking the door and turning on the lights. He placed Sarah's suitcase on a luggage carrier and handed her the key: "Get some sleep, lady. Call me in the morning when you're up. I'll be at the bar 'til noon and I'll join you for lunch. I was hoping we might spend the afternoon together."

She smiled weakly. "You may have to send an army to wake me. Thanks, Tyler. Forgive me for being such a wet dishrag ..."

"As the Lutiguans say, 'not to worry.' Good night, Sarah. I'm glad you're here."

They sat across from each other at one of the tables set up for lunch under the palm trees. Sleep had restored Sarah—gone were the dark circles and pallor, in their place, cheeks tinged with colour, eyes sparkling with vitality. After giving the waiter their order, the two suddenly found themselves stymied by an unexpected shyness and reserve; their attempts at casual conversation were clumsy and stilted, making the arrival of food a welcome diversion. While they were eating, several members of staff including Wash, strolled past on their way to or from their stations, and paused by the table to welcome Sarah back.

"That Wash is such a darling!"

"Listen lady, the help don't usually make this much fuss over a returning guest. That ought to tell you something."

"*Flattery*, sir, will get you nowhere," was her airy response.

In a finger-snap, the awkwardness of their reunion seemed to vanish; a relaxed compatibility, which marked their previous times together, eased back into place.

"How's about a swim after lunch? We could go back to that cove we found the last time."

"Sounds wonderful to me."

After a leisurely swim, they lay side by side in companionable silence languishing in the rays of a bright sun. Reluctantly, Sarah broke the spell and sat up.

"I better throw something on before I get burned to a crisp." She withdrew a light blue cotton top from her beach bag and pulled it over her head, then deftly applied another coat of suntan lotion to her face and arms. "Damn. This sun is wicked and I forgot to bring a hat."

"Hang on a sec. I've got an old baseball cap in the car. You're a *Pirate's* fan, right?"

"Do I have a choice?"

He returned, slipping the cap onto her head and deliberately pushing the brim down over the top of her nose.

"Thanks a bunch, Scranton. I can hardly see. Is this how a devoted *Pirates'* fan wears this thing?"

"Beggars shouldn't be so fussy," he mocked, flicking a handful of sand in her direction; he sat back down beside her, content to watch as Sarah began to draw elaborate curliques in the sand with her index finger. When she spoke again, her voice had none of its former playfulness.

"I must say, Fate has a funny way of arranging things. I only came back here the last time because the situation in Antigua was so intolerable, I couldn't face another day of it. I wasn't ready to go home and <u>Belle Jours</u> was the first place that popped into my head. Then *Voila!* by some miracle, a room was available!"

She went on to relate how her travel agent had booked her into an isolated hotel on Antigua, miles from the capitol. ("My fault, really. I sort of implied I *vanted to be a-lone* .") During her second day there, she realized the Hotel Manager was being much too attentive. "I mean, he followed me everywhere! Always with some excuse. He was a grubby little man, Czech, maybe, or Hungarian. He had these awful beady eyes and he was always rubbing his hands together ... leering at me... One night, after I'd gone to bed, he knocked on my door saying he needed to speak with me. I was really frightened, Tyler. Hotel managers have access to all the room keys! Of course, I wouldn't answer and finally, he went away. I put a chair against the door, but I didn't get a wink of sleep. That's when I called Lutigua... Now look! Instead of carousing in the Big Apple as planned, here I am again. Do you guys at the bar slip something into the drinks, so guests will keep wanting to come back?"

Tyler picked up a stone and hurled it angrily into the sea. "Dirty bastard... . I'd like to wring his neck. But why didn't you tell me this before?"

"I didn't feel comfortable talking about it then ..." she gave him a winsome smile, "but I don't mind now."

The hours flew by and they never seemed to run out of things to talk about (even argue about) while any mention of their personal histories or feelings was scrupulously avoided. It wasn't until later that evening as they sat nursing a nightcap by the deserted pool that Sarah broached the subject of her family.

"Dad's a honey. He's strict with the boys, but he's always been a push-over where I'm concerned... I used to get away with murder. If there was any disciplining to do, Mom did it. I was a regular little tomboy, used to get in the *worst* scrapes. At school, too! Mom saved all my old report cards and when I look at them now, I can't believe how badly I behaved! But eventually, I calmed down ... By the time I was a senior in high school, Mom and I had become very close... and we have been ever since." She described her two younger siblings: Eric, who was 13, "obnoxious sometimes, like most adolescents, but we get along and he makes me laugh," and Arthur, "a love, an absolute whiz at math. He's entering Yale this Fall."

"Sounds as if you have a great family, Sarah. Not everyone's so lucky."

"Now it's *your* turn," she teased. "I want to hear it all! Tell me, Mister Scranton," she asked, parodying the specious voice of a televison interviewer, "were you a holy terror when you were a kid?... And how old were you, sir, when you discovered blondes? (Don't think I didn't notice you making goo-goo eyes at Stacey," she said, laughing at his obvious discomfit.)

"Hey! Gimme a break," he groaned, "you don't wanna hear all those old tapes."

Her grin evaporated when she leaned forward, "I wish you'd tell me about *your* family, Tyler. Really I do. Do you have any brothers or sisters? How old are they? Are both your parents alive?" He hesitated, then began in a flat voice, picking his way through a minefield of emotions, struggling to assert a deceptive casualness. This lasted until he started to describe what happened to his brother Neddie: "It wasn't the truck driver's fault. You see it gets dark in the northeast that time of year. One minute the sun's on the horizon, the next ..." he snapped his fingers, "it's gone. Lots of truckers used to cut through the road near our house because it saved time; afterwards someone told Myra about a state law restricting certain tonnage in residential areas. Of course, it's one of those laws that stays on the books, it's never enforced. Neddie was standing with his bike by the side of the road waiting to cross when the truck swerved to avoid an oncoming car speeding down the middle of the road. Maybe a drunk, I don't know. The trucker never saw Neddie, never knew he hit anything until a fellow in the car behind chased him down. He'd witnessed the whole thing. The state police told Myra it was an accident, no one's fault really, unless you count the car that got away. The driver of the truck was pretty shook up. Sent a big wreath to the funeral. Seems he had two kids of his own." His voice faltered and trailed off. Sarah reached for his hand and squeezed it.

"After all this time ... all these years, it still hurts. I miss Neddie."

"How sad for you and your parents."

"There's only my mother and it damn near killed her. Neddie was the favorite, and after the accident, Myra - that's my mother - sort of shrivelled up like some sort of rare, exotic flower and Neddie, the only one who could nourish it, keep it alive."

"Still, your mother must be happy to have you."

"To be honest, Myra and I never did get along. After the funeral we could hardly stand to be in the same room together. I left home about two years later."

"Is your mother still living?"

"Yeah, she's still around. Look, I don't want to talk about Myra."

Trudging up the hill to the cabin after they parted, Tyler marvelled at how easy Sarah was to be with, how natural it felt to be telling her about Neddie—his death a wound that had never fully healed. He felt a sense of relief, almost buoyancy, as if the immense burden of grief for his brother was lessened by being able to share it with someone. And not just 'someone.' *Sarah's special.* Always in the past his relationship with women had centered on sex, on giving and receiving gratification; but not now. He wasn't even tempted to push for an advantage with Sarah on the few occasions when their hands touched, their bodies casually brushed against one another. Having a female confidante whose company he sought and enjoyed with no amorous strings attached was a new and heady experience for Tyler.

* * * * * * * * * *

Mary dropped by the suite to tell her aunt she'd found a new friend. "I've met this dear girl from the States, Aunt Laura. She's one of our guests, her name's Sarah Locke. I was coming back from the beach when I saw this woman trip over a garden hose lying across the path. The pile of books she was carrying went flying in all directions! I helped her retrieve them and we ended up having a cup of coffee together. We had a lovely chat. I told her all about you and the history of Belle Jours. May I bring her round to tea this afternoon so you can meet her? It's my day off."

"How about a swim around four-ish, Sarah? It's my only free time. Brian's sprained his wrist and I've got to cover for him."

"Sorry, Tyler. Mary and I are invited to tea with Mrs. Foster-Jones."

"You're having tea with the Dragon Lady?"

"That's not a very charitable description."

"I know, but remember, I work for her. F.J.'s o.k., but sometimes ... anyway, come by the bar for a drink after dinner tonight and let me know how it goes."

Laura was aware that her niece was having a difficult time with the staff, but refused to interefere or even discuss it. *She's got Shelby blood in her veins. She'll work it out.* But she couldn't help noticing that the bloom had gone from the English girl's cheeks, that her skin had taken on a sallow, unbecoming colour and at times dark hollows appeared beneath her eyes. To assuage ambiguous pangs of guilt, Laura went to extra pains to see that a lavish tea was prepared and waiting for the two young women.

The hour passed quickly and pleasantly; Mary, seeing the trouble her aunt had taken to entertain her new friend, was grateful to the point of tears.

"Come and visit me again," Laura called to the them as they left the suite.

Before Wash had a chance to clear away the remains of the tea, she asked for 'the usual.' Lately, she'd begun to rely more and more on a few stiff dollops of rum to relieve her ennui and boredom.

"Tyler Scranton, you're wrong as can be about Mrs. Foster-Jones! She set out a splendid tea for us, and was as charming and gracious as anyone could wish."

"That means she must have liked you. I've seen her 'entertain' sometimes when she barely opens her mouth."

"I could tell it meant alot to Mary, too." She shook her head. "Poor Mary. She's so isolated here. I can't imagine what made her accept her aunt's invitation to take on the thankless job of Assistant Manager. She's too young to be stuck in a place where it's all work and no fun. No eligible males, either."

"I rarely see Mary. Our schedules don't match and she hardly ever comes by the bar. It never occurred to me to wonder if she was happy or not."

The next morning he spied Sarah sitting at a table in the shade of a casurina, a spot on the lawn far removed from the noise and bustle of the pool. A small pile of books was at her elbow and she was doggedly writing on a yellow legal pad. He walked up softly behind her. "My, aren't we the studious one!"

"Oh! It's *you*! You scared me!"

"I hope not. Why have you got your nose to the grindstone on such a beautiful day?"

"I'm placating a guilty conscience. I dragged these along to study" she said, pointing to the books, "but thanks to a certain gentleman, I've barely cracked one open since I arrived. You see, before I apply to the Peace Corps, Tyler, I want to check out the countries they serve in. You're allowed three choices on the application, though there's no guarantee you'll be assigned to one of the countries you select. Since I've had five years of Spanish I thought I'd concentrate on Latin America. But first, I need to bone up on its history."

"You're really serious about this?"

"Of course. The Corps needs bi-lingual teachers. And nothing could be farther from Miss Pringles than a *barrio.*"

His immediate reaction was, *Don't go! That's no kind of life for someone like you!* But he caught himself in time. *Hold it, buddy-boy. It's none of your g-d business.*

"I phoned your room, Sarah, and when you didn't answer, I thought you might be at the beach. Look, I have Sunday off - *the whole day*! – and there's a special place here on the island I want you to see before you leave. An amazing story's connected with it. I'll tell you about it on the way. What do you say? Would you like to go?"

"I say 'yes', 'yes,' a thousand times 'yes'! Now scram, please, sir. I need to concentrate and you're a very distracting presence!"

The desire to share Watu–Kai with Sarah had been stirring at the back of Tyler's mind since her arrival. What brought it to the fore was James Mac Arthur's announcement when he arrived to start his shift that his father had taken ill suddenly.

The barman felt a genuine pang of concern for the elderly, gentle Lutiguan: "Was the doctor called in, James? What did he say?"

"Yessir. De Doctor come en he tellin' my Mummy to fix up de turpentine for Daddy's chest en have him to drink plenty of mauby. He order up some medicine, too."

"Turpentine?"

"Yes, sir, Mister Tyler. A turpentine poultice's good for chasin' de fever en coughs away."

"Did the doctor say how long he thought your father would be laid up?"

"No, Mister Tyler. All he sayin' is my Daddy needs to be keepin' to his bed for a time."

News of Wash's illness spread swiftly through the hotel. Darius Owen was hired to carry an enormous basket of food to the Wilson house from Laura, along with the message that Mrs. Wilson wasn't to worry about money: "Tell her James will be bringing his father's wages home for as long as Wash is ill." Others contributed, too: Corbin prepared a pot of rich, nourishing chicken broth, Tyler sent a bottle of brandy and Danielle a basket of the elder Lutiguan's favorite fruits, pawpaw and mango . The rest of the staff chipped in and bought a 'Get Well' card which everyone signed.

At dawn Sunday, Tyler was awakened by a light tattoo of rain on the corrugated roof. *Damn. I hope this doesn't last all day and spoil our plans.* He had plenty of time to roll over and catch another forty winks, but anticipation of his outing with Sarah negated all desire for sleep. He ambled into the tiny kitchenette and plugged in the new hot plate to boil water for his morning coffee.

At the agreed-upon hour Sarah appeared at the front of the hotel in slacks and a long-sleeve shirt; a tote bag was slung across her shoulder containing - as she later described it - a few 'just-in-case' items. Her eyes scanned the cars in the courtyard looking for the familiar Ford. The rain had let up, but the sky overhead was sullen and unfriendly. Tyler appeared fifteen minutes later. (As he was leaving the cabin he found he was down to his last cigarette and raced off to the nearest rum shop to buy a carton.) He pulled around the circle and drew up beside her. Sarah greeted him in high spirits, "Good morning!" Smiling happily, she opened the door and slid onto the seat beside him, "Jeeves, you've kept *Ma-dom* waiting again. Shame on you!"

"I beg *Ma-dom's* pardon. I was delayed by a pressing matter."

"What's more pressing, I'd like to know, than being on time for a date with me?"

"Nicotine, m'dear. Nicotine. I was out of cigarettes."

After a few miles he pointed to the sky, "Look! Over there! The sun! It's trying to poke through that bank of clouds." He slapped the wheel, "Come on, sun. My money's riding on you!"

As they headed across the island towards the Waterfall, Sarah listened intently while Tyler recounted the legend of Watu-Kai, as told by Wash. He didn't mention his encounter with Simon, nor his own reaction to the lovers' tragedy. *There's plenty of time for that when we're closer to the Falls.*

When he was done, she exclaimed, "But they were just children! How terrible." The disturbing tale put a damper on her cheerful mood and she fell silent as she sat in beside him.

Tyler won his bet. The sun emerged triumphant and its probing rays turned the landscape around them into a vivid Impressionistic canvas: splashes of ochre, rippling variations of greens, bright yellows and tomato reds in contrast to the rich bitter chocolate of the soil. They pulled over a few times so Tyler could look at the map. (When he'd first approached the Waterfall, it had been from the East Coast; today they were heading straight north.) After several wrong turns and twice having to back out of roads that dead-ended into dense shrubbery, he saw the familiar sign bearing the legend, Blue Hill, 2 kil.

"Hallelujah! We're here at last!" He stopped the car and turned to his companion. "I had the kitchen make up a lunch for us. As usual, they prepared enough for the Marine Corps. What do you say to having a quick bite and a beer before we start out? We can polish off the rest when we get back from the Falls."

"That's the most sensible idea I've heard all day. I'm famished."

They quickly found the foot path and Tyler, with Sarah close at his heels, led the way into the rain forest. Once in the embrace of the canopy of towering trees the young woman halted, too awestruck to continue. Breathing deeply she slowly pivoted, examining everything in sight, her mind busily storing the scene for future reference. Then she stooped down and exclaimed over a tiny flower partially hidden under a fern. To Tyler's amazement, she seemed to know the Latin names of several species of bromelaids, the herbaceous plants that called this gloomy catacomb of nature home.

"Where'd you learn all this stuff?" he asked admiringly.

"I had a crush on my Botany teacher sophomore year in college. While most of my classmates were into pot and Sylvia Plath, I was memorizing the Latin names of the plants he spoke of in class. I wanted to impress him. A hopeless cause, as I discovered later. Betty Symington, another girl in my class, was doing the same thing and she was a lot prettier and sexier than I. Betty made no bones about her yen for Mr. Peale. You know, I've often wondered if he ever screwed her?"

"Listen, if I were surrounded by a bunch of females even half as attractive as you, I'd have opened a harem. Come on. Let's get moving. We have a way to go."

She didn't utter a single complaint as they stepped along a forest floor made thick and slippery with a coating of mold and wet leaves, navigated rocks hazardous with lichen and moss, vines and branches that malevolently lashed their at bodies. As they started to move upland, away from the sheltering forest, he turned to her, "Stop for a minute, Sarah. I need to tell you something."

Calmly he told her about Simon, "the boy that followed Lord Dunham's daughter and the cook's son."

"You mean he's still alive?"

"Yup, and he hangs around Watu-Kai. He's pretty scary to look at, but he's harmless. Wash says he's 'off his head'; if we see him, let me handle it. Just don't let his gibberish rattle you." A flicker of fear registered in her eyes.

"Relax, Sarah. The rain we had earlier probably discouraged the old guy from coming here. I don't think he'll bother us."

In the near distance the dim, pulsating roar of the Falls reached their ears and Tyler quickened his pace. When Sarah had a hard time keeping up, he grabbed her hand and tugged her along after him. "There ahead! See it!" He pointed to the huge boulder blocking the path. "The Waterfall is on the other side."

Once they broke through the clearing and Sarah could see for herself the mesmerizing cascade of water, Tyler let go of her hand and stepped back, allowing her the privacy of her own response to its grandeur. He lit a

Kool and studied her as she stood like a statue, hand flung against her mouth in wonderment.

Taking a last drag on the cigarette, he stamped it out and flicked the stub into the bushes. Sarah still hadn't moved. Finally, she turned towards him and said something, but words were futile against the thunderous roar of water. He shook his head and pointed to the Falls, then his ear, pantomining his inability to hear above the din. Slowly, almost reluctantly, she walked back to him, and steadying herself with her hand on his upper arm, stood on tiptoe to whisper in his ear, "This place is fantastic, Tyler!" Retracing her steps, she settled herself on the outcropping of rock overlooking the Falls. He joined her and they sat together drinking in the splendor and beauty of their surroundings.

He was suddenly conscious that the brilliant light was fading; glancing at the sky he saw angry clouds racing over the horizon towards them. He tapped Sarah on the shoulder, pointed to the gathering storm and motioned it was time for them to leave.

They made their way back past the boulder, down the steep, rock-strewn incline and were about to enter the rain forest when the first drops fell. Tyler hurried on, worried the storm might hold them captive for hours. Sarah was several feet behind him when she cried out, "Damn. *Damn!* Tyler, help me!" He looked around and saw that she had fallen into a gully, that her right leg was twisted ominously beneath her body.

Oh shit. "Sarah. Are you all right?"

"Don't ask silly questions. Just help me get on my feet. It's so slippery here, I can't get my bearings." He rushed towards her, placed both arms under hers and with a gentle tug, pulled her to her feet. "Your ankle? Can you stand on it?" He held her tightly as she gingerly put her weight onto the injured limb and tested her mobility. "Hey, it's going to be o.k." Relief flooded her face and she smiled into his eyes. "Just let me hold onto you another minute or two 'til I'm sure."

He loosened his grip, aware for the first time of her body, its small bones, its softness, the scent of shampoo in her damp, toffee hair; he looked down at that delicate heart-shaped face he'd come to know so well, as if he'd never seen it before.

Sarah touched his cheek with her fingertips and said in a mocking voice, "My hero." She was about to continue in that same frivolous vein when she saw the look in his eyes. Tyler knew it was time to release her, to let her walk on her own, but a sudden unreasoning urge to kiss that pixy face changed his mind. Softly cupping her face in both hands, he brushed his lips along her brow, her cheek, the tip of her nose, stopping at last to kiss her fully on the mouth. She didn't resist, but neither did she respond. He dropped his hands as if they'd touched fire and backed away from her.

"Sarah. I'm sorry," he mumbled. "I didn't mean for this to happen. Leave it to me to spoil things ."

Seeing the stricken look on his face, she said reassuringly, "You haven't spoiled anything. I rather liked it." She held out her arms to him, "Let's try again, shall we?"

CHAPTER XX III

Supported by Tyler, Sarah was able to negotiate the slippery terrain of the rain forest, but their progress was slow. By the time they'd descended to a spot where the station wagon was visible, the storm had overtaken them in earnest. Torrents of water poured down from the skies. Tyler lifted Sarah off her feet and carried her under his arm as he raced the last several yards to the station wagon.

"We're stuck, 'til the rain lets up. I can't see a damn thing," Tyler said, once they were inside the Ford.

"At least we've got shelter," Sarah answered breezily. "We can have the rest of our picnic right here in the front seat."

"Hey, lady! Look at you! You're soaked to the skin."

"You're no prize yourself. I have a clean dry shirt in my tote, but what about you, Tyler? You shouldn't stay in those wet clothes."

"There's an old beach towel in the back. We can use that to dry our-selves off with. You first."

"What about you?"

"I haven't got an extra shirt, but I'll be o.k."

She crawled over the front seat and handed him the rest of their lunch. He turned his head while she slipped out of her blouse and bra and pulled a T-shirt over her head.

"Take off your shirt, Tyler," she commanded, "I'll wipe you off with the dry part of the towel." She gave him no choice. "The air's warm enough, and you'll be better off if you don't put that wet thing back on."

After one quick glimpse of Sarah's unencumbered breasts outlined against the T-shirt, Tyler kept his eyes focussed on the windshield. They nibbled at their lunch in silence, the spontaneous embrace in the rain forest making them both self-conscious.

"Do you want a brownie?"

"No thanks. How 'bout you?"

"I've had enough to eat. Look, Tyler ..."

He interrupted, "Sarah, what happened ..." They looked away from one another. He tried again, "I think we need to talk about ..."

"No we don't!" Sarah placed the remains of her lunch in a napkin, took off her glasses and placed them on the dashboard. "Tyler," she said with great deliberation, "I want to kiss you again."

He stared at her, nonplussed. She was sitting with her back against the passenger door, legs folded under her body. She leaned towards him across the seat, placing her hands on his bare chest. "What does a girl have to do..." her words lost as he swiftly drew her to him and placed his mouth on hers. It was a long, satisfying kiss, followed by another and another. "You're a great kisser," she whispered. "There're some places I missed," he murmured, running his lips down the side of her neck, stopping at the hollow between her collarbone. The rhythm of Sarah's breathing quickened and he could feel himself getting hard. She surprised him by pulling back and saying, "Not fair. What's sauce for the goose ..." and in one quick motion had shed her shirt. He stared at her enticing breasts accented by the v of her tan where the top of her bikini began and ended. "Oh God," he groaned as his lips caressed one breast, then the other.

"Tyler, help me get these slacks off," he reached out an obliging hand, then froze. *What the hell are we doing?* Her fingers were struggling with the buttons at the side of her pants when he covered her hand with his, saying in a voice thick with longing, "Stop, Sarah. This has gone far enough."

She wrenched back her bare shoulders, eyes widening in shock. She had never looked more beautiful. Sarah stared at him in disbelief until the obdurate expression on his face convinced her he wasn't teasing, he meant it. "Oh God, I've made a complete ass of myself," those lovely, nearsighted eyes of hers filling with tears. "Where's my goddamn shirt," she said helplessly and wrenched it from the floor of the car, turned her back to him and put it on.

"Sarah, don't cry. *Please don't cry.* It's not your fault, it's mine. I should never have let things get so out-of-hand."

"Don't flatter yourself, I'm not crying," she retorted angrily, brushing at her damp cheeks with her fist, then drawing a tissue from her pants' pocket to blow her nose.

"Look, I'm not very good at words, but it's like this: You're the nicest person - *I mean woman* - I've ever met. You're decent and honest and intelligent, besides being damned attractive. And I've never been so at ease, so comfortable with anyone before. But you don't really know me, Sarah. I've been around. I'm no angel, believe me. And I'm not any good at sustaining a relationship. What's more, I can give you the names and addresses of a half dozen women who can attest to that fact. That's not bragging, it's just the way I am."

No response.

He struggled to continue, "What I'm trying to say is that this can't go anywhere. And you can believe it or not, but there's nothing I'd like better than to make love to you. If you weren't the kind of gal you are, I would have tried to get into your pants long before this. Don't you understand? *It's not you, it's me!*"

"I think the rain is letting up a bit. Can we go back to the hotel, please."

They sat in unbending silence during the long journey, a journey made more difficult by water-filled potholes, over-flowing gulleys and the debris thrown in their path by the torrential rains. As they pulled into the circular driveway at Belle Jours, Tyler pleaded, "Let's not part this way. I wouldn't hurt you for anything in the world, Sarah. Can't we still be friends?"

She pulled at the door handle as he braked to a stop: "Thank you for showing me Watu–Kai," she said politely, staring straight ahead. "It's been a day I'm sure I'll never forget." The door closed and she was gone.

Tyler didn't want dinner, "I'm gonna get pissed as fast as I can," he vowed savagely. When he found there was only a half bottle of Scotch left at the cabin, he flew into a rage, picking up an empty glass and hurling it against the kitchen wall. He had the grim satisfaction of hearing it shatter, shards scattering everywhere, and was about to throw another when he thought, *Hell, I can get more booze from the bar when I run out.* He sat himself down on the porch and began drinking generous dollops of whiskey over ice to help erase the memory of Sarah's anger and tears. But instead of dulling the pain - *I really fucked up this time* - he became more agitated.

How *did* he feel about Sarah? Up until the moment she was in his arms, his mouth on hers, he probably would have described her as 'a good friend', the only close *female* friend he'd ever had. But that kiss and the ones that followed, the arousing sight of her bare skin and breasts, had turned his world inside out. He wanted her. *God, how I want her.* Then why hadn't he allowed the inevitable to happen? Why had he backed off? Sarah wasn't the first woman to excite him physically; there'd been others over the years and when he was interested enough, they ended up in bed. This formula, so simple and uncomplicated and yet so ultimately rewarding, had served him well in the past; how could one kiss change all that?

He dragged himself to bed in the early hours of the morning; nothing that made sense had been settled in his mind . He slept fitfully and woke determined to see Sarah, to try to recapture the warmth and informality that marked their relationship before the outing. Confident that he could win her over, that with a night's rest she'd see things differently, he ambled down to the staff's table in the dininghall and ordered a hearty breakfast.

His equilibrium restored by generous helpings of eggs, sausage, biscuits and fresh fruit, he picked up the previous night's receipts from the cash register at the bar and cheerfully headed towards the office. Danielle would know the name of a reliable florist; he'd order a dozen roses for Sarah to make amends.

"Morning, Danielle. How's Lutigua's 'fairest of them all' this lovely morning?"

Her usual smile of welcome was missing. "Did your tongue get stuck in a jampot Tyler?" she said tartly.

"What's eating you, Danielle? Mary giving you a hard time?"

"There's no problem with Miss Farmington."

"What then?" he asked peevishly, annoyed to have her sour words dampen his buoyant mood.

"Miss Locke's leavin' Lutigua," she said accusingly.

"What do you mean, *Miss Locke's leaving*? What put that idea into your head?"

"Last evening, Celene was at de front desk when Miss Locke called on de house phone sayin' she wanted to leave today, and askin' Celene to phone de airlines to see if a seat could be had. But Celene told her how all de airline offices close here at six in de evening, that she'd have to wait 'til morning.

"You're kidding me."

Remembering her own difficulties with the American after he'd had too much to drink, Danielle addressed him like an errant schoolboy, "I'm thinking you're de reason for Miss Locke's wishing to leave Belle Jours in such haste, Tyler."

He couldn't look at her. "It's not what you think, Danielle. Look, I know it's against the rules, but I'm going to her room. I need to see her."

"Don't you go upsetting her now, Tyler."

She answered his knock with a muffled, "Come in."

Sarah was outside on the small patio adjoining her quarters; Tyler saw her through the open glass doors, her back to the room, intent on shoving books into a cardboard box. As he walked towards her - his sneakers deadening sound on the tiled floor - he was chagrined to see the open suitcase on the bed, clothes piled neatly beside it. "Yes, who is it?" she asked, turning to face the intruder. When she saw Scranton, her eyes widened. She bit her lips in distress: "*What are you doing here?*"

"I heard you were leaving the hotel," he said miserably, "and I just ..." He never knew what impelled him to leave the sentence unfinished, to rush forward to gather her in his arms. He buried his face in her hair and murmured, "Sarah, don't go. For heaven's sake, don't go. I know it doesn't make any sense, but I need you to stay. I ... I think I've ... fallen in love with you." His confesssion was a profound surprise to Tyler; it was as if some overwhelming force had dragged it from his sub-conscious, sending the words tumbling from his lips in defiance of a life-long habit of sidestepping serious commitment. Here, then, was the answer to those troubling questions of the night before, here in his arms. What if she'd gone away and he'd forfeited the chance of ever seeing her again?

If his falling in love with Sarah was a revelation to Tyler, it was even more of one to the young woman he held in his embrace. She looked up at him in astonishment, "You what?"

"Look, I'm not supposed to be in your room. Hotel rules. Will you take a walk with me on the beach so we can talk?"

She followed behind him as he unlatched the wrought-iron gate, portal to the long strip of sandy white beach fronting the hotel, and kept herself at arm's length as they strolled side by side, parallel to the incoming tide. Haltingly, he told her about the hours he'd spent since they'd parted trying to figure out why he'd drawn back from her in the car. "It wasn't 'til I saw the suitcase on the bed, saw you packing those damn books, that I realized how I felt. Believe me, it was the last thing on my mind when I came to your room. I just didn't want you to think you had to leave Belle Jours because I'd behaved like such a *fucking* ass." He stopped in his tracks.

"Have you already booked a flight? Am I too late?" He held his breath, waiting for her answer.

She wasn't going to make it easy for him. Bending down, she scooped up a a delicate dove shell from the sand and held it aloft in the palm of her hand. "Look, I've not seen one of these before, have you? Not this lovely mauve color, anyway."

"Sarah! Stop torturing me! Are you leaving Lutigua today or not?"

Ignoring the question, she dropped to her knees to continue searching for more shells. "MMmmm, I'd love to find a few more of this species." His groan of anxiety made it difficult to stifle the bubble of laughter welling up within her; she took her time answering, never shifting her gaze from the beach.

"*Sarah!*"

She looked at him impishly, "I called *Eastern* first thing this morning. Mr. Amos, their agent, said the flight originated in Trinidad and he needed to check the passenger list before he'd know if any seats were available on the afternoon flight... said it would be a while before he got back to me."

"Ring Amos back and tell him you've changed your mind."

"My, aren't we the bossy one."

"You'll stay then?" Tyler was in such a state that he'd totally missed the teasing note in her voice.

"It depends."

"Depends on what?"

"Whether you've given up kissing me."

With a whoop of joy, he scooped her up in his arms. "Never. I promise. Never!"

Hand in hand they continued walking along the shoreline. "I'd already changed my mind before you came charging into my room," she confessed. "First of all, Danielle' was so concerned and sweet on the phone, asking me if there was a problem here at the hotel, and if not, was there anything she could do to convince me to stay on. Then Mary showed up in tears, said I was the only person she could talk to and 'Please, please not to cut short my visit.' It was then I realized I'd gotten to know most of the staff, that I'd miss them: Mr. Marshall in the diningroom ... James, always so polite ... ...Colin."

"But you were packing to leave! I saw the suitcase on the bed."

"Yes, I emptied the drawers and closet right after breakfast, but as the morning wore on, I thought, 'As a candidate for the Peace Corps, I need to get off on the right foot by making peace with Mr. Scranton.'"

To Tyler's proposal that they continue as they had before the outing at Watu–Kai, she replied sensibly, "But we can't go back, Tyler. Things are different now. We can only go forward ... wherever that leads us."

"I want to make love to you, Sarah. Christ, if you knew how badly I want that." His grip tightened on her hand, "but you can't come to the cabin and I'm not allowed in your room."

"*Hotel rules.* I know. But you'll think of something," she said dreamily, rising on her toes to nibble his ear, "I can wait. I just hope it isn't for too long."

That evening he took her out to dinner at the 'Belevedere'. Afterwards they necked in the car, reluctantly pulling away from one another when their ardor threatened to escalate into serious love-making. Both agreed that the front seat of a station wagon was neither comfortable nor romantic; but the strain of abstinence was taking its toll. Sarah adjusted the the straps her dress which had fallen down in the heat of their embraces, while Tyler lit a cigarette to calm himself. Gently, he took her hand and brought it to his lips. "Only two days left... just the thought of your leaving... what am I going to do without you, Sarah?"

The young woman glanced at the travelling alarm clock by her bedside when she heard the light tap on her door. *It's after midnight. Who could it be at this hour?* Sarah wasn't afraid, but she decided to be cautious nonetheless. Turning the book she'd been reading face down on the coverlet, she tiptoed in her bare feet to the door. "Who's there, please?"

"It's me ...Tyler," was the whispered response. "Turn off the light before you open the door so no one can see me." Trembling, she did as he asked, pulling back the chain and opening the door just wide enough for him to slip through. For the past two days they'd barely had any time alone together and Sarah would be leaving in a few hours.

"What are you doing here?" she whispered, "I thought you weren't ..." her words smothered by his hand covering her mouth. "Shush, no talking allowed." In a daze of happiness she melted into his arms as he withdrew his hand and kissed her hungrily. Slowly his fingers moved over her thighs, her buttocks and up her spine easing her delicate frame ever tighter against his body. "Can you stay the night?" she asked breathlessly.

"Most of it. Foster-Jones was invited to a big 'do' at the American Embassy and I decided 'to hell with rules.' I had to see you."

"Darling, I look a sight." He kissed her hard again, "Think I care?" He felt himself stiffen against her and moved back in order to lift her night-gown over her head. "I want to be able to see you, Sarah. I want to touch every inch of you." Not daring to risk the glare of the ceiling light, they settled for the refracted glow of a small bulb inside her closet. Arms at her sides, heart pounding, overcome with shyness as she waited for her lover's scrutiny, Sarah remained still as a graven image while Tyler hastily shed his own clothes.

"You're so delicate, so very, very beautiful ..." Tyler choked on his words, unable to express the longing and desire that held him captive. He leaned over and kissed her breasts, his lips and tongue moving thirstily along her neck and shoulders then back to her nipples. Her whole body shivered. Tyler stopped and led her tenderly by the hand to the bed where his tongue and mouth continued their delicate explorations until Sarah pleaded, "Darling, now. *Please now.*" They made love quickly, urgently, like parched earth welcoming the first drops of rain, unable to control their yearning for one another. At last he withdrew from her and they lay side-by-side, breathless and content.

"Sarah. I love you."

"I know."

"What's that tired old saw, 'I never felt like this before'? Funny, but it's true. You're the best thing that's ever happened to me."

A while later they made love again, this time slowly, deliberately, as if their bodies were new planets and they had all the time in the world to explore them.

CHAPTER XXIV

Tyler slipped from Sarah's room before dawn, exacting from her a solemn promise to return to Lutigua as quickly as possible.

"Catch a flight down as soon as school lets out."

"Oh darling, I can't. The family expect me home at the end of term; after all, I barely saw them at Easter... and, oh! I almost forgot–the Fourth! For as long as I can remember, we've driven up to New Hampshire over the Fourth to a cottage on the lake. It's been in Dad's family for ages. There's always a big picnic, and fireworks. It's sort of a Locke tradition. They'd never understand if I tried to duck out. Besides, my brother will be leaving for Yale at the end of August and it may be our last chance to spend some time together...Tyler! You're scowling! Don't be cross with me."

"Well you can't expect me to dance a jig."

"Wait. *Wait*! I just had a marvelous idea ... could you possibly get free and spend the weekend of the

Fourth with us? I'd love to show you off to my family and vice versa. Oh *could you*, Tyler? It would be so ..."

He interrupted her, "Dream on, lady. There's no way F-J's gonna' let me tootle off for a weekend. Sorry."

"I'll write, darling. I promise. And you know I'll be back as soon as I can."

Miserable at the thought of not seeing Sarah for what seemed like an eternity, Tyler had all he could do to sit through a staff meeting later that morning. *I've gotta get out of here.* It was to the *Bristol* that Tyler fled after Sarah's departure.

As he turned the corner Scranton saw several men standing in front of the pub. *Damn! Just your luck, buddy-boy. The Bristol's closed.* As he came abreast of the group, Isaiah appeared from the opposite direction; he unlocked the front door and ushered them in, greeting the regulars by name. He winked at the American as he entered, "You come at a good time, sir. Mister Robertson docked dis morning."

Seating himself at the end of the bar, Tyler started off with two quick shots of Scotch, then switched to beer, so mired in despondency he was oblivious to the lively scene around him. The bar had filled up quickly and most of the customers seemed to know one another. Gradually, the American became aware of the large crowd gathered at the dart board at the back of the room; good-natured taunts, extravagant boasting and preposterous bets sailed across the smoked-filled room as the players took turns. Without benefit of pencil or paper, a man they called 'The Skipper' kept track of the scores and the money.

I'll ask Isaiah to point out Robertson next time he gets down to this end of the bar. Before he could get the bartender's attention, however, a firm hand gripped his shoulder and a raspy voice at his back boomed, "Hey Yank, how about a go at darts? Loser pays for the next round of drinks."

It was 'The Skipper' himself, Dunc Robertson, who was challenging Tyler. ("How'd you know I was an American?" Scranton asked later. "Because it's only Yanks like you that insist on having their brew served ice cold. No man in his right mind would ruin good ale by coolin' it.")

Thickset and balding, his skin covered with a light sprinkling of freckles, Robertson's 'uniform' consisted of chinos, a crisply pressed white shirt open at the neck (its empty left sleeve neatly pinned at the shoulder), white sneakers and a British naval officer's cap pushed back up on his forehead. He was the by-product of a union between a cook on one of His Majesty's frigates and a girl from the Hebrides. Unlike most shore-leave scenarios, the sailor returned to her bed whenever his ship was in port and after the baby came, he sent money. From his father, Robertson inherited an abiding love of all things English; the *Bristol* was a tribute to his memory.

Tyler lost his first game of darts that day, the next round and the next, and after that, Robertson refused to let him pay for any more drinks. By then the barman was feeling no pain and the pub's owner, having learned he worked at Belle Jours, insisted he down a cup of steaming black coffee before starting the long journey back to the hotel. "Listen, Yank, you don't want to go knocking down some poor sod who's walking along the road."

Several evenings and many rounds later - Tyler's ineptness at darts became an in-house joke at the pub - the American had accumulated a sketchy history of its likable proprietor. He soon realized that underlying the man's geniality and wit lay a powerful, charismatic personality.

Robertson was an ex-R.A.F. pilot, one of the lucky few who survived, only to be confronted with one of those tragic ironies which haunted many a returning British serviceman: his bride of a few months was killed by a German V-1 'buzz bomb,' the infamous weapon unleashed on British civilians in the closing days of the war by a desperate and spiteful enemy. After his discharge the embittered wing commander ignored several lucrative offers to fly commercially, preferring instead to sign up as a free-lancer for a privately-owned cargo line. In the early 60's at the height of the

Algerian war, he was running guns to Oran when his plane was shot up on a runway as he was preparing to lift off. Along with the loss of an arm and all hopes of piloting again, a silver plate in his head destined him to a life-time of recurring headaches and dependence on drugs to alleviate bouts of unbearable pain.

It was never explained how he finally ended up on a small island in the Caribbean Sea, or how he managed to convince the newly independent Lutiguan government to hire him. His formal title was *Deputy Minister of Defense,* impressive until one remembers that Lugtigua's defense forces consisted of less than 50 unarmed men and two ancient Tiger Moth reconnaisance planes donated by the British government to help its former colony scout the shoreline for lost fishing boats and storm damage. Actually, his experience was invaluable when the island came to building and staffing its new airport; the successful completion of that undertaking by a disorganized, fledgling government can be directly attributed to the former wing commander. After the lavish dedication ceremonies Robertson resigned his post to have more time to devote to the pub and his new boat.

Tyler became one of the *Bristol's* regulars, drawn there as much by its masculine, no-nonsense decor, its absence of ear-splitting music as its 'Skipper' and the assortment of characters who frequented it.

* * * * * * * * * * *

In order to get to know the members of his Church in a more informal setting, Peter Callender began the customary task undertaken by new clergy of paying courtesy calls on every household. In setting up the list his housekeeper Mrs. Linton proved invaluable, offering quick sketches of each congregant and acquainting him with the elders and prominent families who should be seen first. Occasionally he brought Tamika along if he knew there would be other children in the household for her to play with.

Josiah Mapp was the fourth name on his list; before setting out he learned that Mapp was a widower -

Linton described him in glowing words - with two grown children living at home, a daughter Danielle and her brother Jacob. As he walked up the dirt path leading to the modest frame house, Callender noticed the well-tended yard and beautiful foliage surrounding the entire perimeter. Josiah was sitting in a rocking chair on the front porch reading the local paper in the fading light of early evening; he rose immediately when he saw his visitor.

"Good evenin'. Welcome to my house, Mr. Callender. If you would please, take de chair over there, we'll have our visit here on de porch where de air is sweeter. Would you be carin' for a cold drink... limeade...mauby... coconut water?"

After a few awkward moments, the two were soon discussing church matters like old friends.

"These cookies are very tasty," Callender murmured, as he helped himself to another.

"Dani, my daughter, she's de cook in de family. Her name's Danielle, but here at home we calls her 'Dani' ."

"En what do your children do, Mr. Mapp?"

"Dani has a big job at a hotel, but I fear she works too hard. My son, Jacob, he teaches at de primary school. They are good children ... good to their Daddy. Perhaps you have seen Dani? She sings in de choir when she is not at her work ."

"No, I don't think I've made her acquaintance. There are so many new faces ...so many names to be rememberin'," he added lamely.

"She'll be coming home soon to fix de evening meal. You can meet her then. Now, tell me more about your program for our young people."

The new Minister wished to provide a monthly activity geared to appeal to the teenagers in the church community. "They're too young to work, en we all know 'bout idle hands en de Devil," said Callender as he launched into an enthusiastic outline of his plan. Midway through his discourse, Josiah interrupted, "Here come my Dani now."

As she stepped up onto the porch, Callender felt a rush of elation. He recognized Mapp's daughter as the lady in the choir, the one who wore the gold-hammered earrings on Easter Sunday morning.

* * * * * * * * * *

"I tellin' you, mon, dese folks, dey holds onto a dollah like a hungry dog wid a fresh bone." 'Legs' Waldrond, one of the regulars who worked the bar, made this observation after a careful count of the change left by a noisy, demanding table of guests.

By mid-May his plaint was echoed in one form or another by all the help at the hotel. The package tours converging on Belle Jours were a breed apart from their winter-season brethern. A New York advertising agency known for its aggressive marketing tactics had developed a weekly 'special' which was touted to travel agencies from Dusseldorf to Houston. So attractive did the promotion prove, the hotel was in the enviable position of having to turn down requests for rooms.

Since the package included everything but liquor, tipping and hotel tax, its participants stormed the coral corridors, beaches and dining hall bent on getting double value for every deutsche mark, shilling and dollar paid out. They arrived early for meals and in Jack-Sprat fashion, licked their platters clean. Before the tours began, Corbin, Osbert Marshall and Laura had wrestled with the problem of large groups converging on the dining hall demanding instant service; the solution, they decided, was to offer buffet-style dining several nights a week. But the buffet proved a mistake from the start: the generous platters of salads and local vegetables, the heated aluminum trays with rice, breadfruit, curried chicken, Kingfish and snapper had to be replenished several times before half the diners had moved down the serving line. Foster-Jones bowed to the obvious: "*Noblesse oblige* doesn't exist for these parasites, she said tartly, "that's supposing they ever heard of the concept."

Linens, towels, ashtrays and silverware disappeared at such an alarming rate that Elsa Vernon, head of housekeeping, declared heatedly that departing guests should be required to bare the contents of their suitcases before checking out.

"I'm sorry, Mrs. Vernon, but we can't do that," Mary said firmly. "It's illegal as well as unethical. I appreciate your concern, but it's a problem shared by hotelkeepers the world over."

"Dat don't mean I has to like it,"

Vernon, a tall, astringent Lutiguan, had been Leona's personal choice. Proud of her status and bent on seeing that her employer get full value for her wages, she was testy and demanding with the local women under her aegis; moreover, she had come to regard every inch of the hotel with a fierce, proprietary air. She respected the heavy Englishwoman and they had worked well together. Mary Farmington was another matter. Tightened lips and a sniff of disapproval followed each of their encounters.

"My Mummy beat me for sure if I was to dress like some of de ladies I seein' here," Cleo giggled as she described to a friend the assault to the eye and Lutiguans' innate sense of modesty that greeted her daily. And indeed, the bikini took a terrible beating at the hands of housewives and secretaries from Tilburg to

Altoona whose aspic mounds of fat spilled over in protest against restricting strings and squares of cloth. Their male counterparts were just as shameless. One and all zealously exposed themselves to the merciless tropical sun in a six-day race to return home with a tan. (The island's sole importer of tanning lotion ran out of stock by the third week in May, and it was only Danielle's ingenuity in rounding up several of the young locals who hung around the beaches and persuading them to to sell the juice of aloe squeezed into discarded rum bottles that saved many a guest from serious burns.)

After the swimming pool - filled with splashing, churning bodies from dawn 'til dark - the busiest center of activity was the bar. Tyler was rarely able to take more than a few hours off despite having recruited extra help. During the late Spring, two attempts were made by guests from Belle Jours to find the Waterfall, Watu-Kai. A party of five from Holland hired a local taxi, pointed to a spot on the map and told the driver to take them there. In keeping with the age-old boycott, the wily cabbie dumped his passengers off a few miles west of the actual path leading through the rainforest to the Falls, offering at best only sketchy directions on how to proceed. While his fares trudged through thick underbrush in the debilitating noonday sun pursued by a posse of hungry mosquitos, the driver dozed comfortably in the shade of a cannon-ball tree. In less than two hours, the disgruntled party were ready to call it quits.

A few weeks later a young, energetic American couple on rented bicycles made a stab at it on their own. Veteran cyclists, they left the hotel well-prepared, carrying with them bug repellent, drinking water and a light picnic lunch. They abandoned their bikes near the spot where Tyler'd left his car and proceeded on foot, taking time to pause and admire the exotic plants indigenous to the forest kingdom. Their pace quickened when they heard the distant rumble of the rushing water; as they came abreast of the boulder, the wife in the lead, Simon, in his self-imposed role of guardian of Watu-Kai, stepped forward to challenge them. In one terrifying moment, their light-hearted expedition became the rudiments of a nightmare.

The startled young woman turned to flee, tripped and fell, smashing a bone in her knee-cap. Unable to move, she screamed in fear and pain. Her husband picked up a heavy stone, the nearest thing at hand, and hurled it at the apparition. His aim went wide, but Simon, seeing that he was being attacked, let out a howl and disappeared. The distraught young man kept his head: he fashioned a crude splint with three pieces of bark held in place by a bandana and managed to piggy-back his wife back to the clearing where they'd left the bikes. The pain was such that she blacked out several times along the way. He left her propped against a tree and pedaled like one possessed to the main road where, after a half-hour's anguished wait, he flagged down the sole approaching car and begged the driver to help him get his wife back to the hotel.

Unnerved by the incident, the hotel posted a notice to all guests, warning them of the dangers of trying to enter the rainforest on their own: TRAVEL THIS AREA AT YOUR OWN RISK.

When he learned of the escapade Tyler had mixed reactions. He was sorry the young woman had been hurt, yet he was secretly relieved that the couple's efforts to reach Watu-Kai had been thwarted. The American had taken emotional possession of the spot and tresspassers were not welcome.

At breakfast each morning, Tyler thumbed through the pages of *The Ledger*, the island's sole newspaper. Not because he had much interest in the local news, but the baseball season was about to get under way in the States and he liked to keep tabs on the *Pirates* and the *Orioles*. Scores for U.S.teams were dutifully carried in a small box at the tail end of the Sports' Section, where headlines and long columns of copy were reserved for soccer and cricket. He stared at the front page headline: POLICE CHIEF MURDERED! Recalling Leona's brave confrontation with Rupert Haynes, he hurriedly read on:

The bullet-ridden body of Lutigua's Chief of Police, Rupert B.Haynes, was found at the bottom of Hangman's Gully late yesterday afternoon by Lester Pilgrim. Mr. Pilgrim, a laborer at Fairfield Plantation, was passing by the gully on his way home when he saw the body. Officials at the scene speculate that Chief Haynes may have been shot with bullets from his own gun. The investigation is continuing. Police urgently request anyone who was in the area of Bank Hall near the gully during the hours of 7.am. to 4 p.m. yesterday to contact their local district station. (More details on page3.)

Serves the bastard right. I'm betting half the population of Lutigua is toasting the killer right now. Instead of hanging the guy, they ought to give a medal to whoever did it.

The chief's murder overshadowed another piece of news that at any other time would have been a front-page item: TWO NEW HOTELS TO OPEN IN '81.

Well, whadd'ya know ... looks as if Lutigua has been 'discovered' at last.

The next morning as Tyler was stepping from the shower, he heard the low, metallic buzz of the telephone. Hastily tucking a towel around his middle, he padded the across the wooden floor to answer it leaving a trail of wet footprints.

"Scranton, here."

"Good morning, Tyler. It is Danielle. A cable, it comes for you early this morning. The boy is on his way to de cabin with it now."

Must be from Sarah. I hope nothing's wrong.

His fingers were shaking as he took the message from Colin and tore open the envelope:

Dear Son, I need you to come home right away. Myra

The wave of relief washing over him quickly turned to irritation. "Shit!" He crumpled the note in his fist and tossed it in the waste basket. *She couldn't be ill or needing surgery. She'd have said so.* Myra had never asked for anything before, not even money. He couldn't ignore the summons, but he was damned if he'd wait until he got to Thompson to find out what was so urgent, why he was needed 'right away.'

I'll phone her to see what's up. It better be major. With guests standing ten deep at the bar, F-J isn't going to let me run off to the States without a good reason.

CHAPTER XXV

On the long flight back to the States, Myra's words re-echo in his mind like a broken record:

"I'm sellin' the house and moving to Wisconsin to live with sister Madge. Your Uncle Henry passed last year and she says the place is too big for one person."

"That's great, Myra. I'm pleased for you. You won't be alone anymore. But why must I come now? The hotel's booked solid and they need me. Can't whatever-it-is wait until I'm due for my leave?"

"No, I need you here in Thompson as soon as possible. Your father left the house to you and Neddie."

"What do you mean, 'left the house'? You mean he's dead? My father's dead?"

"Passed last October, maybe early November? I don't recall."

"Why didn't you write and tell me?"

"It didn't seem important at the time. He's been gone so long, Tyler, I can't even remember what he looked like. After Madge called, I put the house on the market and now I've got a buyer. I need you to sign the papers before they change their mind. Your father left you some land, too. But I'll tell you 'bout that when you get here."

"Jesus, Myra, you wait 'til now to unload all this ..."

"Tyler, you know I don't like to hear the Lord's name taken in vain. I'm going to hang up now. Long distance costs the earth. Hurry and get here, that's all I ask."

He was lucky enough to get a seat to Miami on short notice, but he was on standby to Baltimore. *F-J was damn decent about the whole thing. Said I could take as long as was necessary, but hell, one or two days of being around Myra is about all I can stomach! Whadd'ya bet she starts pickin' on me the minute I walk in the door. At least it'll give me a chance to phone Sarah, tell her I can take the time coming to me as soon as she's free. Better find out what she'd like to do. If only she weren't tied down to that teaching job, we might've been able to grab a day or two together when I leave Thompson. It'd be nice to know how long this business with Myra is going to take .*

He wished he could feel less apathetic about his father's death, but he'd already passed through all the stages that mark the pain of abandonment and loss; it had been especially hard on Tyler when he was in his teens and longed to be part of father-and-son activities enjoyed by his friends—fishing trips, baseball games, camping out. Unlike his teammates, he had no one to cheer him on, pat him on the back with a 'Well done' after a successful track meet. Little by little the bitterness had faded along with the memories and when Myra told him of Hugh Scranton's death, there was only regret for all those lost years.

Night had settled in when the plane touched down in Baltimore. Tyler immediately headed to a phone booth and dialled the number of the apartment Sarah shared with two other girls. No answer. Frustrated because he wasn't able to leave word he was in the

States, or set up a time to call back when she'd be there, he jammed the receiver back on its hook and retrieved his dime. With signs of a headache coming on, he snapped at the girl at the *Avis* counter when she informed him there were no compacts available.

"You're only Number Two, so you work harder to screw the public," he said savagely as he signed the contract for a luxury sedan.

"Yes, sir. Here are your keys, sir. Have a nice day."

As he guided the Buick down the ramp and away from the airport, there was a momentary confusion about which side of the road he was supposed to be on, then he remembered: *Relax, buster. You're back in the good ole U.S. of A.* His fingers roamed idly over the buttons on the radio, stopping once to catch the local weather report before moving on to an FM station featuring soothing instrumentals; on the heels of an old Berlin tune, Bernstein's "Tonight" came wafting through the speakers. *Julie's favorite. Damn, wouldn't you know.* The music unnerved him. In his gut, like a heavy stone, lay an implacable dread of returning to the town he'd avoided so assiduously most of his adult life, a place of bittersweet memories and ravished illusions.

* * * * * * * * * *

Saturday

Julie is lying against him in the curve of his arm, her breath against his neck, her bare right leg holding his captive. They are on his bed in his room where they have been making love all afternoon. Earlier in the day, Myra had boarded a *Shortline* bus to visit her ailing mother in Wilkes-Barre and they have the oyster shingle house to themselves.

"Have you told your parents?"

"Not yet. Soon though. Maybe tonight."

"Why can't I come with you? I should be there when you tell them."

"No. It would only complicate things."

"Are you o.k.? I didn't hurt you or anything before, did I?"

"Don't be a ninny. You can't hurt me. The only difference I can tell is my stomach does flip-flops when I smell fish or garlic and my breasts are a little sore, that's all." Landguidly she raises and arm and squints at the delicate oval face of her gold watch. "Almost time to go." His arms tighten about her. He knows better than to argue. All at once her body tenses against his:

"Look at me Tyler Scranton," she says fiercely, "if my parents give us a hard time, promise you won't walk out on me. Promise?"

He rolls over on top of her and covers her mouth with his. She struggles for a moment, then surrenders, opening her lips to return his kiss.

"Julie, quit that," his voice thick with emotion. "How many times do I have to tell you, I'm in this for keeps. And I'm glad about the baby ...Now look what you've gone and made me do." Gently he moves an arm under her hips and braces to enter her again.

Monday

He and Lyle are in the garage tinkering with a shortwave radio which they are assembling from a kit.

Myra calls from the back door, "Phone for you, Tyler. Some woman."

Oh shit, something's happened to Julie. He races into the house.

"Hello?"

"Tyler Scranton? This is Annadel Webster, Mr. Waterman's secretary."

He struggles to focus on the unfamiliar voice.

"Is that you, Mr. Scranton?"

"What? Yeah, it's me."

"Mr. Waterman would like to speak with you privately here at his office. Shall we say seven p.m. this coming Wednesday?" It is not an invitation, it is an order.

Wednesday

Miss Webster, a tiny woman with iron grey hair and a slight limp, leads him across the worn Oriental rug in the reception room of *Waterman, Swain & Waterman*, past shelves of bound-leather books, a colbalt blue Ming Dynasty vase resting on an antique table and down a dark hallway. The woman reminds Tyler of an etching in a book from his childhood of the witch in 'Hansel and Gretel'. She halts before a heavy oak door and knocks gently. A muffled voice bids them, "Enter."

"Nice of you to come, Mr. Scranton." A hand is extended in greeting along with a slight nod to Miss Webster, who silently withdraws from the room. Having steeled himself for hostility, the youth is disarmed by this civil gesture.

"Please. Make yourself comfortable," indicating a low-slung brown leather armchair in front of an imposing Biedermeier mahogany desk. A stocky figure, dressed in a navy pin-striped suit and maroon silk tie, Julie's father has a face like an image graven on the back of old coins: Roman nose, jutting chin, sunken steely eyes—the austerity deflected by a network of lines around the corners of his mouth and eyes which connote good humor.

On the wall directly behind Waterman's desk is a full-length oil portrait of Julie's grandfather attired in the flowing black robes of his office. The proffered chair is carefully situated so the visitor is unable to escape the judge's aristocratic gaze and overbearing air of rectitude, an arrangement the lawyer finds expedient for dealing with opposing counsel.

Arthur Waterman does not sit at his desk, but casually leans against its front edge, one leg crossed over the other; the polished shine of his imported leather shoes captured by the light from the brass lamp at his elbow. The occupant of the chair is forced to look up at him. It is an old trick.

"I hope this little chat isn't interfering with any plans you have for the evening? Do you mind if I call you Tyler?"

"No, sir. I mean 'no,' I don't have any plans, and it's o.k. if you want to call me 'Tyler.'"

"Good. Now, Tyler, let's not waste time. I'm sure you know why I asked you here." The tone is light, crisp, impersonal. "My daughter tells me you want to get married. I won't say 'have to get married' because that implies pressure exerted by her mother and me, due, shall we say to Julie's present 'delicate' condition.

Believe me, that is the farthest thing from our minds. Julie tells me she loves you and love her." These opening remarks have been directed to the space above his visitor's head, but abruptly Waterman shifts his perspective and looks him sternly in the eye. *"You do love her?"*

"Oh yes, sir. I want to marry her, don't I? Julie's being ... well, you know ...has nothing to do with it." Tyler bites his lower lip, desperate to regain the combatative stance which fueled his long walk across town. *He's up to something, but he's not gonna push me around.*

"Tell me, Tyler," he asks politely, "are you planning to continue your education after you leave Thompson High?"

"You mean like college?"

"Yes. I mean 'like college.'"

"I'd sure like to, but that's out for me, sir. We don't have the money and my marks ...well, they're not so hot."

"The services, then? Lots of young men your age enlist, you know, and Uncle Sam pays for their education."

"No, sir. My Mom, she don't want me in the Army. See I'm the only one left. (His voice drops). My brother Neddie, he was hit by a truck and my Dad ... well, he hasn't been around since I was little. My Mom says there's no way the Army would take me." The lie comes easily. The subject has never come up. Tyler doesn't think Myra cares one way or the other, but he does. He wants no part of the military life.

"I see." A slight frown materializes and just as quickly melts away. Waterman already knows about the accident, about Myra's marital status, where they live and what she earns. He has spent the weekend ferreting out every scrap of information he can lay his hands on relating to "the sneaky bastard who impregnated my daughter." By immersing himself in this quest, he was able to quell a murderous rage that descended on him after Julie's defiant confession.

"I *do* have a job, sir. I make two dollars an hour workin' part-time for Mr. Deever at the Red Checker's Depot, and he's promised to take me on full time when I finish school."

"Meaning, if you're lucky, you can count on $80 take-home pay a week?"

"Something like that." The sum represents a king's ransom to Tyler.

Sharply now. "Did my daughter happen to mention she'd applied to and been accepted at Bowdoin College and St. Lawrence?"

"No, sir. We never discussed anything like that. We just talk about getting a little place of our own, an apartment here in town. Julie says maybe she can be an *Avon* lady, you know, sell cosmetics and stuff to help out. But after the baby comes, I wouldn't want her working."

"And how do you proposed to finance all this—hospital bills, medical care for Julie and the baby, to say nothing of clothing, food and rent on $100 a week?

Perhaps you were expecting Mrs. Waterman and myself to support you?"

Smarting from the insinuation, Tyler jumps up, "No, sir! Nothing like that. We weren't counting on you for a penny. Not one red cent." With fists clenched, chin thrust forward, he heatedly declares, "We don't need your money, Mr. Waterman. We can make it on our own."

"Sit down, Scranton. Relax. I just need to have a clear picture of what you have in mind for the future. Considering what's at stake here - *my daughter's health and well-being* - surely I have a right to ask. Let me see now ..." turning to search among the papers on his desk. "Ah, here it is. I've been doing a little research of my own." He holds two thin sheets of paper against the light. "Shall we begin with the average cost of renting a one-bedroom apartment in Thompson?"

Exerting enormous self-control and finesse, the lawyer guides his daughter's lover to the inevitable conclusion: Tyler is in no position to take proper care of Julie and their unborn child. What then? At this juncture, Tyler no longer perceives Waterman as the enemy.

"What do you think I ought to do, sir?" he asks miserably. "I want the best for Julie."

"Perhaps it would be 'best' for you to step out of her life."

There is silence as Tyler grapples with the significance of these words.

"You mean walk out on her? Leave Julie for good? No, sir, I can't do that." His mouth settles into a stubborn line.

Damnit. I'm pressing too hard. Another hour passes. The youth's only bulwark against the seasoned professional's onslaught is the depth of his feelings for Julie. Bit by bit Waterman turns this sentiment in on itself, equating Tyler's loyalty with selfishness.

Sullenly. "If I leave now, I won't graduate."

"I think that can be worked out, Tyler. Ben Benedict (the principal) and I are old friends. Six weeks isn't going to make that much difference in final grades. I remember during the War, hundreds of young men were called up in the middle of their senior year and still received their diplomas. I'll see you get yours."

The attorney moves away from the desk to pace back and forth under the portrait of his father. Tyler eyes him with exhausted indifference, unaware that the man is bracing himself for the final rout.

* * * * * * * * * *

Engrossed in the exhumation of that fateful evening, he has missed the turnoff for Route 15 to Harrisburg. *Screw it.* Wearily he turns back at the next exit and starts searching for a motel to hole up in for the night.

The air is soft and warm, the trees and lawns of Thompson a viridescent green as he drove into town the next afternoon; but so much that was familiar had disappeared and he made two wrong turns before finding the house he once called home. *The old place looks pretty good.* Stark white aluminum siding had replaced the old oyster wooden shingles; a contrasting gunmetal blue on the gutters and trim lent the simple frame house an air of dignity. Gone were the century old elms from the front yard and in their stead a healthy clump of shrubs stood under the front windows, an unsteady maple sapling nearby.

Come on, buddy-boy, it's the witching hour. Better let the old witch know you're here. Tyler had cabled ahead, telling Myra when to expect him and asking that she set up a meeting with the attorney so he could sign whatever was necessary and be on his way as soon as possible. Reluctantly, he left the sanctuary of the car, walked up the stone pathway and rang the front doorbell.

"Is that really you, Tyler?" Myra studied the caller, her face peering out from behind a chain lock on the partially opened door.

"The one and only."

"Come on in, son, don't dawdle," she instructed, releasing the chain. "There's a nest of wasps just under the outside light and I don't fancy 'em in my parlour." He followed her down the hallway to the livingroom, noticing immediately that the room had been stripped of its former clutter. All that remained were the old

Delft-blue sofa, a scarred end table and a single chair. Mother and son stood in the center of the room eyeing each other with undisguised curiosity.

Tyler could only marvel: This elderly woman, this bundle of dried bones and corn-dyed hair, *this* was his nemesis, the disturber of his dreams? His mother's face was a roadmap of lines and detours around pinched lips and nostrils; she was clutching the collar of a plaid vyella robe with fragile, translucent fingers (the other hand gripping the sash as if any moment she expected an assault against her person). Before he had time to readjust his visual memory to present reality, she said accusingly, "I looked for you an hour ago. We got to be at the lawyers at three and it's after two now."

"Sorry. I got held up outside of Harrisburg. A big tractor-trailer keeled over blocking both lanes." The apology was accompanied by a weak smile. *She hasn't seen me in ten years and in two seconds she's reduced me to feeling like a little kid who gets caught snitching pennies from her purse.*

"I'll be down in a minute. I've had my bath, I just need to put on a dress."

He avoided the couch and sat stiffly on the remaining chair, a part of him registering the sounds of slippered feet on the stair, the muffled opening and closing of closet doors and drawers, the other part of him lost in the past.

Myra never had much savvy when it came to arranging furniture. To a small, active boy the livingroom had been a daily obstacle course with its scrambled-egg assortment of chairs, tables, scatter rugs and lamps, the plundered spoils of rummage sales and flea markets. Cheap ceramic knick-knacks covering every inch of surface were on a constant collision course with knees and elbows. The setting of many a slap and tongue-lashing, Tyler had hated the room with a passion reserved for an animate enemy.

She persisted in calling the alcove at the far end her 'dining room,' although they never took a meal there, not even when his father was around. The only time he could remember it being put to use was the afternoon of Neddie's funeral, when neighbors solicitously covered the oak dropleaf table with plates of cold meat, casseroles, cakes and fruit. At the center someone had placed a bowl of white roses, temporarily banishing a dusty pot of ferns which, it seemed to him, had been there from time immemorial. *Neddie.* As if it were yesterday, his small brother sprang to life: Neddie toddling across the room in faded cotton pajamas, thumb in mouth, the talismantic yellow blanket dragging along the floor behind him. Neddie at the kitchen table, diligently marking ridges with a spoon in a mound of mashed potatoes. He felt a lump rise in his throat.

"I'm ready." Jolted from a cascade of memories, he gazed unseeing for a moment at this stranger who was his mother: Myra, her hair held neatly in place by two shell combs, had changed into a dress of dusty rose with a cream, crocheted collar; at her throat was an old-fashioned onyx brooch. *Except for the dye job, she could pass for a Norman Rockwell grandmother* .

"You look swell, Myra."

With the exception of a few old landmarks - the Union Savings Bank, the Library and the century-old dark brick Presbyterian Church - the downtown section of Thompson had grown and prospered, gussying itself up in the process like an old whore with a myopic client. The law office of Myra's attorney, Jefferson Armstrong, was located on the second floor of the former *Sears'* building which had been converted into a rabbit-warren of suites for professionals and small businesses; a florist and a jeweler's occupied the ground floor spaces facing the street.

Armstrong was a courtly gentleman in his early 60's with a great mane of pure white hair and a slight tremor in both hands. In a meticulous and concise manner, the lawyer explained to Tyler the content of each document he was asked to sign. Not only had George Scranton left the house to his two sons, but, as Tyler read in a document Armstrong handed to him from the clerk's office in Edmunton, Canada, the brothers each inherited 300 acres of adjoining property located near the Pembina River in the province of Alberta. The barman was stunned at the news. *What the hell will I do with 300 acres in the wilds of Canada?*

"When the letters come to the house," Myra explained, "I opened Neddie's and showed it to Mr. Armstrong; he wrote and told those folks about the accident and everything. They wrote back to say since I was next of kin, the land was mine if I wanted to claim it. But who'd want to fool with some old piece of land in a foreign country at my age? I'm turnin' it over to you, son."

"Did he ... did he leave you anything, Myra?"

"Me? What would be the point?"

Tyler could think of any number of reasons why a man who arbitrarily deeded 600 acres to two sons he hadn't cared enough to see or contact for some 30 odd years, should have made a penitential gesture to the woman who'd borne and raised them.

He readily signed over his half of the house in Thompson to Myra and in turn, she relinquished Neddie's portion of the property. *Now, for the $64,000 question: Do I give up my job and start herding sheep?*

When they emerged from the building, Tyler looked at his watch, "I can't believe we've been in that lawyer's office for nearly three hours! It's almost dinnertime and I've got to start back tonight."

"I could fix us an omelet at the house."

"Forget the omelet Let's eat out."

The invitation seemed to rob her of speech. That suspicious frown he knew so well appeared. *She thinks I'm gonna stick her with the tab.*

"My treat, Myra. You pick the place."

She mulled over his words, the hint of a smile brushing her lips as she murmured, "All right, then. We'll go to *Tait's*. No need to take the car. We can walk."

The restaurant was around the corner from the main thoroughfare, its interior decor reflecting a shotgun wedding between *Red Lobster* and *Steak & Ale*. It was early and only a few tables were occupied.

"Care for a drink before we order dinner?"

"A glass of sherry. That would be nice." After he gave their order he watched her carefully inspect the room, nodding to herself from time to time as if checking off a mental inventory.

"Cozy place. Do you come here often?"

"Me? *Tait's?* That's a good one." She gave a dry honk. "You're really out of touch boy, if you think your mother can afford to eat with the hoi-poloi. The Church Street crowd hangs out here a lot. First I heard of it was from Evie McKay. Walt brought her here for their anniversary. You wouldn't know the McKays. They moved to town after you left. Walt's the head butcher at Grand Union."

When their dinners were served, his mother gave all attention to the food on her plate, carefully cutting and chewing her way through two large char-boiled lamb chops, a baked potato with sour cream, salad, vegetable and hot biscuits. An agonizing few minutes were spent over the dessert offerings before Myra finally settled on a double chocolate layer cake with whipped cream. *Either she hasn't eaten for a week or she has some miraculous secret that keeps her thin while she piles on the calories.* She declined a second glass of sherry and pretended not to hear when Tyler ordered another double Scotch.

At last Myra put down her fork and pushed the empty plate to one side, settling back in her chair with a look of feline contentment. "Thank you, son. I enjoyed that."

It was dark when they arrived back at the house. As he took her arm to guide her up the path to the front door, he was suddenly aware that not once had his mother asked about his job or his plans for the future. He waited while she fumbled in her handbag for the key to the lock.

"Look, Myra, I hope things work out well for you in Wisconsin. If you need anything, let me know. And give my best to aunt Madge." He bent down and kissed her lightly on the cheek. "Goodnight. Take care."

Unexpectedly, she reached up and in a familiar gesture brushed a lock of hair from his forehead. "Good night, son." He was halfway down the path when she called after him, "You left here because you got some girl in trouble, didn't you, Tyler?"

He hurried on without answering.

A quarter of a century had passed since he last stood at his bedroom window wiping ignominious tears with the back of his hand as he stared at the snapshot of him and Julie taken the summer before at Camp Devon. "Julie ... Julie ... Look what they've done to us," whispering her name to himself like a litany. At his feet a battered suitcase belonging to his father was stuffed with his belongings; in his back pocket an envelope bulged with a thousand dollars in small bills, more money than he'd ever seen in his life. A letter to his mother was propped up against the lamp on the dresser behind him:

Don't worry about me. I'm o.k. Mr. Benedict is sending my diploma in the mail. Please save it for me. I'll write soon.

Your loving son.

He had agreed to leave town because he didn't for one moment believe the banishment was permanent.

Somehow Julie would convince her parents to accept him; he'd return to Thompson, pay back all the money Miss Webster had handed him from Mr. Waterman. He and Julie would get married and have a wonderful life together. The muffled sound of a car backfiring in the distance interrupted his reverie. Time was running out. There was a bus to catch.

"I betcha within a week they'll be beggin' me to come back" he muttered defiantly as he picked up the suitcase and stalked from the room.

When he spied the public phone booth across from the bus stop, it was too much. *To hell with the bastard.* Despite a solemn pledge not to contact Julie once he accepted the money - she'd been absent from school since his interview with her father - he had to hear her voice one more time, had to tell her how much he loved her and that he'd be back as soon as things were squared away with her parents. With trembling fingers, he dialed her home number. *If her old man answers, I'll hang up.*

"The Waterman residence." It was Mrs. Clute, the housekeeper. "I'm sorry but Miss Julie's not here. She's away on a trip with her parents. Would you like to leave a message?"

Tyler slammed down the receiver without answering. *Sons of bitches.* He bit his lip to contain a fresh surge of emotion. When the bus rounded a curve and lumbered to a stop, its horn tooting, he could barely see it through his tears.

So began a year of such misery and loneliness that afterwards, Tyler managed to black out most of the details. Arrangements had been made for him to work on a stud farm owned by a distant cousin of Julie's mother; he was told the place was roughly twenty miles north of Casper, Wyoming, At first the young Easterner was spellbound by the vast panorama of grazing land, the distant towering majesty of the Laramies; but the scenic wonders of the far West in summertime were soon supplanted by the frigid winds and daunting snowfalls of winter.

Three thousand dollars in payments stretching over a year would be forwarded to him at the farm; leaving meant forfeiting the money. The hours of work were long and hard; he was ignored by the hardened ranch hands and ex-cowboys with whom he shared spartan lodgings; behind his back they called him 'pretty boy.' A bow-legged Indian who worked in the kitchen and called himself Eagle Feathers tried to teach him to ride, but Tyler was afraid of horses and after being thrown twice, refused to try again, further isolating him from his companions, all experienced riders.

Every Saturday afternoon the farm's pickup truck carried those wanting a lift to Casper. (No one mentioned the arrangment to him his first week at work; he spent a wretched afternoon stretched out on his cot counting the cobwebs on the ceiling and missing Julie, reliving that long-ago Saturday when they'd made love in his bedroom at the oyster shingle house.) The first thing he did when he got to town the following week was fill his pockets with change and hunt for the nearest phone booth to call Lyle.

"Hey, buddy, where the hell are you? You o.k.?" The familiar voice prompted such a wave of homesickness, the unhappy youth had to clear his throat before answering.

"Sure. I'm fine."

"The fellows have been makin' book that you and Julie eloped."

"You mean Julie's not in Thompson?"

"Nope. She dropped out of school about the same time you pulled your disappearing act. Ain't she with you?"

"No, Julie's not with me." They talked until Tyler ran out of change; before Lyle hung up he promised to ask around, see if any of Julie's friends knew where she was. Tyler retreated to the darkened comfort of a movie theater and, oblivious to the madcap adventures of Philias Fogg and his faithful Passepartout, made a desperate effort to come to terms with the obvious: Waterman had been ten steps ahead of him all the way. Julie was out of his life forever. He left the theater midway through the second feature and roamed the streets of Casper. At eleven, when the pickup was due to return to the farm, two of the ranch hands went looking for him. They found him retching against the wall in an alley, so drunk he could hardly stand.

Thereafter, he continued to call Lyle once or twice a month, content to hear the sound of his voice, to touch base with the life he'd abandoned so heedlessly. No one seemed to know of Julie's whereabouts and after a while he stopped asking. He spent his free Saturdays by himself, at the movies and later in a bar where he developed a taste for rye whiskey with beer chasers; he was rescued from these solitary pursuits by a cashier at the eatery he frequented. Tyler found solace and the physical gratification he craved between the dimpled knees of Darlene, a local girl in her early twenties (he never could remember her last name). Her tiny, cheerful apartment over a laundromat seemed like Eden compared to the austere barracks at the farm. Three months after he began sleeping with her they were married by a Justice of the Peace. Tyler pledged Darlene to secrecy: "*I promise, sweetheart, soon's this job is over, we'll have a real honeymoon 'n you can tell the whole world you're Mrs. Scranton."* He continued to live and work at the ranch, able to spend only Saturdays with his new bride.

Early in spring, after a particularly gruelling four days of tending to a batch of new foals, the men were given the afternoon off. It was the middle of the week and Tyler hitched a ride to town, elated over the prospect of passing the rest of the day with Darlene in her double bed. At the apartment he walked in on her as she was performing fellatio on one of the restaurant's busboys. The annullment papers were drawn up a week later.

When his year in purgatory was up, Tyler, who had managed to hold onto half the money sent by Julie's father, quit the stud farm and bought a one-way ticket at the *Greyhound* depot to New York.

CHAPTER XXVI

Tyler couldn't wait to put as much distance as possible between himself and Thompson's city limits. On the route back to Harrisburg he passed mile after frustrating mile looking for an open gas station so he could phone Sarah; he'd forgotten the old saw about the sidewalks in rural areas of northern Pennsylvania being rolled up by nine p.m. It was past midnight when he reached a lighted *Texaco* station on the outskirts of a town called McClure. *Too late to call Sarah ... better forget about trying to make it to Harrisburg, too. I need some sack time. I'll ring first thing in the morning. Tomorrow's Saturday and she should be there.* He paid for the gas and asked station's owner if he could recommend a place to stay in McClure.

"'Bout five miles down the road on your right, you'll see a sign, 'Sloane's Slumber Inn.' It ain't much to look at, but the cabins are clean. Friends of mine own it and Dottie, she's the wife, takes a lot of pride in keeping it up."

"Sounds good to me. I'm beat. Thanks."

"I'll call ahead. Tell' em you're coming."

A sleepy female voice answered the telephone Saturday morning; as soon as she heard Scranton's name, she called, "Sarah, come here! Guess who's on the line!"

"Tyler, darling! Is that you? How wonderful to hear your voice!" As succinctly as possible he told her the reason for the unexpected trip, adding that he was on his way to Baltimore to catch a Miami flight that would take him back to Lutigua.

"You mean I'm not going to see you?"

"I wish there'd been time to make a detour and spend a few days with you, hon', but as it is the hotel's jumping and Foster-Jones was a good sport about letting me go." He heard a groan at the other end of the line.

"But listen, Sarah, I've got three weeks leave coming and as soon as you're free, we can spend every second of it together."

"Oh Tyler, that would be wonderful!"

"I'll make the arrangements as soon as I get the go-ahead from you. Where would you like to go, love? Another island? ... the Caymens?... Aruba? ...I hear Bermuda's a nice spot. Or maybe you'd prefer a big city? It's up to you. Whatever you say."

"Since you've given me *carte blanche*, how about Paris? I've always wanted to go to that beautiful city, to make love at the top of the Eiffel Tower. Or London, darling. London would be perfect! Grand passion on the floor of the Albert Hall. Think of it! *The Albert Hall!*...Seriously Tyler, why go anywhere? Why not stay right on the island? Instead of wasting time travelling and having to acclimate ourselves to a whole new situation, why don't you find us a cozy cottage to rent as far from Belle Jours as possible?"

"Do you really mean it, Sarah? You want to meet me in Lutigua?"

"Absolutely! I can't think of a lovelier spot."

"O.K., hon', I'll scout around. See what I can find for us. By the way, can you *cook?*"

"Oh there won't be time to think about anything as mundane as food, darling. I'm going to chain you to the bed and we're going to make love around the clock."

* * * * * * * * * *

Two Sundays had passed since Peter Callender's visit to the Mapp house, an interlude he thought of often and with pleasure. He admired and approved of every aspect of Josiah's daughter: her refined looks, her obvious intelligence, her ease of conversing and above all the respect and affection she showed towards her father. This morning as the choir swept down the aisle to resume their places, she acknowledged his presence with a nod; it was enough to set his heart dancing.

After the service he stood at the front door of the church greeting members of the congregation, hoping Danielle had not ducked out by the Sacristy door as the choir members often did.

Here she comes ...

"Good morning, Miss Mapp. Would you mind staying behind for a moment? I need to speak with you."

Her look of surprise was quickly replaced by, "Yes, please, Mr. Callender. I'll wait for you under the tamarind tree by the gate."

The Horticultural Society's annual Flower Show was scheduled to open the following day and after weighing several options, Callender decided it was the most suitable place for a casual outing.

Flustered but nonetheless gratified that the attractive widower had singled her out, Danielle shyly accepted his invitation to escort her to the flower show on her next half-day off.

* * * * * * * * * * *

"What you puttin' a clean work shirt on for, Mr. Wilson?" his wife asked as she stood in the doorway of their tiny bedroom, arms folded belligerently across her ample bosom. "You think you goin' somewheres?"

"They needs me at de hotel. Ain't a soul there knowin' how to do for de Mistress like I do. She's got her ways en she always sayin' to me, 'Wash, what would I do widout you? You're the onliest one understandin' what I needs before I has to ask.'"

"Doctor Hoyos en't give you leave to go back to work."

"Now woman, we both knows de doctor's quicker den a cockaroach to order you to bed when you're feelin' poorly, 'n slow as mule 'bout lettin' you out of it. I'm feelin' fine, but I'll be sick for sure if I spends one more day lazin' about dis house."

His wife sighed. It was a battle she knew she couldn't win, but she was worried nonetheless. Never a big man to begin with, her husband had lost weight during his recent illness and looked like a stickman in his clothes. Nor was he completely free of the cough which daily wracked his body.

"Here," she said in a voice of quiet resignation, "your collar's turned in. Lemme fix it. En Jeremiah, you needs to call Mr. Cyrus up the gap en have him to carry you to work in his truck."

"I already done that."

When she'd finished putting the breakfast dishes away, Wash's wife sat down at the kitchen table to prepare breadfruit for the evening meal. While her hands were busy at their task, her thoughts slipped away to the past. She and Jeremiah had been childhood sweethearts, had married as soon as he was able to find work away from the plantation where he was born and where his parents labored all their lives. The mutual attraction and passion of youth had matured and ripened over the intervening years, mellowing into strong bonds of affection and devotion. She remembered when her husband first started work at Belle Jours, when all he could talk about at home was "de Mistress," how clever she was, how beautifully she entertained, on and on. She smiled to herself, recalling how she'd storm about the house after he'd gone, filled with unbridled animosity towards Wash's employer: "Dat woman too good to fit." She was jealous, of course. But that was many years ago, and wisely she had put her rancour aside.

"Thirty-seven years," she shook her head in wonderment. "'Cept for de time he went off to work for dat big oil company, Jeremiah en me been sharin' de same bed all those years."

With a wife, two growing sons and a six year old to provide for, Wash searched in vain for another job after Laura Foster-Jones closed down the hotel and went abroad. He watched in desperation as their small savings dwindled to nothing. A cousin working for *Shell Oil* in Curacao heard of his plight through the family grapevine and sent a letter:

They got work for any man who has a mind to earn a decent wage, Jeremiah. But I has to tell you, mon, no matter what sweet words they sayin', de living here's no good at all ... nothin' but a plank board for a bed, a hole in de ground for your shite and food so poor tastin', it'd make a beggar weep. But de pay's good, better than what you makes at home, 'n better'n no pay at all.

Reluctant to leave his family yet realizing he had no choice, Wash contacted the local recruiting agent for *Shell*; along with three dozen other Lutiguans, he signed a two-year contract to work as a labourer in their oil fields on the Dutch island.

He quit 18 months later and returned home after receiving a letter from his wife saying there was a place for him as houseman at the plantation where he was born. Wilson's life on Curacao was one of such hardship and misery that he could never bear to speak of it. But he vowed never again to be separated from his family; his wife had reached the same conclusion: "If I has to work in de cane fields to put bread on de table, I will!"

"The Lord's been good to us," she reflected as she finished peeling and cutting the breadfruit. The two older boys had grown into fine young men, both with good jobs, and James, the apple of his parents' eyes, was a constant source of joy. Now, if only her husband would regain his strength and be truly well again! "Please, Lord, *please*, take care of my Jeremiah."

After a flourishing May, bookings at Belle Jours dropped so precipitously that by mid-June Foster-Jones was impelled to call a meeting of her senior staff.

"Mr. Kissoon, our bookeeper, tells me we cannot afford to keep a full complement of personnel over the next three months. You're going to have to put your people on half-time. I leave it to you to work out the details. And it would also be helpful if each of you would take his annual holiday during this period. Just make certain that whomever you leave in charge is up to the responsibility."

Tyler retreated to the cabin where he spent several hours trying to work out a schedule for his crew; he found it tough going. Over a period of time he'd been privy to a few details about their lives away from the hotel: Sam was supporting four children he'd sired by two different women; with a father languishing in jail, 'Legs' Walrond was the sole wage-earner in a household that included his mother, grandmother and a sister; and Brian handed over his wages to his widowed mother to help feed and clothe two younger siblings. The others had problems too, but the American had no choice: he was forced to lay off all those who regularly filled-in during the hotel's winter season or when the hotel was full and extra hands were needed.

He should have let James MacArthur go too, but after the indignities he'd suffered, Tyler couldn't bring himself to tell the youth he'd be out of work for three months . *James'll just have to be satisfied working weekends only.*

As always, he was uncomfortable with that aspect of his job requiring him to be tough or assertive; given a choice, he would've held off announcing the cutbacks for as long as possible, but knew that word would spread quickly amongst the others. Drained by his struggle to forestall the inevitable, Tyler fixed himself a cheese sandwich and chased it down with two beers, deciding he needed all the Dutch courage he could muster to face the task. *Better spill the bad news when the shifts change this afternoon ... and then, come heaven or highwater, I'm off to the Bristol .*

"Hey, Yank. Where you been hiding yourself, then?"

"Listen Robertson, I'd be down here every week beating the socks off you at darts if it was possible. Don't ask me why, but I really miss this three-ring circus. Last month the hotel was snowed under with package tours, then I had to make a quick trip to the States on family business and I've been bustin' my butt ever since."

"Fancy a little fishing one of these days, you know, get away from it all?"

"Sounds enticing to me. What day did you have in mind?"

"I'm clearing out of here in July, so it will have to be soon. *Sally Anne* and I are headed for Australia."

"Oh? Is Sally Anne a 'special friend' of yours?"

"*You could say that.* She is rather special. Bit on the heavy side of course, but then you can't have everything."

"Heavy side?" *That's a helluva way to describe a gal you're taking half-way around the world with you.*

"Give or take a few stones, I'd say she weighed close to 42 tons."

Tyler frowned in confusion. Robertson doubled over with laughter. "Got you that time, Yank. The *Sally Anne's* my boat, as trim and sweet a lady as a man could wish for. If you can get free next Sunday, I'll 'introduce' her."

Unable to sleep, Mary Farmingham flung off the top sheet and padded to the tiny kitchenette in Leona's old suite to fix herself a toddy, counting on the combination of hot water, sugar and rum to do the trick. Lately she'd begun to feel that her body belonged to someone else. Before coming to Belle Jours, Mary was one of those lucky ones, able to nod off within seconds anywhere, anytime, waking refreshed and full of energy. But these days, her wretchedness is compounded by nightly skirmishes with elusive sleep and mornings when she feels as if she's encased in a strait-jacket. When she does manage to doze off, her recurring dreams terrify her: always there are towering waves of malevolent water threatening to engulf her, and no matter what the setting – a city street, the beach, a walled garden – she is unable to save herself.

The last few tablets containing a mild sedative (prescribed by her London doctor for a sprained ankle) are gone. Getting another sedative means having to see a physician; she met Dr. Harcourt at Leona's farewell party, but she can't very well sneak off to see him without telling her aunt and this she stubbornly refuses to do .

Carrying the warm drink onto the patio, she sinks down in her favorite chair, knees to chin, fervently wishing she'd never accepted Laura's invitation to come to Lutigua. While her mind busily exhumes the sources of her misery, she empties the mug, goes back inside and polishes off the last few inches of rum, knowing full well that dependency on liquor is a false and dangerous panacea.

Feeling isolated, her self-esteem in shambles, what she longs for is a confidante, someone to whom she can unburden herself. *No one on the staff likes me. They don't respect, me, either. And that Mrs. Vernon is so bloody-minded, there are days when I could ring her neck.*

* * * * * * * * * *

"Say, lady, you're looking especially perky and beautiful this morning. What's up? Did you find a pot of gold at the end of the rainbow?"

The Lutigan flushed with pleasure, hugging to herself the secret of her new-found happiness.

"You tease too much, Tyler." Peter Callender had entered her life, courting her with deference and restraint. This evening he would be bringing his daughter to dinner at the Mapp house; for days Danielle fussed over the selection and preparation of the dishes to be served. She'd be meeting Callender's child for the first time and prayed with all her heart that the evening would go well, that Tamika would like her.

"Here's a list of the names of the bar crew who'll remain on the payroll this summer. Is Kissoon in his cubby-hole?"

"No please, Tyler. He's gone to the bank, but I will give him your list when he returns."

The weather – hard driving rains and crushing humidity – was miserable on the days preceding Tyler's fishing date with Dunc Robertson; but late Saturday afternoon, a cooling breeze from the south blew across the island and by Sunday the puddles had disappeared and every leaf and blade of grass looked freshly washed. Wearing white ducks, his captain's hat set at a rakish angle, Robertson, looked every inch the sailor as he greeted the American at the dock where the *Sally Anne* was tied up. In keeping with the flavour of the occasion, he introduced two muscular, capable-looking Lutiguans in their early twenties as 'Ensign Leonard and 1st mate Adrian.'

With a light breeze skimming over the water, the Englishman was clearly eager to be on his way, but politeness demanded that he give Tyler a tour of the gleaming two-masted ketch: the main cabin and additional sleeping quarters were austerely furnished, but every piece of brass had a burnished sheen to it and the bulkhead sported a coat of fresh paint.

They sailed for an hour before dropping anchor on the leeward side of an uninhabited coral atoll, one of many within easy reach of Lutigua. The fish weren't cooperating, and after a time the two men lost interest. Tyler took a leisurely swim and came back on board in time for lunch; it was a simple affair, prepared and served by Adrian: fried chunks of snapper and chubb, pickled breadfruit, marinated cucumbers, fresh tomatoes and to top it off, slices of the sweetest pineapple the American had ever tasted. Completely relaxed, he was content to leave the burden of conversation to Robertson, a ribald and flippant ranconteur. The two men started drinking from a half-gallon jug of rum and by the time they were homeward bound, it was empty. Just as the sun was about to take a final, spectacular bow, the *Sally Anne* nudged into place against the dock.

Turning to his new-found friend, Tyler clapped him on the shoulder: "Thanks, Dunc. As you Brits would say, 'It's been a bloody fine day.' I'm going to miss you, old salt." Only after his feet touched *terra firma* did he realize he'd consumed far too much booze and was badly sun burnt to boot.

"Good heavens, Tyler. You look ghastly! How did you let yourself get in such a state?" Mary Farnham exclaimed the next morning. Tyler's nose, forehead and arms were a lurid, flamingo pink and the dark, puffy circles under his eyes gave him an aura of a boxer who'd gone one round too many.

Suffering the worst hangover in recent memory, the barman was clearly not up to polite chitchat. "Haven't you got more important things to worry about?" he answered curtly, and was immediately repentant.

Mary reared back as if she'd been slapped; a deep flush rose from her neck to the roots of her hair. He could have kicked himself.

"Look, I'm sorry. You didn't deserve that. It's just that ..." without waiting for him to explain, she turned on her heels and rushed down the path towards the sea. His eyes followed her copper hair as she pushed open the wrought iron gate to the beach and disappeared from view.

Well, buddy-boy, that little performance just earned you the prick-of-the-year award. He went to the bar and composed a short apology on the back of an unused drinks' tab, adding that he hoped she'd meet him at the bar – this evening, say around 10? – and let him buy her a drink to make up for his churlishness.

At 10:30 he decided she wasn't coming; at 11, as he was preparing to close down the bar for the evening, she appeared.

He greeted her with a wide grin. "Hey, I'm glad you decided to come. About this morning, I'm really ..."

She brushed her hand in the air to cut him off. "Please ..."

"O.K. What can I get you, Mary?"

"A banana daiquiri would be nice."

"Right. One banana daiquiri coming up." He poured himself a Scotch and motioned to a table nearby, "Let's sit over there."

Silence, like an impenetrable fog, descended between them as they sipped their drinks. Tyler, usually adept at light conversation, found himself stymied by her reserve. He cleared his throat, "How are things going, Mary? Do you like it here? That's some tough job you've got."

"Oh I don't mind," she lied, "I'm glad to be busy. It's just that sometimes ..." She ducked her head and let the unfinished sentence hang in the air.

"Sometimes what?" he prodded gently.

"Actually, I miss my friends in England. (But not the climate, I assure you.) If anyone told me there'd come a time when I'd sell York Minster for 'woman talk', for good chat over a cuppa, I'd have said they were starkers. But I do miss it. I find myself longing for the oddest things in this place. Do you, Tyler?"

"Now that you mention it, I could do with a big, fat pastrami sandwich on rye, please, light on the mustard and I swear I could eat a whole bushel of juicy, ripe Georgia peaches. They'll be coming on the market right about now."

She rewarded him with a wan smile. "If you're going to make that kind of list, I could go on all night. What I meant was, don't you miss the people back in the States, your friends?"

"Hadn't thought about it, frankly." He wasn't about to mention Sarah.

"Oh." She lapsed into silence again. Tyler studied her as she idly swiveled the remains of her drink around with a straw. *Not a bad sort, once you get past those 'rawther nots' and 'teddiblys'. Guess she can't help the way she talks, but it's damn off-putting... Not hard on the eyes, either, but she's definitely not my type.*

By then, like everyone else on staff he knew Mary was Foster-Jones' niece. He admired them both for acting as if the relationship didn't exist. *Must be pretty hard on the kid, though. No one to pal around with. Must be lonesome, too.*

"Can I get you another daiquiri?"

"No. Thank you. I'm off to bed now. Tomorrow I must be up early to catch the farmer who delivers our egg plant and sweet potatoes. Corbin found mold on the last three batches and was very put out about it. He acted as if it were my fault."

"Don't let Corbin get to you. He's a great cook, but he's a tempermental son-of-a-bitch. He'll push you around if he thinks he can get away with it."

As if I didn't know that already. "Thanks, Tyler. I'll keep it in mind."

CHAPTER XXVII

A cable arrived at the hotel which sent Reservations into a tizzy: PLEASE HOLD YOUR FINEST SUITE FOR ARRIVAL OF COUNTESS VOLINSKY AND COMPANION, 7/1–7/23. CONFIRM. Lutigua had not seen the likes of royalty since Edward VII, Duke of Windsor, stepped ashore from the royal yacht to lunch with the High Commissioner.

Colin, the bellhop, was on duty the afternoon of the Countess' unforgettable appearance at Belle Jours.

"Here come de fattest lady in de world, huffin' 'n puffin, tryin' to get outta de back seat of dat old taxi. (When I offer a hand, she give me a look like, 'Who you kiddin', boy?') Den de driver, he come 'round en starts to pullin' on her arms en I see someone from *inside* de taxi pushin' she from behind. Mon, I'm sore all over, pinchin' myself to keep from laughin'. Ain't seen nothin' like it since Dorsey's mule got stuck in de ditch.

"When dey gets she out of de taxi, de lady poke inside dis piece of fur what's wrapped around her en pull out dis runt of a dog. Den she start kissin' it like found money. I swear, de dog's no bigger than a mango stone. How'd she pass dat mutt through Customs, mon, tell me dat?"

Colin's bewilderment was mild compared with the reaction at the front desk to the appearance of a tiny, tan Chihuahua. The hotel had never dealt with the question of whether animals should be allowed on the premises because Foster-Jones sensibly assumed the problem would never arise. In order to keep the island rabies-free, Lutigua enforced a strict quarantine, its guidelines so daunting most holiday-goers, including the animal-loving Brits, were content to leave their pets behind.

"This is Ladislaus the Fourth, darlink," the Countess said by way of introducing the animal to a flustered Cleo. "Ladis is a good boy, aren't you darlink." Her loving gaze moved from the dog to the hapless young Lutiguan, the tender words abruptly supplanted by a tone of icy hauter:

"My Ladis has a very delicate palate. He vill eat nothink but calves liver. Tell the Chef the Countess vould like a small dish of *fresh minced calves' liver* delivered to her suite each day at twelve noon. On the dot. And remind him, darlink, Ladis does not like to be kept vaiting."

A hurried conference was called out of sight in the back office. Laura was away at a luncheon hosted by the Lutigua's Minister of Tourism, so the burden of deciding what to do fell to a reluctant Danielle who could not guess what her employer would say when she learned a guest had (a) brought a pet, (b) the pet required a special diet. She threw up her hands in defeat. "The lady is here. The room, it is paid for. To send her away is impossible."

Tyler had his first glimpse of their royal visitor later that evening when he was on duty at the bar. Foster-Jones, making a rare appearance in the public rooms, walked up to a table on the far side of the diningroom and introduced herself to an extravagantly stout woman with skin the color of a magnolia blossom, frizzy hennaed hair, and whose eyes were hidden behind wing-shaped sunglasses studded with rhinestones. The new guest was swaddled - there being no other word to describe it - in a Wedgewood blue silk version of the African dou-dou, with gold braid trimming. As the woman raised her cigarette holder to heavily painted lips, fleshy fingers displayed an opulent array of diamond, sapphire and ruby rings. Covert stares and whispers followed her every gesture; she was the center of attention, but then she was hard to miss .

How does her royal nibs manage to get around? She's the size of a ten-ton truck.

In contrast, the Countess' travelling companion was thin to the point of looking anorexic; an angular woman with with olive skin, jet black hair tapered close to the skull, she was dressed in a white jumpsuit with matching leather belt and sandals. Her flat, Buddha-like face was devoid of makeup in a calculated bid to appear self-effacing. Tyler noticed that she rarely spoke, but her dark, glittering eyes missed nothing.

After an animated exchange - at one point the Countess threw back her head and laughed with the abandonment of a young girl - Laura excused herself and came over to the bar.

"A magnum of our best champagne for our royal guest, Scranton. And charge it to my account." As she turned to rejoin the ladies at their table, Ladislaus the Fourth, hidden from view in the ample folds of the dou-dou, leaped from his mistress' lap and rushed forward to give the hotel's owner a friendly, welcoming yip. (Tyler recounted the incident to Danielle, "You should have seen F.J.'s face! It was pricelss. What I wouldn't give to have a photograph of it!")

Fascinated by their eminent guest, Laura hosted a small gathering in her honour so Sir Edward, Marianne Pharr and Gideon Moss could meet her. The Countess arrived for cocktails on Laura's private patio with Ladis in the crook of her arm; happily, the tiny dog remained curled in his mistress' lap and was no trouble. Encased in one of her silken tent-like garments, the woman held the group enthralled.

Emboldened by drink Gideon asked, "I confess I'm dying of curiosity. Do tell us, dear Countess Volinsky, how did you manage to get your dog through Customs?"

"It's like this, darlink," she said with a twinkle, "a few hours before ve are leavink, I give my precious Ladis a little pill to make him sleepy. Before ve are boarding the plane, I tuck him inside my stole. I am taking zis stole with me everywhere, darlink ... to Paris in springtime, to Istanbul in vinter." She and her companion, Titania, always insist on three seats together. "Once the airline peoples see the size of Countess Volinsky, there is no fuss," she explains with a laugh. After take-off the Countess slips the sleeping Ladis into her carry-on luggage, made-to-order with air holes so the dog can breathe. Then, if they're travelling to a foreign country and must pass through Customs, the Countess, with Ladis once again safely encsconced in her stole, waits 'til the moment when the Customs' officer asks her to open her luggage for inspection:

"Suddenly, darlink, the most dreadful *tink* happens. My cosmetic bag drops to the ground and *everytink* falls out. Such a mess, darlink! Rollers are rollink, lipsticks are spinnink, talcum is spillink on the floor; I am cryink in a loud voice, 'Oh! Oh!' and clutch my heart like I am goink to faint or vorse.' By the time everythink is back in my bag the line is very long and peoples are cross, so the officer vaves us along.'" Then she gives Moss this big wink and drops the fake accent: "Titania is a genius when it comes to packing."

The Countess' demand that the kitchen prepare a special dish for her dog and deliver it at a certain hour had enraged Corbin. "My ears gone hard. I ain't hearin' what you want, and I ain't doin' it!" When appeals by both Mary and Danielle failed to change his mind, Laura had a word with him privately. Of course, fresh calves' liver was almost non-existent on Lutigua, so the chef grudgingly made do with sheep livers, covering his tracks by presenting the substitute in a sea of gravy which the dog lapped up.

'Fixin' up de calves' liver' became a running joke in the kitchen:

"Hey, mon. You drown Miz Vernon's scrawny cat en that be its liver?"

"No way, mon. It's de gizzard from ole man Landers' pet mule."

On several evenings during her stay at Belle Jours, the Countess held court after dinner, commandeering a settee in a corner of the formal Lounge. She invited a select number of guests from the hotel, ones she'd shrewdly observed seemed articulate and bright. (Titania delivered the invitations. No one ever refused.) With her entourage gathered in a half circle around the chair, she enacted with gusto the leading role in her own version of a European *salon.* Drinks were served - the Countess habitually drank *Chablis* - and the guests were expected to pay for their own and hers as well.

Despite her demands, which were sometimes outrageous, her tips, which were miserly (Tyler dubbed her 'Hetty Green') by the end of her stay, the preposterous woman had the entire staff at her feet.

Having sent a bottle of *Johnny Walker* to Corbin from 'Ladis', she departed in a flurry of luggage and 'darlinks', promising "Ve vill be back next year." It took two men to wedge her into the taxi.

The place seemed infinitely duller without her.

"The Countess, she's a fuss-box," was Cleo's comment to Danielle, "but still, she all de time laughin' at herself en she make everyone else to laugh, too. One fat happy lady, dat's what the Countess is! But Miz Titania, de one wid her, she's stiff as a starched sheet. Do you think *Titania's* her real name, Danielle?"

"Must be so. It's what the Countess is calling her."

Later she asked Tyler what he thought of Countess Volinsky's companion.

"Titania? An odd duck ...so quiet you hardly know she's there. A perfect foil for her flamboyant employer, I'd say. Actually, I'd guess the woman plays half a dozen roles ... personal maid, secretary, a regular Steppin'-fetch-it. Just getting the Countess dressed for the day would be a job in itself!"

At noon on Sunday, the day after the Countess' departure, the S.O.T.S. were gathered as usual on Laura's patio. Earlier, they'd had a delicious time chewing over the Prime Minister's latest peccadillo; although married and the father of three grown children, Lutigua's head of government had the reputation of an incorrigible philanderer. (His transgressions didn't seem to bother the islanders, who returned him to office by a landslide. In fact, it probably accounted for his great popularity among the menfolk.)

"I vote we change the subject," Bill Howard interjected sourly, "I'm sick to death of hearing about the PM's roving prick," this from a man whose wife rarely let him out of her sight.

"Bill' right," Gideon chimed in. "Let's talk about something pleasant for a change. I know! The Countess! Now there's a sizable subject for you."

"Ha, ha. Gideon. Very funny. When God passed out a sense of humor, He must have passed you right by."

"Come, come, dear Marianne. Let's not bicker," Sir Edmund chided. Turning to Laura, he asked, "I understand your royal guest left yesterday. Did she ever talk about her background? Is she a member of an old, titled family?"

Laura smiled benignly. "She *is* something, isn't she? As to being from an 'old, titled family,' I hardly think the Mulligans of Astoria, Long Island, can lay claim to royal blood."

"Mulligan!"

"That's her maiden name. She told me so herself. Actually, it's a remarkable story, especially the way the Countess tells it. One minute she's into that absurd foreign accent and the next she's lapsed into a New Yorkese that would curl a sailor's hair."

"I'm absolutely intrigued, Laura. Tell us the rest, please do."

Their hostess shrugged. "If I go around telling tales on my guests, I won't be in business very long ... nevertheless, I don't suppose she'd mind. She was so open about it all herself. Well ... it seems that shortly after V-E Day (this is in the States, mind you), a friend invited her to a party in Greenwich Village-she was just seventeen at the time and starting secretarial school. At this party she meets the Count, a genuine member of the old Polish aristocracy; he fought with the Resistance, then escaped to London and volunteered his services to the British government. He was in his mid-thirties, a bona-fide war hero. 'Ve look at each other and boom,' she says, 'just like a clap of thunder! It is luff at first sight, darlink.' Her family raised hell, but they got married anyway. They never had any children, but they travelled a lot ...saw most of the world except, of course, his homeland. Sounds like a real love match. The Count died about twelve years ago. 'After my darlink Cosmos is gone,'" simulating her voice and words, "'for two years I cry every day. I do not eat. Then one morning I vake up and I *eat*.'" The Countess goes from size eight to forty eight. "'Some day maybe they vill put me on TV? I vill look into the camera and say, *Vy no one tell me about diet drinks?*' Then she claps her hands together in delight and roars with laughter, even though the joke is on herself."

"That's some story."

"That's some lady!"

"I was sorry to see her leave," Laura said pensively. "She is truly a memorable character... Wash! ... My friends and I are ready for another round of drinks."

CHAPTER XXVIII

In a dream, Tyler is swimming towards shore, towards a small figure on the beach. *It's Sarah! She's come back!* He cannot wait to touch her face, to kiss her and enfold her in his arms once more. He redoubles his efforts, kicking harder and pulling at the water with his cupped hands. He has been swimming for a long time; his arms and legs ache with the strain, but he does not mind. He thinks only of her, of how euphoric their reunion will be. As he draws nearer the beach, she sees him and gives a welcoming wave. *Only a few hundred yards to go,* he reassures himself, aware suddenly of a sharp pain in his side. *Easy, buddy-boy, easy does it.* He slows the pace of his furious breast stroke and is rewarded by the surcease of pain. Emboldened by this small victory, he plunges heedlessly ahead; in a matter of seconds he realizes he is making no progress. Instead of moving forward, unseen hands seem to be pulling at his body and pushing it sideways. *What the ...* Then he remembers: *Jossa's revenge.* It is a name given by the

Lutiguans to a treacherous undertow which every year claims as many as a score of victims, natives and visitors alike. (On first hearing the expression Tyler asked Brian what it meant: "My ole granny tellin' me it's in memory of a slave named Jossa who lived in *her* great grandaddy's time. De Master what owned him was a hard man; he passin' out whiplashes like dey passin' de rum pot at Cropover time. One mornin' de Master's waitin' for Jossa to saddle his horse en bring it along so's he can go to de sea--he swim off Bottle Point most days. Jossa was feelin' poorly, he not bein' so young no more, 'n didn't step lively enuff to suit him, so de Master takes out his big ole whip en lashes poor Jossa's back 'til it cut to ribbons. De Master, he's havin' all de folk round de plantation to watch en when he's done, he's sayin, 'Let dis be a lesson to you! Dis is de punishment for laziness.' Dey carries Jossa to his pallet where he's layin' in such pain, it hurt to look on him. En he never get up from dat pallet. Folks tellin' how just 'fore Jossa die from his great lickin', he spat on his hand en calls up a curse on de Master. De day they puttin' Jossa's to his rest in de ground, de Master himself drowned off Bottle Point. De tide carry him off. Soon, word passin' dat Jossa's curse kill't de Master, en ever since dat long ago time, dat tide's been called *Jossa's revenge*.")

In a panic now, Tyler forgets every lesson he ever learned about aquatic safety and flails about, swallowing several mouthfuls of the bitter, briney sea. He struggles valiantly against the current, refusing to accept that the odds are not in his favor, that it is a losing battle. As he feels his lungs filling with water and is dragged under one last time, Sarah's face appears before him, a look of petulance clouding her familiar lovely, features: "Tyler darling ... Where are you? I've been waiting for so long ..."

The dream haunts him for days, every detail of it etched in his mind.

Until the final weeks at Miss Pringles' when she was caught up in a whirlwind of final exams and posting grades, Tyler could expect a letter from Sarah at least once a week; some consisted of no more than a few sentences describing her loneliness and love for him, others were painstaking chronicles of her daily activities. Writing letters "definitely isn't one of my strong suits" he told her, and while he did manage to send a postcard or two, he preferred to hear the sound of her voice and phoned often.

They spoke together on the afternoon she planned to leave Greenwich and rejoin her family.

"Let me have your home phone number. I'll give you a ring in a few days."

"Tyler, darling, I'd rather you didn't. I just don't want to go through the rigmarole of having to explain about 'that man who called from overseas.'"

"Oh. Well, if it's like that..."

"Please. Don't be cross. I'll tell the family about us in good time. It's just that sometimes my parents forget I'm not their little girl anymore, that I'm a grown woman. They mean well, but I'd rather not have to confess that I'm going away with a man I barely know. But I promise, darling, I'll let you know the minute I can get free and fly down."

"Promise?"

"Cross my heart. Goodbye. Love you."

* * * * * * * * * *

Laura looked around at the familiar faces on her patio with chagrin. Sir Edmund was in England, Gideon visiting his son, and Marianne on one of her annual jaunts. 'The Society of Tipplers' had shrunk to three: *I wish Bill Howard would stop whining about the competition, how hard it is to make a decent profit these days in the jewellery business. Who cares? ... Jane and Bill, such dears... but why can't they show an interest in something other than their grandchildren? I'm sick to death of hearing 'Lolly did this... Derek did that'. We've heard it all before. Just last weekend, as I recall.*

But Laura was 'recalling' less and less these days. Seeking the consolation of her favorite rum drink at an earlier hour each day, she was able to expunge from her mind subjects too painful to dwell on. It spared her thinking about Scully and their shattering reunion, of worrying about her niece and the future of the hotel.

Best of all, alcohol lightened the depression that descended like a shroud every time she gazed into a mirror and discerned the telltale encroachments of age, so humiliatingly on display.

I must get away for a few days. A change, new faces. That's what I need!

"My dears, if you'll excuse me. I must lie down. A bit of a headache, you see." She rose unsteadily to her feet and gave them a perfunctory smile of farewell. "Do forgive me."

* * * * * * * * * * *

It was mid-July; three weeks had passed since the Fourth and still no word from Sarah. Her silence triggered a see-sawing binge of emotions in Tyler. Would there be a letter from her in today's mail? Was it Sarah at the other end of that ringing phone? A rush of blood, a euphoric high, followed a millisecond later by a punch-to-the-gut stab of disappointment. He spent restless nights making an inventory of her features, of trying to recall every word she'd spoken since they'd met. In all his roving years of bachelorhood, he'd never been so deeply affected or emotionally entangled with anyone. *What'll I do if she's changed her mind?*

It was a relief having the cabin to himself; it meant he could read or listen to music on the radio whenever he liked. One thing he was determined not to do, and that was turn to the bottle for solace. More conscious than ever of his body, he undertook a regimen of undemanding calisthenics and added a second swim to his daily routine. In a bid to make the hours pass more swiftly, he asked Marshall, the *maitre d'*, to teach him the African game of *warri*. Business at Belle Jours was so slack that as soon as Foster-Jones left the island, he set up the game at the end of the bar and cajoled other members of the staff to play with him. Still, the hours dragged on, the empty days melding one into the other.

Afterward, he would remember that it was a Tuesday. He'd driven the Ford into St. James to refurbish his stock of paperbacks and Scotch and on the way back decided to make a detour that would take him to a surfers' haven called 'The Sugar Bowl'. Brian had mentioned it and when Tyler expressed an interest in seeing the place, told him it was located at the convergence of the two bodies of water surrounding the island, the Atlantic and the Caribbean.

He parked the car and found a comfortable place to sit overlooking the 'Bowl,' a cove surrounded on all sides by green, rolling hills dotted with 'summer cottages' owned by the locals; below him, massive waves moved in steady panoply towards the shore. Tyler spent a leisurely hour watching a group of young Lutiguans skillfully challenge the sea on homemade surf boards. *What a spunky lot!*

Checking his watch, he sighed. *Time to move on.* But he was reluctant to leave. The cool sea air was bracing and his total absorption in the daring sport had swept his mind clear of disquieting thoughts. He returned to the hotel in good spirits, the weight of the past few weeks seeming suddenly lighter. Reception was deserted. "Hey?" he called out, "Anybody home? I'm back. I'll leave the keys on the counter."

Cleo answered from the back office.

"Yes please. Oh! A package come for you, Mister Tyler," she called. "Colin carry it up to your cabin."

"Thanks, Cleo." When she heard his footsteps receding, the young Lutiguan emerged, with both hands clapped over her mouth to contain an upsurge of giggles: *Wait 'til he see dat package!*

As he flung open the screened door, a voice from the far corner of the porch said quietly, "Must you always keep a lady waiting?"

"Sarah!"

He covered the space between them in two giant steps and pulled her body roughly against his. With the intensity of pent up longing and loneliness, he kissed her hard on the mouth, the kiss lasting until Sarah gasped and disengaged herself. "Darling, that was lovely, *but I can't breathe!*" Unwilling to let her go for an instant, Tyler held her at arms length: "Here. Let me look at you. *Am I glad to see you, Sarah Locke!* I've been a terminal case for weeks. But why didn't you tell me you were coming? I could have met you at the airport."

"I'll explain it all later. Now, sir, another kiss. But please, try not to act like Tarzan when he realizes Jane's a girl."

Later he brought them both a drink, pulling a chair up next to hers so he could hold her free hand while she told him of her decision to 'surprise' him.

"What excuse did you give your parents for returning to Lutigua?"

"Actually, Daddy was out of town and so the only person left to tell was Mother. I said I'd met someone special and that I needed to be sure he felt the same way about me. She was good about not prying, just gave me a quick hug and said, 'I hope it works out for you, Sarah dear. All your father and I want is for you to be happy.' But that's Mom. She's absolutely splendid when it comes to respecting my need to keep some things to myself. Besides," she laughed, "she knows I'll tell her everything eventually anyway."

"Good. I'm glad there was no fuss." They sipped their drinks in silence, overwhelmed by the reality of their being together at last. Sarah finally broke the spell by leaning over and gently brushing a lock of hair from his forehead.

"Cleo seemed really pleased to see me! I've booked a room, said I wasn't sure how long I'd be staying, but she said it didn't matter ... the hotel had rooms to spare. When I learned you'd taken the wagon and no one seemed to know when you'd be back, she and I cooked up that little drama. Now tell me, darling, have you found a cottage for us? How soon can we get away?"

"I asked around right after you left, and Sam has a cousin who leases a place on the East Coast, a mile or two up the road from Bethlehem. He checked to see if it was available, and it was, so I rode out there one afternoon to take a look at it. The place is tiny, but it's clean and has all the amenities, *plus* there's a screened porch with a fantastic view overlooking the ocean. There are a couple of drawbacks, though: the cottage *is* pretty isolated... it's a good five-mile drive to what passes for a grocery store ... and - lest I forget! - the mattress on the double bed's a little lumpy," he grinned, "but I'm hoping we'll be too busy to notice. I wasn't sure when we'd want it, the dates that is, but Sam's cousin seemed glad to take a deposit. My guess is rentals are scarce during the summer months here."

"Oh, Tyler, it sounds ideal! The lumpy mattress just adds to the charm. But you haven't said a word about when we can get away."

"I know. I was saving the bad news for last. I have to give a week's notice, hon'. It's only fair, and ..."

She interrupted, "It's my fault, darling. I should have let you know when I was arriving instead of playing childish games." Her sigh was tremulous, "After all the time we've been apart, I can't believe I have to wait another *whole week* until we can be alone."

He took her hand and brought it to his lips, slowly flicking his tongue over her palm, then sucking each finger before pulling her to her feet and moving his mouth to her neck. "You're not the only one who's good at surprises," he murmured, his voice hoarse with longing. "Foster-Jones is off the island. She's not due back 'til day after tomorrow."

Tyler's shift began at four that afternoon. "Sorry, we won't be able to have dinner together your first night here, hon', but I can't beg off. And since I'm taking three weeks leave, I'll to pulling extra duty. I don't want you to eat alone. Why don't you give Mary Farmington a ring? She's always liked you and would probably welcome the company."

Throwing caution to the winds, he closed the bar down early and took a quick shower before cautiously making his way in the darkness to Sarah's room.

With the door closed and locked behind him, he turned to look at her, his pulse racing, so overwhelmed he couldn't speak.

"Hello, darling. Do you like my new nightgown?"

When he found his voice, it was husky with passion, "Miss Locke, you'd look gorgeous in a gunnysack." He stripped his clothes off quickly as she stood by, watching his every movement. Then he came to her and gently pushed the straps of the gown from her shoulders, letting it slide to the floor. For a few seconds he stared at her greedily, mesmerized by the delicate body that was his for the taking before backing her against the wall and covering her naked body with his.

Tyler watched enviously as Sarah drifted off to sleep. He wished it were that easy. His body was relaxed in the special way it always is after an explosion of sexual tension. But his mind was another matter; it had taken off like a rocket the moment Sarah's breathing confirmed she was safely into her dreams. *It's too soon to expect Sarah to make any promises about the future ...our future ...best to wait until we've spent some time alone together. Real time, not like this hit-and-run business tonight. But I can't imagine a day that doesn't include her in it... If what I suspect about her family is true, though, they won't be too pleased to have a 'bartender' for a son-in-law. I'll have to scout around, find some other job that's a little more respectable. Maybe sales. I wasn't too bad at selling. No one could object to that. ... Whoa! Hold it a minute, buddy-boy. What about the differences in age? I can't be much younger than Sarah's Dad. Now why the hell did I have to open* *<u>that</u>* *can of worms?*

Sarah turned sleepily on her side and reaching out an arm to fling across the body next to hers, found the space empty. The familiar odor of acrid smoke was enough to make her fully alert. "Tyler?" she whispered in alarm. "Tyler, *where are you?*"

"Over here."

Nude, seated on a chair near the curtained patio doors with his legs crossed, his chin cupped in the hand that held a lighted cigarette between two fingers, he resembled a Rodin statue–solemn and brooding.

She hopped from the bed to stand at the back of his chair; playfully ruffling his hair with her fingers, she leaned over and kissed him lovingly on the side of the neck, "Darling, is something the matter?"

"Sarah, did it ever occur to you that the man you just made love to is as old as Methuselah?"

She guessed immediately what was bothering him. Moving her hands down his chest, she hugged him to her, "Don't be a ninny, Tyler. I don't give a damn about the difference in our ages, and neither should you. Where'd this sudden 'age-hangup' thing come from? Please. Come back to bed."

He crept out of her room just before dawn after one last gratifying interlude of love-making. Exiting by way of Sarah's patio, he took a circuitous route back to the cabin, hoping against hope he wouldn't be seen.

From her patio, staring bleakly at the sky as it raced to change colors, Mary Farmington spied Tyler moving hastily across the pool area . *While the cat's away, the mouse dares all. I wonder if I should report this to Aunt Laura?*

Despite the knowledge that he had one night left to be with Sarah before the hotel owner's return, Tyler decided it was foolish to tempt Fate: "Look hon', someone might catch me going to your room, and it's just not worth it." Sarah reluctantly agreed. During the week he was on duty they tried to spend every available moment together around the framework of his schedule at the bar, conscientiously conducting themselves with decorum while on hotel property. But staffers noticed that whenever she was near, Tyler's face dissolved into a weak, foolish grin.

On one of her solitary walks away from Belle Jours Sarah chanced upon a chattel house that had been converted into a bar and restaurant. Lured by the piquant aroma of frying fish cakes, she timidly stepped inside the plain, immaculate room. Brightly painted plank tables with benches were scattered throughout the small, affable interior. She was greeted by Mrs. Toppin the owner, a rotund, jolly Lutiguan, who encouraged her to stay and sample some true West Indian cooking: "Order me pumpkin soup en plantain wid fish cakes, darlin'. Best on de island!" The food was delicious, utterly unlike any the American had ever tasted and she was determined to bring Tyler with her at the first opportunity.

Since it was within easy walking distance of the hotel, Mrs. Toppin's restaurant became their favorite rendezvous. Secure from prying eyes and inquisitive glances, they dawdled over their food and talked about themselves, she sketching for him a secure and happy upbringing in a comfortable milieu, a close and loving family.

"Parts of my life have been such a cliche! When I was ten I fell in love with the boy next door, Tod Jameson. He was fourteen and, of course, never looked at me. Then the Jamesons moved away. At sixteen, I started dating, but for a long time I carried a torch for Tod. While I was at college, I got involved in two 'heavy' relationships. The last one ended badly. Very badly. I was home for the Christmas break my Junior year when Tod walked back into my life. We ran into each other at a dance at the Club; his father had died and he and his mother moved back to town. He and a friend got together and opened an insurance agency. This time, the shoe was on the other foot: Tod fell for me. But I'd been badly burned, and it took a while for me to accept the fact that he was serious. My Senior year was fabulous ...Tod came up to college most weekends. We were madly in love. We even managed to sneak away together a few times ... ."

"You mean you *slept with him?*"

"For goodness sake, Tyler, don't get all Victorian on me! Of course I slept with him, and he wasn't the first. The day the pill came on the market, my dear, it freed us females from that old bugaboo, 'nice girls don't do it 'til they're married.'"

"Then what happened?" he asked sulkily.

"Why Tyler Scranton, you're jealous! How lovely," she said, squeezing his hand. "To make a long story short, Tod wanted to get married as soon as I graduated, but Mommy insisted I work for a year, said I'd always have the experience if I ever needed it later in life. We were going to announce our engagement during mid-term break from Miss Pringle's but Tod, the coward, sent me a letter saying he'd changed his mind, said he 'just wasn't ready to get married,' that kind of rot. I was devastated, of course, so when the girls came up with the idea of vacationing here, I jumped at it. No sooner did I set foot back in Greenwich when Tod was on the doorstep saying he'd made a terrible mistake, etcetera, etcetera. But I'd had plenty of time to think while we were here, and I decided *I didn't want him.* So there you have it, my pet, the sad, sad saga of Sarah Locke."

He responded in kind by revealing his brief marriage to Darlene and the subsequent annulment. Shame prevented him from telling her the reason *why* he was in Wyoming - his abandonment of Julie was too painful to reveal - just that Darlene had been a palliative to the misery and loneliness of his existence at the ranch.

"And you've never been seriously involved since?"

"Close, but when it came right down to it, I just ... *I told you, I have a lousy track record when it comes to commitment.*"

"We'll have to see what we can do about that!"

"When are you due back in the States?"

"Stacy's getting married Labor Day weekend and she's asked me to be a bridesmaid so I booked plane reservations for the last week in August. You remember Stacy, don't you darling," she tweeked his nose, "that gorgeous blonde you drooled over the entire week we were here?"

"Danielle! Have you heard one word I've said in the past five minutes?" Mary Farmington asked crossly. *This whole place is crumbling to bits and pieces. First, Aunt Laura - out of the blue - ups and decides to visit 'a dear old friend' from England who now lives somewhere in the wilds of North Carolina, leaving me in charge of this damn hotel where no one pays the least bit of attention to what I say. Tyler moons around like a lovesick calf and Sarah has no time for me anymore. She spends every second with him. Danielle is the one person I can count on, and half the time lately she acts as if she were under an anesthetic! Bloody hell.*

Indeed, Danielle was still reeling from the aphrodisia of Peter Callender's kisses and declaration of love. Last night, as they embraced in the shelter of a century's old flamboyant tree bursting with scarlet blossoms, he asked her to marry him. With tears of happiness she had given her assent and sealed it by placing his strong, beautiful hands over her heart. They parted with his promise to "speak to your father after the service next Sunday."

As the time for their getaway drew closer, Tyler was as excited as a schoolboy. His biggest hurdle was finding a car to lease; the sole rental agency at the airport reserved their small supply of vehicles for representatives of established overseas businesses or guests of the government. 'Legs' Walrond overheard his boss complain bitterly about the situation: "Only two car dealers on the whole damn island and they don't *do rentals* and those s.o.b.s at the airport turned me down flat!" 'Legs' drew him aside. "Mr. Tyler, dose fellas out de airport way, dey known to come round when dey sees de colour of money."

"Thanks, 'Legs.' Appreciate it. I'll see to it right away."

After her brief hiatus, Foster-Jones was once again poking into every corner of the hotel's operations. Not only would Tyler be absent, but Mrs. Vernon was taking her leave at the same time; trusting nothing to chance, Laura decided to keep a personal eye on both housekeeping and the bar.

In mid-week word reached the hotel that Wash had been rushed to the hospital; a fit of coughing had brought on a seizure . The grim news affected the entire staff. Alone in her suite, Laura's eyes filled with tears when Reception called to tell her.

"Everything's arranged," Tyler told Sarah. "We can skip out of here anytime after breakfast Saturday morning. No need to hurry because the woman who cleans the cottage for Sam's cousin won't be done 'til after lunch."

Determined to avoid any possible delays once they were on their way, he picked up the rental car at the airport, bought groceries and extra liquor the day before they planned to leave. Sarah pursued a personal agenda of her own that day: exacting a promise from Callie, the room maid, to press every item in her wardrobe, she hopped into Darius Owen's taxi for the drive to St. James. It was her first visit to the island's capitol and she found the city not only confusing but exasperating. Darting in and out of several shops, she was appalled at the shabbiness of the goods made locally; an astute saleswoman took pity on her: "Try de 'Green Parrot' round de corner," she advised. "Dats where de white ladies go." (Danielle had passed on the name of a fashionable beauty salon, but Sarah lost her nerve when it came to asking her advice on where to buy lingerie.) After her frustrating morning, she was unprepared for the beauty and elegance of the selections inside the tiny boutique. An hour later Sarah emerged from the 'Parrot' having happily parted with an outrageous sum for a filmy lace nightgown with matching pegnoir bearing the label *Made in France.* The remainder of the afternoon was spent at the salon where, as she said later, "I had *the works!*"

Sarah's door was ajar, but Tyler knocked anyway, "Almost ready, sweetheart?"

"Give me a few more minutes, Tyler. I've packed away some things I won't need. Danielle, bless her, said I could leave them in the office 'til we get back. Come in, love, I want to show you some pictures of my family before I put them away . I meant to do it before now, but somehow you always distract me," she said teasingly, holding up a double leather frame for his inspection. "See, there's Arthur, the one with glasses and curly hair, and that's Evan (it's not very good of Evan, he's much better looking) and that's me, of course. This other photo's of Mom and Dad, taken on their wedding anniversary last year. What do you think? Does my family pass muster?"

Tyler wasn't paying attention. The moment she'd shown him the photos his gaze had zeroed in on the attractive woman in a delphinium silk dress standing next to a man with greying hair. *I've seen that face before. Hell, It's probably just a coincidence.*

"Sarah, what's your mother's name? Her face looks ... I don't know. Like I've seen it somewhere ."

"That's what everyone says!" was her delighted response. "Mom's always being taken for the Weather-girl on one of those early morning talk shows ...Veeva . . Veeva something. I forget. Mother's name is Julie. She has a beautiful face, don't you think? But then I'm prejudiced."

In the split second before the meaning of Sarah's words registered, Tyler decided she was either mistaken or joking. *Hell, buddy-boy, of course she knows her own mother's name.* All at once he couldn't breathe, as if someone had delivered a vicious blow to the solar plexus. Sarah turned to place the folded frame on top of the other items in the box and didn't see the color drain from his face. *I've got to get out of here.* But his body was congealed, unable to move.

"There, that's done. I can close it now. Darling, would you please take the box up to the office and thank Danielle for me? I just need to check the closet and bathroom again to make sure I haven't left anything behind."

Tyler picked up the box, still struggling to find his voice. "Look, hon', I've got to run up to the cabin for a minute; I forgot to pack my swim trunks. Why don't we meet in the parking lot, say in half an hour?"

How can I tell her the whole thing's off, that we can't go away together? How do you tell the woman you love, the only person in the whole fucking world who matters to you now, 'Hey, honey, know what? I once screwed your mother'?

He slammed open the cabin door and ran to the kitchen, remembering as soon as he opened the cupboard that he'd packed the last of the liquor to take with them. What he wished for more than anything in the world was for the earth to open up and devour him—*anything* to escape the reality of that photograph. Instead, he lit a cigarette and paced up and down the porch.

What the hell do I do now? Sarah's waiting for me. I've got to think of something. Maybe I should just forget it, forget I ever saw that damn picture of Julie, not cancel our plans. I owe Sarah that much. Then, when the three weeks are up, just say 'goodbye.' Give her some excuse why it wouldn't work.

But a vision of Sarah's face as he mounts her, that look of joy and wonder, of total surrender and trust, was indelibly printed on his brain, mingled with others: her eyes squinting to focus when she takes off her glasses, the unselfconscious way she puts her hand over her mouth in surprise, a curled lock of toffee hair on a damp forehead after lovemaking, the achingly desirable sight of taut, rosy nipples. *How can I kiss her, how can I touch ... feel ... that lovely body of Sarah's, much less put my cock inside her knowing what I do?*

He couldn't. Tyler slammed his fist against the wall in despair, a desolate, gutteral cry of defeat emanating from his lips.

Walking slowly down the path away from the cabin, he resolved to settle the matter. *There's got to be a way for me to back out of this so Sarah won't be too disappointed, too hurt* . Suddenly, he thought of Watu-Kai, the Waterfall, where Sarah had slipped and fallen, and where everything had changed with that spontaneous kiss in the rain. Sarah had been as touched by the legend of the doomed lovers as he'd been after listening to Wash tell the tale. What better place to say 'goodbye'?

Now all I need is a guardian angel to put the right words in my mouth.

"You haven't said a word since we left the hotel, Tyler," Sarah commented, adding with the assurance of one who knows she's asking a frivolous question, "Not having second thoughts, are you?" She reached up and lovingly brushed the back of her hand against his cheek "Honestly darling, for someone about to embark on a romantic holiday, you're awfully glum."

"Sorry. It's this damn car." It was the first excuse he could think of. "I'm not used to the way it handles. And these roads are no picnic, as you can see."

"O.k. I'll be a good girl. I promise not to say a word so you can concentrate on your driving." Humming the chorus of a favorite Carly Simon song, she gazed contentedly at the landscape and people they passed, waving to two boys heading for the beach with homemade fishing poles, a barefoot young woman balancing a basket on her head and a baby on her hip, an old man resting at the side of the road. Tyler deliberately crawled along, stalling for time, praying for the courage to do what must be done.

"Tyler, isn't this the route we took to the Waterfall, the day we got lost?"

He didn't answer.

"Why are we going there now? I thought we were on our way to the cottage?"

"I want to stop at Watu-Kai."

"Oh darling, can't we do it another day? I mean, we've waited so long to be by ourselves ... let's get settled first."

"Didn't I make myself clear?" he snapped. "We'll go to the cottage *after* we see the Waterfall."

At first Sarah was too stunned by this unreasonable display of temper to react. But as his words and the tone of his voice sank in, she recoiled, hugging herself to contain the hurt.

Out of the corner of his eye, Tyler saw the wounded look on her face, was aware that she had spontaneously moved away from him. *Oh Christ. Now look what I've done. It's not her fault the whole fucking world just got turned around.* "Look, Sarah, I'm sorry, really sorry. You didn't deserve that, sweetheart. I guess it's just the tension of the last couple of days, all that over-time, plus putting the guys at the bar through their paces, and to top it off, the Dragon Lady on my back at all hours." He took her hand, which she surrendered with obvious reluctance, and tenderly kissed the inside of her wrist. "Next time I get on my high horse, sweetheart, I give you permission to box my ears." It was meant to make her smile, but she didn't. *Change the subject, you idiot. Just change the subject.*

"Tell me more about your family, Sarah. Have you always lived in Vermont? What does your Dad do?" Gradually, she relaxed, and after a few spare answers, warmed to the subject. Her father, she said, was President of a small private bank, one which had been in his family for several generations. "But Daddy says they can't hold on much longer. All the little banks are being swallowed up by the bigger ones. It's all part of this merger craze that's sweeping the country." She described for him 'the family traditions' ... the summer vacations in New Hampshire, Thanksgivings with her mother's parents, who lived in a small town in

Pennsylvania – "my brother Arthur is named after Granddaddy Waterman" – the Locke family's annual reunions. She stopped in mid-sentence, "You know, Tyler, I never thought of it 'til this moment, but Daddy's a good fifteen years older than mother. So you see, the difference in our ages is nothing to worry about! Consider it part of the 'family tradition.'"

Passing a familiar landmark reminded him they were nearing the place where they'd left the car the last time, but his mind was still a blank. *Keep her talking.* "How'd your parents meet?"

"It was terribly romantic. Daddy's father was on the Board of trustees at the University of Vermont, where Mom was a day student. There was to be this important Board meeting but Mr. Locke senior was ill and couldn't go, so he sent Daddy in his place. Daddy says he saw 'this vision of loveliness' crossing the campus with an armload of books when she slipped or something and the books went flying. He rushed over to help pick them up. At this point he always grins and says, 'and the rest is history.'"

"Well, here we are, my love." He turned off the motor, but Sarah sat perfectly still, her thoughts a thousand miles away. She said softly, "I never talk about this, but Norman Locke isn't my real father, though he legally adopted me after he and Mom were married. Mommy says mine died in a car accident before I was born. She told me about my father when I was twelve...Said he was quite handsome, that they were very young when they met, that he'd had a sad life and that they loved each other very much. Mommy said after the accident she just wanted to lie down and die, but I came along and somehow she was able to pick herself up and go on. I remember this sort of beatific expression on her face when she added, 'The gods must have taken pity on me because they brought Norman into my life–the kindest, most honorable, most loving man I've ever known.' I say 'Amen' to that. No one could ask for a better father... Well now, that's enough about my family! Tyler, be a love and get my sneakers and the bug repellent out of my bag in the back, would you please, darling?"

As he got out from behind the wheel and went around to the rear of the car, she called after him, "I get six extra kisses for being such a good sport. I'll have you know this expedition of yours doesn't appeal to me at all!"

He handed her the shoes through the open window. When she stepped out of the car, Tyler caught her up in his arms and kissed her too quickly for her to notice his pallor, the sudden tautness of every muscle in his body.

It didn't take a genius to figure out the corollary to Sarah's revelation.

Tyler Scranton was not a religious man. While Christmas and Easter Sunday services were rarely missed, Myra's attendance at church with her two young sons was sporadic at best; whatever faith she had in the Almighty's benevolent love died with Neddie, and after his funeral, she never went back. And while Tyler may have broken a Commandment or two, it was done casually, without reference to any moral or ethical context. When he was in grammar school he snitched a few dimes from Myra's purse, a couple of *Hershey* bars, and a package or two of *Chicklets* from *Woolworth's*; but he never stole anything of value and he certainly never intentionally did anyone harm. With the exception of a one-night stand with a married woman - she being the aggressor - he'd stayed away from other men's wives. With so many available fish in the sea, why go begging for trouble?

Sarah's innocent confession struck him like a white, hot rapier, its double-edged blade slowly and with cruel deliberation eviscerating him. So intense was his agony that he couldn't bring himself to name the vileness of the sin he'd commited with this utterly precious human being. *And if she ever learns the truth! But she musn't! Please, God* ... he humbly petitioned, *forgive me* ...

The inexorable resolve that no one else must ever touch her, know her intimately as he had known her, love her as he loved her, grew stronger, gave him the wit and courage to deceive. He withdrew his mouth from hers and held her tightly, feeling her heart racing against his.

"Look sweetheart," he said calmly, "I know it seems like I've been stubborn as a mule about coming here, but I've always thought of Watu–Kai as being a magic place, a sort of 'lucky charm'. I think I fell in love with you while you were standing on the rock overlooking the Waterfall. I watched you ... the expression on your face... I'll never forget it. We kissed for the first time in the rain forest, remember? Watu–Kai is where it all started, Sarah, where everything changed for us. I just had to come back today. These next couple of weeks ...I want them to be ... perfect."

"Oh, Tyler you should have told me before! I was so cross about not going to the cottage right away. I couldn't make any sense of it, but now I do. Darling, has anyone ever told you at heart you're a dyed-in-the-wool sentimentalist? Who would have guessed? And I love you madly for it." She kissed him quickly, then pushed his arms away and as she started to run, shouting playfully, "Last one to the Falls is a rotten egg!"

His legs were leaden, his chest heavy as he fell in behind her, relieved and grateful when the slippery underpinnings of the rain forest slowed her pace. Arriving at the far side of this tropical phenomenon, they stopped to catch their breath before beginning the rocky ascent to the Falls. Tyler lit a cigarette and with his arm around Sarah stared at the sky, offering up a silent entreaty: *Please, just give me the guts to go through with this.*

He ground the cigarette out with his heel, "Time to move along, hon'."

Obediently she turned and started to climb when impulsively he reached out and drew her back. "Wait, Sarah." Gently placing both hands on her shoulders, he stood as if memorizing the slim body, the contour of her breasts against her damp blouse, the heart-shaped face and tousled hair, the sweetness of her mouth, finally moving his gaze to look directly at her. She was about to offer a teasing comment about his delaying tactics, until she saw the expression of overwhelming sorrow flooding his face. The words he spoke were wrenched from his lips, "Remember, won't you, *I love you, Sarah. I'll always love you.*"

For a brief moment, his intensity frightened her, but then she divined that Watu-Kai and the old legend had an emotional stranglehold on him beyond her ken. She replied gracefully, "Thank you, darling. It's lovely to be reminded. A girl can never hear those words often enough ." She ducked out from under his grasp, eager to resume the journey and be done with it.

The roar of rushing water made conversation impossible. Just before they reached the boulder, Tyler said, "You win, sweetheart. I'm the rotten egg. Let's look at the Falls together." She gave him her hand and they moved cautiously around the forbidding rock with Sarah in the lead.

They were about to gain the clearing when from behind them the mottled white owl Tyler had seen on his first trip to Watu-Kai swooped over their heads and flew gracefully over the cascading water to regain its former perch. The bird unsettled Sarah, but she showed more curiousity about it than alarm, wordlessly pointing it out to her lover. The creature's unexpected presence shook Tyler to the core. Ordinarily a sceptic when it came to matters of superstition, he recalled his instinctive fear and loathing of the fowl the last time, and believed it was an evil omen, a preamble to hell.

Together they moved to the flat rock overlooking the Falls, Sarah's expression one of sheer delight when she saw the rainbow's arc across the sun-dappled waters. She held up her face for Tyler to kiss and as his mouth bore down on hers every nerve in his body cried out to be joined with hers. *This way, we'll never be apart, Sarah my love...Forgive me.*

Quickly he snatched her wrist in a vise-like grip, *Now! Do it now!* He'd made up his mind to take her with him, but as he summoned the will-power to commit this last, irrevocable act, Sarah's face dissolved, became Julie's, her anguished plea piercing his heart: *No, Tyler, no! Don't destroy the only decent, tangible evidence of our love!*

Marshalling every ounce of strength he possessed, he flung Sarah back, away from the rock. Her body slammed against the hard ground, the impact so severe she briefly lost consciousness. In a state of shock, she lay where she'd fallen unable to catch her breath, a thin mewling sound like that of a small wounded animal escaping from her lips. Painfully, she struggled to a sitting position. The flat rock was empty.

From behind the large boulder came the unearthly sound of keening.

CHAPTER X X I X

The morning sunlight pivoted and toe-danced its way through the leaves and branches of generations'-old trees interspersed amongst the crumbling masoleums, crosses and markers in the cemetery adjacent to St.Mary's Chapel. Situated at the crest of a hillock and originally built as a place of worship for slaves from the adjoining plantation, the chapel was twice destroyed by major hurricanes and rebuilt in 1836. A small band of mourners straggled towards the modest stone building with its bell tower. At Laura's request there was no church service; instead, the rector would read the order of burial at the gravesite.

They gathered awkwardly in a semi-circle around the freshly dug grave: Laura and Mary, Peter Callender and Danielle, Corbin and Osbert Marshall, Sam, Brian and James MacArthur, the Gardners from the Sunday group and Mrs. Toppin, the proprietress of the chattel-house restaurant. Funeral wreaths from the staff, held upright on wire staves, dotted the perimeter; a spray of pink roses from Sarah rested on top of the simple wooden coffin. The priest, a balding, morose Englishman from Surrey, glanced over the tops of his smudged glasses to confirm that there were no latecomers, that those assembled were ready for the service to begin.

I am the resurrection and the life, saith the Lord: he that believeth in me ...

At dusk, a phone call from the police station in St. Joseph's was received at Belle Jours' front desk; St. Joseph's was the parish in which Watu-Kai was located. The duty sergeant informed Cleo that a guest from the hotel had been found inside a rented automobile, sitting with its motor running in the middle of the road. The guest, a young woman, was in a 'sorry state,' according to the sergeant, and was claiming there had been some sort of accident. Would the hotel please send someone to fetch her? He hinted that it might be advisable to call a doctor and added that a senior officer would come round in the morning to take a statement, the woman being unfit to make one at present.

The call was switched immediately to Laura, who upon learning the young woman was Mary's friend Sarah Locke, determined her niece should be the one to bring her back. But after a hasty search of the hotel and grounds, neither Colin nor Danielle were able to locate the young Englishwoman. Since time was of the essence, Foster-Jones had no choice.

"Danielle, I need to ask a favor of you ..."

Darius Owen was summoned. It was dark by the time Danielle began the long journey to the district station in his taxi. The duty sergeant and his constable were relieved to see her, to rid themselves of responsibility for their unstable visitor. Danielle was told by the constable that a passing cyclist, a school boy, had found Sarah sobbing uncontrollably at the wheel of a car blocking the road. Using his head, the boy quickly pedaled home and told his mother about 'de white lady in de car'. With no neighbors at hand or telephone of her own, the worried woman had walked the mile and a half to the station to report her son's discovery. When the police arrived, Sarah kept insisting that they go up to Watu-Kai to look for "a gentleman de lady call Tyler. She sayin' some crazy ole man wid a beard's up dere, too, howlin' behind a rock!" He shook his head in disbelief and continued, "She all de time cryin' 'n moanin', 'He can't be gone, he can't be gone.'" The police could make little sense of her story and if, indeed, her companion had slipped and fallen into the Waterfall, it would be several days before his body would surface in one of its tributaries. (They ignored the part about the crazy old man, dismissing it as a figment of her overwrought imagination.) In any event, a search after dark was out of the question.

The only space available for the distraught woman to have some privacy was a tiny, dank cell at the back of the station which is where Danielle found her, huddled against the wall on a bare cot, arms locked fiercely around herself in an effort to contain her misery. Indelibly stamped on Danielle's memory is the look of bewilderment and pain on the young American's tear-stained face.

"Miss Locke? It's me. *Danielle.* I've come to fetch you." Recognizing a familiar voice, Sarah jumped up and with a wrenching sob flung herself into the Lutiguan's arms.

Foster-Jones had the foresight to send Danielle off with a bottle of smelling salts and a flask of brandy; she proffered both in an effort to calm Sarah during the endless ride back to Belle Jours .

I know that my redeemer liveth, and that he shall stand at the latter day upon the earth: and though this body be destroyed, yet shall I see God.

Simon had witnessed it all and it was his terrifying presence, his howls, that goaded Sarah to leave the flat rock, to stumble her way through the rain forest and back to the car where she found the keys resting on the seat. She willed herself to drive, but was able to make it no farther than a half-mile along the main road before collapsing in hysterics. Danielle pieced together this scenario from Sarah's incoherent torrent of words. A tragic accident. It was the only explanation possible.

Sorrow's sittin' like a lump in my heart. Poor Tyler. Miss Locke swears there was no quarrel, no hard words and he wasn't at de liquor. She say 'he was there and then he wasn't there.' Tyler's feet must've come loose from de rock and when he knew he couldn't save himself, he threw her to de ground to save her. Observing the grief locked in Danielle's face, Callender gave a gentle squeeze to the arm clasped tightly in his. In less than three months she would be his wife. He could hardly wait.

Why is it bad news come tumblin' down all at once ...like de wind that tear off a roof in de night, and next day, a fire come to burn de house down? Daddy tells me Mister Wilson is dyin'. 'He'll be passin' any day now,' Daddy says. Truth to tell, <u>Belle Jours</u> *won't be the same without Mr. Wilson and Tyler. That Tyler! With his funny way of sayin' things ... always teasin' ... . . tellin' foolish jokes. He's de first American I come to have as a friend, and he has me likin' de whole country without ever settin' foot in it.*

Man, that is born of woman, hath but a short time to live, and is full of misery. He cometh up and is cut down like a flower ...

On the morning following the grim news, Laura phoned Sarah Locke's parents in Vermont. She explained that a friend of their daughter's had died in an unfortunate accident, as a result of which the young woman appeared to be on the verge of a breakdown. Yes, a doctor had been consulted and sedatives had been prescribed. "Could a member of the family please fly down to Lutigua as soon as possible to escort your daughter home? The hotel cannot assume responsibility for sending her back on her own."

Unlike wintertime, booking a flight to the Caribbean during the 'low' summer season could be done with ease. Less than 36 hours after Laura's call, Sarah's brother, Arthur Locke, was standing at Belle Jours' Reception desk asking to speak to Mrs. Foster-Jones. Acting as his parents' emissary, the slim young man was welcomed by Laura, who noting his strained, anxious demeanor, insisted he have a cup of tea and light refreshment before meeting with his sister. Since he was on an adult's mission, she treated him like one by confiding that Sarah's relationship with the deceased was more than mere friendship. No, Sarah had not been told a family member was en route. No, the body had not yet been recovered. Yes, they were trying to reach the gentleman's next-of-kin, but it was proving difficult, and until they did, it was impossible to know what arrangements should be made for his burial.

Once apprised of the complex situation, Arthur was more sensitive to his sister's grief, more certain of the need to make decisions for them both. At first Sarah refused to leave the island until Tyler's body was found, but her brother protested, saying their parents expected them to return home immediately. Emotionally exhausted, her spirit too broken to resist, she reluctantly agreed. A tearful Callie packed her belongings and with the help of a mild sedative prescribed by Dr. Harcourt, Sarah, with Arthur holding her tightly by the hand, managed her farewells to the staff, breaking down only after the taxi was clear of the circular driveway.

In the midst of life we are in death; of whom may we seek for succour, but thee, O Lord ...

Finding it an effort to stand still for very long in one place and remain awake, Mary Farmington surreptitiously pinched the skin on her upper thigh. Not once, but several times. Since the tragedy at Watu-Kai, the tempo of her fragmentation had accelerated. *Don't let them catch you yawning. This is a funeral for pity's sake. You liked Tyler, remember? Show a little respect, old girl. It's the least you can do for him and poor Sarah. Thank heavens I never told Aunt Laura about the morning I caught him sneaking away from her room.* Those who remembered how vivacious and attractive the young Englishwoman had been when she first arrived on Lutigua, might have had trouble recognizing her now: dark welts under her eyes testified to too many sleepless nights and somnolent days; gone, the sheen to her lovely copper hair and an alarming loss of weight played havoc with the fit of her clothes, which she donned each morning like an automaton. In truth, Mary Farmingham looked like an itinerant scarecrow, one of those hapless remnants of society who wander the city's streets without purpose or hope .

She never asked where I was, why they couldn't find me. But I could tell Aunt Laura was really cross with me. While Danielle and Colin were searching the hotel compound for her, Mary was fast asleep in one of the unoccupied guest rooms. The unbroken pattern of sleepless nights, days when she was so overcome with lethargy it was an effort to move or speak, had taken its toll. Aware since her arrival that she was tolerated by the staff only because they had no choice, her self-esteem had plummeted; but her pride wouldn't let her mention her unhappiness to her aunt. Seeking relief from daily tribulations, both real and imagined, Mary had taken to secreting herself in one of the unoccupied guest rooms where she would fall into a deep, comatose sleep from early afternoon until dinnertime. (There was never a question of asking for a key, she had a set to all the rooms.) No one missed her or even bothered looking for her until the call came from the St. Joseph police station.

By sunrise the next day, everyone on the hotel staff knew about the incident at Watu–Kai except Mary; she learned of Tyler's death after Laura beckoned her to a private meeting in her suite. Her aunt's description of the events of the previous evening came as a severe shock. Before she had a chance to absorb it all, Laura was saying, "Danielle and Colin looked everywhere for you. After all, you were the *one person besides Tyler*, who was a friend of Sarah's. And if ever she needed a friend, it was last night." While she was speaking Laura studied the young woman sitting across from her: *Mary's not herself. How long has she been in this wretched state, and why haven't I noticed before? After this dreadful business is settled, she must return to England. But first, I'll insist she see Harcourt for a thorough examination. What would her parents think if they saw her now?*

"Mary, I need for you and Danielle to go up to Tyler's cabin and look through his belongings. See if you can find his mother's address or a phone number. The poor woman must be notified immediately."

Thou knowest, Lord, the secrets of our hearts ...

Solemnly, the two women entered the empty cabin. On the screened porch floor sat the suitcase Tyler had packed for his holiday with Sarah; a young police constable had returned his and Sarah's belongings to the hotel. Noting her companion's dazed look, Danielle said kindly, "Why don't you unpack the suitcase, Miss Farmington, while I look around in the bedroom?" But as soon as she opened the bag and caught sight of Tyler's favorite sport's shirt, Mary started to cry. Diverted by the sound of her sobs, Danielle came back out on the porch and found her on her knees on the hard wooden floor, her hands clutching Tyler's shirt to her bosom. *She's not fit to pour a drink of mauby*. The Lutiguan returned bearing a glass of water and persuaded Mary to sit down and calm herself.

"But Aunt Laura says I'm to help you."

"Not to worry, Miss Farmington. I'll be fine on my own."

In the bedroom closet, tucked into the pocket of a navy wool jacket suitable for wear in less temperate climes, Danielle found a black, dog-eared leather address book . She stood by the window and opened it, skipping quickly to 'S'. Listed were the names and phone numbers of a restaurant, two males and several females. (two of the latter were scratched out with the notation, 'moved,' 'married,' in red ink.) Foster-Jones had told her that Tyler's hometown was somewhere in Pennsylvania, his mother's name either 'Myrtle' or 'Marge,' she couldn't recall which; (Scranton had mentioned her name when asking for emergency leave in June). Danielle went back to the beginning of the alphabet and painstakingly reviewed each name. She found no 'Myrtle,' but there was a 'Marge' Lewis; her address, however, placed her at a ski resort in Vermont.

Under the 'M's' she found the single word 'Myra' and a telephone number. She dialled the front desk and asked them to ring through to that number in the States; the overseas operator informed the hotel that the number was 'no longer in service.'

Frustrated, she began again at the beginning: *That rascal Tyler! So many ladies' names! For truth, seem like he take to heart that old sayin' of ours, 'A good liv-wid bettah than a bad marriage.' But with Miss Locke, it was different. The Lord as my witness, I know he truly loved her!* As she flipped slowly through he pages, the name 'Lyle' caught her eye, his area code being the same as the number no longer in service.

Thou shalt show me the path of life ...

The unearthing of Lyle's name provided the key to finding Myra's whereabouts. Laura spoke with him and passed on the news of his old childhood friend's death; Lyle, in turn, was able to tell her that Myra had moved to her sister's house, to recall Aunt Madge's married name, plus the fact that she lived somewhere in Wisconsin. With the help of a dedicated long-distance operator, the number for Madge's residence near Eau Clair was finally tracked down. (Weeks later, Laura confided to her friend, Marianne Pharr, "It was the most unsettling phone conversation I've ever had.")

After introducing herself, Laura said, "I'm afraid Mrs. Scranton I have some bad news. It's about your son, Tyler."

"Tyler? What's he done now? He ain't in jail is he?"

"No, *certainly not.* The fact is, there's been an accident ... I'm sorry to have to tell you, Mrs. Scranton, your son ... drowned. Tyler fell off a high slippery rock into a waterfall. The police haven't recovered the body yet."

"You mean Tyler's *dead?*"

"Yes, my dear. Please know how sorry everyone is here at the hotel ... . .Tyler was very well-liked. I must apologize. I know what a dreadful shock it must be hearing this sad news from a complete stranger."

"Tyler's *really gone*? This call ain't some kind of prank is it?"

"I assure you, Mrs. Scranton, this is no prank. Look, I apologize again, but I need to know: when they find the body, do you wish to have it shipped to the States for burial?"

There was a long silence.

"Mrs. Scranton, are you still on the line?"

"I'm here. Just thinkin'. When you say 'shippin' the body,' you mean, put Tyler on a plane and send his coffin back here? That would cost a heap of money, wouldn't it?"

"Why, yes. I suppose so. I hadn't thought about it."

"Then you ain't ever been poor, Mrs ..."

"*Mrs. Foster-Jones..*"

"No, I think it best to leave him right there. I can't see the sense of making some funeral director richer than he already is. Tyler won't know the difference."

"What about his personal belongings?"

"Why I'd have no use for those. You can give 'em to whoever you like, or throw them away."

Her callous response was the last straw. *What a horrible woman! Poor Tyler!*

"Is there anything else I can do for you, Mrs. Scranton," she asked icily.

"Well no, can't think of a thing. I thank you kindly for calling, Mrs... Sorry, I keep forgettin' your name."

When the connection was broken, the old woman in Wisconsin slowly placed the receiver back in its cradle, laid her face down on a withered arm and began to weep.

Unto Almighty God we commend the soul of our brother departed, and we commit his body to the ground; earth to earth, ashes to ashes, dust to dust ...

Laura sighed. *Thank heavens it's almost over.* She had a long-standing aversion to funerals, representing as they did, such a tangible link to her own mortality. *Any day now, Wash will be gone, too, and with him so much a part of my life here. . ... I shall miss him... Dear God, I hate to think what that service will be like ... all weeping and shouting. ... But Wash is an old man who's lived a full and useful life. Not like the one we're burying here today...Tyler had so much vitality, so much of his life left to live . . . . Funny, despite what Leona said about him always 'running away from unpleasant situations,' when the chips were down, he came through. He saved that girl's life.*

Lord have mercy upon us... Christ have mercy upon us ...

It was a full week before the body was recovered from a stream several miles from the Waterfall. In the interim, the events of that fateful night assumed legendary proportions: Mister Scranton was a hero! He sacrificed his own life to save the life of a young woman!

Members of the staff consoled themselves by enlarging on heretofore unknown and unacknowledged acts of selflessness and bravery during his stay among them.

Osbert Marshall, with the wisdom of his years, heard the exaggerated stories with a wry shake of the head. *Mebbe old age done sour me, but from what I seen of him, Mr. Tyler was nothin' special. True, he had a pleasing face en spoke wid a fair tongue, but still ...he was just a regulah kind of man. Truth to tell, if he'd lef' here en move on - quiet like a mongoose - folks forgettin' all 'bout him come de next rainy season.*

Lord have mercy upon us.

THE END

ACKNOWLEDGEMENTS

BAJUN PROVERBS - compiled by Margot Blackman, Montreal, Canada, 1982

BARBADIAN DIALECT - Frank A. Collymore, Barbadian Nat'l Trust, 1992

HISTORIC CHURCHES OF BARBADOS - Barbara Hill, Art Heritage Publications, 1984

THE COOKING OF THE CARIBBEAN ISLANDS - Linda Wolfe & Editors of Time/Life Books, 1970

The Book of Common Prayer of 1928 as amended. The Order for the Burial of the Dead.

ABOUT THE AUTHOR

It was the author's love for and appreciation of her former island home—*its natural beauty, its inhabitants, its history*—that spurred her to write *THE WATERFALL*. Numerous articles and interviews focusing on the West Indies have appeared under her byline, but she acknowledges, "I wanted the freedom, which fiction gives you, to paint with words a broader, more colorful canvas."

Yaeger's recently published children's book, *CONSTANTINE*, is also set on an island in the West Indies.

Printed in the United States
1036300001B